TRIANGLE: QUESTION OF COMMAND

In the same series
TRIANGLE

TRIANGLE:
QUESTION OF COMMAND

a novel by
CHRISTINE SPARKS

from the BBC-TV
series created by
TED RHODES
and BILL SELLARS

Based on storylines by
BEN STEED
and scripts by
COLIN DAVIS
DAVID HOPKINS
SUE LAKE
DAWN LOWE-WATSON
JACK MOTT
and BEN STEED

British Broadcasting Corporation

Published by the
British Broadcasting Corporation
35 Marylebone High Street
London W1M 4AA

ISBN 0 563 20061 8 paperback

First published 1982

Printed and Bound in England by
Love and Malcomson Ltd.,
Brighton Road, Redhill, Surrey.

Chapter 1

The pale blue Saab screeched to a halt with such violence that Matt was jerked forward in his seat.

'Sure there's any rubber left on the tyres?' he asked.

'Positive,' said Kate Laker shortly.

'After that, a force twelve gale seems like a millpond.'

'You did offer to come with me.'

'Why is the Terson home our first stop?'

'I insist on seeing Marion.'

'Insist?' he whistled. 'You've got guts, lady.'

It felt like stating the obvious. The first thing he'd known about Kate Laker was that she had guts. She'd had the guts to take on a whole ship whose crew didn't want her, and win them over. She'd had the guts to take on her own father, the all-powerful George Terson, owner of the Triangle Line of shipping. George had wanted nothing so much as to get Kate out of her job as Chief Purser on one of his ships. Kate had faced him down, and kept her job, made a triumphant success of it too. But it was George who'd had the last laugh – if you could put it that way. In his dying hours he'd married his companion Marion Carter and left her the whole line. To his daughter had gone nothing but the cottage he'd started in long ago.

It might have been the end of something but in fact it had been the beginning. Kate had simply taken up the fight with Marion where she had left it off with her father. Oh yes, this lady had guts. Matt had never doubted that. He supposed it was one of the things he loved about her. But he wasn't blind to the fact that it was going to make her hard to live with – that is, if she ever did get around to keeping her promise to marry him. At the moment he had a feeling that he came somewhere behind Triangle and Marion in her list of priorities. And he was beginning to run out of patience.

'And I know Nick Stevens will be there.' Kate was fuming. 'Since he's become her right-hand man . . .'

'She needs one.'

'She knew what she was letting herself in for.'

'Not so sure about that,' he said thoughtfully. 'Anyway, this was supposed to be a date. You know – you and me? Candles and wine?'

'We're together, aren't we?'

'I was thinking more of some English nosh.'

'There'll be time.'

'Yeah, I forgot. Your business before our pleasure.' His temper was beginning to fray at the edges.

'If you don't like it . . .'

'Not a question of that, Kate. It's *you*, a crazy lady – and I adore you.'

'So – let me get this meeting over. I have a few things to say to Nick and Marion.'

'Here we go again!'

'It won't take long – promise.'

'Believe it when I see it.'

'O.K. I'm not fighting.'

'If it helps any, I'm on your side,' he offered.

'It helps.' She started the car again.

As they drove he reflected. He supposed he should have known their date was a gonner the moment Kate mentioned the name of Nick Stevens. Nick was the young, smart company lawyer who, for the last ten years, had been retained to look after George Terson's affairs. He now looked after them for Marion, a nice middle-aged lady whose only knowledge of shipping lines was what she had picked up from twenty years of living with and loving George Terson. That was a fact that made a lot of people nervous, and it was only the knowledge that Nick was there to guide her footsteps in her early days as head of a giant corporation that made them feel able to sleep at night.

But Matt knew that none of this counted with Kate. To her Nick Stevens was the lawyer who had first told her the contents of her father's will. It was through him that she had learned of the last insult that her father had dealt her. And so Nick was a man to be hated.

Not that Kate was totally out in the cold. She had some shares in the company that she had inherited from her mother, and for a while she had been intriguing with fellow shareholder Jeremy Gates to get herself onto the management team. But that uneasy alliance had ended when Kate made it clear she wasn't prepared to vote to convert Triangle's passenger ships to freight. Gates had argued strongly for freight, in which he saw more profit, but Kate held out.

Paradoxically this had had the effect of throwing her into Marion's camp, for Marion too was determined to keep up the passenger side of the line, in memory of George who had built it up that way. Marion had offered an olive branch which Kate had reluctantly accepted. At least this way she was part of the management, even if her power wasn't anything like what she felt it should have been. It seemed a long time ago now (although actually it was only a few months), but for a while it had seemed as though peace might break out.

It was Jeremy Gates who had thrown the spanner into the works by selling his shares to David West of D.R.W. Shipping – which just happened to be Triangle's biggest rival. What was worse Marion had actually welcomed David West into Triangle. That had been the first of her dubious decisions, in Kate's eyes. The other was to let Triangle 'go public' with a quotation on the Stock Exchange. There was a meeting taking place right now to celebrate both these decisions, and Kate was determined to get there if she killed them both.

'If I haven't already said it, welcome, Mr West.'

Marion Terson had to look up a little as she spoke. David West towered above her and his genial smile seemed to reach down from on high to touch her. He looked confident, sure of himself, genuinely at home in this world of big-money decisions and international business. He looked, in fact, everything that Marion pretended to be, and knew she wasn't.

'David, please,' he purred. 'I prefer a little informality if this is to be a successful enterprise.'

'As you've just bought some shares – I won't disagree with you.'

'Glad to hear it – Marion.'

He said her name in a caressing manner that made her feel self-conscious. She resisted the temptation to glance into a nearby mirror. She had checked the last detail of her appearance before coming downstairs. She looked elegant, well-dressed, well-preserved. But she also looked what she was – a woman in her fifties. That had never mattered with George, who had loved her when she was young, and sworn till his dying day that she had never changed. But George was gone, and she must face a world that saw her as she was, not as she had been and through the eyes of love.

She wondered how many of those here today knew that she was

terrified. Nick, perhaps. He was a tower of strength. But he was a mere boy in his middle thirties, and something deep within her prevented her making a total admission of how confusing she often found everything. Plus, Nick was still an employee. A trusted and privileged employee, but still one with whom, in the last resort, the barrier of seeming confidence must be kept in place.

The same was true of Captain John Anderson who was much nearer her own age, and also a shareholder in Triangle. John still worked for her in the sense that he was captain of one of her ships, and Marion didn't feel sufficiently sure of herself to forget this, even though John was an old friend, who had known her and George in the days when Triangle was just starting. In fact it was George who had given John his shares – £2,000 worth. That had been a lot of money in those days, but they were worth a great deal more now. They'd be worth more yet when the share price started to rise on the Stock Exchange, as David West had assured her it would.

And there, in a nutshell, was the reason she felt she could lean on David as she didn't dare lean on any of the others. He wasn't her employee and he hadn't known her in the days when she was an ill-educated girl from a poor background who'd had the luck to fall in love with a man who was going places, and to win his love. George Terson had taken her to the stars, but some part of her still remained the little girl whose clothes didn't fit properly because they'd been bought at jumble-sales, and whose home was a back-to-back where every penny had to be counted before it was spent. David treated her as an equal, the head of a giant shipping corporation, as big and important as his own D.R.W. Shipping. In fact he sometimes treated her as though she had built Triangle up herself. It made a nice change from the barely concealed concern of everyone around her.

She knew that the others neither liked nor trusted David, but that wouldn't last. When they knew him better they'd see what a gain he was.

In the corner John Anderson and Nick Stevens stood with their heads together. They were discussing David West, and saying precisely the kind of things that Marion feared they were saying.

'Of course I've heard of him,' John muttered, 'but that's the trouble, Nick – his reputation's gone before him.'

'And that worries you?' The younger man also spoke softly.

'Yes,' said John, thinking of the rumours he had heard, the deals in which David West had been involved that had been only just this side of legal, the investigations narrowly avoided. And hadn't there been a highly-paid employee who had left the country very suddenly, for reasons that were never adequately explained? And now this man was a major shareholder in Triangle, the very company from which his own had most to fear.

'Early days, John,' Nick said soothingly. 'Triangle's only just gone public. It's worth giving everything a try – including new shareholders.'

'I agree. But my stomach gives me warning signals . . .' He broke off as he saw Marion and David approaching together.

'I wish all our meetings were as easy to handle –' said Marion raising her drink slightly in David's direction '– and as pleasant.'

'Then *I* could get back on the bridge,' said John.

'Not used to boardroom politics, Captain Anderson?' said David West politely.

'It's a question of preference, isn't it – Mr West?' said John. He hadn't missed the attempt to reduce him from the status of a shareholder to that of a mere employee.

'How are you coping with the transference?' said Marion to John.

'Pretty well. I was delighted with your offer, Marion.'

'I've just given John the flagship,' said Marion grandly to David.

'Chosen your crew yet?' Nick asked.

'It isn't easy, but I'll keep you informed,' said John evasively.

'I didn't know captains could pick and choose,' said David West, curiously.

'Extra bait, David,' said Marion. '*I* provided it.'

'I wouldn't have accepted the new command without it,' said John.

'Why don't we tour the ship?' said Marion suddenly. 'Show David part of what he's bought.'

This idea found favour. John would have accepted any suggestion that allowed him to get out of this plush atmosphere and back onto a ship, where he belonged.

Only Nick declined the trip to the nearby docks at Harwich where the *Anglia* was moored. He was more at home in an office than on board and he suddenly remembered some paperwork that he had to clear up. So Marion, David and John departed together, and Nick was alone when Kate came storming in.

He coped with her as best he could, which wasn't very well if the state of her temper was any barometer. He knew that he was hated, and why. And if that was unjust, well – it was an unjust world. He was an easy-going young man who didn't lose his temper quickly.

'Triangle *is* going public, that's settled,' he explained patiently. 'And whether you like it or not, we're introducing shipboard management.'

'What does that involve?' she demanded.

'It means every ship will be run independently with the captain as its business manager. He'll be responsible for everything from changing the carpet designs to refitting the engine-room – with no recourse to any senior authority.'

'Leaving shareholders with even less control,' she said bitterly. 'I see. I don't like it, Nick.'

'Marion has ideas, talk to her.' He spoke politely but he had no intention of being drawn. His loyalty was to Marion.

'I intend to.' She strode to the door, but turned back to fling her last words at him. 'My father didn't want any of this "Going public" nonsense – *and neither do I.*'

Once outside she hurled herself into the car and slammed the door hard.

'Where are we going?' said Matt as the engine roared into life.

'Harwich.'

The car swung out of the drive so sharply that Matt had to cling onto the side.

'Why?' he demanded.

'Marion's there.'

'Do us a favour, love,' he pleaded. 'Let me drive.'

'No.' She never took her eyes from the road.

'Why not?'

'We want to get there, don't we?'

From which Matt deduced that she intended to break every speed-limit she came across, give him grey hairs and lop five years off his life. And he was right.

Mid-afternoon in the Bellevue Lounge on the *Anglia* was usually a quiet time, and today was no exception. The bar was closed, which left the barman, Barry Peters, free to check his supply list, as he was now doing. The only two customers present were drinking coffee.

One of them was a very tiny lady, somewhere in her sixties. From the way she was dressed she was probably wealthy, but attached more importance to her money as a source of comfort than of elegance. Her only companion was a small Yorkshire terrier who sat on a chair beside her. A lead was attached to his collar, but it could not be said to be restraining him. He sat in devoted silence, his eyes following every movement of his mistress. Now and then she would put down her cup and stroke his head fondly.

Barry Peters looked up from the bar and regarded the old lady with a friendly smile. He liked Mrs Harper. Everyone did.

The other customer puzzled him. She was a young woman, fair-haired and pale-skinned with perfect, elegant grooming, and a face that would have been very attractive but for a certain glacial quality about it. She was drinking her coffee in an absent-minded fashion. Often she did not bother to drink at all, but stared into space. Occasionally she picked up the empty glass ashtray before her, played with it, put it down. Barry watched her. She didn't look the kind who went round nicking ashtrays – but you never knew.

A murmur in the corridor outside made Barry look up in time to see the chief purser, Dougie Evans, ushering in three visitors. Dougie was a huge man, the kind you might prefer not to meet in a dark corner, if it weren't for the all-embracing kindness in his face.

'Plenty of room for a band . . .' he was saying to his visitors, indicating the big lounge. 'We had a Hungarian group last week.'

'There's a noise limit, surely,' said Marion.

'Of course. Fortunately they got nowhere near it. Just as well. I mean, how do you say "Please play quietly" in Hungarian? All right, Barry?' The party had reached the bar.

'Fine, thanks.'

The party moved on, and Judith Harper approached the bar. She was carrying the little dog in her arms.

'Barry . . .' she said in a low, conspiratorial voice.

'Mrs Harper . . .' He leaned over the bar and matched her tone.

'Our purser, Mr Evans, I already know. And Mrs Terson of course. But who were those two gentlemen?'

He leaned towards her over the bar. 'How much is it worth for me to divulge top-secret information?'

She lifted the little dog higher. 'How would you like to feel Mortimer's teeth at your ankles?' she hissed.

Mortimer rather ruined the effect of this threat by licking Barry's nose. Nonetheless he jumped back in theatrical terror.

'You wouldn't do such a thing?' he said.

'I would.'

'All right. One of them's the new captain – the other, I don't know. Honest.'

'Thank you, Barry.'

'You're a hard woman, Mrs H.'

'I know. Isn't it fun? Come along, Mortimer.'

At that moment the young woman, who had been sitting close enough to overhear the conversation, rose and moved towards the bar.

'Afternoon,' Barry greeted her.

She gave him only the faintest smile of acknowledgement. Then, after a moment's hesitation, she left the lounge through the same door as Dougie Evans and his party.

They were well ahead by now, and had reached the shopping arcade which Dougie was showing off as though he owned it. His pride in the *Anglia* shone through every word, John noticed with approval.

'How long have you been purser, Douglas?' Marion asked.

'Since I left college. About fifteen very happy years, Mrs Terson.' The words might have been sycophantic, but they sounded utterly sincere.

'Happy?' Marion queried.

'Yes. Always knew this was the job I wanted, you see.'

'Good for you,' said John quietly.

'Made mistakes though,' the big man grinned. 'Tried to please my old man once. "I want to live up to your standards," I'd say to him. "Never mind *my* standards," he'd say. "Find your own." So I did.'

'Best piece of advice he could've given you,' said John. 'I hope my kids don't feel they have to please me –' he added quietly '– or their mother.'

Marion squeezed his arm. She knew all about the tragedy of John's separation from his two children, owing to the vindictiveness of his Swedish ex-wife who had made them Swedish citizens, and denied him access. John adored his children, and he didn't know when he'd see them again.

'Well, if you'll excuse me.' David West's slightly bored voice broke in on them. 'The office beckons. Nice to have met you Captain Anderson.'

John watched with distaste as David West's Savile Row suit retreated into the distance. He had the feeling that the other man couldn't wait to get off the ship. Nor had he liked the lingering way he had held Marion's hand and said 'Goodbye'.

'I like to know there's a happy crew on George's favourite ship,' said Marion.

'A good omen, eh?' John smiled at her fondly.

'Perhaps. When he died I wanted nothing more to do with Triangle. But he must've thought I was capable of running it on my own?' she added in a pleading voice.

John was too chivalrous to say what he was thinking: that in the last moments of his life George Terson had been more concerned with offering a spiteful insult to his daughter than the future of his company.

He already knew the *Anglia* from previous visits, but he was impressed all over again. It was larger than his last command, and on the whole better appointed and more luxurious. The route, too, was different. Instead of travelling the triangle from Felixstowe to Amsterdam and the Swedish port of Gothenberg, this one travelled the triangle from Harwich to Amsterdam and the Danish port of Esbjerg.

They were moving now through the First Class cabin area, and Dougie suddenly put on speed to the end of the corridor where he could see Judith Harper struggling to find her key while not letting go of Mortimer.

'Here, let me help you,' he said, taking Mortimer from her.

'Mr Evans, how very kind. It's so difficult sometimes, isn't it? I mean, life and everything?'

'Yes, I know what you mean,' he assured her.

'Mrs Harper – how are you?' said Marion warmly.

'I'm very well, Mrs Terson – and so's Morti – aren't you, my precious? Say hello to the nice people.'

'This is your resident passenger, Mrs Harper,' Marion said to John.

'Resident? I didn't know there was such a thing.'

'This is your new captain,' Marion introduced John.

'Where's Captain Adams?' said Judith.

'He has a lot of loose ends to tie up before his transference,' said Marion. 'He's been moved to a freight ship.'

Judith addressed John with dignity. 'Well then, Captain, if there's anything I can do for you, just let me know. Or if I'm not in, leave a message with Mortimer. He'll know where to find me. If you'll excuse me – there's so much to do on a ship, isn't there?'

'Yes, isn't there?' said John, dazed.

Judith retrieved Mortimer and opened her door. Before she had quite closed it behind her John's voice reached her as he walked away, saying, 'A little dotty, perhaps?'

'Oh yes,' said Dougie, 'but quite harmless.'

Judith sniffed disdainfully, wondering what had happened to gentlemen's manners these days. Captain Adams would have known better than to say such a thing. Dotty – harmless – she wasn't sure which was the bigger insult.

'It's a pity, in a way, about British quarantine laws,' Dougie was saying as they turned the corner, out of Judith's sight. 'You see, Captain, when she decided to return to England after her husband died, she discovered she'd be parted from Mortimer for six months. Well, on her arrival at Harwich, they wouldn't let the dog off the ship so Mrs Harper refused to get off without him.'

'A quick re-negotiation of her ticket and here she still is – a permanent passenger,' added Marion.

The tour ended on the bridge where John looked round him in appreciation of the latest equipment. Dougie Evans had left them.

'What do you think, John?' said Marion, making a gesture that included the bridge and the whole ship.

'I'm delighted,' he said sincerely. 'It's a very fine ship.'

'Did you ever have any doubts?'

'No.'

'And with David's involvement on the Board . . . I've always admired the way he runs his companies.'

'D.R.W. has certainly kept pace with the rest of us,' he said non-committally.

'That's why I was delighted that he was the highest bidder for the shares. His ideas, our company – it's a deadly combination.'

John felt that deadly was probably the right word, but Marion had spoken in all innocence. That was just the problem – her innocence.

'You're a fine captain,' she went on. 'I want you to be happy in your work. As happy as your purser.'

'*My* purser?' he said sharply. 'I asked Kate Laker, you know.'

And that, he thought, was an indication of how far he'd travelled. He'd neither liked nor wanted Kate when she came storming aboard his last ship, having got her appointment by stealth, so that her father had never known until it was too late. John had liked it even less when Kate started turning the ship upside down, 'throwing her weight about' as he had put it crossly at the time. But Kate's way had worked. She knew what passengers wanted, and her side of operations had soon shown a seventeen per cent upturn in profits. And gradually she'd won over the crew. Even Matt Taylor, John's chief engineer, the Casanova of the North Sea, had abandoned a life-time of caution to ask her to marry him. John supposed they'd get around to it soon – if they could stop sparring long enough.

And now here he was himself, *asking* Kate Laker to join him on the *Anglia*, as purser. It just went to show . . . something or other.

'What did she have to say?' said Marion.

'Kate made it clear to me she didn't approve of Triangle going public. I think we're going to face a very angry lady, Marion.'

He wondered where Kate was this minute. Somehow he had expected her to be at the meeting at Marion's house, airing her views. It wasn't like Kate to miss the chance to do that.

David West made the same comment when Kate burst into his Harwich office soon after his return. She was breathless and livid, but he faced her calmly.

'We missed you at the meeting his morning,' he said.

'I was delayed.' She spoke icily.

'Well, what can I do for you, Miss Laker?'

'I suppose you think this is just the first step?'

'What?'

'Eighteen per cent of the shares.'

'*My* eighteen per cent now – or will be.'

'Exactly. I'm going to fight you, every inch.'

He shrugged. 'A pity. I thought you would want to move with the times.'

Kate breathed hard. 'Your company has always been in strong competition with Triangle. My father never trusted you. Why should *I* trust you?'

He gave her the smile that never failed with Marion. 'Miss Laker, this isn't a war. The new board of directors will be in a position to . . .'

'The what?'

'With the voting shares split as they are, *nobody* can make any decisions without calling an extraordinary meeting of shareholders, and the new board . . .'

' . . . which you, I presume, instigated. Mr West, I suspected you of sliding in through a back door . . .'

'Not my style,' he said coolly.

'But you've done better than that. You have the nerve to . . .'

'Yes, Miss Laker, I have the nerve. That's why *I'm* the owner and chairman of *my* company.'

She almost spat at him. 'My father was probably running Triangle before you bought your first rowing boat. And what was good enough for him, is fine by me.'

'You mean total power?'

'If I can't have it over a company which rightly belongs to me, I'll make sure you'll never get it.'

'George Terson was the last of the autocrats.'

'Not the last,' she assured him fervently.

'I advise you to think more carefully, Miss Laker.'

'I don't need your advice,' she flashed.

He shrugged dismissively. 'Then if you're looking for Marion Terson you'll find her on board the flagship.' He gave her a slight, mocking bow. 'Miss Laker, it's been – an experience – meeting you.'

Matt was still waiting, standing beside the car. In a hard voice she recounted the meeting to him, then fell silent. Matt too said nothing. He knew that anything he said at this point would be wrong.

'Triangle should have been mine, Matt,' she muttered at last.

He suddenly realised just how tired he was of hearing her say that. If she was going to spend forever brooding about a battle that was already lost, life would rapidly become unbearable.

'Maybe so,' he said. 'But I think you're going the wrong way about things.'

'Do you?' She was staring into the distance, answering him mechanically.

'Yes. So I'll be in the pub over there. When you've cooled down a bit, perhaps you'll join me.'

'Matt,' she called after him, 'I don't think they're open yet.'

He looked back briefly. 'I'll wait. I've had plenty of practise.'

He walked off. She scarcely saw him go.

Jane Anthony studied the girl who was cramming clothes into her wardrobe: Lisa Watkins, eighteen, willing, energetic and basically good-natured, but not, if the way she was shoving those clothes in was anything to go by, particularly tidy. That would have to improve. As a member of the cabin staff it would be Lisa's task to clean the passengers' cabins and keep *them* tidy – and she'd better start by learning how to do the same with her own.

But for the moment Jane was willing to suspend any further judgement. As cabin crew supervisor she had seen girls come and go, and she knew that those who showed the least promise initially often turned out the best.

She herself was a slender, almost thin woman in her thirties, whose face was redeemed from plainness by a pair of beautiful grey eyes that often carried an expression of humour. She resumed reading from a list in her hand.

'And there's another crew member, Barbara Carter.'

'One big happy family,' Lisa had finished stowing her clothes away, and just about forced the door to close on them.

'Let's hope so.'

'Don't worry about it,' said Lisa in a large-minded spirit. 'Me – I'll get on with anybody – just so long as they don't try and lord it.'

'Anything you don't understand – any problems – just ask me.'

'Don't expect any. Except sea-sickness.'

'Don't worry. If it happens to you, we'll give you some pills.'

'Never had it before,' Lisa confided, 'but it's just the thought that puts me off.'

'Fresh air,' said Jane bracingly. 'That's the important thing.'

'My Mum told me to lie down,' said Lisa in gloomy accents. 'Can't believe anything these days, can you?'

'Excuse me . . .'

'They both looked up to see a fair, pale-faced young woman, elegantly dressed in blue, who had appeared in the doorway.

'Can I help you?' said Jane.

'I'm looking for the reception area.'

'I'm going that way. I'll come with you.'

'As they walked along the corridor Jane said, 'It's difficult, isn't it, keeping a sense of direction?'

'Yes.'

'Did you lose your way?'

'Something like that.'

'Took me a while to get used to it,' Jane persisted. 'Your first time on board?'

'On this ship? Yes.'

Jane gave up. This lady plainly wasn't going to give anything away.

'No ties, John?'

John came out of his reverie abruptly. The tour of the ship had ended in his new quarters, where he and Marion had clinked glasses to the future. But there was something about a glass that hypnotised you. You found yourself staring into it and remembering other people with whom you had shared drinks.

The face of Jo Bailey seemed to swim before him. Jo had been the cabaret singer on his last ship. A nice lady, whose sympathy had helped him endure what his wife was doing to him via her lawyers. At one time they'd even thought there might be more between them than that, but then she'd had this offer – the offer of a lifetime. John had refused to influence her decision. He didn't want the responsibility. And that, he supposed, told its own story.

'Pardon?' he said now to Marion.

'I asked you if there were any ties. Jo Bailey. What happened?'

'Jo? Made her own life. On her way to a starry career.'

'I'm sorry.'

'Why? Oh, there was something there, I suppose. A fondness. But it wouldn't have lasted. She knew it, so did I. Anyway, all that money, fame and glamour nonsense – she wanted that more. So, good luck to her.' He raised his glass.

'So you're a free agent?'

'Always was – except for Maya.' Even now the name of his ex-wife had the power to make him shudder a little. 'But with the divorce through as well – yes, I'm a very free agent.'

Free of everything, he thought bitterly. Free of Maya, free of the home I thought we'd built up together, free of my children, because they're now Swedish citizens living in Sweden, and Maya threatened to put the police onto me if I tried to see them. He thought of his little girl, Emily, ten years old . . . and his son Ted, sixteen and almost a man . . .

He slammed the glass down suddenly. Yes he was free, dammit!

'Have you decided on the rest of your crew?' said Marion, tactfully changing the subject.

'I have. I want Matt Taylor – but he won't commit himself. Tom Kelly and Charles Woodhouse.'

All of them names from his last command. Marion nodded at Matt Taylor and Tom Kelly. Tom in particular was an old friend of her own, as well as being a fine first mate. But the name of Charles Woodhouse made her raise her eyebrows. She had not known Charles in earlier, happier days, when he had been married to his beloved Jenny. But she had heard of the change that came over him a year ago, when Jenny had died while carrying their child. After that everything that was cold and ambitious in Charles had risen to the surface.

John caught her look and nodded. 'I know Charles is after my job – but he's an invaluable first officer. And I want him on my side.'

'Your choice, John.'

'Yes it is. I'm prepared to take certain risks, Marion.'

'As long as you know what you're doing.'

'Don't I always?'

He refilled their glasses and they clinked again.

'Then you take over the flagship officially when it berths next week in Amsterdam,' she said.

There was a knock on the door and Dougie's head came round.

'Excuse me, Mrs Terson – but Kate Laker is in the Terminal Building. She wants to see you.'

John went down with Marion. It was about time Kate gave him an answer. They found her out on the quay, her long dark hair blowing about her face as she stared out at the horizon.

'Marion,' she said, 'I waited long enough.'

'If I could be in six different places at once . . .' Marion shrugged.

'It seems decisions have been made behind my back. Triangle – a public company. How could you?'

'I want this company to succeed, Kate. To succeed we must remain competitive and expand – tours – hotels –'

'George Terson built a proud shipping line, not a chain of doss houses,' said Kate brutally. 'And why allow those shares to go to West, of all people?'

'He's less likely to cut our throats now,' said John. 'It's a sensible move, Kate – and with shipboard management we . . .'

'What do you know about shipboard management, John?' she flashed at him. 'You're a sailor, not a grocer in a corner ship.'

'David West has a stake in the company,' said John firmly. 'He doesn't want the whole of the North Sea.'

'I wouldn't count on it,' snapped Kate.

Since John agreed with her but could not say so in front of Marion, he fell silent, while Marion said, 'But can we count on you? Are you going to accept John's offer. Purser on board the flagship?'

'So that I shall be at sea again when decisions are made? And when I'm at sea – how competent are *you*?' This was aimed directly at Marion, and John did not miss the slight way she flinched. 'I have a stake in this company too, you know.'

'But this is different,' Marion pleaded. 'It's a new way of operating the company.'

'No, Marion. With the shares in West's grasp – you in his pocket, extraordinary general meetings – just how much control is being dispersed?'

'He's not the enemy,' said Marion gently.

'Isn't he? It's taking control further away from me and I don't like .t.'

Marion dropped her placating manner and became belligerent. 'So what are you going to do?'

'For the time being I'm staying where I am, Marion. Sorry, John, find yourself a new purser for your flagship.'

'I'm disappointed, Kate,' he said quickly. 'Where are you going?' She had turned away from them.

'Somewhere to think. The hovel my father left me in his will, perhaps. The last thing he gave me and it meant nothing.'

'He loved that place,' said Marion sadly.

'He loved lots of things – ships, properties, objects – but not his daughter.'

'You're crazy,' said Marion.

'Yes, but I'm right – and what you're doing with the company is wrong.'

'I'd buy that cottage from you – pay any price.'

'Any price? From you? I'd rather give it away. For once you can't use your money, Marion. I'll defy your wealth and your power – just as I'll always oppose you.'

'I thought there was a chance at least that we might be allies.'

'Don't kid yourself,' Kate flashed. Then she was gone.

'I told you she was angry,' said John as they returned to the ship.

'She has every right,' Marion admitted. 'She's missing a good opportunity.'

John shrugged as they reached his quarters and he ushered her in. 'Perhaps. But I don't want a half-hearted crew and she's made up her mind.'

There was a knock on the door. John opened it to reveal a fair-haired young woman in blue.

'Mrs Terson?' said the young woman, looking at Marion.

'Yes?'

'I'm Sarah Hallam.'

Marion's face brightened at once. 'John, may I present Miss Hallam? This is Captain Anderson. Sarah's our first shipboard manager.'

'Ah yes – shipboard manager.' John spoke uncertainly. Until this moment he had been under the impression that the manager of the ship was the captain.

'It's a growing commercial concern, Captain,' said Sarah, reading his face with accuracy.

'She'll be in charge of running the management side of the ship,' added Marion.

'With reference to me, I hope,' said John firmly.

'Where necessary, of course.' Sarah smiled at him.

'There's only one captain per ship,' he told her.

'Yes.'

'Nick Stevens recommended you highly, Sarah,' said Marion.

'Thank you, Mrs Terson.' Sarah looked from one to the other. 'I didn't mean to interrupt – just wanted to let you know I was *around* here.'

'Well, we'll speak again soon.' Marion showed her to the door.

'Yes. Goodbye, Captain Anderson.'

As soon as Sarah had gone John whirled on Marion. 'Who *is* she? I thought this Sarah Hallam was an adviser, not a manager.'

'Once my schemes are established, she will be. But for the moment she's a manager,' said Marion brightly.

'Then just who is the master of the ship . . .'

'You're crazy to refuse the Captain's offer,' said Matt.

They were sitting in the pub where she had finally caught up with him.

'I'm crazy anyway,' she said. 'You told me that.'

'It's a job, Kate – only a job.'

'No, it's my company.'

'Become an obsession with you,' he grunted.

'I can't condone the wrong direction Triangle's taken . . .'

He sighed. 'You used to be fun.'

'Things aren't supposed to be "fun" any more.'

He took a deep breath. 'Then I don't think I want to know. You'll stay where you are . . .'

'I'll oppose her. I'll not give up easily.'

' . . . and I'll move on,' he said, scarcely hearing her. 'Shipboard management sounds like a good idea to me. Worth a try, anyway.'

She looked at him as though seeing him for the first time.

'Matt – I thought you were on my side.'

'Look,' he said patiently, 'George Terson's dead, and his ideas died with him. You've got to move.'

'No,' she said flatly.

He looked back into his drink rather than at her. 'Then that's it, isn't it?'

She stared at him blankly. 'What do you mean?'

'You won't come with the flagship – and I'm sure not staying behind to hold your hand.'

'You're against me?' said Kate, defining their positions in the only terms that now seemed to mean anything to her.

'Seems like it. I love you, Kate, but I don't like your ideas. In fact, on this occasion I think you're dead wrong.'

Their eyes met for a long moment. Then a mirthless smile curled her mouth.

'That's funny,' she said.

'What?'

'It's the first time you've ever used the word "love" – just now, when it looks like the end.'

'Yes, I'm rolling with laughter. You're giving us up – for what? Policies, decision-making, power struggles. Well, you can have it. Because for once I'm not on your side. I'm not on anybody's side – 'cept my own. And I should thank you for that.'

They faced each other like two strangers, wondering if they had ever been anything else.

'I demanded loyalty once,' she said.

'Demanded?' he flared. 'Just who are you to demand anything?'

'Someone trying to do their best, trying to do what's right.'

'Perhaps you took too much for granted.'

'Yes,' she said softly. 'Perhaps I did.'

He shrugged. 'Sorry.'

'No. It's me who should apologise. I just thought – well, never mind.'

'Nothing more to be said.'

'Suppose not. I wish – it hadn't been you. I loved you.'

'And it's the first time *you've* ever said it,' he pointed out.

'Too late now.' Her words fell like stones.

'Yes, too late.'

A silence fell between them. Neither was willing to do what must be done next. Finally it was Kate who got to her feet.

'Do you want a lift?' she said tonelessly.

He shook his head. 'Told you. I'm staying right here.' He lifted his glass to her in cheerless salute.

'Matt . . .'

'Yes?'

The words stuck in her throat. With a gesture of despair she turned and left him hurriedly He didn't watch her go.

John had the Bellevue Lounge to himself, which he was glad of as he had a lot of thinking to do. To have Sarah Hallam jumped on him at the last minute had been a nasty surprise, and increased his unease about Marion's decision-making. It was a bad omen for the start of his new command. On the other hand there was nothing to be done about it now, but get on and put up with it.

'Ah, Captain.'

Looking up, his eyes met a sight that surprised him. Matt was weaving his way towards the table with unsteady steps.

'So this is it,' he said as he dropped into a seat. 'Reporting for duty, sir.'

'What?'

'I've decided. I'm throwing it in with you.'

John eyed his condition for a moment, then leaned forward and shook his hand.

'I'm delighted, Matt.'

'And so am I.' Matt spoke rather too loudly.

'Where've you been?' John demanded.

'Finishing off unfinished business.'

'Kate?'

'She's not with me – with *us*. You knew?' Matt hiccuped mournfully.

'O.K. old son. You'd better fill up with coffee,' said John kindly.

'She said something about her inheritance – her father's cottage—'

'Are you all right, Matt?'

'Yes, Captain, I'll be O.K.'

Not today, he thought, or tomorrow. But sometime . . .

'Good.' John spoke gently but firmly. 'Because I wouldn't like to see my chief engineer in this state again.'

Matt closed his eyes. When he opened them again he was alone. He couldn't remember when he had last felt so alone. He'd broken with women before, but never like this. Kate had been the right woman for him in as many ways as she'd been the wrong one. And it was over. Ahead of him lay a return to the old days, trying to live up to his reputation as a shipboard Don Juan, acting as though it still mattered to him . . .

He dropped his head into his hands.

Chapter 2

Who'd have believed Charlie Ryan's son would have turned out so like his father? Matt thought as he approached the figure on the quay in Amsterdam, a week later. And who'd have thought he'd be assigned Charlie's son as an engineering cadet? He was looking forward to it. Charlie had been a good mate in days gone past.

Close up he could see less of the similarities and more of the differences. The chief one was that Charlie had never stopped laughing, whereas his offspring had his face set in sullen suspicious lines. Ah well, that was modern youth for you! For Charlie's sake Matt was glad to take the boy under his wing.

He helped Bill Ryan aboard with his gear, then stood back to take a better look at him. About eighteen, he reckoned, and not bad looking if only he'd cheer up a bit.

'You won't believe this,' he said, 'but you look just like your father. We'll be living in each other's pockets for the next few months. So let's grab a jar before I start kicking you around.'

'What?' said Bill sharply.

'Joke,' said Matt. 'Dump your gear.'

The boy indicated some books he was carrying uncomfortably under his arm. 'If you don't mind, I'll take these with me.'

He clutched the books as if they were gold dust as he followed Matt back off the ship and to a nearby bar. Matt tried to read the titles but couldn't crane his neck that far. Once they were seated Bill downed his beer as though there was no tomorrow.

'Easy,' Matt advised him. 'It's not a race. Plenty of time before we're needed on board.'

'Developed a thirst. Got delayed by customs.'

'Hope you weren't smuggling.'

'Course not,' Bill scowled. 'They probably didn't like my face. Put uniforms on them and they think they're God.'

'You'll be in uniform one day.'

'That's different. I'm me.'

'So?'

'I'll only be an engineering cadet.'

'Who's to know? There's someone else seeing you, thinking the same thing: "Look at him! Put a uniform on him and he thinks he's God."'

Bill shrugged. 'Point taken. Thanks for the lecture.'

'No lecture,' Matt assured him. 'Common sense. How old are you?'

'Nineteen,' said Bill proudly.

'Blimey! A baby.'

'No,' Bill flared.

'All right, son. All right,' Matt soothed him. 'Only joking. Where's your sense of humour?'

Privately he was beginning to suspect that whoever had made Bill Ryan had left that bit out. He had further cause to think so as they walked round Amsterdam, Bill struggling to carry the books, which kept slipping.

'Brought the library, have you?' Matt asked.

'Studies. Engineering mostly.'

'Mostly? What else?'

'Political. That sort of thing.'

Matt didn't waste time asking what Bill's politics were. Anyone so totally lacking in the ability to laugh had to be an incipient revolutionary.

'You won't have time,' was all he said.

'Then I'll make time. Don't care how long I have to stay awake. May as well use the system to my advantage – keep ahead of the right-wing extremists.'

'Oh, I see. So come the revolution you'll be up there in front telling the proles what to think . . .'

'Well . . .'

'Listen, son, I don't care who you are, or how you tick – but your father taught me everything I know in this business. So I owe him – and I'm interested in how you shape up as an engineer . . .'

'Sure, but . . .'

' . . . and if you go waving the flag when you should be on duty, I'll thump you. Just remember, you're answerable to me now.'

'I won't let you down.'

'We'll have to see about that.'

There was a moment's silence as they walked along, then Bill said musingly, 'An officer thumping a cadet? Wouldn't look good for company image, would it? Sir?'

Glancing at him Matt saw that the boy was grinning. Thank the Lord! There was hope for him yet!

After an hour's wandering round the town they fetched up thankfully in a small dock-side bar where they found Tom Kelly and Charles Woodhouse already ensconsed. Tom was indulging in a highly-coloured description of his Irish holiday, and Charles was listening with every appearance of enjoyment. For once he looked human again, Matt thought, as he and Bill joined them at the table.

'Thought I'd find you two old soaks here,' he said. He exchanged greetings with them and introduced his protégé. 'This is Bill Ryan, the engineering cadet.'

'Welcome to the fold, Bill – I'm Tom Kelly.'

'How do!'

Charles' greeting was formal: 'Charles Woodhouse – First Officer.' The instant mutual antipathy between him and Bill was almost tangible, and Charles' next remark did nothing to improve matters. 'So you're the ship's powder monkey, are you?'

'Something more than that.'

'Take no notice, Bill,' said Tom hastily. 'It's what he calls every newcomer to the crew.'

'Tom was just telling me about his adventures in the Emerald Isle.' Charles addressed Matt. He seemed to have forgotten Bill's existence.

'Can't understand, Tom,' said Matt, 'why some little leprechaun hasn't shown you where the pot of gold is hidden . . .'

'How d'you know he hasn't already?'

From nowhere Charles produced an Irish accent: 'Yer wouldn't be keepin' the treasure all to yerself now, would yer?'

'I bet *you* would if you found it,' said Bill. 'I bet most of us would.'

There was a silence. Charles was staring at Bill as if unsure whether to believe his ears. Tom smothered an embarrassed grin. Matt came to the rescue.

'Just been showing Bill some of the sights,' he said briefly.

'All at once?' said Tom. 'Poor lad.'

'He can take it.'

Charles ignored them. His eyes were on Bill's impedimenta. 'Do you always travel with so many books?' he asked curiously.

'Yes. Ever since I cancelled my subscription to the *Times* – never took to fantasy comics.'

'Then we have a bookworm in the crew, gentlemen.'

Matt made a valiant effort to steer the conversation back to light-hearted channels. 'Makes a change – I can never get beyond page three. Cheers!'

'Prefer the *Telegraph* myself,' said Charles.

Bill sniggered.

'What's funny?' Matt demanded.

'Nothing.'

'So – Triangle's flagship! What a turn-up,' said Tom desperately.

'Registered under Danish law, isn't it?' Matt asked.

'Yes,' said Charles.

'Is Esbjerg ready for us?'

'You'll have your hands full with a cadet in tow,' said Charles.

'He'll be okay – keep telling you.'

'Where they dig them up from these days, I've no idea.'

Bill spoke with deceptive politeness. 'Lots of us around, Mr Woodhouse – like manure, you have to spread us evenly to get a good crop.'

Matt and Tom chuckled. Charles' lips tightened.

'A farmer, too?' said Matt. 'Then we've got a bright lad here.'

'Just so long as he knows he will address me as "sir" on board ship,' said Charles.

'Won't forget, will you?' Matt eyed Bill with misgiving.

'Oh no, I won't forget. Sir!'

All John's worst fears about having Marion as a boss seemed to rush in on him when he entered her office in Amsterdam and found her accompanied by a very pretty young girl whom she introduced as her niece Barbara Carter. Barbara was about seventeen, expensively dressed, and looked like a little madam. That would not normally have bothered John, except that in a weak moment he had allowed himself to be persuaded to take her on as a cabin girl. Within a few seconds he knew that had been a mistake.

'Marion,' he said with as much courtesy as he could muster, 'with all respect I prefer not to discuss ship's policy in front of a cabin girl.'

'This is not just a "cabin girl",' Marion protested. 'Barbara is my niece.'

'She is also staff and, as such, I never discuss anything to do with policy . . .'

'. . . in front of a cabin girl – yes, we heard you the first time, Captain,' Barbara interrupted. 'It's all right, Aunt Marion, I don't mind.'

'It doesn't matter what you "mind", Barbara. This is nonsense.'
'No, just a principle,' said John firmly.
'Any chance of a drink?' said Barbara suddenly, looking round her.
'Barbara, we're trying to discuss business . . .' said Marion.
'Sorry, I'm sure.'
'*You're* discussing – I'm not!' said John in a quiet voice.
'John, we're not on board now,' Marion spoke placatingly.
'Makes no difference. If, as you say, Barbara's here to work her way to the top, she'll have to get used to being excluded from certain situations. And this is one of them.' John tried to keep his voice courteous but he could not suppress a sharp twinge of dismay. If this was to be an example of Marion's attitude, then life was going to be difficult for everyone.
The girl gave an exaggerated sigh and stood up. 'I'm going now, Aunt Marion. Do feel free to discuss your secrets, Captain.' She bestowed a brief kiss on her aunt. 'Thank you. Now I suppose I'll find my own way to the boat . . .'
'Ship, dear!' said Marion mechanically.
'Well, whatever. Goodbye, Captain. We'll certainly meet again, won't we?'
'Miss Carter,' he opened the door to her. His hand was itching to give her a good smack as she wafted out.
'Triangle will obviously be her first taste of discipline,' he commented when he had shut the door.
'She'll survive.'
'No doubt,' said John grimly, wondering if the same could be said of himself.
'I want her to learn the nuts and bolts of the business.'
'If she looks beyond her fingernails, it may do her good.'
'Don't be deceived, John. She's really very bright. It's just . . . My brother was a lorry driver . . . When he died, Barbara took it very badly. She adored him.'
'How old was she?'
'Nine. She went into long bouts of depression for a couple of years after that. It was a kind of madness. I felt totally responsible for her by this time and there were the hospital bills to pay.'
'Hospital . . .? I'm sorry.'
'When her – illness – was over, I helped her through school and more or less took charge of her life.'
'Good for you.'

'Even now I don't think she has really got over his death.'
'Well – perhaps the sea is just what she needs,' he said non-committally.
'Be kind to her, John.'
'Of course.'
Marion had been absently opening an envelope as she spoke. She took out a cheque and a letter, which she began to read. Suddenly her face went white. 'I don't believe this . . .'
'What's the matter?'
'It's from Kate!'
'What does she have to say?'
'She *sold* it – the cottage.' Marion sounded as though she were choking.
'Sold it? To whom?'
'Here's the cheque.' She held it up. 'Forty-two pounds!' she said, dazed with disbelief.
'What? It's worth thirty *thousand*, at least.'
'It must be a joke.' She read out. '"I sold it to a retired couple. I thought you might like the proceeds – as you wanted the place so much. I got a good price for it!"'
'No joke! She's serious.'
'It's her way of getting at me. She's *mad*! John, what can we do?'
'Nothing, I'm afraid. It was hers to sell – or give away – or burn down. If she chose. Leave it, Marion. There's *nothing* you can do.'

By the time Barbara had found her way to the 'boat', she was beginning to go off the whole idea. To begin with she had a headache coming on. Then the purser, when she managed to find him, claimed to have no record of her on his list of cabins, and when he'd discovered that she was a cabin girl said that explained it, as though she was suddenly the lowest of the low. And whatever Marion Terson's niece was, it wasn't that.
To cap it all, she'd been handed over to someone called Jane Anthony who looked and talked like a school-mistress, and had made her carry her own bags. And now she was in her cabin she didn't like the look of it. Small wasn't the word – more like minute.
'This isn't the Savoy,' Jane said, reading her expression. 'You'll get used to it.'
'I suppose I shall have to. Still – isn't there anything bigger?'
'You're now a member of the crew and no-one gets special privileges.'

'Do you know who I am?' said Barbara, astounded.

'Doesn't matter. As crew you'll learn to pitch in with the rest. You'll learn – or you'll leave.'

'I see.'

'I'll send Lisa Watkins along. She'll give you a run-down on basic duties.' Jane departed on the words and headed straight for Lisa's cabin, but her progress was fraught with confusion as a crowd of male crew members seemed to be conversing on the same corridor. There were a lot of bags around. One of them clouted her on the leg, and looking up indignantly she saw a face she recognised.

'Tom!' she cried in amazement.

Tom Kelly stared at her. 'I don't believe it. What are you doing here?'

'I've been working this ship since the last refit. What are *you* doing here?'

There were two men and a boy with Tom, none of whom Jane recognised. They seemed impatient to pass. As soon as Lisa opened her door Jane pushed her inside and went in after her to make more room.

'Tom. I'll talk to you later.'

The men passed on. The last one, the boy, attracted Lisa's attention.

'Now that's what I call a dish,' she said frankly. 'Hi there.'

The youngster blushed to the roots of his hair. 'Er – excuse me.'

Jane firmly shut the door. 'Lisa, do something for me.'

'Who was *he*?' demanded Lisa, who had no subtlety whatever.

'A cadet, I think.' said Jane. 'Lisa, pay attention. Go and talk to Barbara in 87. Show her the ropes. Any problems – tell me.'

'O.K. You didn't get his name, did you?'

'No. I didn't.'

'Have to find out, won't I?'

Matt, Tom and Charles had reached their own corridor by now and were taking a momentary breather.

'You do pick your moments to chat them up,' Matt complained to Tom. 'who was she, anyway? Another flight of fancy?'

'Well, no – actually, she's my wife.'

'Y'what?'

'My *ex*-wife.' Tom corrected firmly.

'Didn't know you were married.'

'A fact I've been trying to forget myself.'

'Mind my books,' Bill demanded as Tom shifted awkwardly.

'You still here?' said Matt. 'Look, here's the key, there's the number, back the way we came, past the hold-up point, got it?'

'Right – ta.'

'And stay there. I'll come and get you.'

'Babysitting?' Charles demanded when Bill had gone.

'Leave off,' pleaded Matt. 'Got to work with him, haven't I? And you were young and green once.'

Half way to his cabin Bill once more encountered Lisa. She beamed at him. 'Well, hello again. Took the wrong turning, didn't you?'

'Excuse me,' he said uncomfortably.

'Yeah, know how you feel. You should let me give you a guided tour.'

He fled. Lisa watched him go without dismay. There was plenty of time when the two of you were trapped on a cramped ship. She made her way to Barbara's cabin. The sullen indifference with which she was greeted put her cheerfulness to its greatest test, but she managed to explain cabin-staff duties without losing her temper.

'You've got to make sure that every cabin has a supply of loo paper, soap, face towels. Learn it. People go crazy without those three things.'

'Really?' said Barbara, filing her nails.

If, Lisa thought behind her smile, I get through the next month without stabbing you with your own nail-file, I shall be extremely surprised.

One person who had been watching the arrivals with a certain amount of anxious interest was Judith Harper. She had been perfectly content under the old regime and was sorry to see it changed. On the other hand, as she explained to Mortimer, one had to be open-minded.

'A new voyage, a new crew –' she told him '– just like the beginning of term.'

She paused in crossing the entrance hall and gave a cheerful smile to a man who, she knew by his stripes, must be the first officer. But he did not smile back.

'Passengers should not be aboard,' he said firmly.

'Passengers? Oh, you don't understand. I never get off. You see . . .'

'Why is that dog here?' Charles interrupted.

Judith held up Mortimer who she was holding under her arm. 'This is Mortimer. Don't let the teeth frighten you. He's a dear when you get to know him.'

'Madam, I have no intention of getting to know "him",' said Charles frostily.

'You're not a dog-lover, then?'

He made the mistake of answering this. 'I prefer cats, but that's not the point . . .'

'Oh, but it is. Animals can always tell. They have instinct.'

'A quality which humans can well do without.'

'Really? You think so? I should be most interested to hear your views on the subject . . .'

'Another time perhaps,' said Charles, realising the trap he'd walked into. 'Another place . . .'

'You, as an officer, must know that the sea has strange effects on people . . . like the moon . . . the tides . . .'

Charles thanked a merciful heaven that none of his colleagues could overhear this conversation. He'd never live it down.

'This is an accommodation area, not a debating platform,' he said when he could get a word in edgeways. 'I must insist that you take that animal to the car deck. I'm sure you'll find plenty of places to tie it up.'

'No,' said Judith firmly.

'Please do as I say,' said Charles, even more firmly.

'Very well . . . I've learned to read those stripes.'

'Thank you.'

Charles marched away before she could start talking again. He had the oddest feeling that he hadn't really won that bout at all.

As he had promised, Matt sought out Bill's cabin half an hour later. The boy was arranging his books carefully.

'Got enough to keep you going,' Matt observed.

'Reckon so. College made sure of that.' He faced Matt. 'What was all the red-carpet treatment? Back there. Meeting me – taking me for a drink.'

'Chance. I saw you.'

'I don't believe in special treatment, you know. For anyone. I mean, we're all equal, aren't we?'

'Can't even do a kindness these days without arousing suspicion. O.K. Fine.'

Matt read from the spine of one of the books: '"Ethics of Political And Social Change". Bit young, aren't you?'

'No,' said Bill defensively. 'What's age to do with anything? Just because we can't all talk posh . . .'

'No-one said anything about that.'

'Think it doesn't count?'

'Not arguing with you.' Matt had no desire to be here all night. Before leaving he turned and said. 'By the way, there was another reason for the red-carpet treatment. I was in your shoes once. I remember how it feels to be as frightened and unsure as you are now.'

He slipped out quickly to avoid a further argument, but from the sudden look on Bill's face he knew he'd got it right.

Tom had answered a knock on his cabin door, and opened it to find Jane standing there. He was genuinely pleased.

'It's fate, that's what it is,' he said, letting her in. 'It's good to see you.'

'Say that when the voyage is over,' she challenged him, sitting on his bed.

'But we've grown up, haven't we?'

'Tom, you were as pleased as I was when the divorce papers came through. You've gone your way and I've made a career . . .'

'What we both wanted,' he said, remembering things.

'Right. So I have no intention of letting you – or anyone – barge in and upset things.'

'You're going a bit far there,' he protested.

'Just warning.'

'We know each other too well.' He handed her a drink.

'That's what I'm afraid of.'

'You wouldn't be taking advantage of a poor innocent like me?' he demanded, half clowning, half hopeful.

'Now would I do a thing like that?'

'Don't try it.'

They laughed comfortably together and sipped their drinks. The atmosphere between them was easy as it had never been in the last days of their marriage.

'I'm just grateful we didn't have any kids,' she mused. 'There was a time when I'd have used them to get at you.'

'Your psychiatrist tell you that?'

'No – worked it out all on my own.'

'Good.'

She looked at him. 'Friends?'

'Friends.'

It was true.

By now Marion was also on board, ready for the party she

intended to give to mark the *Anglia's* first voyage under its new captain. She would have given anything, at this moment, to be able to get out of that party. Kate's vindictive gesture in selling cheaply the cottage that had once meant so much to Marion and George left her wanting to howl with impotent rage. But there was nothing she could do except sit in the Bellevue Lounge with a large drink, reading and re-reading the letter. At last she could stand it no longer and with a savage movement she ripped the letter across and across again.

'Mrs Terson.'

Marion looked up sharply, wondering what fool had chosen this moment to interrupt her. She saw a blonde, anxious-looking girl.

'You don't know me . . .'

'You're Christine Harris,' Marion interrupted. 'The new assistant purser.'

'I wanted to introduce myself before the party.'

'Did you?' said Marion unhelpfully. 'Why's that?'

'I'm not very good at cocktail gatherings, you see. Smoke and crowds and you can't hear yourself speak.'

Marion gave a faint smile. 'It won't be that bad, but I know what you mean.'

'I wanted to say – well, it's an honour for me to be working with Triangle – in *your* company.'

'Thank you. I appreciate that.' Marion wished the girl would go.

'It's always been my ambition, you see – I've always admired what you and Mr Terson achieved together.'

'Yes.' (Would the silly little cow never shut up?)

'It's an example,' said Christine Harris desperately, 'for all of us.'

'Thank you.'

'Well, I'm sorry to have interrupted you.' The girl fled.

Marion hardly noticed her go. She had picked up the shredded pieces of the letter from the ashtray, and was dribbling them through her fingers.

'Oh Kate,' she whispered, 'what have you done?'

Dougie Evans, encountering Judith, immediately spotted what was wrong.

'Where's Mortimer?' he demanded, aghast.

'I had to lock him up on the car deck,' Judith told him indignantly.

'Whatever for?'

She gave a brief account of the meeting with Charles.

'Mrs Harper, don't worry. There's been a misunderstanding. Go and fetch Morti.'

'*Can* I?'

'Go on,' he urged.

'There won't be any trouble, will there? I hate trouble in the home.'

'Yes, so do I. Fetch Mortimer. I'll deal with the first officer.'

She wasted no more time on argument, but headed for the car deck at a speed that belied her sixty years. There was a joyful re-union and they made their escape in haste. Once on the upper deck they ran straight into Charles Woodhouse.

'Madam . . .' he said with a fair attempt at restraint.

'Now don't shout at me,' she said, somewhat unjustly. 'I can't bear people shouting. They look so stupid.'

Charles dropped his already low voice a tone lower. 'I asked you to remove that wretched animal.'

'You don't mean that. If it were a cat . . .'

'I'd say exactly the same thing. You have deliberately ignored my request.'

'Request? You *ordered* me.'

'And you disobeyed.'

'What now, First Officer?' She was near to tears. 'Do I walk the plank?'

'Madam . . .' Charles ground his teeth.

' . . . or shall you just throw us both into the brig for a few weeks?'

'Please tie it up on the car deck *immediately*.'

She hurried away – in the direction of the car-deck. Charles tried to tell himself that he'd heard the last of her – but somehow it lacked conviction.

The party was to be held in the large Bellevue Lounge that was normally the domain of passengers, but this evening had been taken over. Officers were converging on it from all directions. John, catching up with Sarah Hallam at the door, made an automatic note that she was looking extremely attractive in a dark blue cocktail dress. Since this was plainly going to be an evening for putting a brave face on things it might also be an idea for himself and Sarah to straighten matters out between them.

'We must get together and discuss policy,' he told her, smiling.

'Yes, Captain.'

'Preferably before we sail. Would you come to the bridge at, say, three o'clock tomorrow?'

She shook her head, charming but determined. 'I don't think so. Why don't you give me a ring to settle on a mutually convenient time? I'll be in the ship's office. Perhaps you'll come and see me?'

She swept into the lounge ahead of him, leaving him dumbfounded and staring after her. Sarah Hallam had shown her battle colours. She was simply not going to be sent for like a subordinate.

'Mutually convenient time,' he muttered crossly as he followed her in.

After that the party was spoiled for him. He supposed it was no worse than other parties. He endured the flowery speeches from Marion and David West. He made one himself. He remembered seeing Barbara Carter there, when she shouldn't have been. Marion's doing again, he supposed. He was sure he'd drunk too much, and when the evening ended he had a splitting headache.

But the following morning something happened that drove everything else out of his head. Dougie looked in to say that there was an urgent message from the terminal where a young lad was causing an almighty rumpus.

'He demands to see you,' said Dougie, carefully impassive. 'He says he's your son.'

Chapter 3

It wasn't until they were facing each other across a table in a quiet Amsterdam restaurant that John managed to take a good long look at his son. He was startled and then hurt at the change in him. At sixteen Ted already showed signs of the man he would later become, which hadn't been the case when they had last seen each other, six months earlier. Six whole months. John silently cursed Maya who had separated him from his children.

As he listened to the boy's story he realised that Ted had developed a determination and independence that any father might be proud of.

'Hitch-hiking right across Denmark, then Holland . . .' He tried to sound disapproving but knew that a sneaking admiration would not be kept out of his voice. 'You must really have wanted to come.'

'I did.'

'Why?'

'You know why,' said Ted, after a pause.

'I don't. Ted, if I knew why I wouldn't have to ask.' The boy turned his head away, and John spoke more urgently. 'I haven't got a lot of time.'

'You've never had a lot of time,' said his son.

John's voice was gentle. 'Being at sea means that you've got to be at a certain place at a certain time. I'm the captain. The captain has to . . .'

'I know, I know,' Ted interrupted impatiently. He had heard it before. 'Some other time. Dad, I'll talk to you some other time.'

'You've come all this way, surely you . . .'

'It's all too mixed up. Too many things to get sorted out. I don't want to rush it. I'd rather talk about it when we've got the time not to make mistakes, not to have more misunderstandings.'

John nodded, but felt impelled to say, 'You know that I've got to send you back to your mother? Under Swedish law, until you're eighteen . . .'

'I know!' Ted rose, suddenly decisive. 'Right. Will you stand me the taxi fare to the railway station?' He grinned at his father's questioning look. 'I've done enough hitch-hiking to last me for life, and someone's going to have to pay for my rail ticket.'

Charles Woodhouse, very conscious of himself in charge during the captain's absence, managed to make his presence felt in all parts of the ship. He was pleased with the effect he produced.

He was less pleased with the sight that met his eyes as he strode through the entrance hall. He waylaid Judith Harper and addressed her in a tight angry voice.

'I asked you, madam, to ensure that that animal was taken to the . . .'

'Excuse me.' Dougie Evans who was with Judith broke in humbly.

'Yes?' Charles gave him a frosty glance.

'You're the first officer, I presume,' said Dougie with a glance at Charles' uniform.

'Charles Woodhouse,' Charles nodded.

'Right. And I also presume, by what you've just said, that it was you who ordered this lady down to the car deck.'

'You know the ship's rules, I presume.'

'She was trapped in a corner down there, frightened out . . .'

Judith tapped him on the shoulder. 'Not exactly frightened out . . .'

Charles let her get no further. 'That's her decision, Mr . . .'

'Evans. I'm the purser.'

' . . . Evans. All I asked her to do was take the dog there.'

'And however terrified the lady was is of no concern to . . .'

Judith raised her voice. 'I wasn't exactly "terrified", Mr . . .'

Again Charles ignored her. 'Rules, as I'm sure you as the purser will agree, are rules.'

Dougie refused to be impressed by this. 'Rules, as I'm sure you as a human being will agree, are for our guidance, not . . .'

'Perhaps I can help.' They all turned to see Sarah Hallam standing there, a faint quizzical smile on her face.

Dougie got in first. 'This lady, Mrs Harper, is a permanent passenger. She has a dog – this one, which she has always, for two years, been allowed to keep in her cabin. This officer insisted, apparently, that she take it to the car deck, where I found her huddled and afraid and . . .'

'If that's what she's been allowed to do, then I can see no reason why we shouldn't continue to allow her to do so,' said Sarah.

Charles broke in. 'I don't know who the hell you are, lady, but I'm not going to . . .'

'Then perhaps you'd better find out who I am,' she said sweetly, and walked quickly away.

Charles regarded her back furiously before striding off in the opposite direction. Judith was left alone with Dougie, who put a protective arm round her. 'Now don't you worry, we'll soon . . .'

'Mr Evans.' Her voice was strong and indignant.

'Yes, ma'am?'

'I wasn't exactly "huddled and afraid" you know.'

'I know. But let's try and get all the sympathy we can. Right?'

He gave her a conspiratorial wink and she smiled back in sudden comprehension. 'Right, Mr Evans. In that case you'd better help this poor little old lady back to her cabin.'

Sarah forgot Judith Harper and Mortimer the minute she was out of sight. She was late for a meeting with Marion Terson, and for this she blamed John Anderson who had not come to see her as she had expected. On the docks she dashed straight for a cab that was drawing up and collided with the passenger getting out. It was the captain.

'You do realise that we sail in . . .' he consulted his watch.

'Yes, I do,' she said briefly.

'And I thought we were going to have a meeting.'

'So did I,' she said in a voice full of meaning. 'The Sonesta Hotel, please.'

She caught sight of John's disapproving face as the cab drew away, then dismissed him from her mind. She was puzzled and worried. What the hell did Marion want that was urgent enough to drag her away at a moment like this?

At that very moment Marion Terson was sitting in a palatial suite at the Sonesta enjoying the feeling that life was good and she was well in control of everything. If only George – but she refused to think of that. If she didn't have George she at least had the legacy he'd left her, and she was going to make the best of it, in every way. And if that meant living in luxurious hotels (which she owned) and being looked after by charming young men like Nick Stevens – well, George would have understood.

Nick was pouring her a drink now. She sipped it absently as she read the newspaper. She always conscientiously studied the financial pages, certain that one day their meaning would become clear. But today her attention was riveted on the full-page advertisement that the company had taken for its prospectus.

'If the rules say we have to publish a prospectus on the first day of trading . . .' she said.

'. . . then let's make sure it's an impressive one. Right?' he finished for her.

They smiled and chinked glasses.

'It was the right thing to do,' he said. 'Going public. The right thing at the right time.'

'Well, of course. We'll have enough capital for . . .'

'. . . anything we want.'

There was a knock on the door and Sarah breezed in, full of apologies for her lateness. She refused Nick's offer of a drink and sat down in a businesslike fashion. The journey had left her feeling hassled and she hoped this meeting was going to be worth it.

'So?' said Marion, smiling at her.

'Pardon?'

'How's it all going?'

'On the ship?'

'Sarah – dear – you are the first company manager ever to take office actually on board – so . . .?'

Sarah subdued her irritation at being called 'dear' and replied calmly, 'No problems at all. I thought you were asking for specifics.'

'Not yet a while.' Marion waited.

'There is just . . .'

'Yes . . .?'

'I'm not sure whether this comes under my jurisdiction . . . I think – and this is only just from walking about, talking to people . . .'

'We realise that it's only an impression,' said Nick helpfully.

'Perhaps we could do more in the area of public relations. I mean, what we're offering, now, is more than just a quick shuttle service between England, Denmark and Holland. Yes?'

'Yes,' said Marion.

'It's an experience, if you like, almost a holiday in itself . . .' Sarah broke off as she realised the other two were exchanging a smile. 'I'm sorry, have I . . .?'

'Not at all,' Marion assured her.

'"Great minds thinking alike" department,' said Nick.

'It's just that – talking of public relations – a journalist is going aboard today who will then write a piece for his chain of magazines about us. A journalist coming on a trip – at *our* invitation – is exactly the same as a PRO man on the payroll,' Marion explained. 'Better, in fact.' Abruptly Marion changed the subject. 'You and John Anderson getting on O.K.?'

'Fine, thank you, no problems there at all.'

'Good.' Marion looked at her watch. 'Well, it's time I was off.' She jumped up and said by way of explanation, 'When I have a free lunch ahead of me – especially when it's on David West – that's when *I'm* never late.' She patted Sarah on the arm. 'You're doing very well, dear.'

'Thank you very much,' said Sarah, resisting a temptation to pull away.

'I'll be in touch, Nick.' Marion flurried out.

Sarah waited till her footsteps could no longer be heard, and smiled ruefully. 'Damned with faint praise,' she said.

'Not at all. It's just her way.'

'And is it also her way to arrange a meeting when what we talked about could have been said on the phone?'

'She likes the personal touch.' Nick gave her a warm smile. 'So do I. Anyway, how were we to know that everything was going so smoothly? You could have had two hours of problems to relate.'

Sarah nodded, unsmiling. 'Well, I'll be getting back,' she said, but she didn't move.

'Problems?' said Nick, seeing her frown.

'I know it's none of my business – as such – who Marion has lunch with . .'

'They *are* partners.'

'Exactly. But there's something about the Triangle/D.R.W. set-up that worries me.'

'What?' He saw her shrug. 'Intuition?' Again that shrug. 'Everything's fine, it's going to be good for all of us.' He made his voice enthusiastic. 'Believe me.'

'From a girl-friend?'

Matt looked up sharply, displeased at the interruption. He had escaped to the on-board pub and provided himself with a large whisky before opening Kate's letter. Its contents had amply justified these precautions, and he would have much preferred to be left alone. Yet here was Tom Kelly's ex-wife standing beside him, full of curiosity.

'What?' he demanded, abandoning manners.

'The letter. In my experience only a letter from a member of the opposite sex can have that sort of effect.'

He glared, furious to know that his reactions had been written so clearly on his face.

'What sort of effect would that be, Miss . . . er . . .?' What the hell did you call an "ex"?'

'Jane Anthony. As if you've been hit over the head with a sledge-hammer.'

He indicated the letter. 'The lady in question has that sort of effect.'

'It happens to us all,' she said sympathetically.

'Yeah, I'm sure. Look, I really don't want to talk about it.'

'O.K.' She looked put-out, but moved off with no more than a shrug.

'Miss Anthony – er – Jane?' He rose and moved after her. 'That doesn't mean I wouldn't like to talk about other things.' She gave him a friendly smile. 'Drink?' he offered.

She indicated the clock. 'When we've sailed I'd love to.'

When she'd gone, Matt finished his drink and carefully folded the letter and put it back in the envelope. He started to put it in his pocket, then changing his mind, he screwed it up. The barmaid's eyes were on him. He gave her a weary smile.

'Yesterday is yesterday, today is today, and tomorrow is tomorrow,' he said, staring into her startled eyes. 'If you know what I mean.'

He rose and made his way out. He felt as if he'd been to a funeral.

They'd be sailing in an hour. Already the great doors on the car deck had opened to let the vehicles roll on, and foot passengers were trickling aboard. Dougie Evans had taken a deep breath, recognising that he'd had his last peaceful moment for some time.

Some trips you struck it lucky, with no troublesome passengers. He knew within the first five minutes that this wasn't going to be one of them. The man who accosted him in the entrance hall was middle-aged, paunchy, and with a face that looked as if it had taken in too much alcohol over the years. In fact, his manner now was faintly tipsy as he informed Dougie of his requirements, which were V.I.P.

'It's not my concern what cabin number I have,' he announced. 'That is not something I have to bother with. What is my concern and what I *can* tell you is that it'll be the best one on board . . . or, to put it another way, it had better be.'

Dougie studied the passenger lists, wondering how much of this assertive manner was put on to impress the girl who was at least twenty years too young to be with this man. She was blonde and cheeky in a Marilyn Monroe sort of way, and at one time Dougie would unhesitatingly have characterised her as 'a bit on the side'. But the lists declared that she was the man's wife.

'You do know that everything I have is first class?' the man went on loudly. '*You do know that*?'

'If you say so, sir. Mr Kevin Warrender and wife. Cabin E – on the boat deck.'

'And that's the . . .'

'Yes, it is, sir,' said Duggie hastily. 'The best on board.'

'Good. And the next thing you can do is to arrange for me to have a word with your captain as soon as possible.'

'We have to set sail sir. It's quite a hectic time.'

'Just do it.'

Dougie consigned them thankfully into the care of Christine Harris and moved off quickly. He saw Sarah in outdoor clothes, evidently having just boarded. A man had bumped into her and they were engaged in mutual apologies. Dougie immediately classed this man as just as unlikeable as the man he'd just left, but in a different way. This one was smooth, urbane, and carried his middle-aged heaviness with oily suavity. He introduced himself to Sarah as James Wootton before she hurried away, and Dougie got the chance to see how his face altered the minute she'd gone. The smile faded and was replaced by an intent look, the eyes darting quickly round. It reminded Dougie of a ferret. Then he returned to his duties and forgot the man.

John had seen Sarah come aboard from his vantage point on the bridge, and now he made his way along to her office. He was trying hard to pull his mind away from his private worries and back to his job. Now, if ever, a captain should give his whole attention to his ship, but he could not drive Ted from his mind – the way the boy had travelled all that distance, and then calmly allowed himself to be despatched back. It was odd, and it was at variance with that determination that John knew his son had inherited from himself.

Sarah's office was empty. When she came in a moment later she found John standing idly looking at a map on the wall. She looked surprised and not pleased.

'We were going to have a policy talk,' he reminded her.

'You were going to ring to arrange a mutually convenient time,' she corrected him gently.

'I'm sorry. I had to go ashore.'

'Snap.'

'Yes.'

There was an embarrassed pause which she was the one to break.

'There's something about this situation that worries you. Is it my being a woman?'

'No, not at all,' he said, a fraction too quickly. 'One must move with the times.' He did not see the slight smile that she tactfully smothered. 'You're right. There *is* something that concerns me. I am the ship's master. There's hundreds of years of tradition behind me and my position.'

'I understand that.'

'What I'm saying is that . . .'

' . . . The ship is your domain?' she helped him out.

'Yes. Totally. Including here, the ship's office.'

'I see.' She was thoughtful.

'That's not personal aggrandisement. That's the way it is, the way it's always been.'

'Mr Anderson – er – Captain Anderson, do I have free access to the bridge?'

'Of course not,' he said at once. Then, realising the trap she had laid for him, 'Miss Hallam, that is entirely different.'

'Is it?' I would have said that a company manager should have domain over everything to do with the company.'

'Being at sea is entirely different from a block of offices in the City of London,' he defended himself.

'Of course it is. So, let's say, shall we, that the bridge is your domain, and this office – poor thing that it is – shall be mine?'

'I don't want to appear pompous, but every inch of a ship is the master's.'

'Pompous? You? That's the last thing you are,' she smiled. 'I *believe*.' The smile became a laugh. 'Oh come on, nothing's changed. We're both on the same side, surely? There's no need for us to clash.'

'My feelings entirely.'

'The point is that this ship is now an independent company committed to making an individual profit. And *I* am the manager of that company.'

'The point is that this ship is still a sea-going vessel, under the total command of its master. Pompous or not. That's the way it always has been, and that's the way it always will be. I won't have

my authority undermined.'
'Which is exactly what I feel about *my* authority.'
John recognised that they had reached stalemate. Looking at his watch was an act of cowardice.
'I'm sorry, it's nearly sailing time, I must return to my . . . domain,' he said with relief.
'I thought we were going to have a policy meeting,' she said gently.
He turned at the door. 'It seems that that's exactly what we've had, doesn't it?'
Luckily the business of sailing kept him and Sarah out of each other's hair until the next morning, by which time he had forgotten his annoyance with her.
One who was less lucky was Kevin Warrender. He was standing by the desk in the main passenger restaurant trying (but not very hard) to keep his temper with the stupid girl who wouldn't understand his position. She acted for all the world as though she'd never heard of him, and it was embarrassing with Penny looking on. A middle-aged man with a young wife couldn't afford to lose his dignity for one moment.
The arrival of Dougie Evans was greeted with relief by both himself and the harassed receptionist.
'Everything is *not* all right,' he said in answer to Dougie's question. 'I should have thought that an organisation as – is "efficient" the word I'm searching for? – would have been used to correspondents travelling by now and . . .'
'The gentleman says that he doesn't have to pay for his breakfast, Mr Evans,' the girl broke in desperately.
'He's quite right,' said Dougie soothingly. 'Don't worry, I'll sort it out.' He drew Kevin away. 'I'm sorry, it's not the girl's fault. We have only just left port and . . .'
'*Penny*!' Kevin Warrender had realised that his wife was not following them. She had remained by the reception desk, an expression of weary disgust on her face. She sighed and followed her husband to their table, but when Dougie had left them she voiced her feelings.
'A boat-trip across the North Sea.' Her tone suggested that a fortnight in sunny Siberia would have been more fun.
'Oh come on,' he said. 'It's better than that.'
'It's not Bermuda though, is it?'
'We take it in turns,' he said hurriedly. 'There's hundreds of trips

for journalists – sometimes it's hot and sandy, sometimes it's not. But I'll tell you something, my sweet, it's always free. There aren't many husbands who can provide their wives with two free holidays a year. And just for writing nice things about them. I mean, it can't be bad, can it?'

She didn't answer. She was beginning to think that it could.

At ten o'clock that morning Shipboard Management had its first formal meeting. At 10.15 precisely John's truce with Sarah Hallam came to an abrupt end. The ridiculous woman actually wanted to slow the ship down so that crossings would take longer. What was worse, her little speech explaining her idea seemed to have infected Matt with the same nonsense.

'Then I'm sure you'll agree with me that a smooth, cheap crossing is what people want,' she finished.

'*And* arriving on schedule,' said Matt firmly.

'And arriving on schedule,' she agreed. 'Which is far more likely if we have a slower crossing time. Then, if we're delayed – bad weather, perhaps, technical fault, anything – then we can be sure of making up the time – and *still* arrive on schedule. *That's* what impresses people.'

'It makes sense, John,' said Matt.

John looked at him bleakly before turning to Charles.

'I'll need time to think about it,' Charles said vaguely.

'Well, let's all do that, shall we?' said John with relief. 'Let's all think about it and discuss it further at the next meeting. I must say, though, you'll have to come up with very strong arguments to convince me.' Before he could proceed to the next business the door was thrust open and Dougie Evans arrived, breathless and full of explanations.

'I've been trying to appease a recalcitrant journalist, who seems to think that the future of Triangle Line rests entirely on us being nice to him.'

'You know something about this?' said John, catching Sarah's sudden smile.

'Mrs Terson mentioned something about it when I saw her yesterday. I gather that after the trip he'll write a report about us in his magazine.'

John spoke coldly. 'I trust that in future I'll be consulted before anything like this occurs again.'

'Of course,' said Dougie, 'but this was arranged before you took command.'

'Not that it really matters. It's all cut and dried before he comes aboard,' said Charles in a world-weary tone.

'What is?' demanded John.

'What he's going to write. All these journalists, going on their free trips, writing reports about it afterwards for the travel and holiday columns in their newpapers and magazines. The fact is they'll write a glowing report no matter what, or else they might jeopardise their and their colleagues' free holidays and trips in the future.'

'I must say Mrs Terson rather implied that,' Sarah admitted.

'Not this one,' said John quietly.

'Why do you say that?' said Sarah.

'Kevin Warrender's his name. I knew him – I was telling Charles yesterday. Oh a long time ago now, but . . . Kevin Warrender's a man of principle, believe me. If he doesn't like anything about this trip, then he'll say so.'

He was still guiltily conscious that he had not yet seen Warrender, although he had received an urgent message to do so. He repaired the omission immediately after the meeting, inviting Kevin and Penny to his cabin for a drink.

He was slightly shocked at the journalist's appearance. Of course it was twenty years since they'd last met, but still – Warrender looked debauched, that was the only word for it. And the wife, whom John gathered vaguely was number three or four or something, she was young enough to be his daughter.

'I must say I was very surprised when I heard you were coming aboard,' he said, pouring Warrender a third brandy. 'I mean, it's been such a long time . . .' He floundered and started again. 'I'll be reading what you have to say about us in your magazine . . .'

'Magazines,' Warrender corrected him sharply. 'I'm syndicated.'

'In that case I'll be reading it with even more trepidation.'

'Will you?' Warrender looked surprised.

'Remembering what you've said about certain things in the past. "Kevin Warrender, the man who writes straight from the shoulder".'

Warrender gave a shrug. He seemed embarrassed.

'Yes, well, things change, don't they?' he said. 'We get older, more cynical – no, more pragmatic. We become feature writers and captains of ships and . . . well, we begin to want to hold onto what we've got, right?'

John frowned as if he was having trouble taking in what he was hearing. At last he said, 'I'm only saying that I wouldn't like to be on one of the wrong sides of Kevin Warrender's crusading diatribes.'

Warrender shook his head and laughed.

'John, John, what I write about the good ship *Anglia* won't cause you to lose a moment's sleep. Any of you.' He winked. 'Promise.'

John had a disturbing sensation, almost akin to disappointment. The hint of corruption in a man he had once admired was shocking to someone as fundamentally straightforward as himself. When he had got rid of the Warrenders he made for Sarah's office.

'Did you arrange Kevin Warrender's trip?' he demanded.

'No. Why?'

'I know it's good for the ship, good for the Line, to have a glowing report written about them. But, I don't know about you, it's the payola bit I can't take. I mean, well, he was a good journalist once and now here he is accepting free trips – free holidays – just as long as he writes nice things about us . . .'

'It's business. It's the big wide world.'

'Which is another reason why I like my job. Out at sea most of the time. The sea is totally uncompromising.'

'Like you?' she ventured.

He gave her a reluctant grin. The phone rang and she turned from him to answer it. After a moment she handed him the receiver.

'Thank you . . .' He listened, then she heard him say incredulously, '*On board*? . . . You're sure . . .? Yes, of course, thank you . . . Yes, I'll be right there.'

He slammed down the receiver, outrage written across his face. 'You'll have to excuse me, Miss Hallam.'

'Trouble?'

'No, none at all.' He thought for a second before saying grimly, 'Not for *me* anyway.'

Five minutes later he was confronting his son in his cabin.

'O.K., Ted, no beating about the bush, no prevarication, no sliding around the facts. What's going on?'

The boy tried to keep his tone light. 'Not a lot. I'm a bona fide passenger on board the *Anglia*. I've bought my ticket and I have a cabin.'

'Where did you get the money?'

'I sold the railway . . .'

' . . . ticket I bought you,' said John in a resigned tone. 'Of course. Plus the money I gave you for food and magazines. So that solves that problem. You've got a ticket, you've got a right to be on board.'

'That's right.'

'Which is a relief,' said John, seeing his worst nightmares recede.

'What would you have done?'

'If you'd been a stowaway, I'd have put you in the brig.'

'You're joking.'

'I'm not. A captain is a captain is a captain. Right, so now we'll start at the beginning. We've lots of time now, no rush.' He indicated for the boy to sit, and when they were facing each other he said, 'Why did you come all the way to Amsterdam yesterday?'

Ted shrugged. 'Wanted to see you.'

'And . . .?'

'O.K. . . .' He sighed. 'I don't like the way mum treats me. I don't like home, I don't like school, I don't even like Sweden much. Do you know what she wants me to do? Study to be a lawyer, a doctor . . . something like that – *anything* like that. As long as it's respectable and establishment and . . .'

' . . . nothing to do with ships,' John supplied.

'Exactly, but I've . . . the sea in my blood.'

'That's romantic nonsense. You've been watching too many films.'

'You're doing it as well. Treating me like a kid.'

'Yes. Sorry. I know what you feel. It's just . . . Ted, there's plenty of time. You should really go back to your mother, sweat it out if you like, pass your exams, then, *if* you feel the same . . .'

'I'm not going to do that. Whatever else I do, I'm not going to go back. That's final. Law or no law.' He saw his father's exasperated gesture and stumbled over the next words. 'O.K., the thing is, you . . . O.K., the thing is I'd rather be with you, than . . . I miss being with you, I don't want to go back.'

Something in his son's fumbling declaration of love clutched at John. He spoke with difficulty. 'That's right, you had to say that, didn't you? I'm being the heavy father, and you had to say that.' He managed a rueful smile, which Ted returned. 'This might – or might not – surprise you. I like you too. I miss being with you, too.'

'Incidentally, it's not against the law. It's only in Sweden that I have to stay with mum. We're not in Sweden any more.'

John nodded. He too had thought of that.

'O.K., so you really want to go to sea?'

'That's all I want. I'll work, do anything . . .'

'That's exactly what I had in mind.' John picked up the phone, and in a moment he was talking to Dougie Evans. 'Are you still short staffed in the galley? . . . Right, I've got you an extra man . . . He'll be coming straight down.'

He replaced the receiver. 'Right, Mr Anderson, you know the purser's office?'
'I'll find it.'
'Then report to Mr Evans, immediately.'
'Aye, aye, sir.'

'What a nice dog!'
Judith turned to see a tall, heavily built, middle-aged man standing beside her. They were in the arcade, where she sometimes brought Mortimer because he so enjoyed looking into shop windows.
'Doesn't mind the sea life?' the man asked.
'He's had two years of it. It was either that or six months nasty quarantine. Heaven alone knows what that would have done to little Morti.'
Warmed by his encouraging smile she told him the whole story of her husband's death and her decision to stay aboard the *Anglia* with her two dogs, one of whom had since passed on. From time to time he made suitable comments like 'Quite', 'That's amazing', and 'A life littered with tragedy'. He was such a nice man.
'Giving up your homeland, with all that that implies, because of your regard for a . . .'
'Many people have gone into exile in the past for the sake of loved ones,' she informed him solemnly.
He nodded, his eyes grave and sympathetic.
'Well,' she said suddenly brisk, 'I must continue with Morti's constitutional. Exercise is so important. Lovely to have talked to you.'
James Wootton watched her go, his face thoughtful. When she had vanished he turned and made for the purser's office which, as he had hoped, he found empty. Dougie, coming in a few moments later, pulled up short at the sight that met his eyes.
'I'm sorry, sir, but would you mind telling me what you're doing?'
Wootton jumped so hard that he almost dropped the passenger list in his hand, but immediately he recovered his composure.
'I'm sorry – but I've lost the room number from my key. Well – the trouble is, I can't remember what it is and – it's stupid, isn't it?'
'I see,' said Dougie woodenly. 'Your name, sir?'
'Wootton. James Wootton.'
Dougie took the passenger list from Wootton's hand.
'You're looking at the wrong page,' he said. 'They're in alpha-

betical order.' He rummaged until he found the name. 'There you are sir – 121, Anglia Deck.'

'Thank you very much.'

Dougie's tone was carefully courteous. 'Next time, sir, perhaps it might be better to ask.'

'Oh, there won't be a next time, believe me. The number is engraved on my mind.'

Dougie Evans made a mental note to keep an eye on Mr James Wootton.

As the day advanced the crew members found their work becoming more or less arduous, depending on the nature of their duties. For Jane Anthony the tough time came early on, when the cabins had to be cleaned out. The overseeing of that was normally a simple task, except that it was being complicated by the presence of Barbara Carter, who seemed determined not to do her work properly and to place the blame on anyone but herself. This morning, for instance, she had neglected to put the up top bunks in cabins 35 to 40, and when challenged with her forgetfulness had taken refuge in unconvincing denial. She had even gone so far as to say that Lisa Watkins must have pulled the bunks down to spite her. Jane had warned her that she'd soon have to pull her socks up, but she doubted the message had got through.

Passing through the shopping arcade she noticed Matt standing by one of the windows, staring moodily out to sea.

'Still recovering from the sledgehammer?' she asked.

'Oh, hullo,' he shrugged. 'Just thinking.'

'Can do you a lot of harm,' she said wisely. 'Too much thinking.'

'You've said a truth there, lady.'

'You were going to buy me a drink after we sailed,' she reminded him.

'I had a lot on my mind last night,' he said uneasily.

Jane decided to take the hint. 'You still don't want to talk,' she said. 'Sorry.'

Matt grabbed her wrist as she made to move on. 'You're a very attractive woman. I don't have to tell you that, but . . .'

'But what?'

He took a deep breath. 'I've been doing some thinking. I like Tom Kelly . . .'

'So do I,' she said, suddenly understanding. 'And that's it. That's as far as it goes. We're separated, divorced, smote asunder. Legally, mentally, totally. That's the way we both want it. Being on the same boat is a coincidence. A nice coincidence, because two old friends usually make good ship companions. But I value my independence.'

'Great,' said Matt. 'That's exactly what I like to hear. The world can't have enough of attractive, independent ladies. Now, about that drink I'm going to buy you.'

They repaired to the Bellevue Bar and chatted for an hour. Matt found himself liking her more and more. Jane had just the right combination of sympathy and humorous acerbity and he found her company pleasant and undemanding, which was all he felt he could stand at the moment, bruised as he was. He made a mental note to see more of her. Just the same, when the time came to leave he let her go alone. He wasn't ready to be seen moving off with her yet. She seemed to understand this, and bade him a friendly farewell before returning to her duties.

On the way she encountered Dougie, bursting to tell someone about his grievance.

'O.K., so maybe I'm imagining things. But I don't like walking into my office and finding someone – passenger or not – going through my private lists.'

'Passenger lists aren't private,' Jane pointed out.

'Anything that's on someone else's desk should be considered private.'

'Maybe Mr Wootton's going to hijack the ship,' said Jane with a grin. 'He's at the moment sabotaging the automatic pilot.'

'With the captain and Mr Woodhouse, bound, gagged and helpless.' Dougie joined in the joke. For a moment he enjoyed the fantasy of Charles Woodhouse at a saboteur's mercy. He hadn't forgiven his behaviour to Judith.

Christine appeared, looking harassed. 'Mr Warrender wants *another* bottle of brandy,' she said crossly.

Dougie shrugged. 'Ah well. You heard the boss. Mr Warrender gets anything he wants – on the house.'

'We're in the wrong job,' said Christine. She turned to go.

'Excuse me.' Jane halted her, and stood scanning her face. 'We've worked together before,' she said at last. 'Haven't we?'

Christine shook her head firmly.

Jane's brow furrowed with concentration. 'I'm absolutely sure that . . .'

'No,' said Christine abruptly.

'I never forget a face. You'd be surprised – ten years later and —' she looked harder at Christine. 'What other ships have you been on?

I mean Triangle ships?'

'I've never seen you before.' Christine's voice was sharp.

'O.K., O.K.' Jane waved her hands in a gesture of defeat and let the girl go. She pulled a face at Dougie as Christine departed, but she hadn't given up. The memory would come to her later.

Lisa Watkins' pursuit of Bill Ryan was not prospering. Cornering him in the crew recreation room she had actually managed to nudge him into fetching her a cup of coffee. But he had placed it beside her and turned away to play a solitary game of cards. He seemed to have forgotten her existence. Lisa sighed frustratedly as she looked at his broad shoulders and narrow waist. What on earth was the matter with him? She knew there was nothing the matter with herself. There'd been boys enough to demonstrate that: boys who'd have sat up on their hind legs begging if they'd received one tenth of the encouragement she'd offered this lad. So what was the matter with him? Not *that* – surely?

The door banged open and Barbara Carter stood over Lisa, scowling.

'All right, so come on,' she stormed. 'What's it all about?'

'Me?' Lisa looked innocent.

'You.'

'What's what all about?' said Lisa, stalling for time. Out of the corner of her eye she had seen Bill's swift jerk of attention the moment Barbara came in. So that was the way the wind was blowing, was it?

'Bit childish, isn't it?' said Barbara with scorn. 'Those bunks, trying to land me in trouble, is that what you're doing?'

Bill had stood up and moved towards them, his eyes on Barbara.

'Trying to get me in trouble with the head prefect, were you?' snapped Barbara.

'What is all this?' Bill demanded.

'Nothing to do with you, Sunny Jim.' Barbara dismissed him. 'Sit down.'

Lisa grinned. Sir Galahad had had his horse shot out from under him and no mistake.

'You think you're so clever,' Barbara sneered.

'And you think you're so hoity-toity.'

The door burst open and Charles Woodhouse stood on the threshold, frowning.

'What the hell's going on?' he demanded. 'I mean, you've got the

right to do what you like in your own recreation room . . .'
'Too right,' said Bill, just audibly.
'I'm not talking to you,' said Charles with a withering glance.
'*I'm* talking to *you*.'
Charles turned back to the girls. 'But when the passengers can hear you shouting . . .'
'You have no jurisdiction in here . . .' Bill protested.
'*Not another word*! So what's the trouble?'
'Nothing I can't handle,' said Barbara. 'Sir.' She made to go past him but Charles took her arm, more gently than she would have expected. 'Fancy a walk on deck?' He gave her a little smile. 'We can talk. All right?'
Barbara shrugged. 'Why not?'
'Officers,' said Bill when the door had closed. 'Think they've got the right to . . .'
'He's a fast worker,' said Lisa. 'I'll say that for him.'
She gave Bill a significant glance but he had resumed his seat and was shuffling the cards again. She sighed. This was going to be harder than she'd thought. Still, at least the little scene had answered one of her questions. Not that it looked like doing her much good.

Nick Stevens would have gone to the stake before admitting to the outside world that he was less than confident of Marion Terson's business ability. But he could not hide from himself a slight unease at her inexperience. Today he had decided to beard her in her lair – to be precise, the Sonesta Hotel.
He refused her offer of tea and cut short the social preliminaries.
'What do you know about the *Fleetway*?' he demanded.
'It's one of our freight liners. It runs between . . .'
'And that's all?' he interrupted, anxiety overcoming his normally perfect manners.
'What else is there to know?' Her wary tone made him even more uneasy.
'I've heard word that men have been looking over it, making enquiries – discreet of course, about the feasability of converting it into a passenger liner.' He paused. 'The men are David West's agents.'
'How do you know?'
'Take my word.' He felt his heart sink. Her evasiveness confirmed all his worst suspicions. 'You know about this, don't you?' He meant

his tone to sound like an accusation, and when Marion nodded he went on angrily, 'So what's it all about? The very best advice that we have to hand suggests that with the way things are at present three passenger ferries are the optimum for Triangle.' He waited for her answer. 'Marion?'

'David West isn't interested in the *Fleetway* for Triangle's passenger fleet,' she said at last. 'It's for D.R.W.' He stared at her, dumbfounded. 'If we sell it to David West and D.R.W., we can use the extra capital to expand our hotel interests.'

'I still don't see it, Marion. We went public in order to expand our capital . . .'

'But that money is for the building of new ships to keep the company viable in the late eighties and beyond.'

He blew out hard. 'I'm not really sure that . . .'

'Don't worry. I know what I'm doing. Everything is completely under control.'

Nick stared at her.

Chapter 4

With the ship due to dock at Esbjerg in an hour Dougie was grabbing a hasty breakfast. He could barely conceal his surprise when the captain dropped into a chair beside him and announced that he was here for coffee. After all, there was plenty of coffee on the bridge, wasn't there?

After a little small-talk John cleared his throat awkwardly and said, 'Now – Mr Anderson – the young man I sent you —'

'Oh yes.' At once Dougie understood, but he kept his face impassive. He was quite happy to play John's game. 'Mr Anderson.'

'How's he doing?'

'Very well, sir,' Dougie was frantically trying to recall which one Ted Anderson was. Finally he shrugged.

'Yes?' said John.

'I mean as far as . . .'

' . . . one can judge when it comes to washing dishes and cleaning vegetables,' John finished with a grin.

'Precisely, sir. But —'

'Thing is, I trust he'll be treated exactly as any other member of the crew.'

Dougie spoke carefully. 'That's exactly what he is.'

'Good. Thank you.' John tapped his cup authoritatively. 'Good coffee this.'

The subject under discussion was occupied in cleaning vegetables as they spoke, surrounded by a large mound of cabbages. Ted Anderson was humming under his breath. It wasn't quite as he had dreamed of coming to sea, but he was happy enough. He inspected a cabbage closely.

'Work of art, that,' he mused aloud.

'What?'

Startled to find he had company, Ted whirled round to find a cabin girl surveying him curiously. He liked what he saw. Lisa Watkins had generous features and generous curves, and to Ted's innocent sixteen years she was redolent of life with a capital 'L'.

'You talking to me or about me?' she demanded.

'Ah,' he recovered quickly. 'I'll need a bit of time for that.'

She grinned. 'All the time in the world.'

'Yes,' he said, backing away hastily from the hint in that grin. 'Actually I was referring to this cabbage leaf.'

'Work of art?' she said, baffled. To Lisa a work of art was that Trechikov thing that her Mum kept over the mantelpiece.

'Look at it. Those veins, those intricate lacy patterns, that symmetry. Have you ever seen anything like it?'

She nodded. 'Every day when I was at school. Used to call them greens.'

'You've got no soul,' he said sadly.

'Maybe not. But there are other things.'

She winked and passed on. Ted gave her a shy smile before going back to his cabbages. He was cross to discover that he was blushing.

Down here he was roughly able to follow the ship's docking procedure through its movements. He remained where he was, getting an odd pleasure from having to stay aboard while the passengers disembarked. It marked him off from them as a crew member. He felt this even though he knew that many crew members were able to go ashore.

One of those who was determined to shake the dust of the *Anglia* from her feet was Barbara. Bill Ryan ran across her in the entrance hall and found his feet rooted to the spot. There was everything about Barbara to rouse his ire. She was dressed more like a first-class passenger than a cabin girl. Strangely none of this occurred to him.

'Er – hullo.' He inwardly cursed himself for sounding nervous. But dammit, he *was* nervous.

'Mm?' She seemed to see him for the first time, and gave a small nod. 'Hallo.'

'Looks like a nice day,' he said. She rewarded this effort with another nod, even smaller than the first. 'By the way, my name is Bill Ryan. I'm . . .'

'Are you?' she said indifferently.

'The thing is, I don't really know your name at all, and . . .' He waited, but she made no response. 'Going ashore?' She nodded again. 'Yes, well, you would. I mean, why not? Thing is, if you've got no-one to – well —'

'What?' There was no mistaking her expression of boredom. Bill's shoulders sagged.

'Just a suggestion.'

'*What* was?' she demanded in puzzled irritation.

'I was saying that – well – if you haven't got anyone to – well, sort of – I thought that I'd —'

He was talking to empty air. Barbara had moved past him, her face alight at the sight of someone. Bill turned to see Charles and Matt, but Barbara's interest was all for Charles.

'My, my,' Charles surveyed her. 'I didn't realise that I was showing the sights of Esbjerg to a princess.'

'Well, you know now,' she told him with a smile.

The two of them swept off together, ignoring the others. Bill realised that Matt was looking at him sympathetically, and immediately he wiped the forlorn look off his face.

'Showing the sights to a princess,' he mimicked.

'Oh, he's got the chat, all right,' Matt agreed.

'Chat! It's just 'cos he's got a few stripes and has the right accent. Doesn't impress me.'

'She's not for the likes of you, my son,' said Matt wisely. 'Out of your class.'

'Cabin girl?' said Bill in disbelief.

'Out of mine too.' Matt winked. 'Believe me.'

Before Bill could demand to know what he meant, Tom arrived and hastily hailed Matt. 'Matt, a favour.'

'For me, or by me?'

'It's a bit of a ticklish one actually. You see I wanted to take Jane into Esbjerg, but the thing is, I don't want her to think I'm trying to – you know?'

'Are you?' said Matt.

'Of course not. Just being friendly. So – would you mind going with me?'

'I was going to take the young lad here —' he met Bill's glare without quailing, '— my colleague here.'

'Why don't we all go together?' said Tom at once.

'Why not? Esbjerg won't know what's hit it.'

Not every passenger went ashore. Judith Harper never bothered, not only for Mortimer's sake, but because she had called at all these ports so many times. To her surprise she found herself joined on the sun deck by James Wootton, who also showed no disposition to leave the ship.

'Seen one port, you've seen them all,' he said in answer to her question. 'I can see for a lady like yourself, the attractions of permanent residence on a ship.'

'There are many.'

'A way of life, I should think, very equable to a lady of discernment.'

'You have a fine insight into people, Mr Wootton.'

'James, please.'

'James.'

'Now it's odd you should say that, because you are certainly not the first person to comment on that aspect of my nature.'

'I wouldn't be at all surprised,' she said wisely. 'What a pity you never knew my late husband.'

'Well —' hc hesitated '— yesterday, when we had that delightful chat, you mentioned that your husband owned a chain of hotels along the Mediterranean coast of Italy.'

'That's right.'

'Would he, by any chance, have chosen that area because of his war-time experience?'

'He would.' Her eyes lit up.

'Monte Gridolfo? Montegaudio? Coriana?'

'That's right,' she said excitedly.

'Would your husband at that time have been Major Bernard Harper?'

Judith could only nod wonderingly.

Wootton drew himself up to attention and spoke with a theatrical flourish. 'Captain James Wootton, ma'am. I served with your husband right through the Italian campaign.'

He had a moment's sinking dread lest he had got some vital detail wrong. He'd had such a very short time to hunt round her cabin that morning while she'd been at breakfast. He hadn't gathered nearly as much information about her as he'd wanted. You might almost call it making bricks without straw. But a man had to do his best, and as he saw Judith's shining eyes he realised that he'd struck the bulls-eye. Within minutes they were walking arm-in-arm round the deck, Mortimer's lead in his hand, which he correctly interpreted as a triumph of no mean order. Gradually he allowed her to persuade him to talk about himself.

'Ended up as a desk wallah, I'm afraid. The Gracie Finance Co Ltd. Don't suppose you've heard of it. I'm an investment expert – pensions, annuities. My job is to make people's money grow.'

They proceeded onwards round the boat deck.

Someone else who had resisted the lure of Esbjerg was the captain, who had accepted an invitation for a drink in Kevin Warrender's cabin. He couldn't deny a quiet hope that Kevin would say something that would cancel out his attitude of yesterday, and reveal that the old crusading Warrender still lived somewhere.

'It's been a long time, hasn't it?' said Warrender when they were both sipping brandy (the ship's best, supplied free).

'I was trying to think.'

'Twenty-two years. Journalists tend to remember such things.'

'Yes. Malta.'

'In that grotty hotel.'

'We used to talk, do you remember?' said John. 'About what we were going to achieve.'

'And now here we are – successful, everything achieved.' Warrender lifted his glass.

John gave a small private smile. 'Oh, I don't know about that.'

'Bank on it. Both on our honeymoons. Stars in our eyes.' Warrender gave a world-weary sigh. 'If only we knew.'

'Yes,' said John shortly.

Warrender eyed him. 'What happened to yours?'

Abruptly John got to his feet and began to move about the cabin. 'One of those things,' he said.

'Mine turned out to be as rough as old nails. And just about as friendly. When we broke up she took the lot.' John shot him a sharp look, which Warrender correctly interpreted. 'Yours too? Yes, well, that's the law, isn't it? So I'll tell you, John – when people sneer at me – you know, "hack journalism", all that sort of thing – I think, deep down here, I've done being honest and decent to everyone – I've had doing the right thing: because you only get kicked in the teeth for it. From then on – and this means relationships, job, the lot – I get what I want. No-one's going to mess me around again. I bet you feel the same, eh?'

John answered him evasively. After that he couldn't wait to get out of the cabin. It had begun to stifle him. He wondered idly why there had been no sign of the young wife. He would have gone white-haired in a moment if he had known the truth – which was that Penny Warrender was being given a personal tour of the ship by an obliging young crew member called Ted Anderson.

Those who had gone ashore were having, on the whole, more success with each other. At Charles' suggestion he and Barbara had gone to the Fishing Museum. Not that watching seals with a seventeen-year-old was Charles' idea of a good time. It was too much like taking a little girl to the zoo – he silenced that thought abruptly. He didn't want to think of little girls or children in any form lest his thoughts career out of control – towards his wife, Jenny, and the child she had been carrying when she died. He would have been a father by now . . .

Somewhere in his mind a frozen door slammed shut. It was only a year ago that Jenny had died, but it had been another life, another Charles Woodhouse, one who seemed to have nothing to do with the cold, calculating man he had become, a man who pursued ambition ruthlessly because if you couldn't have warmth and love you had to find something else. He gave Barbara an indulgent look.

'They've all got names, see,' he said, indicating the plate where the three seals were listed – Brenda, Josh and Winston.

Barbara peered at the plate and pronounced slowly, 'Bre – er– Bre—' she broke off, laughing, seemingly unaware of Charles' puzzled look.'They're really marvellous, aren't they? So clumsy and inept on land, but in their environment, so at ease . . .'

'Just like me.'

'What.'

'Well, look at me. Here I am, clumsy and inept with a beautiful woman but, if you were to see me at work . . .'

'You, clumsy and inept? I've never seen anyone more confident,' she crowed.

'All a front. In here my heart's pounding like a triphammer. Feel.' he held her hand to his chest.

'Feels all right to me,' she giggled.

He put all his charm into his smile. 'Shows the calming influence of your touch.' He offered her his arm and drew her away. 'So what is a girl like you doing in a place like this?'

She preened – idiotically, he thought. 'You brought me, kind sir.'

'I mean struggling along the corridors of Anglia Deck with piles of dirty sheets. With your aunt being who she is . . .'

'Exactly,' said Barbara with feeling.

'You're being very enigmatic.'

'Perhaps that's *my* front.'

'An air of mystery? What's the beautiful heiress doing in such a lowly position?'

'What deep secrets nestle behind the locked bands of her heart?' she went on dramatically.

'Will they one day be revealed . . .?'

'Unlocked,' Barbara corrected.

'. . . by the suave, handsome, debonair . . .'

'Go on,' Barbara giggled.

'. . . charming, svelte . . .' He ran out of words. They looked at each other and laughed. 'You're quite a lady,' he said.

'You're quite a gentleman. One does get fed up with being groped all the time by greasy students.'

'Does one?'

'One does.'

Charles made a noise of mock exasperation. 'That was going to be the next step.'

Even he was not prepared for what she did then. She leaned forward and kissed him lightly on the cheek.

'Don't believe you,' she said coquettishly.

They moved on in perfect accord.

In the Esbjerg shopping precinct there was another merry party. At least, Tom, Matt and Jane were merry. Bill trailed behind, feeling slightly out of it.

'So what do you think I'd look like in that?' said Jane, indicating an expensive coat in a shop window.

'Lovely. Try it on,' said Tom at once.

She shook her head. 'Once I tried it on I'd want to buy it, and I can't afford it.'

'You've got to buy something,' Tom protested.

'I'm just looking, this trip. No more.'

'O.K.' said Matt. 'Let's have an ice-cream instead. Hey Bill, want an ice-cream?'

Bill caught up. 'Not for me thanks.'

'You all right?'

'Fine.' At Matt's air of concern he grew defensive. 'Really fine.'

Matt's eyes widened at something he had seen over Bill's shoulder. 'Hells bells! What are they paying barmen these days?'

Barry joined them, weighed down by a new cine camera. 'I'm telling you, I'm going to be skint till next pay-day – and it's worth it.'

By common consent he joined the party and they proceeded, not to an ice-cream shop, but to a bar. There, while the others were drinking, Matt took the chance to edge Tom aside.

'Now this is going to be a bit difficult, but . . .' he muttered.

'Yes?' said Tom, maliciously enjoying the rare sight of Matt stuck for the right word.

'Jane.'

'Yes?' Tom wasn't going to help him.

'Your wife.'

'Ex.'

'Yes. The thing is, I don't tread on mates' toes and – well —'

'I don't follow you,' said Tom untruthfully.

'Don't make this too difficult. What I'm saying is, if I was to – well —'

'What?'

'Oh hell, why are some things so hard? If I was to walk out – occasionally – with —'

'Ah! With Jane?' Tom was entranced by Matt's use of the old-fashioned expression. Wasn't walking out what you did with the maid-servant in Victorian times? It just showed what a man could be brought to when he was thoroughly embarrassed.

'Yes, with Jane. Would that bother you?'

'No.'

'In any way?'

'Not at all. Jane's a free independent lady.'

'Yes, well, O.K. I just felt I had to – I mean —'

Tom let the quarry escape. He'd enjoyed the joke long enough. 'I appreciate it, Matt,' he said sincerely. 'Thank you.'

The five of them took a taxi back to the ship. Barry sat lovingly clasping his camera as though it were a long-lost child. As they climbed out Tom exclaimed, 'Oh Gawd! Just what we needed.'

The object of his dismay turned out to be a crowd of English football supporters, complete with scarves and placards, who were advancing on the *Anglia*. They had reached the stage of being no more than pleasantly rowdy, but the journey – and the ship's pub – still lay before them.

'Don't worry,' said Matt. 'If they cause any trouble we'll smack their bottoms and send them to bed.'

He realised that Bill was staring at something unhappily. Another taxi had just drawn out, which disgorged Charles and Barbara. The couple noticed nothing but each other as they made their way to the ship, talking and laughing.

'Oh, my son,' said Matt mournfully, 'what with one thing and another you really do make life rough for yourself, don't you?'

The football supporters made a cheerful procession up the gang-way to the ship, but they struck instant dismay into Dougie's heart.

'Oh dear,' he breathed. 'And this is *before* they've been to the bar.' He gave Christine a quick glance. 'I'm glad to see you back fast.' She had earlier pleaded for permission to go ashore for half an hour to make a phone call and he had given it, guiltily aware that he was breaking the rules, since they were both supposed to be on duty. Still, she'd hurried back as she'd promised, so no harm done.

'I'd better go and have a quiet word with them, I suppose,' he said reluctantly.

From the vantage point of the information desk Christine watched him approach the fans who seemed friendly enough at this point.

'Any mail?' said a harsh voice in her ear.

'Pardon?' The sight of Kevin Warrender made her nervous. He always seemed to mean trouble.

'Mail. For me?'

She hunted in the pigeon-holes and finally produced a large packet which she handed to him gingerly.

'It's all right, love, it's not a bomb,' he said sarcastically. 'Excuse me, madame.' This last was directed to Judith Harper whom he had bumped into as he turned to go.

'Some people,' said Judith.

'Indeed,' Christine replied with feeling.

'I wonder if you could tell me where Mr Evans is, please?' Her eyes followed Christine's pointing hand to where Dougie was surrounded by brightly-scarved youngsters. They were ribbing him noisily, but otherwise didn't seem dangerous.

'I only wanted a word with him about my finances,' said Judith. 'I'd like to cash some money.'

'Perhaps I can help. How much?' Judith produced a cheque and Christine's eyebrows went up into her hair. 'In that case perhaps you had better wait and see Mr Evans.'

She was glad when Judith took the hint and departed. She had a feeling it might be a long wait.

John Anderson, entering his cabin, found his son jumping up guiltily from the sofa.

'That's all right, sit down.'

'I was wondering whether it's in order for kitchen staff to pop in and see the captain.'

'No, it's not. Are you off duty?'

'Yes.'

'In that case, you're my son and yes, it's quite all right. Only don't make a big thing of it with the rest of the staff.'

'Don't worry. No-one saw me; I slunk down here like a criminal.' Ted grinned.

'Drink?'

'Please.'

'Funny thing,' said John as he poured, 'perhaps you won't understand it, but one of a father's big dreams is one day to stand with his son and say "drink?"'

'Why?' said Ted blankly.

'I knew you wouldn't understand. You will one day. Incidentally, there's something *I* don't understand. What on earth was going with Penny Warrender? Yes, I've heard about it. At least, I've heard one version from her indignant husband who wasn't pleased to discover that you'd been escorting his wife round the ship half the afternoon. Surely you were still on duty?'

'Yes, but – she didn't give me a lot of choice. I was loading crates of supplies into the service lift when she came along and said she was looking for a guide to give her a conducted tour. I tried to explain that I was on duty but she didn't seem to understand that. And I didn't want to offend a passenger . . .'

'Yes, I get the picture,' said John hastily. 'But you offended her husband all right.'

'Yes, I think I did,' said Ted with a grin, as he remembered the moment when Kevin Warrender had finally tracked his wife to earth. Ted had been quite innocently showing her the view from the boat-deck, but there'd been a fair bit of middle-aged resentment flying around, he remembered, which wasn't surprising when you considered what Warrender looked like, and what his wife looked like.

In fact Kevin Warrender, having suffered a bad afternoon, now discovered that it took an abrupt turn for the better. The package, when opened in his cabin, proved to contain a wad of bank-notes.

'There's a turn-up,' he exclaimed as he read the accompanying note. 'You know how we get these free trips, don't you?'

Penny nodded like an obedient little girl. She was going carefully after her afternoon's adventure. (Although, to be frank, the fun had gone out of it when she'd discovered the boy was only sixteen. There were some things she hadn't descended to yet.)

'By making sure you write nice things about it for your magazines,' she recited.

'Right. Well, here's five hundred quid to write the 'truth' about this trip.' He flapped the wad of notes at her. 'And —' he read from the note, '— that's just the first instalment.'

'And the "truth" means —'

It's pretty obvious what it means, wouldn't you say?' he gave a satisfied sigh. 'I've been taken to task for abandoning my integrity – whatever that means – and now I'm being paid to recover it.'

'So what are you going to do.'

'Do just that, my dear. This report really will lay bare all the drawbacks of a trip on the *Anglia*.'

It was not until the ship was an hour out from Esbjerg that John was summoned to his office to make an unwelcome discovery. Sarah Hallam was there, and so also was . . .

'Marion,' he exclaimed, putting as much welcome into his voice as he could manage.

He couldn't help catching Sarah's troubled eyes as Marion beamed and explained graciously there was absolutely no professional significance whatever in her presence, and even less in the fact that she hadn't bothered to let them know she was coming. It sounded like a carefully prepared speech, especially when it ended with the words, 'So I thought that I'd just, as they say, set the record straight. I'm simply taking a little holiday. After all, everyone needs a rest occasionally, the change to get away from the pressures. So I'll just be a passenger . . . first class, of course, but that's all.'

'Thank you, Marion,' said John heavily. 'Nice of you to take the trouble, but meanwhile . . .'

'Of course, Captain – meanwhile you have a ship to run. And I must go and settle in to my very comfortable cabin.'

She had reached the door when Sarah's troubled voice stopped her. 'Mrs Terson.'

'Yes, my dear . . .'

'You do mean that? That you're just on holiday?'

'Of course.'

Sarah's voice was gentle but firm. 'Because if there was any interference in the way I do my job, then I would have to tender my resignation immediately. To you, and to the board.'

John gave Marion a quick look, but she was smiling. 'It'll never come to that. Promise you.'

With the journey well under way Matt took Bill down to the engine room. Bill followed his mentor round, puzzled. As far as he could see absolutely nothing needed to be done, but the ear-splitting noise and the protective ear-muffs made it impossible to say so.

He got his chance when they had passed into the Maintenance Room, where it was safe to remove the muffs.

'Didn't see much point in us being there,' he complained.

'Keep your fingers crossed that there'll *never* be any point in us being there,' said Matt. 'Now why don't you pop off for your break, and when you get back there's number three generator to look at.'

Bill went off, not to the crew recreation room, but to the Bellevue Bar. He wanted to have a talk with Barry Peters. Of course it was splendid to see the deserving workers able to enjoy the world's goods, but still –

'It's all a question of attitudes, don't you see?' he said to Barry who was phlegmatically polishing a glass. 'When you came back with that cine camera, people made jokes . . .'

'Didn't do any harm,' said Barry vaguely.

'Not as an isolated incident, no. But what it does do, is underline attitudes. If the captain, or that stuffed idiot, Woodhouse, had come back with a camera, there'd have been no jokes about "winning at bingo" or "getting a pay rise" or whatever. They, as officers, are assumed to have a right to the better things in life, while we . . .'

He was talking to empty air. Barry had spotted a hovering customer and moved away.

'May I ask what you're doing here?' said a cold voice in Bill's ear.

'What does it look like?' said Bill, meeting Charles Woodhouse's eyes more bravely than he felt. 'Having a cup of coffee, what do you think?'

'You have a perfectly good crew recreation room to use when you're on duty.'

'I'm having my break.'

'Your break is part of your duty. In future use the recreation room. Right?'

'Why? I'm not doing any harm.'

'The crew recreation room – as you might possibly guess from its name – is intended for the crew to recreate itself in. See that you do just that in future.'

'That's just typical that is. Push the workers to one side, hide them away, pretend they don't exist, so that the officers can swan about in their . . .'

'Don't you ever put a sock in it?' Charles demanded, exasperated.

'Do what?'

'All this claptrap. People like you, Ryan, have been rabbiting on like that ever since I can remember, and, in the end, nothing changes. You'll always be a grease monkey and I'll always be . . .'

'Mr Woodhouse, sir, I believe you're wanted on the bridge.'

Barry intervened diplomatically. He had hastily abandoned his customer when he saw how things were developing.

'How on earth could you possibly . . .'Charles began.

'I think you *are*, sir!'

'Right,' said Charles meeting his eyes. He gave a final glare at Bill and departed.

'What did you do that for? On the officer's side, eh?' Bill sneered.

'No-one's side, mate. Except the side of sanity. If you have a fight with him, he'll be reprimanded, posted to another ship maybe, lose seniority, who knows? But you, you'll be fired.'

'Then that's . . .'

'Make no mistake. And I'll bet exactly the same thing would happen in Russia, too.'

By mid-afternoon the ship had reached Amsterdam. Dougie prepared for a rushed time as a new influx of passengers came aboard, but even so, nothing had made him ready for what he actually got.

The woman who approached the information desk looked harmless enough, even attractive. She was in her mid-thirties, with dark hair and vivid features. She introduced herself as Beth Brooks, and after asking, in an embarrassed voice, whether she could speak to him 'on a confidential matter', she finally blurted, 'I'm looking for Matt Taylor, you see.'

'Yes, ma'am,' said Dougie non-committally.

'He *is* serving on this ship?'

'Chief engineer.'

'Yes. That's what I was told.' She smiled awkwardly. 'Now this is where it could get difficult – is he married, do you know?'

Before he could stop himself Dougie's eyes had flickered to her waist-line. Ye gods, did this kind of thing still happen? What had become of the Pill?

'I'm not certain whether —' he forced himself to stop floundering. 'You're right, it's hardly classified information. No, ma'am, he's not.'

'Is he engaged or . .?'

'Matt Taylor? No, ma'am.' Dougie tried to keep his voice as blank as his face, but significance seemed to creep into every word. He'd heard of Matt's reputation as a ladies' man from Tom Kelly, but for this situation to crop up on virtually the first voyage – that was going it a bit, wasn't it?

'Can I try to find him for you?' he said politely.

'Oh, not at all. I'd like it to be a surprise. In fact I'd be very grateful if you didn't tell him about me – until I've talked to him first.'

That really will be a surprise, he thought, as he watched her depart. If he kept his promise, that was. He was by no means sure that he was going to keep it. Did giving your word to a passenger outweigh your loyalty to the universal male brotherhood? While he was till trying to sort that one out he became aware of Mrs Harper at his elbow, with a much more manageable problem. She simply wanted him to use ship's fund to cash an impossibly large cheque. In comparison it felt like child's play, particularly as he knew of a definite answer.

'Just can't do it, Mrs Harper. You know that I would if I could. But we just don't carry this kind of money. After all, with respect, it's very unlikely that anyone would require it. We're only at sea for twenty-four hours at a stretch, and there's nothing on board to spend such an enormous sum on. Might I suggest waiting until we arrive at Harwich?'

Judith sighed. 'Well, Mr Evans, if that's the best you can do.' She patted his hand kindly. 'It's not your fault, I'm sure of that.'

He watched her go, his face registering amusement and concern in about equal proportions. Christine, approaching the desk, saw his expression.

'How did you get on?' she asked.

'Twenty thousand pounds,' he said, dazed.

'I know, she showed me the cheque. I wouldn't have thought she was worth that much.'

'A great deal more than that, I reckon. Our Mrs Harper is a very rich lady.'

'Ah, now I know why you look after her so well.'

He grinned. 'Yes, but not a word to my wife.'

Jane Anthony hurried up to the information desk. 'Mr Evans, have you a moment? It's about Barbara Carter.'

'What about her?'

'The truth is that if she was anyone else I'd be thinking of getting rid of her.'

Dougie whistled. 'As bad as that?'

'Slip-shod, arrogant, unenthusiastic – I mean, you name it. Do you think you could have a word with her?'

Dougie visibly blenched. 'Me?'

'I just don't seem to be able to get through to her.'

'Don't see what I can do. Especially now that her aunt's on board.'

'Mrs Terson? Here?'

'She says she's taking a bit of a holiday,' said Dougie with heavy significance.

'Oh dear. That's it, then. There'll be no stopping Miss Carter now – whoever has a word with her.'

Just the same, she tried Sarah with the same request, rightly judging that Sarah would probably have more courage than Dougie. The result was that fifteen minutes later Barbara found herself answering a summons to Sarah's office.

'Just thought it was about time we had a little chat,' Sarah said pleasantly. 'How do you feel you're getting on?'

'Getting on? With whom?'

'Sarah suppressed her temper at the girl's truculent tone, and said quietly, 'With your job.'

'My job.' Barbara sounded as though she was hearing news of a distant relative, seldom seen and never thought about. 'All right.'

'You're sure?'

'What is this?'

'All right.' Sarah stripped the mental gloves off. 'Miss Anthony's asked me to have a word with you.' She studied the girl's face. 'Anything you want to say about that?'

'Not a lot.'

'She's also been to see the purser. Now why do you think a cabin girl justifies such high-powered consideration?'

Barbara gave a little smile. 'I wonder.'

'I want you to tell me.'

'You know why.' Barbara shrugged. 'After all, I'm not just a cabin girl, am I?'

'Ah, now that's where you're wrong. As far as I'm concerned you are just that. And if you don't perform your duties adequately, then, just like any other cabin girl, I shall be reluctantly forced to give you your papers.'

'You wouldn't dare,' said Barbara flatly. 'Especially now, with my aunt on board.'

'Are you telling me that you can do whatever you like and I wouldn't dare to sack you? Is that what you're saying?' Barbara shrugged again and Sarah took a deep breath. 'In that case, our respective positions are totally untenable.'

She opened her desk drawer and removed an envelope. From it she took Barbara's employment documents and a wad of notes. These she handed to the girl.

'This is in lieu of a week's notice.'

Barbara stared at her. 'What do you think you're . . .?'

'You're relieved from your post, Miss Carter, as of this moment, for dereliction of duty and insubordination. You will be expected to disembark at the next port of call. Good day.'

Barbara almost snatched the papers from Sarah's hand, and slammed the door behind her. She had no intention of wasting further time on a woman who plainly didn't know the score. A word in her aunt's ear . . . Just the same, she baulked at the prospect of telling Marion that she'd been sacked so soon. The best thing would be for Miss Hallam to be persuaded to put right her mistake before Aunt Marion had to hear anything. Charles would know what to do.

She made her way dazedly to the crew recreation room, where Barry had unwisely allowed himself to be drawn into an argument with Bill and Matt about the great capitalist conspiracy that enabled captains to give jobs to their sons.

'What's the matter with you?' said Matt when he saw her white face.

'I've been given my cards. Sacked.'

'In two days? That must be some sort of record.'

'Very funny,' she snapped.

'That's terrible,' Bill declared. 'We must do something about this. Do you belong to a union?'

'No, of course I don't,' she said dismissively. 'Has anyone seen Mr Woodhouse?'

'No, but then he wouldn't be in here, would he?' said Matt.

She frowned for a moment. Then she departed as abruptly as she had entered.

'You can't go round sacking people just like that,' said Bill, scandalised.

'Don't you think your attitude smacks just the teeniest little bit of double standard?' said Matt, raising his eyebrows.

'What do you mean?'

'You object to the captain's son working in the galley, and yet stand up for that girl's rights to have a job.'

'Why shouldn't I?'

'Don't you know who she is? Why she's too good for the likes of us?' Bill shook his head and Matt leaned towards him conspiratorially. 'Then perhaps I'd better have a word in your shell-like.'

He made his explanation as short and simple as possible, and when he'd finished he had the pleasure of seeing Bill's eyes nearly pop out of his head.

Sarah's first action when Barbara had left her was to telephone the bridge and ask John's permission to come and see him. When she arrived he was standing looking down at the automatic pilot, and she waited for him to finish. He frowned when he noticed her.

'Trouble?' he said.

'Maybe.'

'If it's those football hooli —' he corrected himself with a little smile, '— supporters . . . well, don't brook the slightest disturbance. I'm not going to have a shipful of passengers inconvenienced for the sake of a handful of yobboes. Any trouble, call Mr Evans. He knows exactly what to do.'

'I will, but it's not that. It's . . . well, after what you asked me yesterday – about Marion Tersons's niece . . .'

'Yes?' he said with faint impatience.

She took a deep breath and grasped the nettle. 'I've sacked her.'

'But *why*?'

'With all due respect I have to say that's irrelevant. I'm only telling you, now, because Mrs Terson's on board.'

'What do you mean, "irrelevant"?' he said, exasperated. 'After what I said, I would have thought that's the last thing it is. Good God, she's only been employed for a few days.'

'I am aware of that.'

'Then couldn't you just have warned her?'

'No, I could not. I either do my job or I don't. With Barbara I had to ask myself how I would have reacted if one of the other girls had behaved like her. I had no other choice.'

'Yes you did,' he said angrily. 'You did have another choice. What you did was decide to opt for one course of action rather than another.'

She met his eyes, refusing to be stared down. Then she gave a slight shrug. 'Just thought I'd tell you.'

There were seldom many customers in the Bellevue Bar by 6.15, and Barry had learned by bitter experience that this was the time he was most likely to have his ear bent by the odd one who happened to there. With few excuses to escape he just had to grin and bear it. Tonight's was a prime example. Like a lot of people talking to the 'invisible' barman she was really talking to herself, sorting out the pros and cons of her marriage, which seemed to be little different from those experienced by most women in their thirties, even if few of them were as attractive as this one. Not that brunettes were usually his style, but she had firm features and a nice husky voice that was easy on the ear.

'Oh, it's not his fault at all,' she was saying of the luckless husband. 'I'm not saying that. I mean, I bet all marriages go through the same. I wouldn't be at all surprised if you've experienced the same thing.' Barry hastily adjusted his non-committal smile. 'I mean, he's a good man. A really good man. He's done his duty as he sees it, to me and the kids. He's worked hard, become one of the must successful accountants in Basingstoke – and that's saying something, believe me. I mean, we have a very good lifestyle but – well —' she smiled deprecatingly and held out her glass for a drink. 'And now that he's had to go to America for such a long time, and the children are old enough to – well, you know —'

'Indeed I do, ma'am.' Barry had refilled her glass with Campari, and at her insistence, had poured a lager for himself.

'I felt, well – why not? Go away. Have a holiday. And some – well, a ship on the high seas, it's almost the epitome of freedom, isn't it?'

Barry's private opinion was that if he'd been seeking freedom on the high seas he'd have sought it in the Mediterranean. But perhaps this lady had special reasons for choosing the North Sea.

Her next words confirmed it. Looking hopefully round her she added, 'And who knows? Perhaps bump into an old friend or two?'

So that was it. Barry wondered who the lucky feller was – and whether he knew that he was being hunted down?

Jane had a feeling of defiance when she arrived at Matt's cabin for a drink that evening. It was all Tom's fault, having the brass neck to 'warn' her, earlier that day, of Matt's reputation with the ladies. He hadn't, he said, wanted to see her get hurt. Jane had left him in no doubt that she was big enough to take care of herself, and that if he wanted them to go on being friends he'd never do anything like this again. Tom had retired crushed.

And now here she was, in the lion's den.

'So this is where chief engineers hold their orgies?' she said, looking round.

'If they're lucky. Sit down.'

While he poured her a drink she continued to study his home.

'Very masculine,' she said at last.

'Mm?' He wasn't sure how to take this

'Bare and unadorned.'

'If I need some chintz curtains or cushion covers I'll let you know,' he grinned. 'It's very nice,' he added, handing her the drink and sitting beside her.

'What is?'

'To have an attractive woman in here again.'

'You say all the right things. Mind you, I'm not sure I like the "again".'

'I'm no angel,' he said defensively.

She smiled at him. 'Gets better all the time.'

'And I'm no villain either. Just an ordinary fellow, with ordinary virtues and ordinary vices.' He lifted his glass and became Humphrey Bogart. 'Here's lookin' at you, baby.'

'Talented as well.'

'You've got no idea,' he said fervently.

'Oh, but I have. Why do you think I set my sights on you the moment I came aboard this ship?'

He eyed her suspiciously. 'I don't know whether you're speaking the truth or I'm the victim of an enormous, monumental send-up.'

'Oh no, not insecurities as well,' she mocked him.

'Sorry. But my ego has been rather bruised lately.'

'Hit with a sledgehammer?'

'Right. Don't worry, though. I'll coat myself in an impenetrable veneer of male ego again, very shortly.'

Suddenly she liked him very much. In the same moment she could understand the danger that Tom had tried to warn her of.

'I think I prefer the vulnerability,' she said quietly.

'All women do.' His voice was harsh.

'Do I detect a soupcon of bitterness?'

He indicated a minute amount with his fingers. 'Just that much.'

'We'll soon get rid of that.' She put down her drink. He put down his. They leaned towards each other in practised fashion – just as a fist banged urgently on the outside of Matt's door.'

'Right on time,' he groaned, pulling apart from her.

He opened the door to disclose Dougie, who promptly became flustered when he saw Jane. She was mildly surprised. She'd thought Dougie was more of a man of the world than that.

He reluctantly allowed himself to be hauled inside and given a drink, until finally, accepting Jane's presence as inevitable, he blurted out, 'Matt, were you expecting anyone to come aboard?'

'Me? No.'

'Someone who might know you?'

'I've told you, no. What's all this about?' Dougie shook his head, embarrassed. 'What's it about?'

'She asked me not to say that she was . . .' Dougie muttered miserably.

'She?' said Jane. Under the eyes of both men she developed an exaggeratedly theatrical manner. 'Good gracious me! How many more, she asks herself.'

When he departed a few minutes later Dougie reflected that he could scarcely have made a bigger dog's breakfast of the whole thing if he'd thought about it for a fortnight beforehand. Which just went to show that honesty was probably the best policy after all. Who'd have thought it?

The problem of Judith Harper and her £20,000 had been referred to Sarah, who had an opportunity to talk it over with the old lady in the Bellevue Bar that evening. She was glad of a rare chance to get Judith alone. It was so rare now that you could catch her without the appalling Wootton in tow. With own own eyes Sarah had seen them clinking glasses, and she could have sworn she heard the words 'To us' float towards her.

'That's a lot of money,' she said when the problem had been laid before her from Judith's point of view.

'It's mine. It's in my account.'

'I don't doubt that. It's just that we don't actually hold accounts on board ship. We only hold enough for your day-to-day use. I'm afraid you'll have to wait until you can cash a cheque in the usual way, ashore. May I ask what you need it for?'

'I've had the greatest stroke of good fortune. I've met this gentleman who wants to invest it for me.'

Sarah's heart sank. 'On board?'

'Mr Wootton. He's an investment expert, specialising in pensions and annuities. Now would you believe it? That I should meet him?'

'I think I can just about believe it, Mrs Harper,' said Sarah grimly.

She followed Judith's gaze to the bar where she could now see James Wootton standing next to Charles. He raised his glass in salute, whether to her or Judith, Sarah couldn't tell. Before she could decide what to do the doors burst open and a dozen youths, football supporters by their clothes and behaviour, crowded in.

'You'll excuse me, Mrs Harper? I must do something about this.'

'Be careful.'
As she approached the crowd she just heard Charles mutter over his shoulder to Barry, 'Get Mr Evans. Quickly.'
Instinctively the youths crowded round Sarah.
'My name is Sarah Hallam,' she said politely, 'and I'm the ship's administrator.'
'I don't know about that,' said one, 'but you look a right little darling to me.'
She flinched from his groping hand but managed to keep her tone pleasant.
'Now none of us want to spoil your trip, least of all me. And I'm sure you have a lot to celebrate.'
'Won three-one, didn't we?'
'*We are the champions*!' they all bellowed in unison.
'I'm delighted to hear it.'
'So now we're going to show this stuffy ship how to really enjoy themselves.'
'Ask her to join us.'
'Why don't you join us, love, eh?'
'I'm sorry, I'm on duty.' Again she flinched. She felt she might be sick if they touched her again. She realised that Charles Woodhouse was watching her reactions closely.
'I'm going to have to ask you to keep a bit quieter,' she said firmly
'Oh, hear that?' The little darling's asking us to keep quiet.' There was a roar of laughter, and he slipped an arm round Sarah's waist. She froze. 'Give us a kiss, that'll keep me quiet.'
'Please,' she said sharply.
'Oh hey, hey, she's pleading for it now. That's what I like to hear.'
At last Charles seemed to decide that enough was enough. He moved toward the group and pulled the lout off Sarah.
'O.K. That'll do.'
At once he went down, felled by a kick from behind. Boots began to fly and in a second Charles had vanished. Sarah looked round desperately for help, but the bar was still mostly empty. James Wootton had vanished. Then to Sarah's relief the door opened and Barry came running in, followed by Dougie.
'All right, leave this to me.' With a speed and force that belied his years he pounced on the ringleader and almost got him in a hammer-lock. But the boy managed to writhe free and scuttle away, hotly pursued by Dougie.
If he'd hoped the purser would give up the chase he was dis-

appointed. Dougie hung on grimly through the shopping arcade, where passengers scattered like autumn leaves before them, down a flight of stairs, onto a lower deck, down another flight of stairs. He was running by instinct, with no idea where his flight was taking him, only knowing that he was going lower and lower, praying that some place of safety would present itself.

He crashed into a door ahead of him and flung himself through it, to find that he was in a vast cavern, populated by vehicles. Here he was trapped. The cars rose in 'shelves' and he could only dodge round them, taking care not to get too close to the edge of the shelf he was standing on, for below the railing there gaped a yawning drop. He could see Dougie approaching him, slowly now.

'Now look, mate, it was all . . .' He found it hard to get his breath.

'Just keep still,' Dougie warned him. 'Don't move.'

'Don't mix it with *me*, mate.'

'Not another word.'

The boy dodged, turned, ran. He never saw what happened behind him, he only heard a jingle as Dougie behind him collided with the chain that formed the railing at the edge of the shelf. Then there was a scream that sank down into the drop, and a thud that sickened him to his stomach. Appalled, knowing what he'd see and terrified of it, the boy forced himself to creep towards the edge and look over to where the still twisted form could just be made out in the gloom.

Chapter 5

It took time to contact the Royal Victoria Hospital, and then the line was bad, but at least Tom Kelly had the reassuring feeling that he was talking to a real doctor who'd know what should be done. Inwardly he cursed. When this sort of thing happened in books there was always a doctor available – drunk or struck-off perhaps, but at least one who'd qualified. It wasn't left to a first mate who knew little more than first aid. Please God, let a doctor show up on the passenger list.

'Severe bruising,' he relayed down the line, 'with no sign of bleeding. At a layman's guess I'd say he's cracked some ribs – but it must hurt him like hell or he wouldn't keep passing out.'

The doctor's voice crackled faintly down the line.

'You say the patient is pale, sweaty, has a high pulse-rate and extreme pain in the left upper quadrant of the abdomen? There are certain things you must ascertain. There should be a regular check on pulse and blood-pressure. Also his girth. His waist, Mr Kelly. I want you to measure it as accurately as possible. Every five minutes. I think he may have internal bleeding.'

Tom put the phone down more worried than he had been when he'd picked it up. He realised that Charles and Marion had joined him in the radio room. He pulled himself together and forced himself to be polite to the boss. Normally he liked Marion but he had enough on his plate now.

'Just tell me briefly, what's the position,' she demanded.

'It's complicated, Marion. Charles, look, I'll need to stay in touch with that doctor, at least till we find one aboard – if we do. And I'll be in the surgery. A head-set wouldn't be a bad idea – save me jumping up and down while I'm seeing to Dougie.'

'I'll get Bob to put an amplifier on it,' Charles agreed. 'No wires, then.'

'Tom, just a moment.' Marion put a hand on his arm. 'What do you mean, "complicated"?'

'It's not just bruising or cracked ribs. I've been on to the coastguard. Helicopter's standing by, but there's little chance of them coming out before morning, "because of the weather".'

'It is a bit foggy,' said Charles.

'Meanwhile Dougie's bleeding internally and if there isn't somebody aboard who can cut him open and stop it, he's going to die.'

'*Is* there a doctor aboard?' said Marion.

'I don't know. Someone'll have to check the passenger lists.'

'I'll get Christine Harris to do it,' said Charles. 'Is there anything else I can do?'

'Probably. I think John should be in on this. You may want to confer with him – there could be decisions to make.'

Upstairs on the information desk Christine Harris was coping alone. She knew nothing of Dougie except the fact that he had departed an hour earlier in response to an urgent summons from Barry, and not returned. With a start she noticed that she was not alone. Matt was leaning on the desk watching her with a quizzical smile.

'Don't *do* that,' she protested, laughing. 'Give me a heart attack.'

'Guilty conscience,' he told her. 'Must be something to do with your secret assignation in Esbjerg. Rumours get around, you know.'

'Oh yes? What sort of rumours?'

Matt glanced over his shoulder and leaned forward conspiratorially.

'I'll say just one word – fishing sheds.'

'Urgh!'

He winked. 'Know what I mean? Big trawlerman from Helsingor. Muscles out here – red braces, chews tobacco. Am I close?'

She laughed. 'Miles away. I go for charm and sophistication.'

'Shame. I thought I was in with a chance.'

'Why? What colour are *your* braces?'

'Stop it, Christine, I know you've got a fella . . .'

'How do you know?'

'I can tell. It's all about body language and eye movement, animal instinct, stuff like that. Apart from which, Les told me in the engine room.'

'He would,' she said.

Charles arrived, breathless. 'Excuse me, Matt . . . Christine, we need a doctor. Will you go through the passenger lists, find one, and get him to report to the ship's surgery immediately. It's Dougie Evans. He's had an accident. At least, the young hooligan we slung in the brig swears it was an accident. Says he never touched him.'

Twenty minutes later Christine made her way into the dining-room to approach the only man on board who might be able to help. She found him seated at a table in the corner with a young girl. From the state of the table they had not only eaten a good meal but also drunk a great deal. Christine edged her way close to them, remembering to give a polite smile to Kevin Warrender who was at the next table.

'Mr Nairn? Godfrey Nairn?'

'Yes?' The man was about fifty with a thin, unpleasing face.

'I'm so sorry to interrupt you, but there's been a bit of an accident, and I was wondering if . . .'

'What sort of an accident?'

'It's our chief purser. He's taken a fall – a rather serious fall and —'

'So what's that got to do with me?'

'We thought you might be able to help —'

'I'm sorry, it's out of the question. I'm not a doctor, I'm a vet. In fact I'm not even that any more. I haven't done animal surgery in ten years. I'm an academic. I teach.'

'I appreciate that, Mr Nairn, but you're the best we've got.'

'No. I'm sorry.'

'There isn't a doctor on board,' she said desperately.

'There must be some sort of emergency procedure.'

'Well, yes, there is – but it's a question of time. You see . . .'

'I'm afraid I can't help,' he said with finality. 'I – I don't want to get involved.'

'But his *life* may be in danger.

'I really cannot be held accountable for that. Now, if you'll excuse us . . .' he turned his back on her.

Christine glared at him for a moment before breathing out hard in frustration. As she turned to go she remembered to offer another polite smile to Kevin Warrender. But he was no longer there.

Marion Terson, determined to be of use, had found her way to the ship's office, where she found Sarah going through a filing cabinet, seeking for suitable blood donors among the crew. There was a young boy with her, checking off the names she read out, some of whom were not available because they were on leave. Marion gave him a hard look.

'Haven't I see you before, somewhere?' she said curiously.

'Yes, ma'am – at a dinner party in Muswell Hill. I was much smaller. And not so good-looking.'

'Yes, of course. You're . . . the oldest.'

'Ted.'

'Yes. I didn't know you were aboard. Nobody told me.'

'That's 'cos I'm insignificant. People do tend to ignore me a lot. I get paranoid just thinking about it.'

Sarah intervened hastily to put a stop to this ill-timed flippancy. 'Ted's a new recruit, Mrs Terson – and a very efficient one. Now, is there anything I can help you with?'

'Yes. The young thug we've got locked up in the brig. I want a case made against him. One that'll stand up. Something the police can use. He's not going to get away with this. I won't have it.'

Sarah spoke uneasily, 'There was some horseplay and a scuffle . . . a minor assault on the first officer.'

'Are you serious?' said Marion incredulously. 'I have a chief purser – an old friend – who happens to be *dying* at this very moment . . . and you talk about horseplay and scuffles . . .?'

'With respect, that was an accident – as Mr Evans will tell you. He fell.'

'I don't believe this!

'The offence, such as it was, is being punished by a night in the brig. Which is enough . . . in my opinion.'

'Well. I'm very grateful to you. For your opinion.' Marion's voice was heavy with sarcasm and she turned on her heel to depart. But Sarah's urgent voice stopped her.

'Mrs Terson. Please. Please just think about it. The Press could turn this incident into anything they liked. Rampant hooliganism, grievous bodily harm . . . possibly even murder. Or they could see it as a bit of boisterousness, efficiently handled by the crew, in which an accident happened. Which version is going to help the ship . . . the company?'

'The truth. How about the truth, Miss Hallam? Or doesn't that count for anything?'

'Truth is, it was an accident. You're being emotional, if you don't mind me saying so.'

'I *do* mind you saying so,' said Marion furiously.

'I'm sorry.' Nothing in Sarah's calm demeanour altered, and after staring at her for a moment Marion swept out and slammed the door behind her.

'I think,' said Ted to nobody in particular, 'I've just fallen in love.'

Sarah didn't answer. She'd found what she was looking for: three crew members whose blood group matched Dougie's. She went straight to the surgery, where she found Tom and John. Dougie lay motionless under heavy sedation.

'I'm keeping him out,' Tom was saying. 'It's bad, John. He's ruptured his spleen.'

'And what does that mean in sailor's language?' John demanded.

'It means there's an artery in there pumping out blood, and if somebody doesn't cut him open and tie it up Dougie is going to die.'

'How long?'

'An hour. Maybe two.'

'Do we have the equipment to cope with that?'

'Oh we've got the equipment.' Tom looked round him. 'This is a first-rate surgery. All we need now is someone with the nous to use it.'

'I've checked his file,' said Sarah, coming up to the two men. 'He's group "O". So is the utility steward, the assistant cook – and the captain.' She gave a wry smile. 'Blood is no respector of persons.'

'Well, if it's a pint of blood,' said John, 'I'd be only too happy to . . .'

'Fine,' Tom interrupted. 'But the doctor will need to see your history.'

'It's all in there,' said John, indicating the file.

Christine Harris had come in and heard this last exchange.

'There isn't a doctor,' she said bluntly.

Tom went white. 'There isn't?'

'Just an ex-vet who refuses to co-operate and who's three sheets to the wind anyway.'

In the horrified silence that followed, all eyes were on Tom. After a moment he turned sharply, snatched up the telephone and barked a few remarks into it. What he heard made his face set. He slammed the receiver down.

'The earliest we can get the helicopter is midnight,' he said. 'That is, if the weather drastically improves.'

'Midnight,' said John, appalled. 'That's three hours.'

'*He hasn't got three hours, John.*'

Despite bruises that made him wince whenever he breathed, Charles had returned to his duties on the bridge. With John occupied over Dougie he had no intention of letting it be said that the first officer wasn't available when needed – however good the reason.

He was staring out into the darkness and fog when he became

aware of someone who had slipped onto the bridge behind him.

'Barbara!' he said, startled.

'Don't say it,' she pleaded. 'I know – I shouldn't be here.'

'No, you shouldn't.' He cast an uncomfortable glance at the helmsman, who luckily seemed to have developed diplomatic blindness.

'I've been looking for you everywhere.' Barbara wandered away from him, touching knobs experimentally. Charles hastily stopped her.

'Barbara, what exactly . . .?'

'Are you in charge? Of the ship?'

'For the moment, yes.'

'I never realised.' She smiled up at him prettily.

'I'm the first officer,' he explained. 'It's part of the job.'

'And are you qualified? To be the pilot, or driver, or whatever you call it?'

'I've a master's certificate,' he said, wondering in frantic embarrassment how much of this the helmsman could hear, and how much would be all over the ship next day. 'Look, I really must ask you to – much as I like you being here, I really think you should . . .'

'So why aren't you captain?' she cut in. She didn't seem to have heard a word he was saying.

'Because Mr Anderson is.'

'He's old.'

'Not all that.'

'And boring, and pompous and stuffy. I don't like him. You should be captain.'

He looked at her for a moment, then drew her away into a corner, out of the helmsman's earshot.

'Yes,' he said.

'Perhaps I should have a word with my aunt.'

'Yes, perhaps.'

'In the meantime, perhaps you could do something for me?'

'Why? What's the problem?'

'Sarah Hallam has fired me.'

'Sarah *fire* you? Can she do that?'

'Of course she can't. Who does she think she is? My aunt put me here because she wants me here – and she's the only one who can tell me when to get off. Oh no, that Sarah Hallam's in for a surprise. She's the one who'll be fired.' She hesitated, running a coquettish finger down Charles' lapel. 'All the same . . . I'm not altogether sure that I want to tell my aunt yet. I don't want her to think I can't handle it on my own.'

'And do you think you can?' Charles smiled at her.

'I think so. With a bit of help from my friends.'

'So you want *me* to tell her?'

'No, we'll keep the big guns in reserve. What I'd like *you* to do is put that Hallam woman in the picture. I don't think she realises.'

'So far my dealings with her haven't been all that successful,' Charles mused.

'Then you won't be spoiling a beautiful friendship, will you?'

She beamed up at him.

In the surgery Tom was once again on the telephone to the hospital, urgently relaying details of Dougie's rapidly deteriorating condition.

'The systollic's down to fifty and the diastollic's right off the scale – maybe I'm reading it wrong . . . hundred and sixty . . . Yes.' He raised his eyes at the sight of Sarah at the door, but she only shook her head and he spoke into the phone again. 'I've just heard. We've no medical help at all. No, none.' He put down the receiver.

'I've spoken to the vet,' said Sarah. 'He won't come. He's quite adamant.'

So what's the situation?' said John.

'Well – even if the helicopter were to take off now, which it won't, it'll still be too late.'

'Miss Harris, you've double-checked there's no doctor aboard?'

'Yes,' said Christine.

John turned back to Tom. 'And there's no way we can get him ashore quickly enough? You've explored every possibility?'

'Yes.'

'How certain is the diagnosis?'

'It's certain. There's no question.'

John began to pace up and down. 'Is it a difficult operation?' he demanded.

'Splenectomy? Not for a surgeon, no. Mechanically it's very straightforward. The doctor I've been calling says it's trickier getting the spark-plugs out of a Volkswagon.'

'Mmmm.' John paced some more.

Tom gave him as long as he could before saying, 'It's decision time, captain.'

Abruptly John faced him. 'You know I can't ask you to do it.'

'You can order me not to.'

'How would you rate his chances if . . .'

'If I were to operate? Not very high. There's a lot that could go wrong. But then a one per cent chance is more than he's got if I don't do anything.'

'So there's nothing to lose,' said John.

Sarah felt obliged to say, 'There is a possible legal side to consider.'

John looked at her blankly, then turned his back, his silence a dismissal of her views. 'What would you need?' he said.

Tom considered for a moment. 'Bob's putting an amplifier onto the telephone, so I'll be able to get step-by-step instructions. I shall want that vet – whether he's happy about it or not.'

'I'll see that you get him,' said John. 'I suppose I'd better go and explain all this to Marion. Anything else?'

'Yes. I shall want the cabin staff manager, Jane Anthony, to assist.'

'Does she know anything about medicine?' said Sarah, bewildered.

'No, Miss Hallam, but she knows a helluva lot about me.'

Bad as the night had been so far, the minute John stepped out into the corridor he discovered something that made it worse. Kevin Warrender was standing there making swift notes on a pad.

'It's called newsgathering,' he said, in answer to John's furious glare.

'I call it obscene,' John raged. 'Get out of here.'

For a moment Warrender looked as though he might argue the point, but the sight of John's thunderous eyes seemed to make up his mind for him. He slipped away.

John passed on without a pause to Marion's cabin. He had no time to think about Warrender's betrayal now.

'You want Tom Kelly to perform an operation?' said Marion when the situation had been explained to her. 'Oh no – that's out of the question.'

'Our options are limited, Marion.'

'He's not a surgeon, bless him. I couldn't ask that of him.'

'You don't have to,' said John pointedly.

'There's got to be somebody else, somebody qualified – or something else we can *do*.'

'Marion, we've explored every possibility.'

'I mean what if it went wrong? He'd have it on his conscience for the rest of his life. It isn't fair to expect it of him. I won't allow it.'

'Then Douglas will die,' said John flatly. He softened a little when he saw Marion's shocked face. 'I'm sorry to be brutal, but that's the situation. Anyway, the decision has been made.'

'No it hasn't,' she said.

For one blinding minute he wished George Terson was still alive. Whatever his faults, George would have understood where his power ended and the captain's began. 'It has, Marion,' he said at last. 'It was *my* decision, and I've made it. I know all the arguments against and I've considered them carefully. But there's one compelling argument for – and that's Douglas's life.'

'I don't like it, John. I don't like it one little bit.'

'Neither do I. Now look, sitting up here in your cabin worrying about it isn't going to help anyone.'

'I shall worry whatever I do.'

His next port of call was Godfrey Nairn, whom he found in his cabin, in company with his young companion whose nose was buried in a magazine.

'I'm flattered by your confidence, Captain,' said Nairn when he had heard all John had to say, 'but this is utterly and totally beyond discussion. I mean, have you considered the legal ramifications?'

'Yes,' said John firmly.

'An unqualified person performing major surgery on a patient without his consent?'

'There's no alternative.'

'That's almost certain grounds for a manslaughter charge if it goes wrong, which it most assuredly would. No, no, no, it would be professional suicide – and not just for me. Have you thought what this would do to *your* career?'

'Yes,' said John again.

'Or the shipping line? Can't you see the sort of publicity it would attract?'

John looked him in the eye. Through the other man's attempt at composure he was beginning to detect the unmistakeable trace of fear. He knew now how he could coerce Godfrey Nairn – as unlikeable a specimen of humanity as he had ever met – into giving his help.

'Mr Nairn' he said steadily, 'let's get something clear. I'm not concerned with your career, my career, the shipping line, or criminal charges. One of my crew is dying and there's a chance he can be saved. Now I don't give a damn how remote that chance is, I'm going to take it, and you're going to help.'

'I'm not,' said Nairn flatly.

John looked down at the young girl, who had not lifted her head from the magazine. Then he returned his gaze to Nairn.

'Exactly what sort of publicity are you afraid of, Mr Nairn?'

The other man drew a sharp breath. 'Are you trying to blackmail me, Captain?'

'Yes,' said John for the third time.

Ten minutes later Nairn entered the surgery.

'I'm Godfrey Nairn,' he said to Tom. 'And before I do anything at all I want you to know I'm here under protest.' He glared round him at the sight of Dougie on the table, at Jane, adjusting the blood transfusion drip, at Tom, ready to start the operation. 'Have you ever performed an operation before?' he demanded.

'No, sir.'

'Have you any inkling of what's involved? Do you have any medical experience at all?'

'I'm the medical officer of this ship. All part of the job.'

'First aid!' Nairn spat derisively. 'We're talking about major surgery.'

'Listen,' shouted Tom, 'I'm not doing it because I want to, I'm doing it because it's got to be done. And I don't need telling what the problems are because I have a very fertile imagination. O.K.?'

'It's madness.'

'So are field hospitals in battle areas, with surgeons swatting flies with one hand and stitching the patient up with the other.'

'Does that happen?' Jane was unable to stop herself saying.

'Search me.' Tom gave her an unexpected grin, his moment of temper gone. 'Like I say, I've got a vivid imagination.'

For those with nothing to do but wait, the rest of the night stretched ahead interminably. Sarah had wandered into the Admiral's Pub, and then out again, twice before she heard her name called.

'Miss Hallam! Oh do come and join us! How lovely to see you . . .'

The voice belonged to Judith Harper who, thankfully, seemed to be alone. Sarah gave her a wan smile and dropped wearily into a chair.

'You look worried,' said Judith sympathetically. 'I know it's a horrid, horrid business – but we've got to wait, and worrying doesn't help.'

'You know about it, do you?' said Sarah, remembering suddenly that Dougie Evans was by way of being a special friend and champion of Judith's.

'Well of course I do. Poor Mr Evans. But I'm sure that lovely Mr Kelly will have him up and about in no time.'

Sarah smiled at her warmly. 'You never fail to astonish me, Mrs Harper. Where *is* Mortimer?'

'Mortimer?'

'You said come and join us. I assumed you meant Mortimer . . .?'

Like an evil genie James Wootton appeared armed with drinks which he laid on the table prior to sitting down. He had overheard Sarah's last remark. 'Mortimer's having his nap,' he said. 'He does like a little nap after dinner.'

'It's the port,' said Judith. 'I tell him he shouldn't really have it, but he insists. At his time of life I think he's entitled. He's eleven, you know.'

Wootton grew sentimental. 'The doggy twilight days. A drop of port is something of a must.'

'I'm sure it is,' said Sarah. 'And you must be Mr Wootton.'

'You know him!' said Judith. 'How lovely.'

'I know *of* him, Mrs Harper. In fact I've been meaning to have a word with you . . .'

Wootton broke in: 'Forgive me, but I'm at an obvious disadvantage. Who might you be?'

'Mr Wootton,' Sarah silenced him with a glare before returning her attention to Judith. 'Yes, Mrs Harper, I was a little concerned about your request to change a cheque for . . . what was it, twenty thousand pounds?'

'Concerned? *Is* it your concern?' demanded Wootton.

'It is when, as I understand it, the request was so that you could "invest" the money for her.'

'Oh no, Miss Hallam, you've got it all wrong,' Judith assured her. 'That was my idea.'

'Mr Wootton didn't suggest it to you?'

'Goodness no! He told me . . .'

Wootton broke in urgently. 'I don't really think this is Miss Hallam's business, Judith, do you?'

'Well, I . . .'

'I think it would be much more sensible if you had a word with your bank manager before handing over such a large sum of money to a complete stranger,' said Sarah firmly.

'Of course it would be. I'm not silly, you know. But Jimmy isn't a stranger – he's going to be my husband.'

'Husband? But surely you've only just met?'

Wootton gave her a triumphant smile. 'How long does it take to fall in love?' he cooed.

Sarah finished her drink and departed quickly. She felt sick to her stomach and desperately worried. Her feet seemed to find their own way to the brig. A hooligan would seem like a nice change after what she'd just witnessed.

The youngster had sobered up, and was now thoroughly frightened, as his first question showed.

'How is he? That bloke?'

'Seriously injured,' Sarah told him. 'The chances are he'll die.'

The boy began to gibber in panic. 'I didn't push him. He fell. *Some*body's got to believe me.'

'All right, I believe you.' Sarah spoke coldly. Believing him wasn't going to help Dougie.

She took the chance to have her first good look at him. He was about eighteen with a heavy, not ill-natured face; the kind who would make his mistakes through thoughtlessness rather than malice. She recalled his slobbery features pushed towards her, the smell of beer fumes. But the memory faded in the face of what he had become, a scared little boy.

'If it's not my fault, why am I here?' His voice was full of bewilderment.

'Causing an affray, assaulting the chief officer . . .'

'He was hurting me. He'd got his fist down my collar and his knuckles was digging into my neck – plus I couldn't breathe proper.'

'And you assaulted me,' said Sarah quietly.

The boy jumped as though stung. 'Never. I know I'd had a skinful but I ain't never hit a lady in my life, and if I did it were an accident. Straight!'

'I didn't say you hit me. I said you assaulted me.' Since he looked puzzled she spelt it out. '"Groped" is the word you'd use to your mates.'

Embarrassed, he looked down and mumbled, 'I wouldn't say nothing about it to my mates.'

'And you resisted arrest.'

'I didn't resist nothing. I got the hell out when I see the big geezer coming. The size on him – he'd have killed me. That's the way it was, lady. Honest.' He looked at her, terrified. 'What'll 'appen to me?'

'I don't know.' She got up and went to the door.

'Lady – I'm sorry I assaulted you. I got respect for women,

normal like. I'd had a few too much. And lady – I hope the big geezer's all right.'

'Yes,' she said quietly, and left him.

Tom Kelly could not remember every being so terrified in his life. Gowned and masked he was standing over Dougie's inert form, while Jane, similarly attired, was holding the anaesthetic mask in place. The amplifier was fixed now so that the voice of the doctor from the Royal Victoria Hospital could be clearly heard by himself, Jane and Nairn. The instructions were coming clear and firm but Tom knew that no amount of instruction was going to help him at the terrible moment when he had to lift the knife. His eyes met Jane's over their masks and he knew she was smiling at him. He felt an inexpressible sense of comfort. Whatever there had been between them in the past she had never let him down when he was in trouble. That was why he had asked for her now, and why she had responded immediately, as he had known she would.

'Slosh it on as much as you like,' came the doctor's voice. 'Don't be afraid.'

Afraid, thought Tom as he swabbed iodine over Dougie's exposed abdomen. You don't know the meaning of the word.

'Doesn't worry you at all, does it?' he said to Jane. Incredibly his voice sounded normal.

'What?'

'The sight of blood.'

'Only when it's my own.'

'That's my girl. It's just that there's going to be rather a lot of it, so they tell me. Right, doctor, it's done.'

'Fine. Now, you're clear on principle about what we're trying to achieve?'

'As clear as I'll ever be.'

'Right. Now the cut is from the xyphoid process to the umbilicus . . .'

'Say again?'

'From the bottom of the breast bone to the belly button,' the doctor translated. 'A bold cut, which you will deepen until you reach the peritoneum.'

'And how do I recognise that?'

'It'll appear as thin, filmy membrane.'

Tom's voice became frantic, 'Yes, but what if I . . .?'

And then Godfrey Nairn spoke for the first time since his initial outburst. He had remained at the head of the table, silently furious, coldly unco-operative. But now he said, 'Just do it, Mr Kelly. I'll tell you when you get there.'

Tom's head jerked up. Jane too was staring at Nairn. In that still room the calm, decided voice had the electric effect of a trumpet announcing the advance.

The doctor's voice came again. 'Are you clear on that point?'

Tom picked up the scalpel. He felt suddenly clear-headed and unafraid. 'Yes, Doctor,' he said quietly. 'I'm making the cut now.'

The sudden outpouring of blood was shocking, nauseating, killing all his new-found courage. Then there were Jane's eyes on him, the awareness of her reassuring smile behind the mask. His hand steadied, he drew the knife down in a firm sweep, going ever deeper until Nairn's voice said, 'That's it.'

He stopped cutting as if electrified, and began another cut, cross-wise, until enough flesh was free for Jane to clamp it back and begin to swab the blood away so that he could see inside. As fast as she swabbed more blood flooded into the cavity. Wherever the artery was it was pouring the stuff out. But where the hell was it? Guided by the doctor he began a desperate search. But in the confused mass of organs that faced him he could find nothing identifiable as a damaged artery.

For one nightmarish moment his mind and hand froze. He was aware of Nairn uttering words that were meant to help, but they conveyed nothing to him. The he seemed to unfreeze and force himself into life, but his movements were jerky.

'I can't find it,' he yelled to the doctor.

'Then you're not over far enough. It's as far as you can go. Don't be afraid of it, Mr Kelly.'

(*I wish to God he'd stop saying that!*)

'Have you got it?'

'Yes . . . yes. I think so.'

'Now draw it forward where you can see it . . . it's tough . . . now can you see the pedicle?'

'There,' said Nairn pointing.

'I have it, yes.'

'If you pinch it hard between your finger and thumb the bleeding will stop.'

'Yes.' To his overwhelming relief it really did happen.

'So clamp it. Use as many clamps as you like.'

'Yes.' Tom's voice was faint, and Jane acted at once.

'Just a moment, Doctor. Tom, leave it.' She caught hold of him as he swayed and forced him upright. 'Stand up, a few seconds won't hurt. Tom! Inhale deeply – big gulps.' He did as she said as automatically as a soldier following orders. He seemed to have no will of his own for the moment. 'It's just a machine, Tom – a very clever one, but that's all . . .'

He had been standing still where she positioned him, his eyes closed as he inhaled. Now he opened his eyes and looked straight into hers. He grinned sheepishly.

'Sorry,' he whispered.

'You O.K.?'

'Yes, it's passed.' He became brisk. 'Right, nurse. Clamps . . .'

'Clamps.' She moved back to her place and her eyes reproached him fondly. 'Silly . . .'

'Matt . . . It's me – Beth.'

He froze right where he stood in the corridor, but did not turn round. He kept his eyes tight shut until she touched him lightly on the arm.

'I know.' He opened his eyes and turned to her. 'I was scared to look.'

'And now you have . . .' she gave a little deprecating laugh. 'No, don't say anything. That wasn't fair of me.'

'Oh, Beth . . .' he said awkwardly.

She began to back away. 'I'll go now. You see, I've had time to think – to be ready for this.' She gave a quick nervous smile. 'I – I'll come back tomorrow – or some time . . .'

'Beth . . .' He strode after her. 'Don't go, I . . .' He shrugged helplessly. 'I don't know what to say.'

In truth he hadn't known what he could possibly say ever since Dougie had first told him who was seeking him out. He had come searching for her, not knowing what he would say if he found her, but trusting that the moment would inspire him. Well, it hadn't.

'I know you don't,' she said. 'That's why you need time to . . .'

'No, you don't understand,' he interrupted hastily. 'For *years* I used to imagine how . . . I used to plan what I'd say if . . . like if you came round a corner, or if we just chanced to . . . and now I . . .' he faltered to a halt.

'And you think I was any different?'

'But we had whole conversations. Beth, you wouldn't believe . . . I even went back once or twice . . .'

'Me too.'

'Just to see. I was sure you'd be there.'

'I often was.'

'But not at the same time,' he said with a touch of sadness.

'Matt, I'm going now. I'll see you tomorrow.'

'Yes.' He let her go a few yards, then seemed to remember something. 'But Beth – what about Rebecca?'

'Tomorrow,' she promised.

He made his way back to his cabin, pulled out a small trunk and began to work methodically through its contents, which were mostly papers, personal and official. His birth certificate was here, plus all his qualification certificates, but he flung them aside, until at last he came to what he was searching for.

He sat and gazed at the battered old photograph. It showed a girl of twenty, dark-haired and vividly pretty, and with something in her face that was still recognisable in the woman he had just left.

He looked at it a long time, smiling.

After leaving the brig Sarah had gone directly to her office where she might hope to bury herself in work and take her mind off Dougie. She entered to find Charles there, studying a huge wall-chart that she had pinned up behind her desk.

'It's a total efficiency chart,' she told him. 'American idea. Doesn't make a lot of sense unless you know what the factors are.'

He gave her a little smile. 'I wasn't really taking it in, anyway.'

'Before you say anything – and before I forget – thank you.'

'What for?'

'Rescuing me back there.'

'That's all right. I would have done it for any lady.'

'Now spoil it,' she smiled.

'... Or any damsel in distress.' He rubbed his stomach ruefully. 'Think I'd only do it once, though.'

'Any news from the surgery?'

'No. I haven't been in. It's "no entry" at the moment.'

'So what can I do for you?'

He took a deep breath. 'It's Barbara Carter.'

'Oh.' Her smile vanished.

'I suppose you could say I'm interceding for her.'

'Did she ask you to?'

'No ... not at all. I just felt ... maybe ... your decision might have been a little hasty.'

'It wasn't.'

'Or at least a little harsh.'

'Mr Woodhouse . . .'

'I know it's none of my business – and I'm sure you had your reasons – but . . . I don't know how to say it . . . Look, over the last few days I've . . . well, I've got to know Barbara. She's not a bad kid. Okay, so she's young and there are certain things she hasn't got right yet – but she's just feeling her way. Stretching her wings in the big bad world if you like . . .'

'So we put it down to the follies of youth?' she said quietly.

'That's all it is.'

'And I reinstate her?'

'Yes.'

'No.' She faced him squarely. 'I've just been talking to a young man. A short while ago he'd had a few drinks, a bit of a laugh with the lads. Things escalated and got out of hand. Now he's in the brig frightened sick that he'll be charge with manslaughter. The follies of youth?'

'That's different,' he said lamely.

'Yes, it's very different. That young hooligan has learned something. You could release him – and I'd personally advocate that you do – because he'll never do anything like that again. Self-knowledge, remorse, a willingness to change . . . even the courage to say sorry . . . Not apparent in Barbara Carter.'

He glared at her, tapping his head. 'It's all in here with you, isn't it? And there's nothing here.' He tapped his heart.

She looked away from him. 'That isn't true,' she said quietly.

'Yes it is. All part of the super total-efficiency chart. Factors, equations . . . it's all a big balance sheet. Crime plus remorse equals innocence? Life just ain't that simple.'

'I didn't say it was. Now if there's nothing else to discuss, perhaps you'd . . .'

As he looked at her something clicked in his brain, something connected with the flinching distaste he had seen on her face when the yobboes pawed her. Of course no nice girl liked being fumbled over, but still . . .

'Do you know what's suddenly occurred to me?' he said. 'You've never had a man.'

She looked at him sharply, then down at her fingernails.

'And how is that – assumption – relevant to the point at issue?' she demanded.

'It isn't relevant at all,' he said. He had spoken quite without malice, more with a kind of pleased discovery of his own shrewdness.

'Then why say it?'

'I don't know. It just struck me as a truth. I'm sorry . . . it's not my business.' He left her quickly, embarrassed by what he'd done. He had a feeling she was on the verge of tears.

He arrived on the bridge half an hour later to find Matt and John pacing.

'They've nearly finished,' he told them. 'Tom's stitching him up now.'

'You haven't been in?' said John.

'No. Just stopped by at the radio room to disperse the crowds. Some bright spark discovered that the radio link could be amplified. There were about a dozen of 'em in there – listening to a blow-by-blow account.'

'That's disgraceful,' said John.

'"Sick" is the word I used. I told the radio officer I'd be mentioning it to you.'

'Yes, I'll have a word with him.'

'I'll get back.' Matt turned to go.

'No. Matt . . . since you're here.' Charles spoke to both of them. 'It's this shipboard management thing. Perhaps I'm being unusually thick – but I was under the impression that *we* are the management.'

'Yes, with Douglas Evans and Miss Hallam,' said John.

'So how can Barbara Carter be fired without our being consulted? Can Sarah do that John?'

'It's in her contract.'

'Can't you countermand it? Or can't we? As a management team?'

'I don't think so,' said John. 'I must confess, the whole thing is acutely embarrasing.'

'With Marion?' said Matt. John nodded. 'I take it she knows?'

'I certainly haven't told her,' John admitted, 'and until this other business is over I'm not going to.'

'Mind you, I'm sure Sarah had her reasons,' said Matt vaguely.

'I don't doubt it. She's never short of those.' There was a bitter edge to John's voice.

Charles picked up the buzzing phone. 'That was Jane Anthony,' he said after a minute. 'Tom's finished.'

In the surgery, Godfrey Nairn, watching Jane clear up, was moved to remark, 'I can't pretend I'm not impressed.'

'You're very kind,' said Tom. 'But it's early days yet.' Just the same, he was trying not to give way to a sense of triumph at merely having brought the patient through alive.

'Sure it is,' agreed Nairn. 'I still wouldn't give him a prayer – but I could get round to it. You must admit the whole thing was all slightly unreasonable.'

'Ridiculous, but there you go. What choice did we have?'

'I just want you to know, I'm sorry for being so . . .' Nairn faltered.

'That's all right, Mr Nairn,' Tom said at once. 'I'm sorry we had to press-gang you into it. If Dougie survives I'll make sure he thanks you.'

'It was almost comic to see the way the other man's face fell at this prospect.'

'No – I think actually I'd be happier if we could just – let it drop.' He began to move towards the door. 'Look, if there's nothing else I can do, I'll just . . . you did a good job, Mr Kelly,' he finished desperately, and fled.

'Funny feller,' said Jane.

'Yeah. I shouldn't have thought modesty was among his more obvious virtues. Still . . .'

They abandoned the uninteresting subject of Mr Nairn and looked at each other. Jane stroked the side of Tom's face affectionately.

'You know, you're still a good man, Tom.'

He smiled at her. 'And you're still a very lovely woman.'

'Is it all right for me to come in?' John's voice from the door caused them to jump slightly apart.

'I think perhaps it's as well that you did, Captain,' said Jane.

'I mean – so far as Dougie —' John was embarrassed.

'I've dressed the wound,' said Tom, coming to everybody's rescue. 'If there's any infection it's there already. He's still alive. There's no way of knowing where it'll go from here. Latest word is that the helicopter won't be here till morning – just to drop off the doctor. There's no possibility of moving him now.'

'Is there anything I can do?'

'Not really. It's just a matter of sitting here with him, in case.'

'In case of what?'

'I don't know.' Tom gave a crooked grin. 'Underneath this impressive fancy dress I'm just a sailor boy.'

John cleared his throat awkwardly. 'No. Something more than that, Tom.'

Then, feeling that he was verging on the dangerously sentimental, he made a hasty departure.

Matt found Beth without trouble the following morning. She was sitting alone at a table in the coffee bar. She smiled when she saw him, and again he was struck by the echo of the photograph he kept with him. It was almost indecent for a woman to have aged so little in fifteen years. He wondered what she thought of him. Right this minute he felt no different inside from the gauche boy who had loved her, given her a child, and lost her because the sea was his first real love.

'Things look different in the morning, don't they?' she said as he sat down. 'You've had a shave for a start.'

He leaned forward so that she could sniff his after-shave.

'Paco something or other,' he said. 'I had a duty-free squirt in passing.' He leaned back and looked at her. 'You don't look any different.'

She gave him a mischievous grin. 'You planned that one.'

It had, in fact, been the spontaneous expression of his thoughts, but a sudden unexpected shyness made the old macho act come dancing on-stage.

'You're right,' he said. 'Rehearsed it a couple of times in the mirror. Did it sound right?'

'Very convincing.'

'Still true, for all that.'

'Well, you don't look the same. You've improved. Not so lean and gaunt . . .'

'Yeah, the acne cleared up too.'

'You never had acne,' she frowned.

'Just testing. Lean, gaunt . . . you might have been thinking of somebody else.'

'I've never thought about anyone else,' she said seriously. The look of alarm in his face warned her and she laughed hastily. 'That *wasn't* planned. It slipped out.'

'And how's Geoffrey?' he said, moving the conversation to safer territory.

'Fine.'

'Non-committal.'

'He's in America.'

'And – Rebecca?' he did not look at her as he asked after his child. The answer mattered.

'She's fine too. I brought you a picture.' She pulled it from her handbag and placed it face down before him. He did not touch it.

'Scared again?' she said lightly.

'It's all too much . . .' he seized the picture abruptly and looked in silence.

'Well?'

'She's beautiful,' he said softly. 'Blonde.'

'Not really. She's fair, but she's at the age of experiment. I won't let her cut it.' He offered her the picture. 'No, you keep it.'

'How does she get on with Geoffrey?' he asked, gazing at the picture again, trying to understand that this was his daughter.

'Oh, he's a perfect father. Sorry —' as Matt winced. 'He's a perfect everything, though, isn't he?'

'Yeah, perfection always was one of his strong points.' He rose to his feet. 'I'd better get below.'

'No —' she stopped him quickly. 'Matt – not like this . . .'

'I'll see you later, O.K.?' He waved the picture. 'And thanks . . .'

He had looked forward to meeting her that morning, and now he was only anxious to escape. Perhaps in a nice simple engine room he could unscramble his feelings.

For a moment nobody moved. James Wootton, standing on the threshold of his cabin, his hand still clutching the door-knob, was rooted to the spot at the sight that met his eyes. Christine Harris, who had whirled at his entrance, was also motionless, petrified at the sight of him. Only Sarah Hallam was unperturbed, and she had her back to Wootton. She was crouched down, going through his clothes cupboard, and seemed riveted by something she had just discovered.

When he could find his voice he managed to say, 'You've over-reached yourself this time, Miss Hallam.'

'Is that so?' she said over her shoulder. Only then did she rise and turn round. She was composed and not in the least troubled by the compromising situation in which she found herself.

'Breaking and entering . . .' he began furiously.

'Show me the break.' Sarah pointed to the cabin key which was still in Christine's hand.

' . . . Illegally entering a private cabin,' he spat at her. 'The police are going to have a field day. And the papers. This time your sickening interference has landed you right in it.'

'That's fine with me —' Sarah studied the passport she was

holding in her hand, '— Mr Jennings.' She held it up, open at the page that bore his picture, and that of a woman.

'What I call myself is my affair.'

'Of course it is,' she agreed.

'You have no right – absolutely no right – to come into my cabin and . . .'

'Read your ship's ticket, Mr Jennings, then tell me my rights,' she cut in coldly. 'So far as the police are concerned, the charge will be attempting to obtain money by false pretences. They don't take kindly to sharks who dupe little old ladies – and nor does the general public.' Sarah tossed the passport onto his bunk. 'I'm sure *Mrs Jennings* will agree.'

She walked passed him to the door.

'You will make your excuses to Mrs Harper. You will get off at Harwich, and you will never board this ship again. Is that understood?'

He looked at her for a long moment, clenching his fists. For a second Christine thought that he would strike out at Sarah standing so coolly in the doorway. But then his shoulders slumped and he turned away.

'All right,' he said sullenly.

The two women left. As soon as the door had closed behind them there was a thumping noise from within the cabin. Neither halted. Both could clearly recognise the sound of a passport being hurled at the wall in a rage.

Matt took a long look at the specimen of humanity that met his gaze as soon as he stepped into the brig. It wasn't, he decided, impressive, and the less he saw of it the better. But John had asked him to do this.

'I've come to suss you out,' he said.

'What does that mean?'

'Eh, now watch it – we'll have a bit of respect.'

The boy's brief attempt to assert himself collapsed. Realisation of the spot he'd landed himself in seemed to crush him.

'Yeah, sorry,' he mumbled.

'I've been asked by the captain, no less, to decide whether we, as a shipping line, hand you over to the law, take civil action against you, or let you go. So if you want to louse up your chances, just carry on as you are. Right?'

'I said I was sorry,' the boy sulked.

'You didn't convince me.'

'How's the fella? The big bloke.'

'Alive.'

There was a faint but audible sigh of relief, then he said, 'So what's going to happen to me?'

'Well,' said Matt, 'the first officer – he's the one you slugged in the stomach – is undecided. The business with the purser would seem to have been an accident, so there's no case to answer. And Miss Hallam – the lady who spoke to you last night – is of the opinion that you should be released. The captain wants a second opinion.'

'Look, I promise you . . .'

'Yeah, yeah,' Matt waved him aside. He wasn't interested in protestations of reform. 'Forget it. I'll tell you what you're going to do. You buy the first officer a bottle of Scotch, Miss Hallam the biggest box of chocolates you can find – and you'll write letters of apology to everyone concerned. And for what's left of this trip you'll smile sweetly at all the passengers, open doors for old ladies and generally behave like a perfect gent. Got that?'

'Yeah – I'll do all that.' The youngster stumbled over the words in his anxiety to get them out.

'And if there's one whisper – just the faintest whisper – of any more trouble from you, I shall personally and privately take you down to the car deck and thrash the living daylights out of you.'

Chapter 6

Bill Ryan found Sarah leaning over the rail of the sun-deck watching the ambulance that was taking Dougie to hospital in Harwich. It seemed as good a time as any to challenge her.

'I've been told you're in charge of staff appointments on the ship,' he said, when the preliminaries were out of the way.

'That's broadly true, yes.'

'What about Ted Anderson? Way I see it, taking him out of the galley and putting him in your office doesn't solve the original problem. It's still nepotism, isn't it? Whatever way you look at it, he wouldn't be on this ship if his dad wasn't the captain.'

'That's true,' she conceded. 'And if he wasn't a good employee his Dad could be Lord High Admiral of the Fleet and he'd still get the push.'

'That doesn't make it right, though. Like, there's three million unemployed and he's got a job because of his family.'

Sarah sighed. 'I'm not paid to solve the unemployment problem. I'm paid to run an efficient business and Ted Anderson helps me do so.'

He played his big card. 'Perhaps the union will think differently.'

She gave it only the briefest attention. 'I'm sure they will. Is that all? Hallo . . .' she turned with relief to see Matt who had walked up behind them.

But Bill hadn't finished. 'There's also the problem of Barbara Carter,' he persisted.

'I'm sorry, Sarah. Is he sounding off again?' said Matt with a grin.

'No, it's quite all right.' Sarah looked at Bill indulgently. 'Go on, what about Miss Carter?'

'You had no right to fire her.'

'Hey now,' said Matt at once. 'You're out of order there, sunshine.'

'No Matt, really, it's all right. Let him say what he wants to,' said Sarah.

Bill felt himself expand with importance. At last this lady had realised she wasn't dealing with a nobody.

'Well, it's in *your* interests,' he said generously. 'Makes no difference to me. I shall be raising it with the union anyway. I'm just giving you a chance to reconsider, that's all. Will you take her back?'

'No,' said Sarah.

'O.K., that's your decision.'

'Yes it is,' Matt cut in hurriedly. 'Now come on, we've got work to do.'

Sarah held up a hand to detain them both. 'For the record, all employees, including yourself, serve one month's probation, during which time they may be dismissed without notice or explanation. The unions all have a file copy.' She looked kindly at Bill. 'Did you realise that?'

Plainly he had not, but he struggled to make a recovery. 'I can't see the owner of the company taking it too kindly. Sacking her niece,' he said lamely.

Sarah gave him a pitying look before delivery the *coup de grace*. 'So what are you suggesting? That I reinstate Miss Carter because her aunt owns the company? Isn't that nepotism?'

The boy flushed under her gently teasing tone. Matt put a friendly hand on his shoulder.

'You walked right into that one, didn't you?' he said.

Bill thrust the hand roughly aside and stalked off.

'Was I cruel?' said Sarah.

'No. Do him good. I'm just sorry he bothered you with all that stuff.'

'No bother,' she smiled. 'You're very fond of him, aren't you?'

'Never thought about it. Takes me back, that's all, to when I was a cadet.

Returning to her office Sarah took a detour past the information desk to see how Christine Harris was coping now she was without Dougie. To her surprise and pleasure she found Barry Peters there, giving the girl a hand, and was about to pass on when a hand was laid on her arm, and a voice said, 'Sarah.'

'Hello, Nick. To what do we owe this?'

His good-looking face made a grimace. 'Regal summons. I didn't need it, if the truth be known.'

'Mrs Terson?'

He held up a bulging brief case. 'I think she wanted me to bring the mail across. I'm not stopping anyway. Flying back this afternoon.' He became suddenly alert, muttering in Sarah's ear, 'And here's one who invited himself. *'Morning, Mr West.'*

David West appeared out of the crowd, greeted them in passing, and turned his attention immediately to the information desk, where he ordered a car 'for myself and Mrs Terson' in half an hour. When he had gone Nick and Sarah looked at each other.

'For myself and Mrs Terson,' Nick repeated slowly.

'You don't like it, do you?'

'Do you?'

'No.'

John Anderson didn't like it either. He had arrived in Marion's cabin fifteen minutes earlier to find the unwelcome presence of David West, and the even more unwelcome news that Marion was about to sign a contract selling David the *Trianglia*, John's old ship. In John's presence Marion had scrawled her signature with a triumphant flourish, and David West had let it be known that he intended to convert the ship to cruise the Mediterranean. In view of Triangle's own Mediterranean interests John had been appalled but had managed to hold his tongue.

'Come on now, John,' said Marion when the door had closed behind David. 'You can speak your mind with me, surely?'

'It's not my place to, Marion.'

'Oh, that's silly. You're a shareholder. And now that we've gone public you could even be called a major shareholder. If it's not your place to speak, then whose is it? You're upset about the *Trianglia*?'

'No. I daresay that's just nostalgia. It just seems to me – or seemed to me – that our Mediterranean interests were poised to – well, to go somewhere. I just wondered about giving the opposition any kind of encouragement.'

'But David's not opposition,' she said quickly. 'He's one of us.'

'And frankly that's where I get confused. D.R.W. Shipping *is* the opposition – and yet D.R.W. himself isn't. I can't see the difference.'

'Surely, just because we're in competition doesn't mean we have to be tearing away at each other all the time?' she pleaded. 'Can't we compete – and at the same time co-operate? When it's mutually beneficial?'

Nick's arrival saved John from having to make a reply that he would have found difficult.

'Now perhaps I can show you some of the advantages,' said Marion. 'Did you bring the Munkjeberg package?'

'I did.' Nick removed it from his briefcase.

John turned to the door.

'Look, Marion, I'm sure that what you say is absolutely right. You don't need to show me anything – and anyway, I must be pushing along now. Going ashore.' He nodded pleasantly at Nick, and went.

He would have been interested to know that his dread of the unknown contents of 'the Munkjeberg package' was shared by Nick – except that Nick knew the contents and dreaded them even more. It seemed to Nick that Marion had chosen a crazy time to buy a hotel, and a crazy hotel to buy. He spread the brochures out and studied them, while Marion hovered excitedly, waiting for his reaction.

'It's certainly a nice place,' he said at last, without enthusiasm.

'Is that all you can say? Oh Nick, it's a *beautiful* place! Isolated but accessible – and just look at that view. It's going to be the loveliest place in Denmark.'

'And what does that say? I mean, the loveliest place in Austria – or even Scotland . . .'

'Now you're being deliberately boorish.'

'No, I'm just being – cautious.'

'And you think I haven't been? You think I've just gone out and squandered a million dollars on a hotel like I'd buy a new dress?'

Privately that's exactly what he thought, but didn't dare say so.

'Believe you me, we've been into this very thoroughly. It was the right place, the right time, the right price – and it's got class, Nick. This is the company image.'

'Don't get me wrong, Marion. I've got every confidence in you and you're most probably right, but . . .' He hesitated then came to a decision. Sometimes you just had to dare. 'Actually, that isn't true.'

She frowned. 'Nick —?'

'I don't have that much confidence,' he said quietly.

Marion's voice had a dangerous note. 'What are you saying?'

'I don't know. I'm just a lawyer – ask me about commercial law – but business on this kind of scale is – well, it's . . .'

'Nick, just what are you trying to say?'

'I just wonder if you're not out of your depth. You've got to admit, Marion, that until – until George Terson died you had no experience of these kinds of decisions.'

'Do you think I make them alone?'

'I'm sure you don't, but . . .'

'I am surrounded – no, I'm *smothered* – by advice from every quarter. Nick, this proposal was put up by our managing director, it was voted in almost unanimously by the board. As chairman, I had nothing to do with it.'

'Except approve.'

'Of course I approved,' she said, exasperated. 'I wanted you to approve it too.'

'Why should my opinion matter?'

'Because you're always so damned *honest*, that's why. Your opinion does matter – and I *demand* your approval.' She had been working herself up into a rage with every word, but now, with the final explosion, she stopped and seemed to hear herself for the first time. She gave a weak, deprecating smile. 'At least, I wish I could.'

He sighed. 'I wish I could give it.'

Suddenly she laughed. 'Oh, let's not squabble. I'll tell you what we'll do. We'll go over there. In fact, we'll have a conference. Get everyone together, and you can see for yourself. And then you'll believe. All right?'

'If you say so,' he said heavily. He knew she hadn't taken in a word he'd said.

Matt found Beth where he had told her to be, waiting for him on the dock, sitting on her suitcase.

'I thought you'd forgotten me,' she said, as he put her case in the car.

'I'm sorry. Car wouldn't start.'

'And you an engineer.'

'She's always temperamental after I've been away. I think the salt in the air makes her ratty.'

'What happened to the M.G.?' She settled into the passenger seat beside him.

'Passed on to the great breaker's yard in the sky. And that's going back some.'

'Shame,' she said sentimentally. 'I always thought of that car as being a part of you, somehow.'

'I always saw it as being a part of *us*. We pushed it far enough between us.' He started the engine. 'Where shall we go!'

'I don't mind. You choose.' She laid her hand on his. 'Matt?'

'Yeah?' He had a sudden sense of danger.

'Aren't you going to kiss me?'

He looked at her for a long time before moving towards her. The moment he took her into his arms he knew his instinct for danger hadn't failed him. He should have stayed well clear of this. But it was too late now, and he wasn't sorry.

After that there was never any doubt about how they were going to spend the day. Matt drove without stopping until he was well out of Harwich and into the surrounding countryside. When he was sure they were safely alone he stopped the car.

They lay back in the long grass, her head against his shoulder, and talked of days long ago, when they had sought just such secluded spots because they had no money to go anywhere – and because neither of them wanted anything but to be with the other. Long sunny days, and long sweet nights – that had ended in her marriage to Geoffrey Brooks.

'At the time it seemed the right thing to do,' she said when they had finished reminiscing. 'And Mum used to preach at me all the time. It was always Geoffrey this and Geoffrey that. If ever I mentioned you she'd clam up and go into the sulks. It wasn't until years after that I realised she fancied you rotten herself.'

'Your mum? You're kidding.'

'I'm not, you know. She got tiddled one Christmas and it all came out.'

He breathed a prayer of silent relief that it had had the decency not to come out while he was around.

'But still,' he reminded her, 'you said it seemed the right thing to do.'

'Yes.' She hesitated. 'Perhaps I panicked – with Rebecca on the way . . . and I could never have told Dad . . .'

'*I* would have told him.'

'But I didn't know that. I didn't know that you'd stand by me . . .'

'Oh Beth.' He didn't know what else to say to cover the sudden rending sense of loss and futility that afflicted him.

'Well, I didn't, Matt. You never said anything . . .'

'I didn't have to. It was all understood – at least, I thought it was.'

'But there are some things that have to be *said*. No matter how close you are you can't hit on a day and an hour to get married without *talking* about it.'

'There wasn't any urgency though, was there?' he said with masculine incomprehension.

'Only a baby on the way,' she said gently.

'Yeah, well – if you'd told me about that maybe I'd have . . .'

'You'd have felt obliged,' she broke in. 'That's the whole point, Matt.'

He sighed. 'So that's all it was. Seems ridiculous.'

'Of course that isn't *all* there was to it. Maybe it wasn't panic so much as instinct. When there's a baby growing inside you somehow your priorities change. Security seemed more important than . . .' she faltered.

'Than what?' he demanded in a hard voice. 'Love?'

'Yes,' she said quietly.

'You said you loved Geoffrey that day I came back,' he reminded her. 'It was the first thing you said.'

'I did. I do. But . . .'

'Still?' Strange how it hurt.

'We've been married fifteen years, Matt . . .'

'So why are you here?'

'Because . . .' She sat up and looked away from him. He could see that she was twisting her hands together. 'What *do* you think of me now, Matt? Honestly?'

'I think you're every bit as lovely as I remembered you,' he said truthfully. 'Your voice is the same. The way you move your head. Is that what you wanted to hear?'

Instead of answering directly she half turned and lay beside him, propped up on one elbow, so that he could see her face slightly above him.

'You know, we were all supposed to be going to America,' she said. 'Geoff was going for business, but we were going to make a family holiday of it. Except Rebecca didn't want to come. She went youth hostelling with some friends.'

'So?'

'So – I don't know. I'm panicking again. I panicked when she came and I'll panic ten times worse when she goes. I don't know what it's all about. I mean, how old will I be? Thirty-six? Thirty-seven?'

'Perhaps.' He refused to help her. Wherever this was leading she had to get there by herself.

'It's not even half-way, and everything's done. Where does it go from here? We've already got the house, the hover-mower, the automatic washing machine . . . Geoffrey's golf handicap hasn't changed in years – it's not going to improve now. And then Rebecca goes. What do we do? You can't go back – and there's nowhere forward left to go. I don't *feel* like sitting back contentedly for forty years.'

'There's always the garden,' he said, grinning wickedly.

'Geoffrey does that.' She smiled back at his teasing. 'And you haven't changed either.' She took a faint breath. '*That's* why I'm here.'

'You've got tired of the security and now you want the romance back. Yeah, well, I'm the lad, aren't I? Life on the briney, exotic foreign ports . . .' There was a bitter edge to his voice. He was being used, there was no doubt of it. And his sudden sharp sense of disappointment told him how close he'd been to making a fool of himself.

'Freedom . . .' she echoed.

'You could always leave him.'

She looked at him for a long moment, trying to read in his eyes if he was serious. She seemed to decide that he wasn't, for after a moment she sighed and turned away. He pulled her down beside him and kissed her, but somehow the heart had gone out of the day, and he remembered that it was nearly time for him to take her to the station to catch her train.

As they walked back to the car, her hand in his, she said sadly, 'Two precious hours, and all I've done is talk about myself.'

'I'm not complaining.'

'It wasn't what I planned. I don't know . . . I had this sort of idea about staying on the ship for the whole time Geoffrey's away.'

'I wouldn't complain about that either,' he said truthfully. 'But it isn't what you want.'

'Oh, it is, Matt. Believe me, it is. But I'd still have to go back to Basingstoke at the end of it. I think I'll go quietly mad.' She smiled up at him. 'You're a lovely feller.'

'Yeah?'

'I think part of me was secretly hoping you'd have got older, settled down, become more like Geoffrey. It would have been much easier that way. But you haven't changed a bit, have you?' When he didn't answer she looked down and said, half-uneasy, half-hoping, 'Will you want to see Rebecca?'

'Oh sure.' He frowned. '"This is Matt Taylor, one of my old school chums." Can you picture it? "Hey mum, you had some weird mates when you was a kid."'

'She wouldn't think that.'

'No, you were right first off. She's Geoffrey's kid. Has been for fifteen years. What's my contribution compared to that?' He tried to see her face. 'That's what you wanted me to say, isn't it?'

'Yes,' she said quietly.

'Come on,' he said in a decided voice. 'Let's get you to the station.'

But she held back. 'Matt – was it a really stupid thing for me to do? Seeing you again?'

'Yep,' he said without hesitation. But when they were seated together in the car he added gently, 'But then we always were really stupid. That's what made it so much fun.'

He saw her off at the station. They made no attempt to drag out the goodbyes. The real goodbye had already been said – fifteen years ago.

From the station he went straight to a small pub that was well known to him, and sat drinking in a bored fashion. It was not the same kind of drinking he'd gone in for when he parted from Kate (although he realised to his dismay that the feelings that were plaguing him were almost exactly the same). Then he had wanted to get drunk. Now he intended to keep a clear head for the arrival of one Roger Powell, who had asked him, by letter, to meet him here for the purpose of making him "an interesting proposition". Matt had told no-one about the letter, and to the last moment had pretended to himself that he had no intention of keeping the appointment. And yet here he was.

'Matt Taylor?'

He looked up to find a burly, dark-haired man at his elbow. The man was in his forties with a naturally heavy face that he was making efforts to lighten into friendliness.

'You got my letter?' he said. 'Do please forgive me for all this cloak and dagger stuff.' He sat down. 'I'm sure you appreciate the need for discretion – on your part as well as ours. So what do you think of our proposition – in principle?'

'Look, I've just come along out of curiosity. Right now I don't think anything about it either way. I don't even know who it is you represent.'

'Well, of course at this stage that's really neither here nor there.' Powell cracked his face into a smile. 'People might question the ethics of this kind of recruitment – though in a sense, if it benefits you and it benefits us what the hell does it matter what anyone else thinks? However, this is just a tentative approach. Obviously, if the idea appeals we can be more specific later on. Would you describe yourself as a loyal man?'

'Loyal to Triangle Line?'

'Yes.'

'Yeah. Yeah, I would.'

'And do you think you could be equally loyal to another company? Should the situation arise, should you see your way clear to making the move?'

'I can't answer that, can I? Loyalty is something that grows over a period. Triangle have always treated me right.'

'Although they're paying you twenty per cent less than we're offering you?'

Matt didn't waste time asking how Powell knew his salary. This was the sort of man who would.

'The salary's more than enough for me. I don't think about it,' he said. This wasn't strictly true, but his hackles were rising: why, he couldn't have said.

'But you wouldn't object to more?'

'I'd be a mug if I did, wouldn't I?'

'Then there's the limitations of the North Sea.' Powell mused.

Something stubborn in Matt made him block every ball Powell could send down.

'I dunno,' he said. 'One stretch of water's much the same as another when you're in the engine room.'

Powell gave his imitation of a smile again. 'You're a difficult man to tempt, Matt. What does it take?'

'If I knew the answer to that I'd tell you. Look, I'm sailing in fifteen minutes . . .'

'We'll leave it at that, then, shall we? I'll report back that you're not opposed in principle, that you'll think it over and let me know in due course. Then we can starting discussing ships and contracts in specific detail.'

'Fair enough,' said Matt without enthusiasm.

'You've got my card. I hope you decide in our favour, Matt.'

In another part of Harwich, in an establishment as different from a dockside pub as the Taj Mahal is from a tent, Marion Terson sat with David West, feeling enjoyably guilty. David could always make her feel that way with the care he lavished on her. He could speak to her as a business colleague on equal terms, while at the same time suggesting that she was something infinitely precious and feminine. It was such a delightful change from the barely concealed scepticism that she detected constantly from her colleagues at Triangle.

She knew they were all watching her, certain that she was going to make mistake after mistake and fritter away George Terson's empire. Nick's outspokenness today had only been the tip of a very upsetting iceberg. Only David could make her feel that she could do justice to George's memory.

And that was where the guilt came in. Could it really be wrong to enjoy the company of a man again, so comparatively soon after George's death? Surely George would have understood that she was taking the best way to protect what he had left her. And surely, too, he would have understood the aching void of loneliness within her that had to be filled up somehow? She tried to tell herself so, but at these times George's features always became blurred, and his voice faint.

Today the conversation had touched on the lightly personal when Marion had ventured to ask a little about his past.

'Of course I have no objections, Marion, other than a natural chivalry. A gentleman doesn't discuss such affairs with . . .'

'Not your *affaires*, David.' She broke in with a little giggle. 'Goodness, I wouldn't dream of prodding about in such murky waters.'

'You misunderstand,' he grinned. 'Deliberately, I think.'

'Go on.'

'Very well, if you insist. I was married at the age of twenty. We separated after three weeks and had to wait five years for the divorce. All things considered, it was an ill-advised and somewhat pointless experience.'

'And have you seen her at all since?'

'Yes. She married a capstan lathe setter and now lives in penury. Or was it Hackney? Both probably.'

'While you've gone from strength to strength?'

'Indeed.'

'I've always been attracted to success.'

'Most women are. There's something almost primeval about it – the desire to mate with the strongest and fittest in the herd. It's nature's way of ensuring the health of the strain. Civilisation has merely broadened the meaning of strong and fit.'

'So I needn't feel guilty about it?' she said, almost to herself.

He looked at her closely. 'Do you feel guilty about being a woman?' She smiled and shook her head. 'Of course, the same principle applies in the world of commerce. D.W.R. Shipping is a thriving healthy company. So is Triangle Line.'

'Now you've lost me,' she said, still in her dream.

'Have I? I don't think so.' He called to a passing waiter. 'More wine . . .'

John Anderson had two jobs to accomplish before sailing, one fairly pleasant, the other not at all so. He decided to fortify himself with the easier one first.

'Ah, Tom,' he said when Tom had obeyed his summons to the bridge, 'Just thought you'd like to know. I've had the hospital on about Dougie. They said his condition was "serious".'

'Thank heaven for that,' said Tom unexpectedly.

'That's good?'

'It means they think he'll live. "Critical" was the word I didn't want.'

'They also said you were to be commended for doing a difficult job in impossible circumstances.'

Tom grinned. 'That could describe the first mate's job the world over.'

'And apparently Douglas was concerned because he never got the chance to thank you and Jane.'

'I'll tell her.'

'How are things there? Between you and Jane?'

'Fine. Why? How should they be?'

'I wasn't meaning to pry or anything. Just that word gets around, you know. Somebody said you were thinking of getting back together again.'

'No chance,' said Tom fervently.

'You seem to get on very well together.'

'We always did. Getting on was never a problem but . . . Did you realise she was a feminist?'

'Aren't they all nowadays? You make it sound like some kind of disease.'

'I suppose I'm basically old-fashioned.'

'Why didn't you just agree to differ?'

'Because when it came to the question of who has the career and who has the kids she'd get illogical. I'd say "*You've* got to have the children because *you've* got the equipment for it." She'd say that wasn't fair. Well, fair or not, that's the way nature organised it. No amount of trendy egalitarian thinking will make *me* pregnant, will it? Still – it's all water under the bridge now. She's a lovely woman for all that.'

Reluctantly John pulled himself away and forced himself to pass on to his next job. He was hating it, but it couldn't be put off any longer. What he issued this time was not a summons but an invitation – to Judith Harper, to come to his cabin, with Mortimer. Not that John had specified Mortimer, but he knew he'd come without being asked, and on the whole he felt his moral support would be useful.

'Isn't this exciting, Mortie?' Judith hissed as they were shown inside. 'Do you know, Captain, in all the time Mr Adams was captain he didn't invite us once to his cabin.'

'There is a purpose for my asking you, Mrs Harper. Do please sit down.' When she had done so he said uncomfortably, 'It's about Mr Wootton . . .'

'Oh yes, what a lovely man. did you get a chance to meet him?'

'Not personally, no.' He could not meet her glowing eyes.

'Well, next time we shall introduce you. You'll get along famously, I'm sure. Real gentlemen always do.'

'You're very kind, but I'm afraid . . . well, you see, the point is there won't be a next time. Mr Wootton won't be coming back.'

'Won't be –? You don't mean he's —?'

'Oh no, no, no – nothing like that. He's perfectly well, but he just won't be coming back.'

'But he said . . .'

'I know he did. It's a long, involved story which he explained to Miss Hallam. He asked that we should offer his deepest apologies and tell you that he will always hold your memory in fond affection. It's for the best, believe me.'

Her lips trembled. 'Could he not have told me himself?'

'He wanted to very much. But the opportunity didn't arise,' said John, improvising madly. He touched her arm gently. 'Morti will look after you, I'm sure.'

She got to her feet, clutching the little dog in her arms. 'Yes, Morti alway looks after me.' She drew herself up to her full height, which was about five feet. 'Thank you, Captain. I'm sorry you should have been involved in my little problems.'

He showed her to the door and closed it quietly behind her. Then he leaned against it, hoping devoutly that a hurricane would hit him before he had to go through such a moment again.

Barry Peters raised an eyebrow when he dropped into the crew recreation room for a quick break that evening. He distinctly remembered that someone had told him Barbara had been sacked – and yet here she was, sitting at a table with Bill Ryan, drinking coffee and listening to music from the juke box. Bill was trying to engage her in conversation but Barbara had an abstracted air that should have warned him he was wasting his time.

Barry dropped down into a chair beside them, and proceeded to go into his best clowning chatter. He was hardly aware of what he was saying. He talked to take his mind off a certain nagging worry of his own that couldn't be confided to anybody. He'd left the under-barman in charge of the work for a few minutes because he'd go mad if he didn't have a short break, but he wasn't happy about leaving the bar . . .

'Did you know that right at the top of the funnel there's a little cabin?' he told the other two brightly. 'What people don't realise is that the North Sea is so shallow that if this tub sinks anywhere in it the top of the funnel will be poking out. So the captain doesn't actually go down with the ship. He legs it up to this little cabin and waits for help to arrive.' He looked round for the applause.

'If I had my way, this ship would be at the bottom of the ocean, funnel and all,' said Barbara. 'And everything else to do with this lousy Triangle Line.'

Barry made an airy gesture. 'What's a hundred million quid between friends?'

'A hundred million?' said Bill blankly.

'I figure that's what Mrs Terson's share is worth,' said Barry. He winked at Barbara. 'One day all this will be yours – or some such. If you haven't wished it to the bottom of the sea.'

'A hundred million pounds?' said Bill again. 'You're joking.'

'Work it out for yourself. Add up the ships and hotels, divide approximately by two and a bit. I could be a few million out either way, but that's just a trifle.'

'And you stand to inherit that?' said Bill to Barbara, outraged.

'Yup,' said Barry before Barbara could reply. 'We're sharing a table with some heiress.'

'And she's not lifting a finger to earn any of it. That is really obscene.'

Barbara had had enough. She looked Bill straight in the eyes. 'And you're just a sickening little juvenile creep,' she snapped. 'Who the hell cares what *you* think? Why don't you just shove off and grease something?'

Barry waited for the great revolutionary to annihilate the capitalist parasite. Then he looked at Bill and saw that he appeared to be on the verge of tears. In another moment the boy had vanished, stomping hurriedly out of the room and banging the door behind him.

'That was a shame,' said Barry quietly to Barbara.

'He deserved it,' she said petulantly. 'Sometimes he really bugs me.'

'Yeah, and what you don't know is that he's been doing his damndest to get you your job back.'

She stared at him. 'How?'

'He's had a go at everyone – Matt Taylor, Jane Anthony, Sarah Hallam. I'm surprised he hasn't bawled the captain out. He certainly said he was going to the union about it at Harwich.'

'I wasn't to know that.' She was pale and Barry had the satisfaction of seeing that she was really shaken.

'What are you doing here?'

They both looked up quickly to see Sarah standing angrily over Barbara.

'I happen to be waiting for the first officer,' said the girl belligerently. 'Any objections?'

'Yes. I told you to disembark at Harwich.'

'I did disembark at Harwich. Then I bought a ticket and re-embarked. You didn't think I'd spend the rest of my life in Harwich, did you? I mean, let's get this in perspective. You're just the manager of one little boat – and you won't be that for very much longer.'

'So you're a passenger?' said Sarah grimly.

'Right on. I'm a passenger.'

'Then might I ask what you're doing in the crew recreation area?'

For a moment Barbara was taken aback. Then she performed a movement so exactly like Bill's as to be funny, getting to her feet and slamming out without a word.

'Thanks a bunch,' said Barry cheerfully. 'I've ten minutes of break left and nobody to talk to – unless you'd care to join me?'

The grimness in Sarah's face had not relaxed. 'You're very kind, but I want you to join me.'

'How do you mean?'

Her next words fell on him like boulders. 'We're going to carry out a stock check in the Bellevue Lounge Bar.'

He tried to keep his voice normal but it was hard when his lips seemed to have frozen. 'When?'

'Now.'

'But the bar's open to customers.'

'Then we shall have to close it.'

'At this time of the evening?' You're joking!'

'Try me.' She began to move off towards the door.

'No, wait – Miss Hallam,' he called after her desperately. She came and sat beside him. 'You know, don't you?' he said in a defeated voice.

'Yes,' her voice was firm, but not unkind. 'Are you going to tell me?'

After a long moment he said, 'I took fifty pounds from the till. But I was going to put it back. I'd have had to Friday anyway, because that's when I'd adjusted the receipts forward to. I wasn't stealing it – I was just borrowing it.' His shoulders sagged. 'They always say that, don't they? What are you going to do?'

'What are *you* going to do?'

'I'll put it back Friday,' he said eagerly. 'I get paid then. That's what I was going to do anyway.' When she did not reply, he said, 'How did you know? The cash tallies with the register – and the daily takings vary by far more than I took.'

'The total receipts vary but the ratio between sterling receipts and kroner receipts is consistent,' she told him, 'to the point where any variation above two per cent is suspect. You took only sterling. It upset the balance.' She stood. 'I'll let you know what I intend to do. I want to think about it.'

When she'd left he didn't bother to finish his coffee. It had lost its taste. He wandered back to work, making sure he passed the information desk. It wasn't really on his route, but that way he got a glimpse of Christine. Not that even that did him much good, he reflected gloomily. He'd taken her out casually while they were in Harwich and she had (equally casually) let it drop that somewhere there was a man she was really interested in. Barry, it was plain, was just for passing the time.

'Where's all the fizz and bounce?' she demanded lightly when she saw him.

He grimaced. 'I dunno. I'm fed up.'

'Strange. I'd have said you were the one person aboard who never gets the dumps.'

He shrugged. 'I'd better get back to work – while I've still got a job to get back to.'

She watched him go with a faintly pitying expression. She knew how he felt about her, but it was no use. Not Barry Peter nor a thousand like him could blot out the memory of the man she thought of night and day. She lived for their meetings, brief as they were, and planned each one days in advance. She knew already that when the ship next docked in Harwich she would run to be with him, to demand reassurance for the jealousy that gnawed her. She would say again, as she had said so many times before, 'It is just business, isn't it, darling? You don't really care for her?'

And he would say, '*Care* for her? Marion Terson? Sweetheart, are you serious?'

And she would say, 'Oh David . . .'

She came out of her dream with a start. Charles Woodhouse was standing beside her, with a quizzical look on his face.

'Listen,' she said hurriedly, 'could you hold the fort for a couple of minutes? I've been trapped in here for hours.'

'Sure,' he grinned. 'I've nothing better to do.'

The night was unusually calm when Matt stepped out onto the deck and went to lean on the rail. It was ten o'clock and he was still on duty, but he felt entitled to a short spell in the cool air before returning to his hot noisy job. Down below everything was going well, and there was nothing that his subordinates couldn't cope with. So he lingered, breathing in the peaceful air and enjoying the glint of the moon on the black waves below.

He knew he was not alone. A little further along Sarah Hallam stood, also looking into the sea. She did not appear to have noticed him and he debated how best to approach her. Sarah intrigued him. Her air of cool, understated sex was not what usually drew his attention. It was too far removed from the brunette flamboyance that had attracted him in Beth Brooks a long time ago, and Kate Laker, more recently, and the worldly sophistication he liked in Jane. Sarah's quiet air of introspection made him think of a nun (at least, he supposed that was what he meant. Nuns weren't a class of female he normally had much to say to.)

After toying with, and abandoning, several lines of approach, he finally settled for simply walking up beside her and saying 'Hello.'

'Oh, hello.'

'Nice night.'

'Isn't it?'

'I've often wondered where you got to when you weren't working.' When Sarah didn't rise to this bait, and in fact gave no sign of having heard it, he said, 'You're very thoughtful.'

'There's a lot to think about,' she said.

'Tell me.'

For the first time she looked at him properly. 'You wouldn't be really interested,' she said with a wry smile.

'I would. I'd be very interested.'

For a moment he thought he'd made contact, then she turned away and said, 'No,' as though slamming a door in his face.

'Why do you do it?' he demanded. 'Why do you lock people out?'

'I don't.'

'Yes you do. You're doing it now. Do you want me to go?'

'If you want to.'

'I don't want to.'

'Then don't,' she sighed gently. 'I don't know what you want me to say.'

'Anything. Anything at all. Just so long as it's about yourself.' But she said nothing and he gave a short embarrassed laugh. 'It's funny. I've been through all this before. In my head.'

'With me?' she said, staring at him.

'Yes.'

'Why?'

'Just thinking about you, I guess, and it sort of worked itself up into a conversation. I told you we all built walls around ourselves, but yours was so high I couldn't see over the top. And I want to.'

'Perhaps there isn't anything to see,' she parried.

'Or perhaps there's something so precious you're frightened to share it,' he said gently.

She gave him a smile of real amusement. 'Did you say that too – in your head?'

'No, that was a straightforward, off-the-cuff, chat-up line.'

Immediately he knew he had blundered. Her smile faded and she turned back to the rail.

'And how should I respond? You see, I don't know.'

Astounded, he realised that she was perfectly serious. 'You say whatever you feel,' he said. 'It should be very easy.'

'But it isn't. Maybe I should see an analyst.'

'Ah well, there's a clue. Something personal. You've spent time in America?'

'One brick out of the wall,' she said. 'I studied business administration at Harvard. There, that's another.'

'Any more?'

'I worked there for three years, advising companies on planned economic growth. Things like that. It's very boring.'

'And they're also very little bricks,' he pointed out. 'In a very big wall.'

'I know. I'm sorry.'

'So let's try a few bigger ones,' he persisted. 'Have you ever been married?'

'No.'

'Engaged?'

'No.'

'Go on.'

'Go on where? Oh, I see what you mean? No, I've never married, never been engaged, never anything.'

'Never anything?' he said with an involuntary inflection that made her start and turn to go.

'And that's too many bricks,' she said firmly.

'No, don't go.' He grabbed her arm and pulled her back to face him. Her eyes were anguished.

'I don't know what you *want* from me.' She brushed a hand hastily across her face. 'Now I've got something in my contact lens.'

He dropped his hand and stood, shocked by the way he had inadvertently hurt her, yet not really understanding. After a moment he touched her arm with gentle fingers.

'I'm sorry, Sarah.'

While she surreptitiously dried her eyes he tried to think of something to say to distract her, and found himself going over this afternoon with Beth. There was something about Sarah that made him feel he could confide in her.

'She was the first in a long and shameful succession,' he admitted sheepishly. 'And because she was the first I guess I'll never get her out of my system completely.'

'And where did Kate Laker fit into the scheme of things?'

'Kate?' He winced. The name still had power to hurt. 'Well, she was something else again – and far too recent to talk about. There has to be a decent time-lapse before a gentleman talks about his lady friends.'

'Are you still seeing her?'

'Nope. And I don't suppose I shall. Last I heard was a letter the first day out of Amsterdam confirming that we were through . . . just in case I hadn't got the message.'

'Were you sorry about that?' She was watching his face closely.

He shrugged. 'There's no point in bleating, is there? So that's my grisly story – and you've got no excuse for not telling me yours.'

His abrupt change of tack confused her. 'I shall need more time,' she said. 'To screw up courage.'

'Why, are the details that lurid?'
'No, you'll find it all very boring.'
'So why the courage?' he persisted.
She moved a little away from him, as though finding him overpowering.
'Matt, please be patient. I feel safe behind my wall. You can't knock it down in one night. I haven't talked to anyone like this since . . . I don't think I ever have.'
'Then you must be very lonely, Sarah.'
'I think I am.'
Knowing what he was risking he leaned forward and took one of her hands. She made no effort to draw it back and he moved closer.
Suddenly his hand tightened hard over hers. She jumped, but realised immediately that there was nothing romantic in the gesture. He seemed almost to have forgotten she was there. His head was cocked to one side and he was listening to the noise made by the ship's engines. Even to Sarah's ears there was something wrong about that noise. It was sluggish and painful.
'Oh hell,' he said violently.
'Matt . . .'
But she was talking to empty air. He had dropped her hand and vanished down the stairs towards the bowels of the ship, leaving her alone with the night and the brilliant stars.

Chapter 7

'So what happened?' demanded John when Matt finally appeared on the bridge, hot and oily after three hours spent in the engine room.

'I've fixed it – for the moment. It's sluggish, but it'll last till we get to Amsterdam.'

'*Three hours late*! I want to know why, Matt.'

Matt grimaced. He didn't like what he was going to say and John wasn't going to like hearing it.

'O.K.,' he said. 'There's a lid on top of the oil filter – the oil filter being the same principle as a car. Well —' he shrugged '— the cap on the filter came loose. Which means that a lot of oil escaped – at speed. You should see the mess.'

'And —?' said John impatiently.

'And nothing. What should have happened, as soon as the oil pressure dropped, was that an alarm tripped and the engine cut out, before any damage could have been done. But that didn't happen.'

'Which means,' said John with bitter emphasis, 'that the engine was damaged, and accounts for our three hours' loss of time?'

'That's it in a nut-shell,' Matt agreed reluctantly.

'Right. Now for a few questions. How? How did the oil filter cap come off? I presume it's held down securely?'

'With eight one-and-a-half inch nuts?

'So?'

Matt looked about him uneasily. 'This had better be discussed quietly,' he said.

John nodded curtly to Charles. 'Take over for a few minutes please, Mr Woodhouse. Matt, come with me. We'll talk in my cabin.'

When the cabin door was firmly shut behind him John said in an ominous voice, 'O.K. So now it can be discussed quietly. We've lost three hours. I want to know why?'

'Maybe we should have listened to Sarah Hallam,' said Matt

reluctantly. 'When she talked about re-scheduling. You know, giving ourselves long enough to make up lost time if necessary . . .'

'I do remember,' said John, dismissing the subject. 'Now . . .'

'About the oil filter?'

'Yes.'

Matt shrugged. 'Sabotage.'

'*Sabotage*?'

'It's got to be, John. Those nuts didn't undo themselves.'

'But who on earth would . . .? he stopped. It was a waste of time. 'Right, next question. What about the alarm? The one that should have tripped and cut the engine?' Again Matt shrugged. 'You're doing a lot of shrugging, Matt.'

'Sorry. Could have been sabotage as well, or . . .' He just stopped himself shrugging.

'Just malfunctioned?'

'Maybe.'

John's voice was hard. 'Because of sloppy maintenance?'

'Or bad luck,' said Matt quickly.

'Yes, well, we'll leave it at that. Last question. Where were you? When this happened.'

'Having a breath of air . . .'

'Having a . . .' John began incredulously.

'I have the right. I'm not obliged to be in the engine room twenty-four hours a day, any more than you have to be on the bridge twenty . . .'

'Yes, point taken. So who was in the engine room?'

'Bill Ryan.'

'The cadet? An engineering *cadet* was left in charge?'

'There were two qualified engineers there as well.'

'Skiving off, playing cards no doubt.'

'That's very unfair. Sir.'

'I don't feel very fair at the moment. You know how important scheduling is for a passenger service such as ours. It should be important to you as well.'

'It is,' said Matt, stung. 'And you've known me long enough to know that. We're alone, so you listen to me – sir. I can allow for every eventuality under the sun – check and double-check anything – everything on the whole of this ship – every washer, piece of wire – but, just like an assassination, if some nut really wants to drop a spanner in the works, *then there's nothing anyone can do about it.*'

'What we *can* do is have a full management meeting. First thing after breakfast tomorrow morning. This morning, I suppose I should say, since it's already two. Now go and get some sleep.'

Matt slept badly and then overslept. He skipped breakfast and made do with a coffee in the Bellevue Bar, where Jane found him sipping morosely.

'It's all right for some,' she said, sitting beside him.

'All right for some,' he said crossly. 'If you knew . . .'

'I do. I'm sending you up.'

'Sorry. My sense of humour is at a low ebb.'

'Can you tell me what happened?'

'Not really. We're having a full-scale management meeting soon to decide just that.' He remembered his manners. 'Coffee?'

'No thanks. I've got to get back to work.'

'Conscientious?'

'In every way.'

'I'm waiting to be given proof of that.'

'I'm waiting to be invited,' she said, remembering how the last occasion had ended. Dougie's interruption had effectively put the dampers on what had promised to be a pleasant evening.

Matt smiled at her. 'So how are you?'

'All the better for sitting down and talking with you.'

'I'm feeling a lot more relaxed too. The soothing touch of a woman's hand across the fevered brow.' She looked at him quickly. 'Metaphorical. I'll take a rain-check on the actuality.'

'Can't wait,' she chuckled. 'I wish you could see the images I've got in my mind. You, down in the bowels of the ship, stripped to the waist, covered in oil, a handkerchief knotted around your neck . . .'

'Like a bit of rough, do you?' he said, leaning back to get a better look at her.

'Oh yes. Very tasty.'

He gave her a suspicious glance. With this lady you could never be certain if she was sending you up. But her eyes were innocent.

Sarah had been about to leave her office to attend the meeting in John's cabin, when trouble erupted in a form she had been half expecting.

'I don't want to make a big issue of this Sarah,' said Marion, her feet planted four-square, 'but I demand to know what's going on. We're three hours overdue, and that is something that happens so rarely with Triangle Line that when it does, it becomes a matter of some importance.'

'I understand that, Mrs Terson. It's a matter of "some"

importance to me too. But as of now I don't know the reason. Captain Anderson hasn't told me yet. I've no doubt he will.'

'I want to know what's going on,' said Marion firmly.

'As a passenger, Mrs Terson, you have no more rights . . .'

'I'm . . .'

'A passenger,' said Sarah firmly. 'Now that's what you told me. Insisted on telling me. Remember?'

She could see that Marion did remember, and also that she wasn't too pleased at being reminded. She pressed on.

'And do you also remember what I told you? That if there was any interference – *at all* – in the way I do my job, I'd resign?' She paused to let this sink in. 'Now, I am telling you everything that, as a passenger, you have a right to know. We have a spot of engine trouble which has now been put right that has made us three hours late. We apologise sincerely for the delay, but it was totally out of our control.'

Marion seemed to be fighting an inner battle with herself. Finally she gave a small tight smile, and said, 'Thank you, Miss Hallam.'

She departed with dignity. Sarah tried to believe that the matter was closed. But she couldn't convince herself that Marion was going to let things rest there. It was partly for this reason that she had omitted to mention the meeting. John wouldn't thank her if Marion gate-crashed that – which she was quite capable of doing.

When Sarah, Matt, Charles and himself were settled in his cabin John came straight to the point.

'There's only one item on the agenda. Matt thinks we have had a case of sabotage. Thinking it over, I have to say that I agree. So what we have to decide is what to do about it. But let's take it step by step, shall we? First of all, who could have done it? By that I mean, what sort of person? Matt?'

'Anyone,' said Matt flatly.

'Please be more precise.'

'I am being precise. I literally mean anyone. A child – *if* he knew what to do, that is.'

'Ah. So it presupposes a knowledge of engines?'

'Not at all. It presupposes that someone was told, or spent five minutes reading a book.'

'This act of sabotage was as simple as that?' said Sarah.

Matt nodded. ''Fraid so.'

'Then perhaps it should be made less simple,' she suggested.

'As I said to Mr Anderson, on a ship this size, if anyone is out to do us harm, then they can do it.'

'So, anyone could have done it,' said John heavily, 'given that they possessed some rather fundamental information.'

Matt gave a small grin. 'I think perhaps we can rule out Judith Harper. I don't suppose that scruffy little dog of hers likes the smell of oil.'

'My sense of humour is rather stretched at the moment, Matt.'

'Sorry.'

'So what are you suggesting, John?' said Charles. 'If, as you say, this is a case of sabotage. The police? The port authorities. And if so, where? Amsterdam? Esbjerg? Harwich?'

'If I may . . .' Sarah broke in. 'Then I would advise, no. I think we should play this very close to our chests. Apologise . . .'

'As we have been doing,' said John bitterly.

'As we have been doing, and just say, "engine trouble". The public, I'd have thought, would think twice before travelling by a line if they believed that persons – known or otherwise – were trying to sabotage it.'

'Point taken. The official line, then, is engine trouble. And that's for every passenger. I'll say that again, ladies and gentlemen, *every* passenger.'

His eyes met Sarah's in an unspoken bond of understanding. There was no need to mention Marion by name.

The meeting broke up. Sarah went wearily to her office. It felt like a million years ago that she and Matt had stood beside the rail talking but it had only been last night. Today they had spoken in the meeting as impersonally as though that other conversation had never taken place. Perhaps it never had. Perhaps she had only imagined the way she had let him edge dangerously close to that self she kept a secret. With one part of her she blessed the saboteur who had stopped the engines and saved her from revealing any more.

She sent for Barry Peters. She'd had time enough to consider this decision and there was nothing to be gained from thinking about it any more. He said very little when he came in, but sat down where she indicated and waited like a prisoner listening to the judge's summing up.

'I've had to think about this a lot, you understand that?' She kept her eyes on his nervous tight-lipped face as he nodded. 'And I think, well, all right, I think you're telling the truth.'

He could hardly speak for relief. 'Thank you, Miss Hallam.'

'And I think you intended to put the money back.'

'I did,' he almost gabbled.

'I believe you. It's not even a question of giving you the benefit of the doubt. I believe you,' she smiled. 'Apart from anything else, it was too much to expect to be able to get away with it.'

'And whatever else I am . . .'

' . . . you're not a fool. Right. Nor are you a thief. So, as far as I'm concerned, and as far as your record is concerned, it's all over. Never happened.'

'Thank you.' He didn't know what else to say.

'Now, another matter, nothing to do with what we've just been discussing. I know that petty fiddling does go on, always does in this sort of institution, be it hotel, leisure centre, large ship, or whatever – wherever there are tills and stores of food and crates of drink . . . But, Mr Peters, the petty fiddling on board this ship is going to stop. *Isn't it?*'

'Definitely,' he assured her.

'As of now?' She looked him in the eyes.

'As of now.' He looked back.

'Good. Well then . . .' There was a knock on the door and Ted Anderson put his head round. 'Ah, yes, Ted. We've finished our business.'

'I just popped in to see if it was all right for me to take my break now. I've booked myself a sauna.'

'At your age?' she laughed.

'Try anything once.'

'All right. Go on.'

When he was comfortably stretched out, sweating, on the bench, Ted opened an eye to take in his surroundings, and through the steam made out the unfamiliar company of Bill Ryan.

'Haven't see you in here before?' he ventured.

Bill looked at him. 'Some of us don't get a lot of time for swanning about in saunas,' he said.

Ted resisted the obvious answer, and grinned.

'You look whacked,' he said.

'You would be if you spent your time keeping this ship moving,' Bill grumbled.

'I'm sure I would.'

'I mean, you people think that all you have to do is pick up a phone or write on a piece of paper and, surprise, surprise, miracles happen, and this ship starts and off we go.'

Ted considered this. 'You having a go at me?' he asked amiably.

Bill also considered. Then he shook his head. 'No, mate, not so's you'd notice.'

'I mean, who do you think I am?'

'I know who you are. You're Ted Anderson, the captain's son.'

'That's right. And you're . . .?'

'Bill Ryan. Engineering cadet. I keep the engines going.'

'Is that why you come in here? To melt that chip?' Bill stared at him. 'The one on your shoulder. I mean, what do you think I do around here? I'm a worker as well, you know.' Bill grunted. 'I work in the ship's office.'

'Oh la di da,' said Bill, seizing on this. 'You, sunshine, are the captain's son. So you're going to ponce around for a few months in the office, getting preferential treatment, before poncing off to some other cushy little number.'

'Preferential treatment?' said Ted, outraged. 'I started off in the galley.'

'So I noticed. For two days. What did he tell you, your dad? "I want you to start at the bottom and work your way up to the top. Take a fornight over it if you like"?'

Ted grinned. 'By God, you really have got hold of the wrong end of the stick, haven't you? Do you think my dad was born a captain? Is that what you think? Captain's stripes on his nappy? Do you want me to tell you where he started from, how hard he worked?'

'O.K,' said Bill wearily. 'So you love your dad. Fact is, feller like me works my knickers off in the engine room, while a feller like you sits in the office and swans off to the sauna whenever he feels like it. Do a hard day's work, you, and you'd . . .'

'Want a bet? I'm pretty fit, you know.'

'Fit? Don't know what it means. Want to do a bit of boxing, mate, like me, play football . . .'

'O.K.,' said Ted. 'Put your money where your mouth is.'

'Do what?'

'You reckon you're fitter than me? I'll race you.'

'Race me?'

'Five times around the deck. Loser buys the winner the best meal the Codan Restaurant has to offer.'

'You're on.'

It was a rough day – on everyone. The passengers were furious at the hold-up. The crew recited 'Unavoidable delay – minor engine trouble – apologies —' like a batch of cracked records. Christine

Harris knew she would remember it as the worst day of her life.

At one point she'd thought she might be lynched, with the mob led by a rough-neck in his late thirties who identified himself as Jack Reagan, and seemed to think that she personally ought to get out and push the ship.

At the height of the row Judith Harper had intervened to say in a voice unusually forceful for her, 'May I say something, please?' When she had everybody's attention she dropped her tone to its usual gentle, wistful note. 'I was just wondering if – well, if you can tell me what happened to that nice Mr Wootton.'

'I beg your pardon?' said Christine, totally thrown off balance by this unexpected change of subject.

'You must remember,' Judith persisted. 'That very charming gentleman – in insurance?'

'Oh.' Christine gave Judith a little smile. 'Yes. He disembarked at Harwich, I believe.'

'Oh, did he? Now that is a pity. Well, more than a pity actually.' Judith addressed Reagan confidentially. 'One makes so few really good friends in this world.'

To Christine's relief Reagan seemed too baffled to reply. While he stood there going red in the face Judith sighed, and added, 'And believe me, you have to hold on to the few you make.' She tapped Reagan's shoulder like a schoolmistress. 'You'd do well to remember that, young man.'

She trotted off. Christine regarded her fondly. The old dear might be dotty but she'd defused a potentially nasty situation. Reagan seemed incapable of taking up the attack again, and went off to seek the bar. There he poured out his grievances into the ever-open ear of Barry Peters, who, after his reprieve, was feeling cheerful enough to put up with anything.

He was glad, though, when Barbara, who was drinking morosely at the bar, roused herself to tell Reagan a few home truths and send him off with a flea in his ear. Barry grinned delightedly as Reagan vanished.

'If you want to get rid of someone, the easiest way is to be rude,' said Barbara flatly.

'Unfortunately, as a member of staff . . .' he shrugged.

'That's the advantage of not being one any longer.'

'Enjoying it then, are you?'

'To be honest with you I wouldn't be sorry if I never see another ship again. And this one can go to the bottom of the sea, and take that bitch Sarah Hallam with it.'She stared into her glass.

'That's a bit unfair,' said Barry awkwardly. 'She can be a very understanding lady.'

'Then I hope she understands that I'd like her to go to hell.'

'All I can say is that she's been very fair to me.'

'Then all I can say is "lucky old you".' Barbara shrugged.

He leaned close to her ear. 'I borrowed some money from the till to – well, I needed it for a while. Don't look at me like that. Everyone does it. Tide them over till they can pay it back. Now, after Sarah Hallam found out, doesn't matter how, she had a choice: either believe me and let me pay it back, or disbelieve me and . . .'

'Fire you?' Barbara was watching him closely.

'Precisely. Yes, sir . . .' Barry moved away in answer to a customer, leaving Barbara staring. After a moment her face became thoughtful.

I still feel guilty,' said Sarah.

She was talking to Matt, who had dropped into her office for a chat. She was glad of the chance to clear the air.

'No need, I promise you,' he said.

'If I hadn't kept you talking on deck, perhaps the whole thing mightn't have happened.'

'I just popped up for a breath of air. It wasn't your fault. The big question is, who did it?'

'Oh, I know that,' she said absently.

He stared at her. 'You're not joking?'

'Oh no. I know who it is. But I can't tell you yet. Knowing's one thing, proving it is another. And I'm not going to put my head on the chopping-block of a slander suit until I'm sure.'

'You can tell me,' he protested, feeling injured.

She hesitated, then shook her head. 'There's someone I've got to talk to before I can say anything at all. The one person I know I can trust. Nick Stevens.'

'The *one* person you know you can trust?' he said huffily.

For a moment she appeared not to understand him. Then she smiled and touched his arm.

'I'm very slow to make friends, Matt. Very slow. But when I do . . .'

He nodded. He could see it was going to take time with Sarah, and he wasn't going to ruin things by rushing them.

On his way out he nearly collided with Barbara, who was in a hurry, and in a temper if her face was anything to go by. She slammed the door behind her, shutting him out.

Sarah looked up coldly as the girl planted herself four-square in front of the desk.

'I want to know why I was fired for something totally trivial . . .'

'That's a matter of opinion.'

'. . . while another employee, caught red-handed with his fist in the till, is reinstated.' She waited. 'Well?'

'I don't care to discuss other employees' business with you or anyone.'

'Don't give me that,' Barbara snapped.

'Just as, when you were an employee, I wouldn't have discussed your affairs,' Sarah went on, unperturbed.

'You've had it in for me ever since I came aboard.'

'That just isn't true.'

'Then *why* sack me, and not Barry Peters?' said Barbara fiercely.

'There's a difference.'

'I bet there is.'

'There's a difference between an employee who for four years has given excellent service and been very popular both with passengers and crew, and one who from the very first moment she came aboard was rude, supercilious and arrogant. *And* showed no desire to change or, in fact, to be employed by Triangle Line in the first place. Does that answer your question, Miss Carter?'

For a moment Barbara stared at her, then she spoke in a deadly quiet voice. 'Yes, it does. Now you listen to me. There's a certain passenger on board who I could have talked to about this matter a long while ago. You know who I mean?'Sarah did not reply but gave Barbara a cool look that the girl found unnerving. 'I've chosen not to, hoping, I suppose, that either you'd come to your senses of your own volition, or I could eventually persuade you. As obviously neither of those things are going to happen, I'm now going to talk to that certain passenger – my aunt, Miss Hallam.' Still that unmoved look: 'Mrs Terson . . .' Sarah nodded. 'So you'd better start clearing out your desk. Because in one hour you'll be looking for another job.'

An hour passed without anything happening. Sarah refused to look up at the hands of the clock. She would not let Barbara have the satisfaction of worrying her – even if the girl didn't know about it. And she was fully prepared to leave her job rather than allow herself to be dictated to.

When the ship docked in Amsterdam she forgot the matter. There was too much to do. Infuriated passengers streamed ashore, and the comments that reached Sarah's ears were not reassuring.

When the ship had been docked for an hour the phone rang on her desk. Miss Hallam was politely requested to go to the bridge, immediately. It crossed her mind briefly that she might find herself confronted by Marion and John jointly demanding that she reinstate Barbara, but then she dismissed the thought. She would not be drawn into speculating. That was just playing Barbara's game.

As soon as she arrived on the bridge it became plain that Marion had heard nothing from her niece. She was present, but her attention was fully occupied with something she was reading in an English newspaper. John, Tom and Charles were peering over her shoulder.

'What is it?' said Sarah.

'An article under Kevin Warrender's by-line,' said John. 'He was on board for a week or so.'

'Ah, one of those,' said Tom knowingly.

Sarah nodded. 'A free first-class trip – plus the best of everything when on board, so that he'll write a glowing report about us.'

'That's what I thought,' said John.

Marion made a sceptical noise under her breath.

'And to be fair, Marion, so did you,' said Sarah at once.

This intervention earned her a grateful look from John and a glare from Marion who passed the paper to him and said hastily, 'Well, go on. Read it out.'

John began to read. '"Amateur surgery on the high seas".'

'What?' Tom sat up.

'That's just the headline,' John explained. 'It's a long article.'

'Paraphrase it,' Marion commanded.

He did so. 'It concerns a medical operation carried out by an unqualified seaman and a retired vet aboard this ship.'

'Nothing wrong with that,' said Tom. 'We saved his life.'

'*You* saved his life,' put in Sarah.

'But that's not all,' said Marion. 'Right, John?'

John tried to continue. 'He – Kevin Warrender —'

'Your friend,' she put in bitingly.

'My acquaintance of twenty years ago. And it wasn't *my* idea to invite him on the trip,' John flashed back at her.

'Go on,' said Marion after a chagrined pause.

'He goes on to say that he got the distinct impression that the company image was of greater importance than – what's the phrase?' He read aloud, '"... Greater importance than the life of the unfortunate hireling of the company as he hovered precariously between life and death".'

'Good God, do people still write like that?' said Charles in disbelief.

John resumed reading. '"All of this, I might add, took place aboard a sea-going ferry of rather dubious efficiency, rather average comfort, and rather slapdash service."'

There was a moment while this sank in. Finally Sarah could not resist saying, 'And this was one of those journalists who was always supposed to write nice things in return for his free first-class trip?'

Marion threw her an unforgiving look. 'You've already said that, "dear". What I want to know ...'

John burst out, 'Tom Kelly did a first-class – almost unbelievably first-class – job under the most trying circumstances. The doctor who eventually came on board told us that he most likely saved Mr Evans' life.'

'I know about that,' said Marion. 'What I want to know, now, is how my flagship, on its first commission under our revolutionary new management, could fail so dismally?'

'That's totally unfair,' said John angrily.

'Not only do we have bad publicity ...' Marion began.

'Surely you're not going to take this seriously?' said John.

'... but we limp home a dismal and pathetic three hours late. And whether I take that seriously or not is a matter of no importance. What does matter is that a million readers *will*.' Marion faced John. 'I'm going to be holding a board meeting in Munkebjerg, and I want you to fly there with me.'

'But ...'

'Company helicopter, so it won't take long. Mr Woodhouse, meanwhile, will take command for the Amsterdam/Esbjerg trip. Any questions?'

She waited the briefest possible time to ascertain that there were none, before sweeping out. She left a stunned silence behind her. It was Sarah who finally voiced what everyone was thinking. 'So much for "I'm to be treated only as a passenger".'

'I think we all took that with a large pinch of salt,' said John.

'Well, I'm going to say it, even if no-one else is,' said Tom angrily. 'The implication, hanging in the air, that somehow it's all John's fault is very unfair.'

'Thank you, Tom, but I am the captain. Taking responsibility is one of the things I get paid my exorbitant salary for. But anyway, thank you.'

'I agree, particularly about the newspaper article,' said Sarah.

'Oh, I don't know, Sarah,' John was trying to be fair. 'I did go on to him about when he was a crusading journalist. I think I made it quite plain to him that I disapproved of what he'd become. A payola writer. So, perhaps he thought, "Right then, I'll show him".'

'Ah, but that's not it,' she said at once. 'I don't think your disapproval – or anyone else's for that matter – would have distracted the likes of Kevin Warrender from his life-long vista of free trips and first-class treatment.'

'What had it to do with, then?'

'Our erstwhile crusading journalist was *bribed* to write that article in that way.'

'Oh, come on,' Charles burst out.

'No, it's just occurred to me,' Sarah insisted.

'First of all he's bribed to say nice things about us, then he's bribed to say nasty things about us . . .'

'What are you on about, Sarah?' demanded John.

'I'm not sure. Give me time to think it over. I want to be certain before I say anything more.'

She refused to be drawn. Before leaving the ship she put through a phone call. Then she slipped ashore and took a taxi to Amsterdam's zoo. As she had expected, Nick Stevens was waiting for her. He paid their entrance fees and escorted her past cages filled with animals, listening intently while she used the privacy of the crowd to voice her fears about Marion Terson.

'She told us she was there as a passenger and she was to be treated as such. But I think she feels a bit insecure. So she decided to find out what really goes on, without having to make decisions, and where nothing that goes wrong is her fault. And what better way to do it than coming on board as a passenger?'

'Very perceptive of you,' he approved. 'And very clever of Marion.' After a moment he shrugged unhappily. 'Look, she's always been very good to me, so . . . But I have to say that I don't think some of her recent decisions have been very sound. Business-wise, I mean.'

'David West?'

He nodded. 'David West. I think he's getting too big a hold over her. And another thing, selling that Triangle ship to D.R.W. – I really don't think that was a good move on her part.'

'Another example of David West's hold over her?' Sarah mused.

'What do you think? Now look, I'm not suggesting anything underhand . . .'

'More personal?'

'You think so too? But then that opens another can of worms.' He took a deep breath. 'What do you think David West's game is?'

'I really don't know. Why should he want to damage Triangle when he's a shareholder?'

'Damage?' he looked thunderstruck. 'What do you mean?'

She hesitated, nervous now she had come this far. Then she said, 'I'm talking to you like this because I think you're the only person I can really trust.'

'Thank you,' he said lightly.

'I hope I'm right, because I upset someone quite badly by suggesting that very thing to them.'

'You are right.' He watched her face. 'Well?'

'David West was behind that newspaper report I was telling you about, and the sabotage,' she said bluntly.

He stared at her, disbelief written all over his face. 'I think that's going a little bit too far, I really do,' he said with a brief laugh.

She made no attempt to defend herself but walked on beside him in thoughtful silence. As they passed an ice-cream stall he caught her sudden flicker of interest and solemnly presented her with a cone. Not until they were sitting side by side on a bench, eating ices together, did she elaborate her statement.

'When we were in Esbjerg, a local bank called the ship about some documentation detail. It was to do with £500 they were providing against a cheque for the purser's office.'

'But it's not done like that.'

'I'm very well aware of that,' she said with a slight touch of asperity.

'Sorry. It's just that . . .'

'But I didn't tell the bank that, 'cos as well as being perceptive I'm also very curious.' She gave a small mysterious smile.

'So would I have been.'

'So what I did was find out who had cashed the cheque at the bank. It was Christine Harris. The deputy purser.' She saw that she had his riveted attention, and went on, 'So later on when I was in the purser's office, I noticed a package for Kevin Warrender.'

'You've lost me.'

'The journalist who wrote the magazine article.'

'Ah!'

'A package that hadn't come the usual way through the mail.'

He drew in his breath. 'That's all a bit . . .'

'Circumstantial?'

'No court of law . . .'

'This isn't a court of law, this is you and me sitting here, eating ice-creams, talking.'

'All right, so what's the connection between Christine Harris and David West?'

'That's what I'd like to know. What I do know – found out – is that Miss Harris worked for several years at the European.'

'The hotel?'

She nodded: 'In Brussels. It's owned by D.R.W.'

Nick pulled a face, indicating, 'Well, that's something.' He looked thoughtful. 'And the sabotage?'

'Ah. Well, that depends on me being right about the connection between Christine and David West. West has the motive, Christine the opportunity.'

They rose and walked on again. He was sunk in thought, from which he eventually roused himself. 'Anyone else and I'd say that, at best, you were seeing things that weren't there . . .'he said.

'And at worse?'

'That you'd flipped your lid.'

'But you do know me.'

'Which is why I listen to you. If I wasn't prepared to do that I wouldn't have got you the job in the first place. But – no, Sarah. It's all too vague . . . it's all too . . .'

'I know I'm right,' she said stubbornly.

He could not repress a snort. 'You? Feminine intuition?'

'I am feminine,' she said, unperturbed.

'I'm very well aware of that,' he assured her fervently. 'Make no mistake. It's the intuition part that doesn't sit easily on your shoulders.'

'I know exactly what it sounds like, you haven't told me anything I don't know. Which is another reason why you're the only person I've told. She looked at him and repeated slowly, 'But I also know I'm right.'

It was an exaggeration to say that Bill was pleased to look up from his work to find Ted hovering over him.

'Come to find out how the other half lives?' he jeered.

'Just interested, that's all. I like to see how everything works.'

'Find out as much as you can, eh? So that you'll be ready to take your seat on the board on Wednesday week?'

'Never give up, do you?' said Ted amiably.

'You want to bet on that, mate. Make yourself a fortune.'

'So what about the race then?'

'Backing out?' Bill spoke a fraction too quickly.

'Me? No.' So did Ted. 'You?'

'What do you think?'

'Thought perhaps you might have had second thoughts.'

'Hoping, you mean,' said Bill.

'Never.' Ted paced a little then said with sudden resolution, 'O.K. We're in dock. No-one about . . .'

'*Now*?'

'Why not?'

'You might not have noticed, but some of us have got to work.'

'Ah.' Ted pounced. 'So you do want to back out?'

'One hour,' said Bill grimly.

'Oh, I'm sure it won't take you that long to run . . .'

'From *now*,' Bill interrupted, glaring. 'We'll have the race one hour from now. Meet you by the brig.'

'Right.'

'You'll get the thrashing of your life.' Ted grinned and began to move away. Bill called after him, 'And that meal we'll be having tonight . . .'

'I'm looking forward to accepting your hospitality.'

' . . . at your expense. Champagne, I hope.'

For each there was a secret relief in getting the race out of the way while the ship was in dock and relatively empty. During the trip that had just finished each had tried to put in a spot of practice with embarrassing results. For Ted there had been the awkward moment when his father had yanked him, gasping, into his cabin and demanded a rational explanation of his behaviour. Ted had managed to avoid giving it, and thereafter had done his running in another part of the ship.

Bill's experience had been even worse. It had seemed a good idea to do running on the spot in the engine room. How was he to know that he'd been clearly visible to Matt, via a closed-circuit television link in the room above? Matt's hilarious comment, 'You won't push us there faster by doing that, sunshine,' hadn't improved matters.

'You're sure this is a good idea?' Bill made one last try when they were standing together on the deck.

'Yes,' said Ted untruthfully. 'Of course I am. Not trying to cry off again?'

'I'm not – and I haven't tried to cry off. It's just that running round and round . . .'

'I thought you were a free spirit . . . didn't give a toss for your superior's opinions?'

'You'll wish you hadn't said that when you lie panting and begging for mercy in a few minutes time. Right?'

'Right.'

By the end of the first lap they each knew the practice had been worthless. By the end of the second they knew the whole thing was a monumental mistake.

'Three – laps – to – go —' Ted got the words out painfully.

'Feeling – the – strain – are – you?' Bill heaved.

They were still side by side as they started on the last lap; still together half way down the side of the ship when a figure appeared from nowhere and stood patiently while they skidded to a halt, missing her by inches.

'Good afternoon, Ted,' said Marion calmly. She looked at Bill. 'Good afternoon.'

She was neither surprised nor offended when neither of them returned her greeting. Judging by the noises they were making as they fought to support themselves in an upright position, it would have been more surprising if they had.

At last Ted managed to summon the energy to wave a feeble hand in Marion's direction, and address Bill.

'This – is —' he wheezed violently, and reversed the procedure. '— and – this – is —' He gave up.

Marion took pity on him. 'It's a good job I'm just a passenger. I shudder to think how I'd react if – for instance – I was the owner of this vessel.'

She smiled sweetly on them both, and sailed off, stately as a galleon. Bill and Ted turned haggard eyes on each other.

'Who – was – that?' Bill managed.

'The – owner – of – the – vessel.'

Now if ever was the time for Bill to make a speech about unfair distribution of wealth. Surprisingly he didn't. He just said 'Oh', before collapsing beside Ted on a nearby bench, and staring vacantly into space.

Marion took a last look at both of them before turning the corner out of their sight. At such a distance she could allow herself a little smile, although she would never have let them know that she was more amused than annoyed. She had just returned from seeing David West, and was enjoying the feeling that he always gave her of being a born executive with her finger on every pulse. Even the newpaper article by Kevin Warrender had faded in importance when placed next to the prospect of the forthcoming conference at the hotel in Munkebjerg. That was something she was looking forward to.

She knew she had another little problem to sort out first, though. Plainly Barbara wasn't going to let her aunt get off the ship without waylaying her. Marion had already dodged her niece once that day and was interested to see how Barbara would deal with the situation the second time. Not for the world would she have let on to the girl that she knew what it was all about. A chance remark overheard from one of the other cabin girls had been all that was needed. After that Marion had sat back and waited.

'I've got about three minutes,' she said when Barbara appeared in her cabin. 'A lot of important things have to be decided in the next few hours. And to do that I've got to get to Munkebjerg.' She had started her packing and barely spared Barbara a glance.

'You did say that I could talk to you if anything went wrong.'

'Did I?' Marion took some blouses out of a drawer.

'Yes. Don't you remember? When —'

Marion held up her hand. 'I'm sure you're right. What is it?'

Barbara shrugged and spoke lightly. 'Thing is – I've been sacked.'

'Where did I put that —?' Marion was searching on her dressing-table. 'Ah.'

'*Aunt Marion* —'

'From what?' Marion seemed to return from a great distance.

'From that job I had on board the ship.'

'Oh yes. Cabin girl, wasn't it?'

'That's right.'

'Ah well, can't be helped. These things happen.'

'It was very unfair.'

'Character-building, isn't that what they say?' Marion smiled sweetly.

'I wasn't given a chance. And yet other people, other members of staff, are given all sorts of second chances . . .'

'No matter,' said Marion soothingly. 'I'm sure you'll sort it out all right.'

'Me?' Barbara jumped.

'Of course. Now what else will I need?'

'I was hoping that you'd . . .'

Marion patted her arm. 'I'm sorry it's all such a rush, Barbara, and I'm very pleased that you popped in to keep me abreast of what's going on, but now you'll have to excuse me. I really am in a terrific rush and I'm sure we'll be able to sit down and have a really long chat when I come back on board.'

Half an hour later Barbara stood outside Sarah Hallam's door, trying to pluck up courage to knock. It seemed a lifetime away that she had dashed into this very office, angrily demanding to be reinstated. Yet it was only a few hours ago. And everything was so different now. At last she took a deep breath, knocked and walked in without waiting for an answer.

'Can I have a word?' she said, trying to sound braver than she felt.

Sarah took a deep breath. 'As long as it's just that.'

'In private, please.'

'Ted, do you mind?' said Sarah.

'Of course not.' He looked at his watch. 'I've got a dinner date, as it happens.'

'Good for you.'

He grinned. 'With a feller, I'm afraid.'

His departure changed the atmosphere at once. Both women had a feeling of the seconds having left the ring.

Sarah spoke first. 'Right, Barbara. Now I have to tell you that my position is uncha—'

'I went to see my aunt,' Barbara cut in desperately. She knew she was unwise to interrupt Sarah but her courage was running out of the soles of her feet.

'Yes?' said Sarah.

'She didn't want to know.' Even as she said the words Barbara felt a kind of renewed disbelief that they could actually be true.

Sarah paused a moment. 'I could have told you that, if you'd have listened,' she said, not unkindly.

'Treated the whole thing as being a bit beneath her.'

'Which I suppose . . .'

'It is,' Barbara finished. 'Truth of the matter, Miss Hallam, is that I don't really like my aunt. In fact, if you really want to know, I hate her.'

'Look, I'm sorry to appear unsympathetic, but your family relationships are really none of—'

'Can I have my job back?' Barbara blurted the words out before they choked her. The following silence was unnerving. She knew Sarah was looking at her steadily, but she didn't dare to meet her eyes. '*Please*. I apologise for my behaviour. I apologise for my attitude. I apologise for my slackness.' Suddenly Barbara departed from her prepared speech and relaxed into a kind of despairing spontaneity. 'Everything you said about me was right,' she said with a shrug. 'I knew it at the time, but I thought my aunt would protect me.' She took a deep breath and returned to the speech. 'The fact is that my behaviour was intolerable. You reacted in the only way possible. What I'd like is the chance to prove to you – to everyone – that I'm not really like that.'

Sarah said nothing. She was studying her hands on her desk. She had been more impressed than she'd expected to be – not by the words, which had obviously been worked out beforehand, but by the palpable effort it had cost the girl to force herself on to the end.

'You'd have to apologise to Jane Anthony,' she said at last.

'I would have done that anyway.'

'O.K.,' said Sarah. She saw Barbara staring at her as though she had spoken gibberish. 'You can have your job back,' she spelled out.

'Thank you very much.' Light broke over Barbara's face.

'On probation, you understand.'

She cut short Barbara's thanks and got her out of the office. To prolong the interview could only be embarrassing for both of them. But she had a pleasant feeling of having done the right thing. There were good qualities in that girl that might start to emerge, given the chance.

Ted had spruced himself up for his dinner in the Codan Restaurant with Bill, taking as much trouble over his appearance as he would have done for a girl. He didn't want Bill Ryan thinking he was too knocked out to face the world. But as the food and drink mellowed him he didn't mind admitting, 'I have never been so knackered in my life.'

'Nor me,' Bill conceded.

'If Mrs Terson hadn't stepped out then, I think I'd have run straight over the side.'

'So that was Mrs Terson? The big white chiefess?'

'The same. Only she's incognito. Or so she keeps telling people,' said Ted gloomily. 'She also keeps telling people that she's just here for the trip.'

'I bet.'

'*Right*. As soon as Dad makes a slip she suddenly stops being a passenger and leaps on him like a ton of bricks.'

'In trouble, is he?'

'I don't know,' said Ted, frowning. 'It's to do with the – well – the engine trouble.' He poured out some champagne. 'I'm glad I'm not paying for this all on my own.'

'So am I,' said Bill fervently.

They clinked glasses, momentarily joined in the cameraderie of failure. Then Bill remembered something.

'Just because I'm sitting here, eating with you, and finding out that you're not a bad fellow, doesn't mean that your class still isn't a total enemy to me,' he said hastily.

'Of course.'

'I mean it.' Having hitched his revolutionary credentials into place Bill felt free to clink glasses again.

'Hallo, hallo, hallo!'

'Hallo.' Ted looked up to see Barbara looming over him, her face beaming.

She swooped down and kissed him on the cheek. 'What a wonderful world,' she carolled, before skipping off. She had not even not even noticed Bill.

'What did I do to earn that?' Ted mused.

Bill scowled. 'See what I mean? Boss's son, and you get *all* the perks.'

Ted was about to reply lightly that Barbara was a perk he could take or leave, when he noticed that Bill's face had not relaxed. Indeed, the scowl seemed set there for all eternity. He wasn't joking. Ted sighed. The *entente* hadn't remained *cordiale* for very long, and it was all Barbara's fault. Women were nothing but trouble. He felt very wise.

Chapter 8

John disliked the Munkebjerg hotel on sight. It was a featureless monstrosity, indistinguishable from a hundred others, except that it was set down in a fairly remote part of Denmark. But what John hated about it most was that it was wasting his time.

'Marion, I should be on the bridge,' he complained when the two of them and Nick had met up in the palatial conference suite. 'What am I doing here?'

'I wanted to make certain facts clear,' she said.

'And a telephone call wouldn't have been sufficient?' said Nick, who had made no bones about his disapproval of this enterprise.

'It's not the way I work, Nick. You know that.' Marion's manner became businesslike. 'I was very unhappy with the outcome of the maiden voyage and the sabotage attempt . . .'

'Try stopping a dedicated fanatic – whoever it is – from doing whatever they do,' John protested. 'It was unavoidable.'

'We can't keep a constant security check going,' Nick confirmed. 'There's not enough staff. We have to take chances somewhere.'

'Why would anyone want to do something like that anyway?' she demanded.

'Obvious,' said John. 'They have a grudge against the company. It was lucky no-one was hurt.'

'I cannot afford to risk the company's reputation and the flagship's esteem,' she retorted. 'And you call us "lucky". I've always valued your services, John, but you're not indispensable.'

Before he could reply to this the phone rang and Marion listened to the voice on the other end with a pleased look.

'Ask them to come up now, please,' she said at last.

'Visitors?' said Nick in faint alarm. He was beginning to discover that you never knew what Marion had up her sleeve. You only knew that you probably wouldn't like it.

Her next words confirmed his worst fears. 'Our new managing director.'

'What?' said John in disbelief.

'Someone who'll provide ideas, fresh experience – and he'll need to be convinced.'

'Convinced?' said Nick. 'What of?'

'That passenger ships should be Triangle's chief concern,' said Marion.

'What else do you suggest in its place, Marion?' said John. 'White elephants?'

As he spoke he made a gesture at their surroundings that left no doubt of his meaning, but Marion missed it. She had her eyes fixed on the door for the moment when David West entered, accompanied by a burly man in his forties. She turned to make the introductions.

'David West you already know. Now I'd like to introduce you to our new man – Roger Powell.'

Somehow John and Nick remained polite throughout what followed. Greetings over, they all sat and listened while Roger Powell outlined the ideas he thought best for the company. John was not a businessman, and retained only the haziest idea of what was being said. He only knew he had a gut feeling that everything Roger Powell wanted to do with Triangle was the exact opposite of what George Terson had had in mind when he built it up. Whatever you felt about George he never forgot about the human element. Powell seemed never to have heard of it.

After exchanging an appalled glance with Nick, John got out into the grounds as soon as the meeting showed signs of breaking up. Here he was able to light his pipe and smoke it in peace. He didn't envy Nick Stevens, whom he guessed had got into an argument with Marion as soon as he could get her on his own.

After a while he saw Nick emerge into the grounds and make in his direction, with exactly the same air of making an escape that John guessed he had himself.

For a while they strolled in companionable silence before John asked, 'How did this Roger Powell get on the Board?'

'Voted in.'

'Not by me, he wasn't. Someone's pulling rank. Marion, perhaps?'

'It's likely, but not on her own. David West's involved,' Nick mused.

'In collusion, you mean,' said John sharply.

'Something like that.'

'You don't trust him.'

'Do you?'

John answered this obliquely. 'Then perhaps Kate was right, taking the stand she did.'

'Morals and a business sense – what a combination!'

'Well, I hope we've all got that. You've got to admire her, Nick.'

'Oh, I do – as you might admire any deadly species,' said Nick, the memory of his brief acquaintance with Kate Laker making him shudder.

'Not that bad, surely!' John grinned.

'No offence, but not my cup of tea, that's all! And our Mr Powell . . .' Nick shrugged.

'Have to wait and see.'

'Marion's schemes are going off on tangents, leaving us all behind.'

'Might've called it enterprising once, but now . . .'

John forced himself to say it. 'Erratic is nearer the mark.'

'Perhaps I should talk to her.'

'Well, you're nearest the throne.'

'That I doubt!' They walked on a bit before Nick said, 'So what do you think of your white elephant?'

'My what?'

'This!' Nick made a gesture at the building behind them. 'Bought by the money she made selling a ship. Belongs to Triangle now – belongs to you and me.'

'I don't believe it.' John was aghast.

'Fancy yourself as an innkeeper, Captain Anderson? It's all part of Marion's plans to expand the company.'

'*This?*'

'Get used to it. It could be the first of many.'

'Nick, does she know what she's doing?'

The question hung in the air between them as they looked at each other.

Stephen Draper leaned on the rail, and stared gloomily at retreating Esbjerg. He was a small, thin man, with a rat-like face that bore an almost permanent expression of misery. By his side was a large carrier bag that he kept tight hold of.

'On our way at last.'

He looked to see who had spoken. It was an elderly woman with an air of determined cheerfulness that made him feel (if possible) more miserable than before. In her arms she clutched a small dog.

'Yes,' he said blankly.
'What a time we've been.'
'Really?'
'I've never known the ship be this late. I can't remember such excitement since the waiters wore roller skates at dinner.'
'Hmmm.' He wished she would go away. He couldn't have cared less if the waiters had worn suspender belts and pink satin bows in their hair.
'May I introduce you to Mortimer?'
'Your dog?'
'Yes, we're inseparable, I'm afraid.'
'I don't like dogs.'
'I'm convinced Mortimer isn't actually a dog.'
'Isn't he?' he said bleakly.
'No, he's a very dear friend of mine come back, you see. Reincarnated.' She saw how his eyes never left the horizon. 'Are you feeling all right?'
'Perfectly. Excuse me.'
He moved off abruptly. Judith watched him go, baffled.
'The world is full of *very* strange people, Mortimer,' she whispered into his ear. 'Have you noticed?'
Up on the bridge, Charles Woodhouse had assumed command in no uncertain fashion, and was determined that no-one should miss the fact.
'With all the excitement going on, I don't suppose anyone realised the doors of the car deck were four minutes late in opening,' he said pompously. 'I timed them.'
'There was something wrong with the hydraulics, yes . . .' said Tom reluctantly. He'd reported the matter to John and he knew it been passed on to Matt, but Matt had had other things on his mind since. Tom had made a mental note to give him a quiet friendly nudge whenever he saw him, but plainly it was too late now. Charles was in his stride.
'Next time it will be six minutes,' he went on, 'then ten, then . . .'
'Hold on, Charles . . .'
'It was reported in the captain's log. Why hasn't it been fixed yet? What has our engineer being doing?' Charles reached for the phone. 'I want Matt Taylor up on the bridge – *now*,' he snapped into the receiver.
Tom kept silent, but his heart sank as he left the bridge. He had hoped that Charles' "Captain Bligh" phase had been left behind,

but evidently that was not so. It was becoming increasingly hard to remember Charles as he had once been – friendly, good-natured, easy-going; the Charles who had existed in Jenny's day. Jenny's death seemed to have killed him too, and left in his place a crudely ambitious man, ready to exploit any loophole to get himself to the top.

'Matt, why have the doors not been fixed?' demanded Charles as soon as Matt appeared.

Matt hit his head with his hand. 'I *knew* there was something I had to do. I'll forget my head next. It slipped my mind with all that sabotage business.'

'Slipped your mind?' said Charles coldly. 'Is that your excuse?'

'Come on, Charles, I'm as sick about it as you are . . .'

'How would it look if I stayed in my cabin all day because it "slipped my mind" to come to the bridge? I had a very irate first mate on my hands because it "slipped your mind" to do your job.'

'Tom Kelly?' said Matt in disbelief.

'He was delayed four minutes, and in that four minutes the heavens were called down on you.'

'Are we talking about the same Tom Kelly?' Matt demanded.

'I have enough to do on the bridge without coping with angry officers . . .'

'Then be careful, Charles, because you might have to cope with another one – *me*.'

'You're on duty on the bridge. You will address me as "sir".'

'I don't believe any of this,' said Matt to the air.

'I'm not interested in your beliefs, Chief Engineer. I'll tolerate no slackness and no unprofessional behaviour while I'm captain of this ship.'

'Permission to leave the bridge – *sir*?'

'Permission granted, Chief Engineer.'

Matt went straight to the car deck, where he found Tom waiting.

'*Now* what's wrong with these doors?' he demanded abruptly.

'Hydraulics again, I think,' said Tom easily. 'Take a tin opener to it. That should do the trick.' He grinned, but to his puzzlement he met no response. 'Matt?'

'Yes?'

'You all right?'

'No, I'm not. I don't like the way you went crying to our "captain" about this.'

'What are you talking about?'

'If you've got something to say, say it to *me* – especially when it concerns my job.'

'You've lost me, Matt.'

'All that bad temper with our first officer 'cos the doors don't work.'

'Bad temper? Me? It was nothing like that.'

'According to Charles – pardon, the captain – it was. Why stir up trouble, Tom?'

'Stir up —?' Tom stared at him. 'Think about it, Matt. It wasn't *me* doing the stirring up.'

Then he left. It wouldn't hurt Matt to have a little time to think it out.

'Miss Anthony —?'

Jane wasn't pleased to turn and discover that the person calling her was Barbara Carter.

'What are you doing here?' she said.

'I've been reinstated.'

'Oh.' Jane made no effort to stop her face falling.

'Yes, I thought you'd be enthusiastic,' said Barbara before she could stop herself.

'*Barbara* . . .'

'I should apologise,' the girl interrupted hastily.

'*Should* you?'

'All right. I *want* to apologise. I haven't behaved very well.'

'No. But let's forget it, shall we?' said Jane, deciding to make the best of it. 'But do remember you're still on probation.'

'I don't think I'm in a position to forget that.'

'No, you're not,' said Jane, and went into the crew recreation room, feeling that a cloud now hung over the day.

She approached Lisa, whom she found with her feet up, watching Bill and Barry play cards.

'As you're still on duty, why aren't you working?' she asked her.

'Finished everything, haven't I? All without Lady Muck's help.'

'Barbara Carter has been reinstated,' said Jane wryly.

Lisa took her feet down. 'Lucky for some. See what happens when you're the owner's niece?'

'Or the captain's son,' said Bill without turning round.

The others stared at him, to see if some explanation of this remark would be forthcoming, but none was.

'May I remind you all that Captain Woodhouse will be inspecting crew quarters?'

'Again?' said Lisa, groaning. 'We had a monthly inspection just last week.'

'Well, they should be weekly inspections,' said Jane. 'But most captains take their crew on trust.'

'And "Captain" Woodhouse doesn't?' said Bill. 'That's typical.'

'Captain Woodhouse likes to do things by the book,' said Jane formally.

'Likes to crack his authoritarian whip, you mean,' said Bill.

'You should see my cabin,' Lisa wailed. 'Looks like an elephant's stampeded through it.'

'Then the Captain is justified in making his regular checks, isn't he?' said Jane inexorably. She moved away.

'Lackeys,' Bill muttered. 'Dunno what's worse. Them or the bosses.'

'Well, it's all part of the oppression of the workers, isn't it?' said Lisa, suddenly inspired.

'What?' Bill stared at her as though he didn't recognise the words.

'Been studying, have you?' said Barry with a grin.

She ignored him. 'It's true. What right has a first officer got to come poking into our cabins?'

'I agree.' Bill jumped up.

'He's only playing while Captain Anderson's away,' Barry tried to soothe them.

'The whole question of cabin checks ought to be reported to the union,' said Lisa, confident that she was in the right groove at last.

Bill beamed at her. 'It's good to see someone else who's aware of the inequality of the system.'

'Is it, Bill?' she said breathlessly.

'Yes, it is – and I think you've raised some valid points. Hasn't she, Barry?'

'Yes,' said Barry. He was eyeing Lisa with new respect. Till now he'd thought he'd seen girls use all methods, but this was a new one. Good luck to her. If Bill was daft enough to fall for it, it was no more than he deserved.

The cabin inspections, when they got under way, produced a rich crop for Charles. By mid-afternoon no less than five crew members were down to report to him the next day. Lisa, passing Barbara's cabin and seeing her through the open door, sitting with her nose in a book, was feeling sufficiently in charity with the world to put her head in and ask, 'Bulgy Bear passed this way yet?'

'Who?'

'Our "captain". On inspection tours.'

'Just this moment,' said Barbara.

'Bet you got ten out of ten from him,' said Lisa with cheerful malice (there was a limit to charity).

'Well, my cabin's not exactly a pig-sty, is it?'

'Say that again,' Lisa conceded, looking round the neat cabin. 'What are you reading?'

'Oh – *Alice In Wonderland*.'

'Hey, my favourite. Mad Hatter's tea party, the Queen's croquet game . . . always wanted to fall down a rabbit hole just to see for myself.' She regarded Barbara's bookshelf. 'Got quite a few there, haven't you? Bet you haven't got *Wind In The Willows*.'

'Er – no, I haven't.'

'Tell you what – I'll lend you mine.'

'Oh well, thanks. But you won't get it back for a while.'

'That's all right. I'd better go before Bulgy Bear reaches my cabin.'

She vanished. Barbara sat there, not moving, her hands nervously clutching the book. Her eyes were appalled.

Judith sat at the bar in a cheerful mood. There was nothing like a pleasant drink among pleasant people, and Morti did so enjoy the company. Not that Morti was very keen on the man who was standing near her tonight, and who was holding forth in a noisy manner. He was large and had a face that might have been pleasing if it hadn't been suffused with drink.

'Like I said,' he announced to anyone who would listen, 'the referee was out. Not only that, he was blind. Everyone could see it wasn't offside. Even I could see that – and I'm short-sighted.'

'Are you?' said Judith sympathetically. 'Shouldn't you go to the optician? I mean, it's awfully dangerous. You might bump into a bus or something.'

Lennie Baines beamed on her. 'No danger. Wear these glasses, don't I? Except I don't Make me look like an owl. Ugly things.'

'Oh, I think owls are rather beautiful,' she protested.

'No, glasses are ugly,' he explained. 'My glasses in particular.'

'At least you can still see things. Just think if you were really blind.'

'Lady, we mustn't be depressed. Let me buy you a drink.'

'That's very kind, but no, thank you. One cocktail before dinner is my limit. And I must take little Morti for his evening stroll before it gets too dark.'

She made for the exit. On the way there she noticed the little sad-looking man she had met that afternoon, and gave him a friendly nod to cheer him up. But he didn't seem to notice. He had his eyes fixed on Lennie Baines at the bar.

She slipped out into the cool early evening and began to stroll along the deck. Her thoughts became gradually more wistful. It was on just such evenings that she had strolled with that nice Mr Wootton, who had vanished so suddenly, leaving her with only Morti for companionship. Still, she was used to that. She and Morti had been everything to each other for so long now, perhaps it was best that way.

She placed him gently on the deck. He preferred to be free to wander around in his own way, and he knew this ship inside out. She watched him fondly as he sniffed in odd corners. His ears pricked at a faint noise that was coming from a distance. He scampered a few steps ahead.

'Morti,' she called, 'don't go too far.'

He scarcely heard her. He had broken into a trot, then a run, and in another moment he had vanished from sight. Judith clucked in disapproval. If he was going to be so naughty she'd have to put him back on a leash, and that would make him cross.

She began to run, calling him, 'Morti, Morti, come back . . .'

The noise was louder now, a wet whooshing sound. And all of a sudden she realised what it must be, and fear gripped her. In another moment she had turned the corner and seen what she most dreaded – a deck-hand wielding a high-pressure hose, Mortimer dancing joyfully towards him.

'*Mortimer*,' she screamed in anguish.

Another second and the little dog had vanished into the spray. Judith screamed again and again, so that her agony reached the deck-hand and he switched off the hose abruptly. The thunderous noise ceased, the water vanished, and there was just the two of them standing alone on the empty deck.

Christine caught up with Charles and Jane in the corridor where they were making yet another crew-quarters inspection.

'Mortimer's gone overboard,' she announced. 'Mrs Harper wants to know why we haven't turned the ship round to search for him.'

'How absurd,' said Charles irritably.

'Will you talk to her, please?'

'If I must.'

When he could get a word in through Judith's tearful pleading he said bluntly, 'I have no intention of turning round, Mrs Harper. We're running behind schedule already.'

There was a light touch on his arm. Sarah had joined the little scene.

'You're making a wrong decision,' she said softly.

'The dog is lost, Miss Hallam, if not dead already. It would be a waste of fuel to turn back.'

'I know that. But think what it means in terms of good publicity – establishing Triangle as the company with a heart,' she countered.

'You surprise me,' he said satirically.

'Dogs and children. They're winners. Look, we can turn back and circle for an hour before it gets dark. And if we find the animal, great. If not . . .' she shrugged. 'At least we tried. More important, it'll be down on record . . .'

He nodded. Sarah had said the magic words. All this made good career sense.

For an hour the ship circled in the increasingly poor light, while Judith's hysteria gradually gave way to a white-faced despair, and Sarah made useless attempts to comfort her. When the search was finally abandoned, having yielded nothing, Sarah took the old lady to her cabin. She offered to stay with her, but Judith only shook her head and asked to be alone. Sarah's last glimpse was of her sitting frozenly on her bed, staring at the wall while tears slid unnoticed down her face. Sarah sighed when she had closed the door. Her attitude had not been nearly as cynical as she had allowed Charles to believe. It had been largely a question of using the arguments that would affect him. Just the same, it *would* look good for the company – and she felt slightly ashamed in the face of Judith's grief.

Lennie Baines' first action on waking was to clutch his head which felt as though someone had beaten seven bells out of it. He knew he had only himself to blame. He kept promising himself he'd lay off the drink, but somehow . . .

He had a confused memory of the night before – he'd lurched back to his cabin and got undressed somehow. Just as he was passing out someone had come in, a miserable-looking man with a rat-face, that he had seen in the bar. The man had said something about sharing his cabin. After that Lennie remembered no more.

There was the noise of gargling coming from the bathroom. Lennie hauled himself painfully out of bed to investigate, just as the rat-faced man appeared in the bathroom door.

'Who are you?' Lennie demanded. 'What are you doing in my cabin?'

Stephen Draper regarded him kindly. 'You don't remember? You said I could sleep here. Had too many jars last night, didn't I? Couldn't find my cabin. You helped me look for it – talk about the blind leading the blind – then you came up with the answer. Sleep here, you said. So I did.'

'I don't remember.'

'Not surprising. You almost passed out. Had to carry you back . . .' Draper had been dressing while he spoke. 'Just get my stuff together. Then I'll be on my way. I'll do the same for you one of these days . . .'

He gave a grin which cracked his sad face oddly, and disappeared. Lennie sat down heavily, trying to recall anything that tied in with the man's story. But his mind was a blank. Finally he forced himself to dress, and tottered out to find Christine. To her he poured out his woes.

'Last night I distinctly remember his saying that we were supposed to be sharing,' he said. 'But this morning . . .'

'Would you recognise him again?'

'I'm sure I would – and with his carrier bag. That's what made me suspicious, you see.'

She snatched up the phone and got through to Charles.

'Captain, I think we have a problem you should know about . . .'

Perhaps, she thought, if he had a real problem to think about, he might stop making people's lives a misery to them.

In the crew dining room Matt had reluctantly sat down to have his breakfast at the same table as Tom and Jane. He would have preferred not to eat with Tom while he was feeling sour with him, but Jane had made it impossible for him to refuse. He sat in silence eating his meal while the two of them sparred. Tom, he noticed, was inclined to get sentimental about Jane.

'Bit like old times,' he said, 'having breakfast together.'

'This is hardly cosy domesticity, surrounded by hundreds of people,' she pointed out.

'Nearest thing we'll ever get to it.'

'Let's keep it that way, shall we?' she said, a little sharply.

'O.K. – no need to snap!'

'Sorry!' She looked at Matt. 'Our chief engineer is very silent this morning.'

'He was taught not to speak with his mouth full,' Tom quipped.

'I was also taught not to go whining to the captain,' said Matt sulkily.

Jane looked from one to the other. 'Gentlemen, what is this? Disagreements over breakfast?'

'He thinks I complained to Charles about his work,' Tom told her.

'And did you?'

'Of course not.'

'And you don't believe him?' she said to Matt.

When he shrugged without speaking she went on: 'Let me tell you something: if it was a choice between a power-hungry officer and this man here, I'll tell you who I'd believe – and it isn't because I was married to him for too many years . . .'

'You're probably right,' said Matt reluctantly. Now that his sense of proportion was returning he felt a bit of a fool.

'Probably? I *am* right – and you know it.'

Tom looked at her, his head slightly on one side: 'Er . . . what do you mean, "*too* many years"?'

She put one hand over his. 'Not in front of six hundred people – "darling",' she cooed theatrically.

'She has a point, Matt,' said Tom. 'All that "captain" business seems to have gone to Charles's head.'

'Nine of my crew staff have to report to him today,' she said.

'Why?' Matt demanded.

'You name it! Toothpaste out of alignment in the shower room . . . bedroom slippers showing too much fluff . . .'

'Think I owe you an apology, Tom.'

'Forget it! We're all in the same boat.' The other two groaned. 'Sorry!' he said hastily.

Breakfast over, he quickly discovered that Charles had discovered something real on which to vent his megalomania – a "blind" passenger, i.e. one who had slipped aboard without paying for a ticket; that plus a message from shore to say that the police were searching for a wanted criminal who might have slipped aboard. Put the two of them together and what did you get? You got a first-class excuse for Charles to search everyone's cabin again, that was what you got.

Lennie Baines, as the only man who had a clear idea what the criminal looked like, was the hero of the hour. He accompanied Tom and Matt on the hunt, and finally identified his cabin companion sitting in the Bellevue Bar.

'There he is,' he yelled, thus alerting Draper, who jumped to his feet and fled before Tom and Matt could get near him. They gave chase but lost him almost immediately. Splitting up didn't help either. After half an hour they joined forces again, breathless and empty handed.

'Lost him,' Tom gasped.

'Damm it.'

'He's a thin guy. He could be hiding anywhere.'

Matt breathed hard. 'There's a chance . . . Come on. I've had an idea.'

He led the way to the anchor housing, a low-built claustrophobic area, that had Tom gulping. And there they found him, filthy with grease and panting with fear. Matt grabbed him and hauled him from his hiding place by the scruff of his neck, but it was obvious that Draper was going to offer no resistance. In minutes they had him before Charles, who eyed the dirty smelly little man with distaste.

'Stephen Mark Draper,' he said, reading from the passport that he had found in Draper's abandoned carrier bag. 'This is him all right.'

'What are you going to do?' Draper sounded terrified.

'Put you in the brig till we reach port – then hand you over to Interpol.'

'Can I have a scrub first?' Draper pleaded, indicating his filthy condition.

'Don't see why not. Tom, put him in the shower – *lock* him in. And take his clothes.'

'Yes, sir.'

Half an hour later Tom was again facing Charles, making his lame explanation.

'*Escaped*?' Charles roared. 'How? Did you lock him in?'

'Yes. But he must've turned the lock from the inside and prevented it from catching. It can be done, sir.'

'Then he must have moved and thought like lightning.'

'Shows what we're up against.'

'You took his clothes?'

'Yes, sir.'

'So we have a stark naked criminal on the loose?'

'Well, it won't be too hard to spot him.'

Christine's hasty entrance saved Tom from a reprimand for facetiousness. She had a piece of paper in her hand.

'I found this lying on the information desk,' she said. 'It's from him. He says, "I know there's no escape and I can't go back to prison. Don't look for me. By the time you read this it'll be too late. I'm going over the side." Captain, what shall we do?'

John sat alone at his table in the hotel dining-room. He was feeling as depressed as he could ever remember being in his life. That very day another English newspaper had carried the story of the sabotage attempt, which he had fondly hoped had been kept a secret. To make matters worse, Triangle's shares had dropped in price, and Marion had declared her intention of returning with him to the ship, 'as it seems I'm the only trustworthy person around at the moment.'

Last but not least of his woes was the fact that the lobster he had foolishly eaten was beginning to disagree with him. And if anything could make things worse than they already were, it was the sight of David West oiling his way to the table and sitting down opposite him.

Remembering his manners John offered him a brandy, and ordered one for himself.

'See if it'll settle the stomach,' he said.

'Not feeling so good?' said West sympathetically.

'Touch of indigestion. What is it you want to say?'

'Nothing specific. But I always welcome the chance to get to know Triangle people personally. But if you're not feeling . . .'

'I'm in for a restless night anyway. I've had a disagreeable meeting with the boss, and I've only a hotel bed to look forward to.'

'Sleep better on board, eh?'

'It's the only place I ever find any peace and quiet,' said John grimly. He swallowed some brandy. 'Then of course there's the comradeship you find on board. I've always appreciated that.'

'Something you don't often come across in business, I'm afraid.' West spoke heavily as though he yearned only for the simple life.

'I can imagine,' said John with a wry smile.

'How long have you been at sea?'

'More years than I care to remember. Joined when I was a lad. Been on a ship of one kind or another ever since.'

'Mainly with Terson's?'

'Always with Terson's. That's why I find this sabotage doubly upsetting.'

'Unpleasant business.'

'Unpleasant? It's potentially disastrous. I can't think of anyone who stands to gain from it.'

He could not help himself casting a sideways glance as he said this, but the other man remained expressionless.

'You've never fancied a change? From the sea?'

John sighed wearily. 'Mr West, it's a long time since I've been interviewed.'

'Forgive me. A purely academic interest.'

'I see,' said John, eyeing him steadily, 'Well, what else could I do?'

'I don't know. Let us suppose, for example, that Triangle were to shift its operations —' he looked at John's sudden grimace. '— Are you sure you're all right, Captain?'

'Ironic, isn't it? A sailor who can't eat the fruits of the sea. The lobster.'

'It's always been delicious when I've had it.'

'It was perfect. You'll think me very foolish but I'm allergic to shellfish. Every so often I can't resist indulging myself. It's entirely my own fault.'

'Oh dear. A doctor, perhaps?'

'No, no, I'll be all right. Carry on. If Triangle diversified.'

'Yes. Say, ran down the shipping and concentrated on the hotels —'

'Good God.' John stared at him, 'Is Marion seriously considering that?'

'I'm sure she isn't,' said West in an indulgent tone. 'I'm sure she isn't. A hypothesis only.'

'Mr West, I'd relish sitting behind a desk as much as you'd relish becoming a stoker on a banana boat. Does that answer your hypothesis?'

'Perfectly.'

'I'd rather retire.' He thought for a moment. 'I could afford to.'

'So I understand.' Abruptly West shifted tack. 'How are you getting along with Miss Hallam?'

'We've had our differences. It's not personal: I'm just not convinced that shipboard management can work.'

'Oh, it can work. With the right manager.'

'Are you sure you're not interviewing me?'

'I've discovered your loyalty to Triangle. I like that.'

'I've never really known anything else.'

'It means a lot to you?'

'Everything,' said John after a moment.

'For the last time,' Charles raged, 'I am not – repeat *not* – turning this ship around.'

He glared at Tom and Sarah who were standing with him on the bridge.

'But he *could* have jumped, man,' said Tom. 'You've got to!'

This was a mistake, as he instantly recognised. Charles eyed him coldly to say, 'I haven't *got* to do anything.'

'You've read the note,' said Sarah. 'He's obviously unstable. We must give him the benefit of the doubt.'

'There *is* no doubt. He's bluffing,' said Charles.

'You can't be sure. He did say he'd rather die than face prison again,' Tom reminded him.

'Then we'd be doing him no favours by finding him, would we?'

Sarah gasped. 'This is a human being we're discussing.'

'Draper is a common criminal,' Charles snapped. 'He's not cut out for heroic bids for freedom. I *know* he is on board this ship.'

'We can't take the chance. I insist you turn round and search,' said Sarah.

'Do you? I would remind you, Miss Hallam, that up here I am the master.'

'Don't we know it!' Tom muttered. Even he, who thought he had known what Charles was turning into, was taken aback by this.

'Searching for a man at sea is a major operation,' said Charles.

'So you're not going to try?' Sarah demanded.

'You know the rules, Charles – we *have* to look,' said Tom.

'And you ought to know that searching in broad daylight is hard enough. In the pitch dark it's impossible.'

'We should at least inform other shipping,' said Tom.

'Inform them of what? Look, I've already been on one fool's errand, looking for a damned dog,' Charles glared at Sarah, 'against my better judgement. With luck and no more interruptions I can just about make up the lost time.'

'The publicity will be disastrous!' she told him.

'Stopping for a dog but not for a man . . . It will look bad,' Tom confirmed.

But they both knew it was no use. Charles was beyond listening. He went on smoothly, 'This ship is supposed to be a commercial enterprise, not a charity. In the morning, I shall instigate a thorough search for Draper.'

Sarah looked at him in the eyes. 'I'd hate to be on a sinking ship of yours.'

'You'll leave the bridge *now*, please,' said Charles, tight-lipped with fury.

'I have never known such arrogance.'

'Thank you for your advice. Good night.'

Sarah slammed the door behind her, but not before she had heard Charles say, 'That woman is asking for trouble.'

She stopped dead on the other side of the door, shaking with anger and almost in tears. Matt, who had approached the bridge in time to hear raised voices, viewed her with concern.

'What's going on in there?' he demanded.

'Mr Woodhouse refuses to turn round and look for Draper,' she choked.

'*What?*'

'Says he's still on board.'

'But he knows the rules.'

'He won't listen. He ordered me off the bridge.'

'Did he? We'll see about that.'

'Please, Matt, I don't need gallantry. I can take care of myself.'

'I'm a professional seaman,' he said, stung. 'My only concern is the proper running of a ship. And I've some more news for him that he won't much like. Excuse me.'

But once on the bridge, confronting Charles, Matt found himself up against a stone wall.

'How many more times?' Charles raged. 'I am not stopping this ship!'

'I don't understand you,' said Matt.

'English is your native tongue, isn't it?'

'Cut the sarcasm, Charles. I agree that the chances are Draper is hiding somewhere, but we have to cover all possibilities.

'The courage of your convictions, Matt.' Charles' voice took on the suspicion of a taunt. 'It's what makes a captain.'

'One day, Charles —'

'Pack it up, you two,' said Tom. 'I agree with Matt. I think you're making a big mistake.'

'It's a captain's perogative to take risks. Now if there's nothing further . .'

'There is,' said Matt. 'The fault in the hydraulic doors, it's a specialist job. I can't repair it.'

'Must I take responsibility for everything?'

'Are we going to be able to get the cars off?' Tom demanded.

Matt shrugged. 'I've done what I can.' He looked pointedly at Charles. 'It's another risk we'll have to take.'

'Is that all?'

'Yes. Apart from Draper.'

'He's not going anywhere. Let him stew. I've said there will be a thorough search at first light. Good night.'

Chapter 9

Charles' search took the form of going through the cabin of every crew member and every passenger. In this manner he succeeded in generating a good deal of ill-feeling, and that was all he succeeded in doing.

He was standing morosely on the bridge the following day, feeling that the moment of truth had arrived. The ship had docked at Esbjerg and at any moment he would have to let the passengers off. Christine Harris appeared.

'Well?' he said sharply.

'A blank,' said said.

'I don't understand it. He's *got* to be on board.'

'Everywhere's been searched. The engine room, the hold, every cabin. Including yours. Beginning to look ominous, isn't it?'

'I refuse to believe he jumped,' said Charles stubbornly.

'We all make mistakes, you know,' she said, in a voice that contained just the faintest trace of self-satisfaction.

'It's too late for me to have doubts now, Miss Harris,' he snatched up the ringing telephone. 'Bridge.'

It was Tom. 'Car deck here. We're ready for disembarkation.'

'Right. I want every single vehicle checked. Understand? I don't care how long it takes.'

'Let's just hope the hydraulics behave themselves.'

'That's your problem, Mr Kelly.'

Tom raised an eyebrow. 'Thanks very much – *sir*!'

He put the phone down and nodded to a rating who pressed a button. He crossed his fingers as the doors began to move, wincing at their grinding and scraping. But they continued all the way across, and at last he allowed himself to sigh with relief.

'Well done, Matt,' he muttered.

On the bridge Charles was giving further orders. 'Right. I want officers stationed at all the exits to check every single passenger disembarking.'

'Should I notify immigration?' said Christine.

'I suppose you'd better. Just in case he slips through. Oh, by the way. All shore leave is cancelled.'

She looked unhappy. 'What? That's a bit short notice.'

'I can't help that. This is an emergency. If he isn't caught trying to get off then the whole ship will be searched again.'

As the disembarkation got under way Matt stationed himself by one of the passenger exits. He studied every face that passed him, but none was remotely like Draper's. After a while Sarah joined him. She took the opportunity to say. 'I didn't mean to be ungracious last night.'

'No problem. Charles gets a lot of people that way.'

'He is extremely sure of himself, isn't he?'

'Doesn't understand compromise.' Suddenly Matt spotted Judith in the queue. 'Hello, where's she off to?'

'Mrs Harper?' Sarah called.

She raised a pale preoccupied face to them. 'Mmmm? Oh, good morning.'

'Not leaving us, are you?' said Sarah.

'I am allowed ashore?'

'Of course, but it is a little unusual for you.'

'There's nothing to keep me on board at the moment, what with poor Morti gone,' she said sadly.

'I see. You won't get lost, will you?' said Sarah gently.

'My dear young lady, I'm not completely ga-ga, you know.'

'Of course not.'

'But you will keep an eye on the time, won't you?' said Matt.

'I might. I might,' said Judith distantly and floated on.

'Oh dear,' said Sarah as they both looked after her.

Then Matt spotted a face he did recognise.

'And where d'you think you're going?' he demanded of Bill.

'Ashore, of course. I'm off duty.'

'All shore leave is cancelled.'

'Why?' Bill demanded, outraged.

'We all stay on board until Draper is found,' said Sarah.

'That's not my problem.'

'It's everyone's problem,' Matt told him. 'If necessary the ship will be searched *again*.'

'Who the hell does he think he is?'

'Watch your tongue,' said Matt.'

'Matt, Matt. Quickly.'

The cry came from Jane who had dashed up to him, breathless.

'What is it?'

'Mr Woodhouse wants you. He's found Draper.'

'Right!' Matt took to his heels, following Jane to the deck, where they found Charles waiting for them impatiently. Tense as he was Matt had to suppress a smile. Charles was standing outside a cupboard, a fire extinguisher in his hand, held as though it were a gun.

'Shush,' he said as they came up.

'He's in there,' said Jane dramatically to Sarah who had followed Matt.

'Keep back,' Matt commanded.

They could all hear the sound of indeterminate noises coming from within the cupboard. Charles called, 'O.K. We know you're in there. Be sensible, and no-one's going to get hurt. Right, Matt. *Now*.'

He wielded the extinguisher in a threatening manner as Matt reached forward and flung wide the door.

For a moment they all stared, their eyes riveted on the apparently empty cupboard. Then a noise from the floor made them look downward to where Mortimer surveyed the world, with his head on one side.

When the limousine carrying Marion, John and Nick to the docks reached the terminal building Marion was first out. The place was swarming with police and she could see passengers being checked, even sometimes frisked.

'What on earth's going on?' she demanded.

Voices reached her from passengers hurrying past. They said things it churned her stomach to hear.

'That's the last time I travel with them.'

'I felt like a criminal, being searched.'

'I'm glad I didn't bring the car, it'll be ages before they get off.'

'What are all these police doing here?' Marion demanded.

'I'll go and check with the office.' Nick raced off.

A departing passenger accosted Marion. 'Take my advice, lady, go by air.'

'I hope this isn't anything to do with Triangle,' said Marion, but she did not speak as though she had any real hope.

'Marion, you're becoming paranoid. Why should it be?' John demanded.

'Why shouldn't it be? Everything else is going wrong.'

John reeled suddenly under the impact of someone colliding with him. 'I'm terribly sorry . . . oh, Mrs Harper.'

'Ah, Captain. A friendly face.' Judith beamed at him.

'What's our permanent passenger doing ashore?'

'Avoiding hoodlums.'

'I beg your pardon?'

'Apparently there's a dangerous stowaway on board. They've been searching the ship.'

'Stowaway?' said John, sceptically.

'Are you sure, Mrs Harper?' said Marion.

'Oh, I know you think I'm a dotty old lady —'

'Of course not,' John soothed. 'But you have had a very upsetting time lately.'

'I can see I'm a dreadful nuisance, so I'm getting out of your way.' Judith prepared to depart, thoroughly affronted, but paused a moment as Nick dashed up, bursting with news.

'Bad news, I'm afraid,' he gasped. 'There's a man called Draper on board. Wanted for robbery with violence.'

'You see, Captain? I may be dotty but I'm not deaf,' Judith declared in triumph. She stalked off.

'There's worse,' said Nick.

'There had to be,' Marion muttered.

'There's a rumour he might have thrown himself overboard. And they didn't stop to search.'

For one blazing moment Marion stared at him in disbelief. Then she turned on her heel and strode off to the ship, leaving John and Nick to hurry after her. Five minutes later Marion and John were confronting Charles on the bridge.

'Can you imagine what this is going to do for Triangle?' Marion demanded. 'Passenger missing, presumed drowned!'

'Mrs Terson, I was convinced – *am* convinced – that Draper did not jump overboard.' Charles looked only slightly uncomfortable. He was far from losing his confidence.

'How can you be so stubborn?' snapped John. 'All the evidence is against you.'

'It's not impossible he slipped off unnoticed.'

'Why are you so certain, Charles?' said Marion.

'Instinct. Men like Draper only want to save their own skins. And why write a note? Why not just jump?'

'It's a point, John,' said Marion.

'You're a trained officer, Charles. You don't run a ship on

instinct!' said John.

'It was pitch dark: you know there isn't a hope. Besides, I was running late, and I had the distinct impression it was vital to be on time.'

John wasn't impressed. 'Why were you running late?'

'Because I listened to Miss Hallam.'

'What do you mean?' said Marion.

'She thought it would be good for our image if I danced about on the high seas looking for Mrs Harper's dog.'

'Which was on board all the time, I hear,' John was unable to suppress a little smile.

Charles gave a small embarrassed cough. 'As it happens, yes.'

'Like Draper, I suppose.'

'You've nothing to be complacent about, John,' said Marion. 'It seems to me that Charles has handled a difficult situation very ably.'

'That remains to be seen.' A spasm of pain made John's face contort.

'Are you all right, sir?' said Charles.

'I am perfectly all right, thank you. I am simply appalled that you seem to be unaware of a captain's responsibilities.'

'I would say that Charles is quite aware of his responsibilities,' said Marion. 'He made an executive decision, and the ship arrived on time.'

'Is that all that matters to you, Marion? I credited you with a little more humanity.'

She turned on him. 'Let me remind you that on your first command this ship was sabotaged and we received disastrous publicity which directly resulted in our share prices plummetting.' She emphasised her last words. 'Which fact alone ought to concern *you*.'

John stared at her, too shocked by the injustice of this to speak. To his relief Christine Harris came in at that moment. She addrssed herself to Charles in a respectful voice. 'I thought you should know that all the passengers have disembarked, Mr Woodhouse.'

'I *am* back on board, Miss Harris,' said John coldly.

'I'm sorry, sir.'

'Are all the cars off?'

'Yes, sir.'

'No sign of Draper?' said Marion.

Christine shook her head.

'Thank you.' When the door had closed behind Christine, Marion heaved a sigh and said, 'I don't know – I've a damned good mind to get out of shipping altogether.'

The last words reached Christine clearly. She stood quite still for a moment, until she was sure that Marion was going to say no more. Then she raised a quizzical eyebrow and sauntered off. She did not see Nick Stevens watching her.

Matt dumped Morti on Sarah's desk.

'I thought you'd better look after him until Mrs Harper gets back,' he said.

'Yes, we don't want him to go missing again, do we?' she cuddled the little dog to her. 'Well, little feller, at least we found you.'

There was a knock on the door and Bill came in.

'I'd like to talk to you,' he said to Sarah. 'It's important.'

Matt went to the door. 'Don't be long, will you? It looks as if there's going to be another search.' He departed.

'D'you like dogs?' said Sarah, depositing Morti in her out tray.

'They're all right. That one gets a better life than some humans.'

Sarah gave a little sigh. Bill never let up and it got monotonous. 'What's your problem?' she said.

'Not just me. I'm speaking on behalf of all crew members.'

'All?' She eyed him cynically and he had the grace to blush.

'Well, quite a few. We don't like the way we've been pushed around the last few days.'

'Who's pushed you around?' Sarah demanded.

'Well, Mr Woodhouse, for one, has been a bit high-handed.'

Sarah was privately so much in agreement with this that it was a moment before she could reply formally. 'If the crew have a complaint there is a perfectly adequately liaison procedure through the union.'

'I'm not talking about unions. I'm talking about the way we're treated.'

'What exactly is it you want?' she said, determined to stop him waffling. To her mind half Bill's trouble was that for too long he had been allowed to get away with vague talk, without having to trouble himself about specifics.

'What I'm suggesting is that we should have a voice in the running of the ship.'

'*How?*'

'Look, you've got shipboard management. Why not a shipboard committee with a representative at the weekly meetings? We should have a say in every decision.'

Sarah drew in her breath, feeling that she had been hoist with her own petard. This was being specific with a vengeance. 'I disagree,' she said at last.

Nick's head came round the door. 'Oh. I'm sorry, I'm interrupting,' he said.

'Oh, hullo, Nick. No, Mr Ryan is just leaving.'

Bill scowled at this cavalier way of dismissing him. 'So you won't listen?'

'Go away. Then come back and convince me,' said Sarah.

He left without another word – chiefly because he was speechless.

'Trouble-maker?' said Nick.

'Just a minor irritant.'

He indicated Morti. 'Who's your friend?'

Sarah chuckled. 'A dangerous criminal called Draper. Sit down, I'll explain. It's good to see you, Nick.'

'How's Christine Harris been behaving?'

'I can't complain,' she said reluctantly. 'Efficient, helpful. I must be losing my judgment.'

'Not you. But I'm afraid Marion might be. Lately she's becoming much more interested in the hotel side and less enamoured of the shipping. Frankly, I'm worried.'

'So you should be,' she said. 'There has to be an optimum balance between the two. And we've reached it. We need the ships, Nick.'

'Right. But it's my feeling that someone's trying to persuade her. That's why this trip has got to be a success.'

He opened the door to leave and found Christine Harris standing there. She was smiling and not in the least perturbed.

'It's Judith Harper, I'm afraid,' she said. 'I've checked my passenger list and she hasn't returned. We sail in twenty minutes.'

'I knew I shouldn't have let her go alone,' said Sarah worriedly. 'I'd better have a word with the captain.'

She found John on the bridge with Marion. Reluctantly he agreed to delay departure by fifteen minutes, no more, which caused Marion to say snappishly, 'John, if we're late arriving there's only one man responsible. And nobody's indispensable. Think about it. I want this to be a perfect trip. Understood? Perfect.'

When she had gone John permitted himself another small grimace of pain.

'Are you all right, sir?' said Tom, who had been watching.

John almost shouted, 'I have never felt better in my life.'

Tom refused to be intimidated. Five minutes later John found himself sitting in his cabin while Tom took his temperature and pulse rate, pronouncing them both up. Twenty-four hours in bed to sweat out the allergic reaction to the lobster was Tom's prescription, and he had never given a more unwilling one, because he could see the inevitable result. Charles was going to be in command again.

Marion, who had come bustling into John's cabin, confirmed at once that Charles would take over while John was indisposed, and Tom just managed to suppress a moan. Was there to be no peace?

Then, just as he thought life had dealt them its last blow, Christine Harris entered with news that made Tom blench. Immigration had called to say that Draper had been found in the boot of a car. When Tom pictured Charles' likely reaction to that he wondered if he should give up the sea and leave immediately. And when he met Charles and Marion on the bridge ten minutes later he knew he should have done just that.

'Of course,' said Charles smoothly, 'he would have been picked up earlier if all the vehicles had been properly checked.'

'With respect, sir,' said Tom with pardonable malice, 'the search was called off when you apprehended Mrs Harper's dog.'

'Ah.' Charles became gracious. 'Well, I'll overlook it this time.'

'The Woodhouse way with dogs, Marion.' Tom couldn't resist saying.

When Marion had left Charles said coldly, 'I don't think we'll mention the dog again, Tom.'

'No, sir.' Tom looked innocent.

Charles looked at his watch. 'We ought to be sailing now, you know.'

'We're waiting for Miss Hallam, sir. She's gone ashore to look for Mrs Harper.'

'I can't help that. She's well aware that it's a passenger's responsibility to be on board in time.'

'Captain Anderson's orders, sir,'

'But Captain Anderson was a sick man when he gave those order. We sail at once.'

In the engine room Matt and Bill were making preparations for sailing. The sight of the boy's sulky look (not that that was anything new) prompted Matt to ask, 'How was your meeting with Miss Hallam?'

'Did I ask you what *you* were doing there?'

'Look, son, you're here as an engineer cadet, that's all you're concerned with,' said Matt wearily. Working with Bill was beginning to feel like living with a stuck record.

'I'm concerned with people, too,' Bill countered.

'When you get back to college they're going to want a report. On engineering, not The Rise of the Working Classes.'

'I happen to believe in industrial democracy, O.K? It's a principle.'

'Your dad was a man of principle, but he was also a conscientious worker.'

'Boss's man,' said Bill contemptuously. 'And what did it get him?'

Matt slammed his hand down. 'He was his own man and a damned good engineer. And frankly the only reason I'm concerned for you is the debt I owe him.'

'Don't do me any favours.'

'I don't give a damn what your politics are on shore, but on board ship you do what you're told.'

'Reactionary!'

'If that means taking pride in my work, then O.K. I'm a reactionary. We're not all hungry for power, lad.'

'No? But it doesn't half stick in your gullet when you have to take it from people like Woodhouse and Anderson, doesn't it? I've watched you. And when you see people like me getting off their backsides and doing something . . .'

'The only thing your backside needs is a damn good thrashing!'

Matt could feel his temper closer to breaking point than at any other time with Bill. He had actually clenched his fists when the door opened and a burly vacuous-looking individual rolled in.

'Hello, sailors. Anyone at home?'

'I'm sorry, this area is forbidden to passengers,' said Matt shortly.

'Maurice Barker's the name. Mozz to my friends. My card.'

Matt took it, and his eyebrows rose. 'Are you the engineer?'

'For all those little hydraulic jobs, I'm your boy.'

'Can I go?' said Bill.

'Yes, you can go on deck and carry out a check on the lifeboat engine,' Matt told him.

'Now you're just making work.'

'That is an order, Cadet Ryan!'

When Bill had stormed out Matt said, 'Right, let me show you the problem, Mr Barker.'

The big man gave a fatuous chuckle that set Matt's teeth on edge. 'Hold on, what's the rush? Got to find me sea legs first.'

'I'm sorry?'

'Come on, you're a man of the world. This job's a bit of a holiday for me, away from the wife and the boss —'

'You are here for a purpose,' said Matt tight-lipped.

'Don't worry, you'll get your doors done. I envy you, you know. You sailors have a lovely life. Know what I mean, eh?'

'A girl in every port, I suppose,' said Matt cynically.

'That's it! 'Course, with me it's the other way round: I try to get a port in every girl! Eh? Eh?'

Matt closed his eyes. This was going to be a trip he'd prefer to forget, even before it started.

It was the merest good luck that enabled Sarah to find Judith Harper almost at once. Her taxi drew up outside a pub just as the old lady came tottering out. She was plastered. Sarah had a momentary pang as she pictured her spending the afternoon in lonely drinking, while Morti was safe all the time.

It was immediately obvious that a few hours in the arms of Bacchus had left Judith in a difficult mood. When she heard Sarah's voice calling her she merely sniffed, waved her aside, and lurched on.

Sarah made a sound that was somewhere between a chuckle and a curse, told the taxi driver not to go away on any account, and raced after her. She made her explanation as best she could and found herself faced with a wall of alcoholic disbelief.

'It's a fiendish plot,' Judith declared.

'Morti's been found, I promise you.'

'Without him, Miss Hallam, you know what my life is? A hollow mockery, that's what it is.'

'He got shut in a cupboard.'

'Cruel,' Judith wept. 'He was swept to the arms of Neptune.'

'Why should I lie?' Sarah pleaded.

'Because I'm a wealthy woman. Triangle needs my money. I know, I hear things.'

For a mad moment Sarah considered picking Judith up bodily and making a dash for the taxi. She settled instead for saying 'Look – if he's not there, I promise you can travel free for the rest of your life.'

Judith considered for a moment. Then she hiccuped.

'C'mon then,' she said, as though unable to understand why they were wasting time.

'Only we must hurry,' said Sarah desperately.

'D'you think he missed me?'
'*Of course he did. Please, Mrs Harper.*'
Judith made a grand gesture. 'I shall return.'
Sarah bundled her into the taxi before she could think up some fresh difficulty. She looked frantically at her watch. If the taxi went fast they'd just make it.
They had just two minutes to spare as the taxi swept onto the docks and halted at the *Anglia's* berth – to disclose a sight that Sarah couldn't believe.'
'Oh no,' she gasped. 'He said he'd wait.'
Judith joined her at the rail, to look at the ship that was about half a mile away by now. 'Oh Morti,' she wailed.
'Missed the boat, Miss Hallam?' The voice was Marion's. She had been standing watching the ship depart, with Nick Stevens.
Sarah's eyes glinted. She hadn't missed the note of satisfaction in Marion's voice.
'Mrs Terson,' she said furiously, 'you heard Captain Anderson. He promised to delay departure for fifteen minutes.'
'Captain Anderson is unwell, so Mr Woodhouse is in charge, and he's a stickler for punctuality.'
'But what about us?'
'What can I do, dear?'
Sarah looked at her steadily for a moment. Then she spoke to Judith. 'Would you like a little adventure, Mrs Harper?'
'In for a penny . . .' said Judith with tipsy grandiloquence.
'Come with me.'
'Where are we going?'
'To charter a boat.'
Sarah nodded a hasty goodbye to Marion, grabbed Judith by the hand and ran.
'She's resourceful, I'll say that,' Marion admitted.
'You've got a down on her, haven't you?' said Nick.
'I can't stop the ship.'
'I wonder if you realise what an asset you have in Sarah,' he sighed.
Sarah remembered that ride till the day she died – supporting Judith's unsteady footsteps into the launch, avoiding the grins of the harbour staff, then the sweep over the water, with Judith trying to stand up like Brittania breasting the waves, and calling, 'It's all right, Morti, Mummy's coming. Hold on.'
But in the end it was worth it to see Judith sway ecstatically

towards Ted, who was holding the little dog out to her, crying, 'Morti, oh Morti, I thought you'd gone for good.'

Charles, watching the little scene on the deck from the bridge, grunted and muttered an uncharacteristic remark. 'That's going to be one happy old lady.'

'And one not so happy shipboard manager,' said Tom, wondering how long it would take for Sarah's wrath to decend about Charles' head. He had every intention of being there to see it. He felt he'd earned a little entertainment.

The door of the bridge banged open unceremoniously to disclose Christine Harris, breathless. She had evidently been running, and was big with news.

'Mr Woodhouse, there's something you should know. There's a meeting going on in the recreation room. It sounded like union business.'

'*What!*' Charles exploded.

'They were all complaining. It was pretty angry.'

'Who's involved?' said Tom.

'Well, the one doing most of the talking was Bill Ryan.'

Charles' voice was tight with anger as he snatched up the phone. 'That young man has gone one step too far.'

'I thought I heard Barbara Carter. But I may have been wrong,' said Christine.

Charles' lips tightened and he stared at Christine, uncertain how pointedly the remark had been directed at himself. At that moment Matt came on the phone in the engine room.

'Matt? Where is your engineering cadet?' barked Charles.

'Ryan? I sent him on deck to check the lifeboat engine. Why?'

'For your information, Mr Ryan is at present holding a union meeting, with a view, no doubt, to bringing this ship to a Marxist standstill.'

'*What?* Then he's disobeying orders.'

'Quite. Get up here fast.'

Matt was there in minutes, his face set with anger.

'I knew that little prole would be trouble,' Charles raged. 'Frankly, Matt, you've got something to answer for.'

'Now hold on —' Matt was determined, if possible, to prevent Charles from making a meal of this for the sake of his own ambitions, but he could see it was going to be hard.

'If he'd been kept busy he'd have had no time for politics.'

'And if you weren't so damned high-handed —' Matt flared.

'The bridge door opened. It was Sarah and she too was angry.

'Mr Woodhouse, I trust you have an explanation?' said Sarah with icy calm.

'You what?' Charles sounded as if he couldn't believe his ears.

'Did you deliberately countermand the orders of a senior officer – and put an elderly passenger to considerable inconvenience?'

Charles glared at her. 'Frankly, madam, I couldn't give a damn if she'd had to swim!'

He left without saying more. Matt followed, not even giving Sarah a glance. For once he could see her as John saw her – as an outsider who knew nothing about the running of a ship.

Outside the crew recreation room the two men halted and eavesdropped shamelessly. This was no time for polite behaviour, but for finding out how far a bad situation had gone. They heard the inevitable voice of Bill Ryan.

'As you know, I tried to approach Miss Hallam with our proposals but she had more important things to do.'

'Typical.' That was Lisa's voice.

'So what I'm proposing,' resumed Bill, 'is that a deputation of us insists on seeing the captain. Now.'

'He's ill,' came a voice that sounded like Barbara's. 'You can't disturb him.'

'I'm talking about Mr Woodhouse, since he's in charge and caused most of the trouble.'

Charles' face became grim and he put his ear a little closer to the door. Matt could scarcely bear to listen any longer to what Bill was doing to himself.

'We make it quite clear to him that unless our demands are met at once, then the crew of this ship will cease to carry out its duties.' There was a rumble of agreement. 'But we've got to be quite sure that we're all together. Because you know what this means?'

Without waiting any longer Charles and Matt erupted into the room and stood facing the startled crowd as an uneasy silence fell on them.

'I'll tell you what it means, Ryan,' said Charles quietly. 'It means mutiny.' He looked round, his eyes sweeping over Barbara's face without appearing to see it. 'You will all return to your duties. Mr Taylor, I want to see that man on the bridge at once.' He indicated Bill with a glance. Then he strode out.

Lisa yelled after him. 'You can't barge in on people whenever you like.'

'Shut up, Lisa,' said Bill.

'I sincerely hope that in an emergency your politics keep you afloat,' said Matt coldly.

Two ratings had followed Matt and Charles into the room. Now they went and stood impassively behind Bill.

He nodded to the ratings who took Bill's arms and marched him out.

'He doesn't mean any harm, Mr Taylor,' said Lisa, suddenly frantic.

Matt ignored her. She was another one who didn't understand that the rules were different on a ship. Ted came in just in time to watch the little procession leave.

'What's going on?' he demanded.

'Look at him, all innocent. Coppers' nark.' Lisa jeered.

'What're you talking about?' said Ted, taken aback by her hostility.

'She means someone must have told Mr Woodhouse about the meeting,' said Barry.

'You don't think it was me?'

'Your daddy is captain,' said Lisa.

'What'll they do with him?' Barbara asked.

'Dunno,' said Barry.

'A dressing down, that's all,' Ted reassured them.

'Could lock him up,' said Barry.

'If they do,' said Lisa, 'then they really will have a strike on their hands.'

On the bridge Bill was truculent as he stood between the two ratings and faced Charles, Tom and Matt.

'You can't arrest me for holding a meeting!' he declared.

'You don't realise, do you, son, that what you've done is illegal?' said Matt. 'A meeting in working hours and with the intent of, I quote, "ceasing to carry out your duties".Not that you were carrying them out too well, anyway,' Matt added.

Bill ignored him and addressed Charles. 'You're really enjoying this, aren't you? Bashing the working classes.'

'I couldn't care less if you're Eton and Balliol. You're a mutineer.'

'Don't come all that old Bounty stuff.'

Matt spoke quietly, 'It's not a joke, Ryan. You've let me down badly.'

'You need a lesson and one which I fancy you'll learn only under lock and key,' Charles snapped. 'Mr Taylor?'

Tom started forward. 'Not the brig. Come on. That's a big strong. He's only a kid.'

'Kids don't start strikes,' said Charles.

For the first time a note of uncertainty crept into Bill's voice. '*You* can't put me in there. Only the captain can do that!'

'While Captain Anderson is ill, *I* take the decisions,' Charles informed him.

'Matt, tell him he can't,' Bill pleaded. But Matt stared at him impassively. 'You'll have a strike on your hands when the rest find out.'

'I'll chance that,' said Charles. 'You'll remain in the brig for the duration of the voyage, when proper proceedings will be brought against you.' He nodded to the ratings. 'Take him away.'

Chapter 10

The following morning Lisa Watkins got herself admitted to the brig at exactly nine o'clock. She was with Bill for ten minutes. Within an hour the effects of that meeting had made themselves felt.

One of the first to learn about it was Mozz Barker who arrived in the deserted bar and waited for Barry – or anyone – to appear and serve him. When nothing happened he turned to the only other individual there, a heavily-built man in shabby clothes who also bore a look of impatience.

'Where is everyone?' he demanded.

'I heard rumours of a strike,' said the man, whose name was Mike.

'Blimey! I knew something was up. Didn't expect this, though. We could always nip over the bar and help ourselves.'

'Tempting,' Mike agreed.

They looked round them. Mozz gave a sideways glance at his companion.

'You – er – drive a lorry then?' he said. He had seen the man with a heavy goods vehicle the previous day.

'That's right.'

'Get around, do you?'

'Enough.'

'Know Chelmsford.'

'Drive through it every trip,' Mike grunted.

'Ah! That's useful.'

'Is it?'

'What sort of stuff do you carry?'

'Machine parts, mostly.'

Mozz lowered his voice. 'Like to do me a favour? I'll make it worth your while.'

'How much worth?'

'A thousand.'

'Go on.' Mike's eyes widened.

Jane's appearance put an end to the conversation. Before their horrified eyes she put up a sign reading 'Bar closed'.

'Sorry, gentlemen. Temporary admin problems.'

'Told you we should have helped ourselves,' said Mozz with a grin.

They moved off. Jane followed them. There was work to be done in the galley – and no staff to do it. So the sooner she got started the better.

On the bridge Sarah was trying to cope with a furious Charles.

'But what they're doing is illegal,' he fumed. 'It must be.'

'I'm not disputing that. But it's happened,' she said patiently. 'The crew are on strike.'

'I've never known anything like it on any ship I've worked.'

'The only thing I'm concerned about is what's best for the company,' said Sarah, trying to keep him to the main point.

'They should *all* be disciplined.'

'We're three hours from Harwich,' Sarah pleaded. 'Wouldn't it be better to release Bill, get everyone back to work, then discipline them later when the passengers are safely ashore?'

'Release Ryan now?' said Charles, aghast. 'That would look as though their actions carry some weight around here. I don't think we should give in to them so easily.' He appealed to Matt, who had just appeared looking thoroughly harassed. 'Matt would support me on this, wouldn't you, Matt?'

'Hmm? Suppose so. At the moment I've got other problems. There's a distortion in the main drive shaft. It means we may only be three hours from Harwich, but once we get there, we may have to stay.'

'I think I'm starting to believe in jinxes,' Sarah groaned.

With Bill unable to do his own negotiating the job of union 'spokesperson' seemed to have devolved on Barry Peters. Half an hour later he was facing Matt, Sarah and Charles on the bridge. Matt, who had always thought of Barry as a reasonable sort of bloke, tried his powers of persuasion.

'It's mutiny, Barry, you must see that,' he said.

'No, I don't,' said Barry. He set his chin with the obstinacy of a weak man who's going to cling on to the one thing he feels sure of.

'You are acting illegally, Mr Peters. You'll have no backing from the union over this,' said Charles frostily.

'If Bill's released, of course we'll return to work.'

'Bill is in the brig for a very good reason,' said Matt.

'There he'll remain until we dock,' Charles confirmed.

'Then no-one works. Sorry, sir.'

Charles stared at him. 'Sorry? You do this to me and that's all you can say? "Sorry"?'

'Surely if Bill were disciplined later . . .' said Sarah.

'Yes, I suspected you'd be on their side,' said Charles bitterly.

Matt tried again. 'You have to give one week's notice of industrial action, Barry. It's the law. And you're breaking it.'

He realised suddenly that Charles was no longer listening to anything that was being said. He could see something that the others couldn't, and was staring at it as though it was Banquo's ghost. As one, the other three turned and saw Bill Ryan standing there.

'What are you doing here?' demanded Charles when he had found his voice. 'Who let you out?'

The question was immediately answered by the appearance of John, right behind Bill. He looked ill, but his face bore a look of determination. '*I* did, Mr Woodhouse. And what the hell is everyone doing on my bridge?'

'Captain . . .' Sarah began.

John ignored her and spoke to Barry in a thunderous voice that few of his crew had ever heard him use. 'Peters, get off here and go back to work – *now*! Anyone caught not doing their job will be fired personally by me.'

Barry recognised the unmistakable voice of authority. '*Yes, sir!*' He got out – quickly.

John turned his attention to Charles, his voice lower but just as deadly. 'Mr Woodhouse, you're not fit to wear that uniform.'

'Sir!' Charles stared as though doubting his ears.

'I can't leave you – *any of you* – for five minutes without trouble.'

'Captain, you're not well,' said Sarah.

John seemed to notice her for the first time. 'As for you, Miss Hallam – the sea's in my blood, and so are the superstitions. *A woman on board brings bad luck.*'

Sarah looked at him quietly for a moment before leaving. Matt broke the uncomfortable silence by asking, 'How did you know? About Bill, I mean?'

'My son told me. Now go away – both of you. Leave me.'

'Sir . . .' Matt tried one last time.

'Matt, you're the best engineer I've ever come across. Just stay out of politics, will you?'

When she had checked that normal work was resumed Sarah made her way to Christine Harris's cabin. There was no point in putting this off any longer.

She knew at once that the girl was nervous. She also had an indefinable feeling that Christine had shoved something hastily out of sight before bidding her enter.

She came straight to the point, watching Christine's face as she spoke. 'There's something – someone – on this ship that wishes it and the company all possible harm.'

'Really?' Christine's face was a careful blank.

'Someone who takes time to magnify problems, leaks them to the press – even attempts sabotage,' Sarah continued in a level voice.

'What's this to do with me?'

'Oh, everything, Christine. Absolutely everything.'

Christine just stopped herself flicking her eyes towards the cupboard where she had hastily stowed the camera before allowing Sarah to enter. Her mouth was dry.

'Are you suggesting . . .? You think it's me, don't you?'

'I don't *think* it's you – I *know* it's you.'

Again Christine had to fight for control of her eyes. After a moment she said, 'Prove it.'

'Give me time. I will.'

'I doubt it. Because there's nothing to prove.'

'Tell me something . . .' said Sarah in a voice that was almost casual. 'Why did you assist in trying to recruit Matt Taylor for another company?'

Christine gulped. That was a nasty one. Just how much did this lady know?

She said, 'Is that what you think I did?'

'It's logical. There's no reason why I shouldn't think it.'

'Reason?' Christine's mind was beginning to work again. 'What do you know about reason? You're a total innocent, Miss Hallam. A total innocent. And you really are in for a surprise.'

Sarah left it at that. She reckoned she'd done as much as she could for the time being. Within half an hour they'd reach Harwich and her duties would keep her occupied. After that she'd get to see John – for a reason that would surprise everyone if they knew.

When the docking procedure was complete John returned to his cabin, glad to get off the bridge. He still felt ghastly, but there'd be no let-up for him yet. The call he had put through to Marion in Denmark was ready for him. Marion wasn't going to be pleased to know that the ship would be laid up in dry dock for the next two days.

'It's not a major catastrophe,' he said when he had listened to her wearily for a minute. 'You're making too much of it.'

'I hold you personally responsible, John – you and Sarah Hallam. Let me just warn you, Captain, that if anything else should go wrong – anything at all – you may be looking for another command.'

David West, sitting in Marion's lounge listening to her end of the conversation, raised his glass in salute to her. He was feeling pleased with himself. That very morning he'd gently suggested to her that their two companies should consider a merger. True, she had rejected the idea, which was not more than he had expected. But when he'd asked her to think about it more deeply she hadn't refused. On the whole he felt he'd made as much headway as was possible for the moment. And the news that Marion had just received from the ship had sent her confidence plummeting down still further. Which just suited him.

John replaced the receiver and sat staring at it. Marion's words still rang in his ears, but he felt too ill to care much at the moment. Damm the lot of them for dragging him out of bed before he was ready.

'Come in,' he said reluctantly, answering a knock on his door.

To his surprise the visitor was Sarah, bearing a glass of green watery liquid that instantly filled him with suspicion.

'Captain, I've brought you something.' She proffered the glass.

'What is it?' He made no move to touch it.

'It'll put you right. Drink it.'

He took the glass and eyed it uneasily.

'I don't think . . .'

'*Drink it!*' she commanded.

He gulped the liquid down, wishing she wouldn't speak so loudly. It tasted odd but not so bad as he'd feared. He grimaced anyway, on principle.

'It isn't that bad,' she said ruthlessly.

'Are you going to tell me what it is?'

'Home-made brew. My grandmother was a wow with herbs. And I've got a miniature garden in my cabin. If you die, they'll burn me as a witch. If you live, they'll burn me as a successful witch.'

He realised that he was being sent up – not unkindly – for his 'woman on board' remark. 'I apologise, Sarah. Pressure and ill-health – pretty deadly combination.'

'If you need any more, let me know.'

'I've never had a herbalist on the crew before.'

She regarded him. 'Know a lot about them? Your crew, I mean?'

'As much as I can, in the circumstances.'

'Oh, Captain – you sound like a wary politician.'

'Did you want something, Miss Hallam?' He felt he'd had as much as he could take.

'Yes, I wanted to talk to you. Do you know what causes unhappiness, and stress and human misery?'

He leaned back in his chair. 'Surprise me!'

'Breakdown in communication. People unable to talk to each other.'

'That could be one of the reasons.'

'Why do you think we had that strike?'

'We'll discuss the problem at the next management meeting – and decide what disciplinary action needs to be taken. Sarah, I appreciate hearing your views. Next time, you don't need the excuse of bringing me medicine to express them. Just knock on my door. Better still, I'll leave the door open. That way anyone will feel free to drop in and chat, won't they?'

'Yes, John,' she said with an apparent meekness that made him shoot her a suspicious glance. He returned the glass to her.

'By the way,' he said with surprise, 'I'm feeling considerably better – thank you.'

The meeting to decide what to do about Bill Ryan was something he had deferred for several reasons. For one thing he wanted to take control of it himself, which meant giving himself a little more time to recover totally. For another he wanted Matt to be present, which he couldn't be if he was giving all his energies to repairing the engine. So when, two days later, the *Anglia* was in its last preparations for departure on its trip to Amsterdam, the whole question of the strike was still hanging fire.

One person who had enjoyed the excitement was Judith. During the short strike she had managed to get behind the bar to serve some drinks, and – if she said it herself – she had done it rather well. It had been quite disappointing when the fun was over so soon.

The two days in Harwich had bored her to tears, and now it looked as though the ship was about to get under way soon she was consumed with impatience. It was too soon yet for many other passengers to be about, but Judith haunted the reception area seeking signs of life, like a bird-watcher hoping for the first swallow of summer. At last she was rewarded by the sight of a scruffy middle-aged woman. The woman – who looked as if she made a habit of drinking too much – wore the aggressive air that is common to those who feel out of their depth and don't want the world to know it

'Shop!' she called. 'Where is everybody? Bleedin' ghost ship, this.'

'It *is* irritating, isn't it?' Judith sympathised.

'Where are they?'

'The chief purser's off sick, the assistant purser's in the conference room, and another assistant's dealing with an hysterical passenger. As far as I know.'

'Know a lot then, don't you?'

'So here we are, left to fend for ourselves,' said Judith brightly.

The woman was looking about her, eyes wide. 'Never been on one of these before.'

'They are fun. When you get used to it.'

The woman sniffed. 'Well, I'm not one for having "fun" in this life.'

'What a pity.'

'I'm on me own, you see. Widow. Family up and left. And what with me back and these headaches I get – no-one's suffered like I have.'

'I am sorry.'

The woman peered at her. 'You're one of them well-travelled people, aren't you?'

'Yes, I suppose I am.'

The woman sniffed again. She sniffed often. 'Can always tell. Pride myself on being an expert on human nature. I've seen a bit of life in Stepney, I have. Experienced, that's what I am.'

'I'm sure,' said Judith politely.

'I'm looking for my daughter. She works here.'

'What's her name?'

'I call her Bee. But it's Barbara – Barbara Carter.'

Two hours out to sea, they met in the conference room to decide what was to happen to Bill. The meeting settled itself along predictable lines. John was growing increasingly glad that he had waited till he was able to take control and overrule Charles.

'Who thinks Bill Ryan should be charged with mutiny right now?' he demanded, knowing the answer.

'We ought to show them once and for all who is in authority,' said Charles at once. 'After all, it *was* mutiny.'

'Back to keel-hauling days, Charles?' said Sarah.

'Certainly not. Just – discipline, that's all.'

'What do you think, Matt?' said Christine.

'Forget it.'

'Exactly,' said John. 'Let us forget this word 'mutiny'. It's out of all proportion. We are discussing one adolescent engineering cadet.'

'Make a mention on his records, then go on as usual,' was Matt's suggestion.

'Sounds like sweeping under the carpet,' Charles grumbled.

'Providing there's no further trouble . . .' Matt shrugged.

'Put it down to youthful fervour,' said Sarah. 'Misplaced ideals.'

Matt seized on this. 'Sarah has a point. God knows, I made plenty of mistakes when I was young.'

'I think we should concede to their requests, John,' said Sarah. 'Have a member of crew sitting in on management meetings.'

'And when it comes to discussing confidential matters? It's not a good idea,' said John.

'But that's what it's about, surely. A question of trust. Treat them like responsible adults, not naughty children, and they'll respond.'

'Exactly!' said Matt. 'We're a team, John. No-one can function without the others' help. And that goes right across the board from cabin girl to captain.'

John pursed his lips, his face unyielding.

'I vote we give Sarah's idea a try,' Matt finished.

'I can't agree,' said John. 'I'm sorry. No argument.'

As he had expected Sarah opened her mouth to argue. It was a relief when the bleeper on his lapel shrilled and saved him from her – for the moment. He seized the phone and listened for a moment before rising to his feet decisively.

'That was the radio room,' he said. 'Received a mayday call – ship in distress. Meeting closed.'

Everyone moved on the word. In this situation each knew what was expected of them. Within five minutes, Tom, Charles, John and Matt had assembled on the bridge.

'It's a Russian vessel,' said John. 'That's all we know so far.'

'We have a fix on her position, Captain,' said Tom. 'Twenty minutes away. Twenty-five at the most. And she's not moving.'

Charles, who had been talking on the phone to the radio room, slammed down the receiver and said, 'Gas cylinder explosion in engine room. It's holed the ship. And the bilge pump is damaged.'

'Repairs to hand?' said John.

'That's the trouble,' said Charles. 'An inexperienced engineer. He doesn't have the knowledge and their stores don't hold the parts anyway.'

'How long have we got?'

'Not long – they've started to sink.'

'Tom, set course. Matt, I want maximum speed. Then stand by to carry out repairs.'

Matt stared. '*Russian* vessel?'

'A ship in distress,' John corrected.

'Yes, sir.'

'Action, gentlemen.'

Nick Stevens could feel his hair turning whiter by the day. He was sitting now in the lounge of the Terson mansion in England, watching Marion. She was on the telephone, her face tightening as she listened, until at last she slammed down the receiver.

'Now what's happened?' he demanded in alarm.

'The papers have printed another story. This time complete with photographs. A strike on the flagship. They've used words like "mutiny" and printed photos of officers serving drinks.' She clenched her hands. 'Nick, when will this stop?'

'It'll stop when the person responsible is caught.'

'I regret giving the flagship to John,' she muttered.

'Now, Marion, you know he's the best person,' Nick pleaded

'But nothing has gone right since he took command. Share prices have fallen, a sabotage attempt, the ship just out of dry-docking. The whole thing is jinxed. There's nothing anyone can do.'

'A run of bad luck. It'll improve, you'll see.'

'No! I wanted to believe that once. I've spent hours trying to convince myself. But it's too much, Nick. I don't think I'm prepared to continue in this way.'

'What do you mean?' he said with foreboding. Marion's decisiveness was rapidly becoming more to be feared than her indecisiveness.

'David has made an offer of a merger. I discounted it at first. Now I'm not so sure.'

He stared in disbelief. 'A merger with D.R.W. Shipping?'

'He said I should give myself time to think about it.' She was throwing some papers into a briefcase.

'What are you doing?' said Nick.

'Going to Amsterdam. We'll sort this business out one way or another.'

The Russian trawler turned out to be a small battered-looking vessel whose crew were almost as suspicious of their rescuers as glad to see them. They refused the offer of a loan of a bilge pump, preferring to buy it outright, a course of action that would enable them to depart more quickly. John declared himself willing to sell his vessel's spare pump. The only problem was that no-one could find it . . .'

Tom Kelly, waiting in the pilot's entrance to greet the boarding party, found himself facing a huge bearded man carrying a plastic container filled with liquid, and a small fierce creature that could have been anything and turned out to be female. She announced that she was Katia Platonovitch, the captain.

'Where is yours?' she demanded.

'On the bridge,' Tom told her. 'He's waiting for you.'

'Good. I must speak at him.'

She stomped off, leaving the bearded man, whose name was Anton, to follow, carrying his plastic bag.

From this point on the problems multiplied. In the absence of the missing bilge pump the only course was for Matt to board the Russian vessel to repair theirs. This Katia definitely did not want. She finally agreed on condition that Matt came alone.

'Come,' she announced. 'Or no time soon – my ship go down like your British dollar.'

To Matt's relief she relented to the extent of allowing Bill to go aboard with Matt, chiefly, Matt suspected, because Bill's eyes were shining with fervent revolutionary admiration. He sighed. Bill was going to be very hard to live with after this experience. But then – when wasn't he?

Two hours of concentrated work got the Russian pump working again. Matt regarded his efforts with satisfaction.

'That just leaves this hole to patch up,' he said, indicating the side of the trawler, 'and you're shipshape again.'

Katia threw a fit. Through a stream of verbiage in which every second word seemed to end in Z, and a good deal of arm-waving, Matt gathered that he must leave the hole for the Russian crew to mend. But he must lend them his tools. He shrugged. He was tired anyway. As he edged Bill away he gave him a quick pat on the back. Bill's work over the last two hours had gone a long way towards redeeming him in Matt's eyes.

'This will take an hour, I think,' Katia told Matt. 'You will join me for a drink?'

Matt was taken aback. 'Well, that's very nice, but – why don't you come for a drink on our ship? You and Anton? You'd be most welcome.'

The two Russians accepted with alacrity. Bill's eyes were shining again. Matt grinned to himself. Once back aboard the *Dana Anglia* Bill was plainly going to plunge into a lot of deep talk with this pair. Matt would give anything to be a fly on the wall.

John, looking down at the trawler from his vantage point on the bridge, heard Charles come up behind him.

'We're three hours behind schedule, sir.'

'Don't look so pleased with yourself, Charles, it can't be helped.'

'With respect, sir, it could have been.'

'It's the first rule of the sea, Charles, to help others in distress.'

'Those Ruskies weren't in any danger, sir.'

'They were sinking, for God's sake.'

'So slowly you had to persuade them to let you aboard. Dammit, John, they didn't want your help. They wanted a pump, which you didn't have.'

'So you think I should have left them there, to help themselves?'

'Yes. As a good company man, looking to the best interests of Triangle, I think you should have.'

John regarded him in disgust. 'I'm a human being first, Charles. The company man comes second. Now, if you'll excuse me . .'

Charles looked after John as he left the bridge, and muttered, 'You've got your priorities all wrong, you know.'

Mrs Carter finally ran her daughter to earth with the help of Jane Anthony. One look at Barbara's face caused her stomach to knot within her. She had hardly dared to hope that the girl would be glad to see her, and the truth was worse than she had feared. Barbara's expression was one of sullen hostility. To cover her nervousness Mrs Carter cast a look round the Bellevue Lounge, where they had confronted each other. Her glance was at once admiring and sceptical.

'It's a bit of all right, isn't it? All this?' she said.

'It's a ship, mother,' said Barbara sullenly. 'It's my career.'

'Career! What do you want with a career? What about your old mother, working all hours on that stall to keep body and soul?'

'Mother!' Barbara wished the earth would swallow one of them up.

'Should be at home, looking after me. Not chasing a career! It's all her fault!'

'Who?'

'My sister-in-law, Marion Terson. Yes, that's it – gave you too many ideas. Always knew ideas was your downfall.'

'Mother, if you've come all this way just . . .'

'I want you back, Bee,' said Mrs Carter suddenly. She looked at her daughter as she spoke, and her face was open and defenceless.

'What?'

'Back where you belong. With me. With your mother.'

At sight of that naked vulnerable face Barbara felt a twinge of pity and guilt. To cover up she spoke in an abrupt voice. 'Don't be ridiculous.'

'Oh, ridiculous am I? That's very nice. Insults from me own flesh and blood.'

'I didn't mean . . .' The girl ran a hand through her hair. 'You know it wouldn't work.'

'Why? Tell me why it wouldn't?'

'Well . . . mother, we're strangers!'

'But you're all I've got,' said Mrs Carter, again with that pathetic simplicity that wrung Barbara's heart and in the same moment made her brutal. 'Ideas above your station – that was always your trouble.'

'Mother!' Barbara hissed frantically.

'Don't know what you've got to be so grand about – and with what you've got to hide.' She looked Barbara straight in the eyes. 'Wouldn't look good, would it? If I told that Anthony woman what I know about you?'

'You wouldn't,' said Barbara, white to the lips.

'I know your little secret, Bee. I'm your mam. And you're all I've got.'

Barbara felt as though something was choking her. This suffocating helpless affection from a mother she did not feel close to, and had nothing in common with, embarrassed her and made her feel guilty. As soon as she could, she saw her mother to her cabin – the cheapest the ship had to offer – and escaped from her.

She went straight to her own cabin and took up the copy of *The Wind In The Willows* that Lisa had lent her. She stood for a moment holding it indecisively, but she knew that if she did not do what was in her mind, then she would be her mother's prisoner for ever. She went and knocked on Lisa's door. Lisa was in and greeted her in friendly fashion

'I'm returning your books,' said Barbara in a thin voice. 'Thanks.'

'Good, wasn't it?'

At the last minute Barbara's courage failed her. This was where she had meant to speak the truth, but instead she said, 'Yes,' in a whisper.

'Loved that bit about Toad in goal, and hot buttered toast.'

'Yes.'

'And Ratty and Mole and . . .' Lisa peered at Barbara's pale face. 'Are you all right?'

'I – it's no use, Lisa. I didn't read it.'

'Why not? You had plenty of time.'

Courage came flooding back – the courage of despair.

'I can't.'

'What?'

Barbara took a deep breath. 'I can't read it. I can hardly read anything.'

'Why not!'

'I'm dyslexic.'

'What's that when it's at home?'

'I can hardly spell, can't form words, can't read – it's a kind of blindness.'

'Word blindness?' Lisa sat up, alert.

'I suppose that's it.'

'Is that all? My cousin got it too.'

Barbara stared. 'Has he?'

'He's taking lessons – reading, spelling. Come on, it's not that bad.'

'It's bad enough.'

'Can you tell the time?'

'Yes.'

'You'll be all right. You should see David, my cousin. Poor thing can't tell right from left, can hardly count.'

'I've never told anyone before,' said Barbara shyly.

'Look, there are groups, classes. I'll call my mum when we get ashore. She'll know about them.'

'When I pick up a newspaper, all I see are the pictures. Everything else is just a jumble. Can't read books, can't read a menu, can't write a letter – and now my mother . . .'

'Take it easy. I'll help you.'

'Oh, Lisa, if it were that easy . . .'

'We'll make a start, use those alphabet books you've got. Yes, I've seen them. Cheer up. We'll have you reading backwards in no time.'

'I think I do that already,' said Barbara ruefully.

Abruptly she rose and left Lisa. Their talk had given her the courage for what she needed to do next. She went quickly to Jane's cabin, praying that she would find her in. She did.

It was harder to tell Jane than to tell Lisa, but somehow the words came out, and a sense of freedom possessed her that she hadn't known for years.

'So that's it,' she finished. 'I never went to university. I can't read, I can't spell. I'm a fraud.'

She looked down at the drink she was holding in her hand. She had a vague recollection of Jane having pressed it there. Jane was sympathetic to distress when she saw it, and she appreciated honesty, however belated. She refilled the glass and gave Barbara her friendliest smile.

'What do you want me to say, Barbara?' she said kindly. 'That you're a hard worker, a nice person . . .'

The girl was near to tears. 'But I've lied, told fibs, *pretended* . . .'

'Do you think we don't all do that, one way or another?'

'No – yes – but —'

'Dyslexia isn't the end of the world. As for the rest, your mother – well, children do feel ashamed of their parents. It's quite common. You'll get over it.'

'It doesn't help the way I feel *now*.'

'We spend our lives kidding ourselves – pretending we're something we're not. God knows, I've done it myself.'

'I don't believe that.'

Jane shrugged. 'Either you start to believe the lies you're telling yourself – or you don't. And when you don't, the pretence gets like a weight around your neck.'

'Yes,' said Barbara with feeling.

'So, we do what you've done. Confess and start again.'

'I feel so awful.'

'You'll recover, believe me. Meantime,' Jane consulted her watch, 'you're six minutes into your duty roster.'

Barbara smiled. 'Slave driver.' She gulped her drink.

'Yes,' said Jane, smiling back.

'Thank you.'

'You're welcome.'

In the crew recreation room, an hour later, Ted heard Barbara's story and was sympathetic.

'Never mind, we've all got mothers,' he assured her. 'If mine was on the boat I'd push her over the side.'

And that wasn't so far from the truth, he reckoned. So far there'd been no word from his mother, although his father had written to her. The long silence unnerved Ted as he knew his mother too well to imagine that she'd accept his defection without a fight.

Lisa and Barbara fell silent when they saw Sarah Hallam enter, obviously looking for Ted.

'Can I interrupt your break and drag you back to work?' she said pleasantly.

'You mean you'll save me from the clutches of these two beautiful women?' He pantomimed vast relief.

Sarah smiled, but said, 'I've got a rather grotty job for you, but it is urgent.'

'Fire away.'

She took him quietly to one side. 'There are two large items missing from the engine room. The spare rectifier, and the donkey pump.'

'Stolen?'

'We don't know. We only found out they were missing when we went to help the trawler.'

'But you want me to find them?' he said, blenching.

'I'm pretty sure you won't. What you have to do is check the records of all the spare equipment we carry. Find out if there's anything else missing. And look up the value of everything that's gone. And if that bores the pants off you, you can play the detective and tell me where the lost items have gone.'

In John's cabin a party was getting under way.

Bill, invited in on the strength of his work on the trawler, took the chance to mutter to Anton, 'I'm not used to this. The working class aren't allowed in here.'

Anton looked puzzled.

Katia presented bottles of vodka to John and Matt, then proceeded to kiss John on both cheeks and give him a bear hug. This brought applause from everyone present.

The drinks went down, the laughter mounted. Someone mentioned spies amid much laughter. Anton looked horrified.

'If we spies – I not want to go to North Sea – too cold. I think I want to be in Mediterranean – with yacht – like Mr Onassis. Then I'd spy on topless girls.'

Amid the general laughter Matt said to Katia, 'You like our ship?'

'Yes, it's a good ship. I don't see boats like this in Tallin.'

'Tallin?'

'Yes. We are from Estonia.'

'Not Russia?'

'Is part Russia.' Katia sounded reluctant.

'But we hate all Russians,' Anton announced.

Bill looked perplexed. Matt read his expression and said with pardonable malice, 'Bill's interested in Russia, aren't you, Bill?'

'Yes I am. In fact you're the first Russians I've met.' Bill looked excitedly from one to the other. 'You see I like the idea of the Communist system.'

Anton's eyebrows rose into his hair. 'You *do*?'

'Would you like to see round the ship, Anton?' said Matt diplomatically. 'If so, Bill will show you.'

He gave Bill a wink.

Mrs Carter had succeeded in tracking down the one person on board whom she felt would offer her a sympathetic ear. She was right. Judith was riveted by the tale of Mrs Carter's misfortunes as they sat together on the boat deck.

'So that was it. I lost him. Thirty-two I was. Barbara was nine. It weren't fun, I can tell you. Trying to look after 'er was a full time job.'

'It must've been a strain, but I'm sure she must realise.'

'I 'ope so.' Mrs Carter did not sound as though she placed much faith in this hope.'She 'asn't forgotten it, being little, I know that. She 'adn't 'ad it wiped out of 'er mind, like they say, but . . . she pretends it never was 'er. All that being poor . . . and such . . . My own fault, of course.'

'*Your* fault?'

'I 'ad friends. Men with a bit of money, 'elp pay for the lino, I used to say. Not for my sake, 'ers. She 'ated 'em. She was really rude. Despised me, you see. So I let Marion 'ave 'er. Suited the both of 'em.'

'You mean the Marion Terson who . . .?' Judith waved her hands vaguely to indicate their surroundings.

'Yeah, that's right. These was all 'is boats, not 'ers. She 'ad no more sense of business than I do, dear. Just fell on 'er feet instead of 'er you-know-what . . . I know I sound jealous. I am, might as well admit it.'

'And Marion brought up your Barbara?'

'Give 'er everything she wanted. Everything,' said Mrs Carter with bitterness.

'It's an awful decision. I mean, it was awful for you to have to take.'

'She still despises me, so it didn't do me no good. I mean, I know I'm common, dear. I embarrass 'er, that's the size of it. She's ashamed to be seen standing next to me. But – whatever 'appened when she was little – she is still my daughter. And I still love 'er, and I don't want to monopolise 'er, breath down 'er neck . . . I'd just like 'er to come 'ome, and see me now and again, to want to do it . . . only now and again, it wouldn't 'urt 'er.'

'Tell her, like you told me,' Judith urged.

'She makes me feel that common, I can't find words.'

'She should understand that. She's old enough by now, I think.'

Mrs Carter sighed.

Anton's conducted tour of the ship was proving a disconcerting experience for Bill. Instead of expounding on the glories of the just and equal society of which he was a product, Anton wanted only to linger in the shopping arcade. Bill got him at last to the crew recreation area, where he sat him down with Barry, Lisa and Barbara. He had looked forward to confronting Anton with Barbara.

'Barbara's auntie owns the boat, you know.'

'Really, you do?' Anton looked at Barbara with respect.

'No, no, not Barbara, her auntie,' Barry corrected. 'Be hers one day.'

'It's happy for to . . .' Anton's English, always limping, stumbled to a standstill. He looked at Barbara. 'I don't believe it,' he said simply.

''s true,' Barry insisted.

Anton looked round. 'No, I can't believe anyone could own this much.'

'I agree with you, Anton, it's disgusting,' said Bill fervently.

Anton gave him a look. That was not what he had meant. 'I would like to own just one trawler. That would be enough for me!'

'You saving up, then?' said Lisa.

'No, no . . . it's not possible,' Anton said sadly.

'Costs too much, does it?' she asked sympathetically.

Anton shook his head. 'It's not permitted.'

'Why's that, then?' said Barry who felt he must be misunderstanding Anton.

'That's obvious, surely?' Bill broke in. 'If people can own that much, a trawler, they can own a boat like this. Before you know where you are, you're back to capitalism. Right, Anton?'

Anton took refuge in evasion. 'I'd like a trawler, I tell you.'

Barry laughed. 'So there, young Ryan, belt up.' He turned back to Anton. 'You've seen our boat?'

'Yes, I have. But I would like to see your shop again. That was fun! It's not the same in Russia, you know,' he added mournfully. 'In Tallin where I live, fun . . .' every eye was eagerly fixed on him '. . . is a trip to the ballet!' he finished dolefully.

Having hauled Ted away from his lunch break to find the thief Sarah hauled Matt away from the party for the same purpose.

'Find the thief, please – before we reach Amsterdam,' she said. 'It shouldn't be that hard, not if he's still on board.'

'You mean he'll wear a badge with "thief" on it?'

She sighed patiently. 'Look, the items were stolen from the engine room. So we rule out all the passengers and most of the crew – they never go there. That leaves either one of your engineering staff or . . .'

'Or someone we wouldn't notice down there.'

'Does that narrow the field?'

'You could say so,' said Matt grimly. He knew now who they were talking about. He went straight to the pub, where he found his man.

'O.K. where's the stuff?' he demanded at once.

Mozz Barker looked at him innocently. 'What stuff?'

'One spare rectifier. One donkey pump,' Matt recited. 'Missing from the engine room. You nicked it.'

Mozz gave him a quizzical look. 'What was it again? A rectifier? And a donkey pump? That's big stuff, isn't it? Heavy stuff?'

'Very.'

'So what am I supposed to have done? Put 'em in my pocket? Come on, Matt – you know better than that.' He took another long drink as though hoping that when he put his glass down his tormentor would have vanished. If so, he was disappointed.

'You had help, Mozz,' Matt went on. 'One of the lorry drivers, I reckon, took it off ship for you.'

'Get away.' Mozz managed a laugh.

'All right, look at it from my angle. Somebody had it, right? I know damn well it wasn't one of my staff. You're the only other bloke to have set foot in the engine room.'

'Anyone on ship could've gone there.'

'They'd have aroused suspicion.'

'If they were seen . . . You're a clever sod, aren't you? Top of the class in logic. Where d'you go to school?'

'Miss Hallam's Academy,' said Matt grimly.

'She taught you about needing to prove things, I suppose?'

'All the time.'

'So why bother when you can't, eh? Why try and take it on? You can point the finger, Matt, but you can't prove a thing.'

'Don't bank on that. We've got a list of all the lorries that come on and off the boat. The police'll trace your accomplice, no sweat.'

'Oh, and then what? D'you reckon that driver's going to admit to something that puts 'im inside? When there's no need to, no evidence, nothing? He'll deny the lot, you see.'

'He just might lose his nerve. Then where'd you be.'

Mozz had finished his glass and was opening another bottle. 'Get the evidence, Matt,' he said. 'Then charge me. If not, leave it out.'

Matt rose to his feet. 'That sounds like a confession to me.'

'You think I'll say what I said to you to anyone else? Don't be a fool, you're talking slander, my friend. You've no leg to stand on. Cheers.'

Matt turned as he reached the door. 'I won't drop this, believe me.'

'Please yourself.'

As he led Anton down the corridor to his cabin Bill was still starry-eyed, still talking nineteen to the dozen. Anton said little but stared around him in awe.

'Now to me, coming from a working class background, I say why? Why should some people in my country have everything going for them from the day they're born? Better homes, better schools, best jobs, first pick – all because a small proportion of them own most of the wealth. That's why I look to Russia – for an example, whatever its faults.' He halted at his cabin door and let Anton in. 'I'm sorry, it's not very grand in here. You get a bit more luxury in the officers' cabins.'

Anton was looking round him, bemused. 'Is very good,' he said at last. He sat on the bed, clutching his booty like a child that had just raided a sweet shop. 'I'll smuggle this into Tallin,' he said with glee.

He studied the shelf. 'Your books?'

'Yes, they're socialist books,' said Bill proudly. To his disappointment Anton showed no eagerness to study them further, but fixed him with a puzzled eye.

'I think you dream about Russia,' he said.

'I'd like to visit it.'

'You think we are best. Plenty Russians think same about you.'

'They don't know, though.'

'Do you?' said Anton significantly.

'Are you telling me you're not socialist? You don't like it?' said Bill aghast.

'I live with. I don't swim away.'

'Why not?' said Bill.

'You think is all good in Russia? Look, workmen on ship, Katia's drinking beer. Some lucky. I must go now.'

Bill rose. 'Yeah, of course. It's been good to talk to you.'

'And you. Good shopping.'

As they went out Bill looked at Anton's precious parcels and made one last try. 'You really can't get all that in Russia?'

'*Niet*,' said Anton firmly.

By eight o'clock that evening things were more or less back to normal. The Russians had gone and Matt was working flat out to pick up speed. To his dismay he realised that the engine was responding badly to his efforts. The repairs at Harwich had not, as he'd hoped, sorted out all the problems and he was faced with having to tell John that an even longer spell of dry dock would be needed in Amsterdam. Inwardly he groaned, knowing he'd be blamed for something that wasn't his fault, and that John in turn would be blamed by Marion.

Coming out of the engine room into the ante-room he was not entirely surprised to see Mozz Barker waiting for him. He shut the door to the engine room and removed his ear-muffs.

'What the hell are you doing here?' he demanded.

'Felt like a word with you.'

Matt looked round. 'Come over here.' He took Mozz down a flight of steel steps to where they were out of earshot of any of the engine-room staff.

Now it came to the point, Mozz didn't look happy. 'So what's going to happen about the stuff?' he said uneasily.

Matt shrugged. 'What do you expect? I make out a report. It goes to the police and the insurance. They can do what they like with it. Now I'm busy, if you don't mind.' He made as if to turn away, but Mozz stopped him.

'What can the police do, Matt?'

'Nothing, I expect. They'll go through the motions, like me.'

Mozz took a breath. 'Look, I can do without all that police stuff. Being interviewed, you know, cautioned, told I'm a liar.'

'Your problem, mate.'

'They're bound to let me go in the end, you know that.'

'I don't care. Nor should you, I reckon. It's a small price to pay.'

'Matt, suppose I told you I'd rather not pay that sort of price?' Matt cocked an inquisitive eyebrow, but said nothing. 'But I wouldn't mind sorting out something with you.'

There was a long silence before Matt said, 'What do you mean?'

'Look, what's happened here? Two or three blokes made a few grand.'

'Just a few!'

'Your company's not losing. They're insured. The insurance company expect a few claims – that's their business! So they don't mind. No harm's come to anyone, really.'

Matt looked him in the eye. 'What're you offering, Mozz?'

'Cash. If you keep my name off that report. £1500.'

'Oh, I don't know.'

'£2000, then. I can't do better. What do you say?'

Matt looked at his watch. 'Look – I'm off duty at nine. Come to my cabin then. Maybe we can sort something out,' he winked. 'All right?'

Chapter 11

It wasn't an accident that caused Barbara and her mother to bump into each other in the arcade that evening. In fact Mrs Carter had been there for over an hour, sitting by one of the windows, drinking steadily, until it was an effort to rise and confront her daughter. The attempt to sound casual was almost beyond her.

'Oh, 'ello, dear,' she managed to say in an approximation of a light voice.

Barbara's face did not brighten. 'Hello.'

'Why don't you try "'ello, Mum"?'

'I'm out of practice,' said Barbara sullenly. Impatience was written on every line of her, but her mother resolutely ignored it.

'Sit down, dear. I'll get you a drink.'

'I've got things to do, you know.'

A hand gripped Barbara's arm suddenly. 'Please, for me.'

Barbara dropped into a chair with a resigned gesture, but said, 'I don't want a drink, thanks.'

'Nor do I, I suppose.' They sat facing each other until Mrs Carter said painfully, 'It's nice to see you.'

'Is that what you wanted to say?'

'No. You're just making it difficult for what I wanted to say.'

'Which is?'

'You. Mean a lot.'

'I find that very hard to believe.'

Mrs Carter flinched. For a moment she seemed about to give up but she drove herself on.

'I want to talk to you, Barbara. Nice and friendly. I got lots of things to say to you, you'd be surprised.'

Barbara frantically tried to shush her mother. 'Can we talk tomorrow, when you've sobered up?'

'I'm quite all right, thank you. Just the ship's rolling. Anyway, tomorrow's too late. I'm seeing 'er tomorrow. Your auntie. The great Marion Terson.' She tried a tipsy wink but was too far gone, and only managed to screw her face up grotesquely. Barbara felt a rush of nausea at the sight.

'What about?' she said.

'Ha . . . Terson! She's a Carter by blood, love. His sister – you're dad's, poor sod . . .' she trailed off into mumbling.

'Mum,' said Barbara urgently, 'tell me, why're you seeing her? Money, is it? Money, or me?'

Mrs Carter gulped. 'Course it's . . . No.'

'Are you sure?'

Suddenly Mrs Carter shouted, 'No. No, I ain't,' and burst into noisy tears.

Barbara leaned urgently towards her mother, desperate to shut her up before they were noticed by someone who knew her. 'Oh God, what's got into you?' she muttered.

Mrs Carter began to gulp through her tears. 'What's got into me . . . is . . . What's going to come to her . . . she's in for a . . . Oh she's . . She's . . . goin' a . . . I'm going 'a beg the bitch . . . Beg for some bloody money from the . . . I don't want 'er filthy bloody money, but I . . . I'm going to be begging the cow for it 'cause I'm in the gutter.'

Hurriedly Barbara produced a hanky and thrust it into her mother's hand. 'Here. Keep your voice down, please.'

'You . . . couldn't . . . You never wanted to come but now . . . It's not fair, I'll never see you . . . I'm living in a hovel. No money at all. Well, if she doesn't want 'er sister in law 'anging around 'er like a smell, then she can pay up. Let me just get my 'ead up, then . . . That'll be all . . . I won't ask again. But I can't take it like it is now, dear. It's up to 'er. She's got to do something, never you mind, never . . .' She stopped abruptly and looked at her daughter with eyes that were dreadfully clear and sad. 'Ashamed of me, aren't you?'

'Miss Carter, if you have a moment.'

Barbara jerked up at the sound of the voice and found herself looking at the last person she would have chosen to witness this scene. Charles' smile gave nothing away.

'Miss Carter, I've got a job I'd like you to do,' he said.

A moment ago she would have given anything to escape. Now, perversely, she felt a rush of loyalty towards the helpless unattractive creature that was her mother.

'I've got to go,' she said awkwardly. 'If you're all right now.'

Mrs Carter nodded and made no effort to detain her. She seemed to have no spirit left. When they were out of her sight Barbara faced Charles.

'Sorry about, that,' she said. 'Well?'

'Nothing actually. I just thought you needed a rescue.'

'Thanks,' she said shortly.

'Damsels in distress. It's my line.' He looked at his watch. 'Look, I've an hour before I relieve Tom on the bridge. How about a walk round the deck?'

'Actually, Charles, I was on my way to the disco.'

'Oh no, you weren't.'

'I was.' She set her face stubbornly. She hated him for doing what she had secretly wanted and for forcing her to feel ashamed of herself.

'I've been watching you. Before you met your mother. You were coming away from the disco.' Charles smiled at her, pleased at his own cleverness, oblivious of the fact that his words were falling like stones.

'Thank you very much,' she said sweetly. 'I was going to fetch my escort. Ted. He's a nice chap. See you.'

He watched her go. He wasn't certain what had happened, but his parting call of 'Have a good time, won't you?' sounded lame in his own ears.

Alone in his cabin Matt watched the hand crawl to nine o'clock. He was annoyed at his own tension. He knew what he was doing, didn't he? He'd thought it all out beforehand. He knew exactly what the risks and opportunities were. Well, then – stop worrying.

Just the same, he jumped when the knock sounded on his door. And before opening he called cautiously, 'Who is it?'

'Me. Mozz,' came the voice from the other side.

'Come on in.'

Mozz shut the door quickly behind him. 'I'm that loaded I thought I'd be mugged,' he grinned, patting something just inside his jacket. 'You and me got a deal then?'

'I've been thinking . . .' said Matt uneasily.

'Come on, Matt. We made a deal.'

'Only to talk, Mozz, you know that.'

Mozz seated himself comfortably. 'All right, Matt, what do you want to talk about?'

Matt dropped down on the bed and faced him. 'What do you think? The risks,' he said.

'There's no risk.'

'Look mate I've got a position to think of. Here. I won't play ducks and drakes with it, whatever you do. So, where did the stuff go?'

Mozz stared at him for a moment, then light dawned on his face and he broke into an expansive chuckle. 'Matt, what do you take me for? Stupid?'

'Either I find that out from you, or we don't have a deal.'

'We don't have a deal,' said Mozz at once. He rose and turned to the door. He had his hand on the knob when Matt gripped his arm to stay him.

'Hold on, hold on . . . I understand . . . all right? But I've got to know something more. As it stands at the moment, you could get caught for all I know. Then my name comes out . . .'

'Won't happen,' said Mozz, coming back into the room.

'Mozz, what do you take *me* for?'

'Look, it went out on a lorry. In Harwich, right? I told the driver to take 'em to a mate of mine, who'd pay him there and then. So he's clear now. There's nothing on him.'

'And your mate?'

'My mate knows the ropes, Matt, don't you worry. It can't be traced, none of it.'

Matt sighed, not too happily. 'All right, I'll believe you. Thousands wouldn't.'

'You'll never make an easier couple of grand, feller. I can promise you that. We got a deal?'

For a moment Matt seemed unable to move or speak. He stood there, his face a mark of indecision as Mozz patted his jacket and grinned.

'Deal,' said Matt at last.

Mozz beamed. 'Right.' He slipped his hand into his jacket and pulled out a wad of money. 'Here.' He held it towards Matt's outstretched hand. At precisely the moment when both men were touching the money a blinding flash seemed to fill the room, making Mozz spin round and rub his eyes in furious disbelief. When he could see clearly, a bellow of rage broke from him.

'*You bleedin'* . . . ' He launched himself towards Sarah who stood in the bathroom door, keeping firm hold on a camera. But Matt's vice-like grip restrained him.

'Never hit a lady. Try *me*.' He didn't relax his hold on Mozz.

'Your idea of a clever trick, is it?'

Matt pointed to the money which Mozz still clutched. 'Yeah, and that's yours.'

'We have two witnesses to your confession, Mr Barker,' said Sarah, 'so it won't matter how many times you deny it. With luck I've also got a picture of you bribing the chief engineer. I'll need your passport, sir. The police will be waiting in Amsterdam.'

After a moment Mozz's shoulders sagged and he sank down onto the bed in defeat. But Matt wasn't watching him. His eyes were on Sarah, and they were full of admiration and curiosity.

They celebrated their victory together at the bar, with Tom and Jane. Matt told the story in a way that made Sarah a heroine. Sarah said very little, but her eyes watched Matt constantly.

'Oh, by the way,' he said, producing Mozz's passport, 'what about this? I'd better not keep it in my pocket.'

'Can you give it to Christine?' said Sarah. 'It belongs in the purser's safe.'

'Oh.' Jane sat up suddenly. 'You know I said I wondered where I'd seen Christine before? Well, I've remembered. It was in 1975, just after our divorce. I went on a course. It was either June or July. There were several courses, all to do with different aspects of shipping, and I was on management, and Christine was on something else, which I can't remember, but I do remember that it struck me as odd.'

'How was it odd?' said Tom.

'Well, at the time I thought it was more of a man's course.'

'You mean a sort of radio officer?' said Matt.

'No. Lots of women do that.'

Tom regarded her sceptically. 'Well, I never thought I'd hear you making the distinction between men's jobs and women's jobs.'

'Where was this course?' said Sarah suddenly.

'In the Hague,' said Jane. 'Place called the POHL Conference Centre.' She turned her attention back to Tom. 'Do you know, I think you men spend more time thinking about women's lib than women do.'

At once they were plunged into one of their old arguments. Sarah never heard them. She was sunk deep in thought.

Ted knew his worst fears had been realised when he was summoned to his father's cabin and John held out to him a letter from Maya.

'What's happened?' said the boy.

'Nothing dramatic, or I'd have let you know before. It was waiting for me in Esbjerg. I've given it a lot of thought before confronting you.'

He held out the letter but Ted turned away. He didn't have to read the words. He knew his mother. 'So she wants me back. I'm not going. That's flat,' he declared.

'What she says is: Either you're *sent* back to her, or she'll make it difficult for me to go on seeing Emily.'

'God, that's sick,' he said violently. 'That's disgusting. What's Emily think about it?'

'Emily doesn't say.'

'Maybe she couldn't care less, then. Sorry. But can . . . can Mother do that, Dad?'

'She can make things very difficult indeed, Ted. The law in Sweden's on her side. But I wouldn't want to twist your arm.'

Ted paced the cabin but almost immediately gave up. It was too small for melodramatics. 'I don't want to twist yours,' he said miserably. 'But . . . God, what a choice! *She's* twisting yours.'

'Yes, and it hurts, but . . . I will stand by you, Ted. So long as you're sure you're doing what you want.'

'I always was sure, Dad. After that, I'm even more sure.'

'On rational grounds? Not just temper?'

'If you didn't want me to get upset, you shouldn't have shown me that . . Oh . . .' He banged on the wall with a savageness that made his father wince.

Before John could say anything there was a knock at the door, followed immediately by Barbara's entrance. 'Oh, sorry,' she said when she saw John, and started to back out.

'Don't mind me,' said John hastily. 'I'm just going.'

'Well, I just popped in to suggest a disco but . . .'

'Come in!' said Ted. 'We're only having a family discussion.'

'I can come another day.' She started to back out.

'You're here today,' said John. 'Come in. You're the same age as Ted – let's have your opinion!' John put a playful arm round her shoulders. 'Barbara, this young man, my son – an independent-minded young runaway – has got a problem . . .'

'It's not your mother, Ted?' said the girl at once.

'Bingo!' he confirmed gloomily.

'She wants you back, I suppose.' She looked at John. 'And she's using your other children as some sort of a lever – on you.'

'So, what do you think?' said Ted.

Barbara spoke slowly, her thoughts coming uneasily, and with some pain. 'Well, I expect she finds you've grown away from her, and . . . you can understand she . . . wants you back, but . . . she doesn't do it . . . nicely . . . She uses blackmail, and . . . Although you try to understand that – why she's feeling like that . . . It's not fair, is it? It doesn't help you. And it may not be good for her either, to get away with it. You can't be forced into love, can you?' Her voice sank on the last words.

John looked at her, vaguely comprehending that there was more behind Barbara's words than there seemed. He had never seen her so serious, or liked her so well. 'Well,' he said to his son, 'I've got to go and reply to this mother of yours. I think you two could do with a night at the disco. Excuse me.'

'That means I've got a reprieve, I hope,' said Ted.

'Yes, of course.'

When they were alone, Ted said hopefully, 'Well, disco sounds great tonight.'

Her face did not brighten. 'No thanks, Ted. I've changed my I mind. I think I'd rather go to bed.'

'Oh.'

''Night.'

'Hey . . . say . . .' She halted at the door, and waited for him to continue. 'Didn't you have a good thing going with Charles?'

She wrinkled her nose. 'Not that good. See you.'

Marion's trip to Amsterdam had not proved a happy experience. The ship was not, as she had expected, waiting for her. Instead she was greeted by the news that once more it was late, and was due for another long spell in dry dock when it arrived.

And now here she was, sitting in her office, staring at a wall-chart that contained more bad news. It contained two lines: one indicated the price of shares, starting high and sliding downwards; the other meant bookings, and it too was falling. Roger Powell was explaining everything to her. Not that he needed to, she thought gloomily. Any fool knew what lines going downwards signified.

'One day,' she sighed, 'I shall become immune to bad news. Until then – tell me gently.'

'It can't be that gentle, Mrs Terson. But I'll do my best. You see, this line here – bookings – shows a far more worrying trend than the share price line, here.'

'It's all downhill,' said Marion.

'Yes, but as David West explained to you, the share price line is a problem but not the end of the world. It won't affect you, for example, unless you want to sell your holding in Triangle. But the trend in bookings is serious. That's turnover. Cash. Profitability. And look at it!' He swept a hand dramatically down the line.

'That's just one day's bookings, though. I'd . . .'

'The computer throws out a number of figures each day: the bookings of the day before, which may, of course, be affected by a number of factors; but also bookings for the last three days, for the last week, month and so on. So we get a pretty fair picture of booking trends. Mrs Terson. And that's bad news – no question.'

Her shrug was weary, almost apathetic. 'So I eat, sleep and drink bad news these days. I don't understand it.'

Before Powell could embark on further explanations Nick hastened in. He looked both angry and worried.

'Good morning,' he said tersely.

'Oh Nick, hello,' said Marion. 'You're just in time for some more bad news.'

'So are you, I'm afraid.'

'*What?*'

'This.' He yanked a newspaper from under his arm and thrust it at her. 'You read it. I picked it up when I drove past the airport, coming in. There's another article on the shortcomings of Triangle Line.' Nick began to recite. 'Like the flagship that stops to look for dogs, and throws parties for Russian fishermen, but doesn't care if the passengers are late or never arrive at all.'

'What's all this about parties?' asked Marion.

'Marion, you're missing the point,' said Nick. 'All this is supposed to have happened on the voyage from Harwich to Amsterdam, which isn't yet over. *So – how did the paper get hold of the story?*'

Powell shrugged. 'Obviously there's a newspaperman on ship.'

Nick rounded on him. 'And how did he get the news ashore? Carrier pigeon?'

'Sarah Hallam,' said Powell at once.

'That's preposterous, Roger, and you know it,' said Nick.

'Do I? What's preposterous about it? For a start she's the company manager and the buck would stop there anyway. On top of that . . .'

'How can you hold Sarah responsible for sabotage? Or for the accident of meeting with a ship in distress?'

Marion snapped, 'That had to be John's decision.' When Nick

stared at her she added, 'To go to the ship.'

'It had to be right, Marion.'

'Look, Nick, I don't want to blame John but . . .'

'Why should you? There is such a thing as bad luck, you know.'

'Not in my book, Nick,' said Powell. 'Or if there is, good company management will allow for it. You expect bad luck some of the time, that's life.'

Marion butted in quickly before Nick could argue. 'When is the ship going to limp in to port, Nick?'

'She'd caught up a lot, the last I heard. Down to an hour and a half behind schedule. I'd say she'd be in around now.'

'Thank you.' She started gathering things together hastily.

'Where're you going, Marion?' said Nick.

'Somebody's to blame for this, Nick. Somebody's head's going to roll. So where do you think I'm going?'

Ted scurried into Sarah's office first thing in the morning, and dropped a paper onto her desk.

'No sooner asked for than got,' he said. 'All the radio phonecalls made since we left Harwich.' He leaned over her shoulder to explain the columns. 'These, with sums of money in the columns here, are crew members' calls, debited against salary. And these are passengers' calls, paying cash. What do you want these for?'

'I'm anticipating a problem which hasn't happened yet – I hope.'

Half an hour later she called him back to her office.

'I've checked out most of these calls, which don't lead me anywhere, except –' she pointed to the list '– for this one here.'

'Ah, passenger call,' he said wisely.

'Yes, but there's no cabin number against it. So I can't find out who made it, or who it was made to.'

'Well if it was my job, *I'd* ring the number and ask who it was at the other end,' he said brightly. 'Then I'd say wrong number.'

'Good thinking.'

He preened as he lifted the telephone. 'So do it, eh?'

'Unfortunately, I've already done it, and they wouldn't say who it was.'

'Try the exchange,' he said, dashed.

'They won't say either.'

'Think of everything, don't you?' he said admiringly.

''Fraid so,' she said, picking up some phone directories. 'That only leaves this – the most soul-destroying job I can think of – for you.' She pushed the books at him. He groaned. 'All you have to do is find this number in one of those.'

'It'll take for ever,' he moaned faintly.

'Couple of days at least,' she confirmed. 'Make a thorough job of it, mind.'

'I can think of more pleasant ways of going blind, Miss Hallam, but for you – anything.'

He exited with a flourish, somewhat spoiled by a collision with Christine Harris in the doorway. Her eyes opened a little at the sight of the directories.

'Message from the captain, Miss Hallam,' she said. Her voice died away as she noticed the telephone list on Sarah's desk.

'Sit down,' Sarah told her. 'I'm just checking the telephone bill.'

'It's just that we're going to be delayed for further repairs in Amsterdam, that's all.' Christine's voice became hard. 'As for the telephone bill, I hope you've time to check it thoroughly, Miss Hallam, because time is running out, for *you*.'

Nick Stevens arrived in the doorway in time to overhear this last remark. He stood aside to let Christine depart.

'What did than mean, I wonder?' Sarah mused.

'They're all running scared of you, my dear,' he told her. 'They want you out. David West has been running you down to Marion.'

'Then we'll have to hurry up, Nick, and find out why.'

'What was all that about phone bills?' he said, coming into the office and closing the door behind him.

'I have the feeling there'll be some more unwelcome newspaper publicity . . .'

'There already has been.' From his briefcase he produced the newspaper carrying the story he had already shown to Marion. 'This appeared while the ship was still at sea.'

'Proving my suspicion that a call must be made from the ship. So I've had Ted checking the calls,' she said. She glanced briefly over the paper. The story was bad, but no worse than she had expected. Then she returned to the explanations.

'There've been seventeen radio phone calls made since we left Harwich. Six of them by crew members and each one of these has been accounted for. Ten calls have been made by passengers and everyone paid cash. All cash has been receipted by the purser's office. Look.'

She handed him a bunch of receipts which he flipped through. There were sixteen.

'So?' he said. 'The seventeenth?'

'Wasn't receipted. Apart from the number called, which appears on the radio officer's log, of course, there's absolutely no record of it. By the way, it was an Amsterdam number.'

'So now you ring the number?'

'I've done that, naturally. But I've been quite unable to find out who they are at the other end. They're giving nothing away and it's a pity I've probably had to raise alarm signals. The radio officer is quite certain all the calls were made by women. I'm sure it was a crew member who had a particular reason for not wanting the call recorded on her salary debit. It also had to be a crew member who was able to ensure no cash receipt was made out and no copy on file. So that person had to be from the purser's office. There was only one person on duty at that time. Look, Nick. We both know it was Christine. We simply have to prove it.' She waved a hand at all the papers. 'Here's our evidence.'

'There is one small sticky fly in our ointment,' he pointed out. 'We don't know who the call was to. Only that it was an Amsterdam call. And this –' he lifted a corner of the newspaper as though its touch would contaminate him '– is printed in London.'

'We'll find out,' said Sarah calmly.

Within half an hour of the ship's docking at Amsterdam John found himself confronted by Marion and Roger Powell, on the bridge. Charles was also present, which was something John could have done without, as Marion was in one of her most unreasonable moods, demanding that he produce explanations out of the air.

'Look . . .' John began in exasperation.

'At what? The share-price plunge? The computer booking forecast Mr Powell here has just shown me? The press coverage we've been getting?'

'You were asking for an explanation,' said John, tight-lipped.

'And about to receive it? Splendid. I'd like it immediately, in my office, not here. I hope it's one that doesn't over-tax my gullibility, because my patience has, I feel, been abused.'

John indicated the control-panels. 'I have my job to do, Marion.'

'I am under the impression that that is what I have been asking you to do.'

'I have to see that this ship is unloaded and into dry dock. Those must be my priorities,' he remained, stiffly polite but his face unyielding. He could not recall being so angry with Marion ever before. It was indenfensible of her to intrude on to the bridge and speak to him in such a way before his subordinates.

There was pure saccharine in Marion's voice as she turned to Charles. 'I think these things can safely be left in the first officer's capable hands. Are you happy about that, Charles?'

'No problem.' Charles' face might have modelled for the cat that got the cream. 'It's in all our interests to – er – get it all sorted out.'

John did not spare him a look. 'Right. I'll inform Sarah there's a meeting ashore.'

'Sarah will not be present at this meeting,' said Marion. 'I shall see her later.'

Unwillingly, but having no choice, John accompanied Marion off the ship and into the terminal hall. Because he did not wish to talk to her he allowed himself to fall a couple of paces behind, and was unhappily aware of the picture this presented. He found himself accompanied by Roger Powell, which was another thing that didn't please him.

Out of the corner of his eye he saw a scruffy middle-aged woman detach herself from the crowd and approach Marion.

'Excuse me, Mrs Terson – Marion–'

Marion stared at her blankly for a moment, before light dawned on her face.

'Oh! I hardly expected to see you here –' Marion seemed embarrassed. 'I'm afraid I'm rather . . .'

The scruffy woman was perspiring under the effort of holding her luggage and keeping some semblance of dignity.

'I must talk to you, Marion, please – it's urgent . . .'

John, who had come to a halt a discreet distance away, did not miss the look on Marion's face. Whoever this woman was, Marion knew her well and was ashamed of her. Powell was looking supercilious.

'I'm afraid I'm very tied up at this moment,' came Marion's voice. 'Could you give my secretary a ring and fix an appointment?'

She swept on without waiting for a reply. John was forced to follow her, but he turned sympathetically in time to see the woman staring after them, a look of desperation on her face.

In Sarah's office Ted was having no luck. He too had telephoned the number and tried to prise a name from the man who answered. But he had got nowhere.

Sarah decided the time had come for desperate measures. With

Christine ashore it was a golden opportunity to search her cabin. Nick's lawyer's soul revolted from such an unethical move, but somehow he found himself drawn into Sarah's determined web. However, the search revealed nothing.

'Exactly what were you hoping to find?' Nick demanded.

'I wish I knew, that's the devil of it. Any little piece of concrete evidence that might have saved the exhaustive investigation I've now got to make. And save time. Just a lead. Anything.' She was rummaging through the locker as she spoke.

'Do you think it's the same reporter behind all these stories?' said Nick.

'No doubt about it. It's Kevin Warrender. He's being bribed, obviously.'

'Then I'd better fly over to England and scare the pants off him.'

'It *could* work,' she said doubtfully. 'But not now, please. I need you. I'm going to need all your moral support when I'm under fire from Marion later today.'

'I never thought I'd live to hear you say you needed moral support from anyone.'

At that moment the object of their attention was sitting in a corner of a dark wine-bar in Amsterdam, being thoroughly kissed.

'Missed you.' said David West as soon as he could speak.

'I'm glad.'

'And now this is all we've got.' He looked round. 'Nice, but not quiet enough for my inclinations.'

'I know. And I can't stay long.'

'How I loathe all this subterfuge. Ugh. Makes me feel like some cheap gigolo, crawling round that woman, pretending I can't keep my hands off her,' he shuddered.

'It's a case of ends justifying means,' she said softly. 'When it's all over, it'll have been worth it.' Her tone teased him. 'Only a few dinners and the odd pounce in a taxi!'

'I do as little pouncing as possible, I assure you. Give me her great limousine with a chaffeur for a chaperone any day. The lady does not turn me on.'

'Glad to hear that. She's hardly the sex kitten of Amsterdam, poor old Marion. What's she doing now?'

'Ah-hah. Giving John Anderson a bad time. And when she's finished him off, she'll be grilling Matt Taylor. Then Sarah Hallam. Our shipping magnate lady is having a busy day.'

'I'm not happy about Sarah. She certainly knows something, but how much I don't know, and it makes me uneasy. So much so, I was unsure whether I really ought to have kept this date with you. I feel I ought to stay aboard as much as possible. Be around.'

'I think you're worrying unnecessarily. Sarah Hallam's days with Triangle are numbered. The newspaper article was the final straw, and Marion's fit to be tied. Very off Miss H., she is.'

'Mm. Maybe.'

'She'll kill the goose that lays her own golden egg. All we have to do is watch and move in at the right time. Don't worry. It's all in the bag.'

He would have been even more pleased if he could have heard what was being said in Marion's office at that moment. Roger Powell was proceeding with the slow murder of Captain John Anderson.

'Leadership is an oddly fragile quality, Captain Anderson. A man can seem – can *be* – very competent and decisive for years and then suddenly he can seem to lose his grasp, and there's no very rational explanation why. It can happen in war. It seems – forgive me – to be happening now.'

'There are times . . .' said Marion. 'I have very seriously been forced to consider promoting Charles.'

John shrugged. 'You could do worse. He'd make an efficient captain.' He felt suddenly too bone weary to show, or even feel, any more emotion.

Marion began to fiddle with a pencil on her desk. She had an uneasy sensation that she was not behaving well, but was too confused to know what else to do. 'Look,' she tried again, 'our association, yours and mine, has been a long one. You were George's valued friend. This is all very painful. I simply do not understand what has been happening to you or your ship – my ship. Now *why* did you feel it necessary to throw a cocktail party –' she pointed to the newspaper article, '– instead of pressing on to keep up your schedule? It all seems so inexplicable.'

'I was hung up, Marion. Don't you see? While part of our equipment was being used to repair the hole in the trawler's hull. The trawler was hove to and until we could help repair their damage and retrieve our own equipment we had to be hove to as well. It seemed common courtesy to entertain the master of the other ship, and perhaps because they were Russians one felt one might be doing an especially delicate job. May I ask how you knew they first declined Matt's help?' he added.

'I was told. Naturally.'

John smiled faintly. 'I must say, Charles never misses a trick, does he?'

'That can be a positive recommendation,' said Powell.

'You must see. His ambition gives him something to strive for,' said Marion earnestly. 'It gives him the edge over someone like you.'

'Well, if that's what you want . . .' John shrugged.

'It is.'

'Then perhaps I am out of my element. Times have changed, Marion, and possibly my values haven't kept pace, but that's the man I am and I like to keep my relationships clean.'

She had a vague uncomfortable feeling that John had judged her and found her wanting. And this meeting was supposed to be the other way round. 'I don't think there's anything further to say at this point,' she said. 'We seem to be on different wave lengths. That's all for now, John.'

The next one to be sent for was Matt. He stared at Roger Powell. He had seen Powell but once before, in a dimly-lit Amsterdam bar. But there was no doubt about it. This was the man who had tried to wean him away from Triangle. And yet here he sat, near to Marion, plainly in her employ. Matt exploded.

'My God. I've heard some grotty things in my time but this beats 'em. I think I've had enough.'

'Now cool it, cool it . . .' said Powell. 'Don't get so steamed up.'

Matt paced the office like an angry tiger. 'If I understand you correctly, that "interview" you gave me was to see whether I was the kind of rat to leave an apparently sinking ship. Yes?'

'I prefer to put it: to establish your loyalty.'

'And was my loyalty so suspect, then?'

'Calm down. You passed with flying colours.'

Matt's scorn should have blasted Powell from his chair. '*Passed.* Thank you very much. Do I get a diploma? I get and keep my jobs on my ability. I'm a bloody good engineer. If I've got a boss whose mind works on that kind of schoolgirl level she can keep her job and I'll find another.'

'Now come along, Matt,' said Marion. 'You're being both rude and deliberately awkward. You must see we had to determine who could stand up and be counted – for the sake of Triangle.'

He turned on her. 'What sort of tricks have you got up your sleeve for the others? Is Charles to be put through the fire? I'd just like to know the company I'm in.'

'Matt! You are being personally insulting.'

'I think it was more than a little 'insulting' to fake interviews to see my reaction.'

She said unexpectedly, 'I'm sorry. Maybe we were a little insensitive this end.'

'Paranoid, more likely,' he muttered, unsure how to take her sudden collapse.

'I think honestly, Roger, we went to unnecessary lengths,' she said. 'I never would have doubted Matt here.'

Powell looked as though he might be prepared to dispute this but the door opened to admit Sarah and Nick.

'That will be all, Matt,' said Marion. 'We seem to have cleared it up.'

'Matt can stay,' said Sarah. 'I know what I've come to hear and I have no objection to his hearing too.'

Marion's voice was all ice. 'Very well. Perhaps you would explain?'

Sarah stood and faced her from the opposite side of the desk. 'I shall let you have my full report, explanation and recommendations as soon as I have completed it, Mrs Terson,' she said.

'I am not prepared to wait.'

'I am afraid you have no alternative,' said Sarah calmly.

The atmosphere in the office became suddenly tense. Nick straightened up from where he had been leaning against the wall. Powell appeared not to react but he had gone very still. All three men were watching Marion, waiting for her explosion. None of them doubted that Sarah had pushed her luck to its limits.

At last Marion spoke. 'Miss Hallam. I put you in a position of unparalleled authority, to ensure the success of an operation which has proved an almost unparalleled failure. If I left you to continue the way you have begun, frankly the Line would be out of business in six months. I have examined every aspect with absolutely meticulous care . . .'

'Are you sure?' said Matt, unable to stop himself.

'Sh, Matt.' Sarah waved a hand at him.

' . . . meticulous care and fairness,' went on Marion, 'before coming to this decision and I have consulted with my managing director and other members of the board. You have left me with no option but to ask for your resignation.'

None of the three men listening to her guessed that behind her businesslike demeanour Marion simply wanted to burst into tears.

The new world that had seemed to hold out such promise to her was collapsing in confusion, and those she had trusted seemed to have betrayed her. Worst of all was the feeling that her failure was a betrayal of George Terson who had trusted her with his life's work. Only Sarah noticed that the hand still playing with the pencil was shaking.

'Now look, Marion. This simply isn't . . .' Nick had been startled into protest.

'Thanks, Nick, but I can deal with this,' said Sarah, pleasantly but firmly. She returned her attention to Marion. 'I am sorry. But no, I shall not resign.'

'I see. Very well. Then you may consider yourself under notice to leave,' said Marion.

'Mrs Terson. I could hardly say that I have enjoyed or am enjoying working for Triangle. Were my personal inclination all, I would gladly leave my post today. But I have begun a job of work and I propose to finish it. My contrast stipulates a month's notice, and there is also a twenty-eight day waiting period before an extra-ordinary general meeting may be called to vote me off the board.' Without warning she turned her stare on Powell. It contained a weight of contempt that made him flinch. 'If I have not analysed and solved this company's problems within a week I shall be extremely surprised. I think that is all. Good day.'

She departed so quickly that they were left staring at the closed door as though she had vanished from their midst by magic. Matt was the first to speak.

'The day that girl leaves, Triangle will be losing the best thing that ever happened to it,' he said deliberately. Then he followed Sarah out.

The last person John had expected to appear while he was staring gloomily down into the waters of the canal, was Barbara Carter. He would rather have been left alone with his thoughts. But he responded to her shy greeting with a friendly 'Hello.'

Barbara spoke in a hesitant voice. 'Did she – did my aunt give you a bad time, sir?'

He smiled. 'I'm not sure I ought to talk about that with you.'

'I'm sorry. A cabin girl ought not to speak to her Captain like that. Forgive me. I still over-step the mark sometimes.' She gave an embarrassed laugh.

'Not so. I was thinking more that I shouldn't be too frank with my boss's niece. Still, never mind. None of it matters much any more, anyway.' He stared moodily down into the waters, and after a moment he noticed that her reflection had joined his.

'You make that sound –' she looked at him for a split second, then returned her gaze quickly to the water '– very negative. If you'll forgive me saying.'

'Perhaps I feel a little negative.'

'You should never feel that,' she said quickly.

He gave her a brief glance, both amused and touched at her lecturing him, but she was not looking at him.

'All for positive thinking?' he said. 'Yes, of course you're right. Only . . .'

'Only what?'

'I was going to say that possibly it's easier to be positive at eighteen than at – my age. Then —' he shrugged '— it sounded patronising. And I thought how boring and depressing I used to find it when I was young and older people said self-pitying things about their own age.'

Abruptly she faced him. 'You are *not* old.'

'I think I said "older"!' he corrected wryly. 'But I felt a hundred and one until you turned up and I think you may be in the process of rejuvenating me.'

'I read in a magazine that it's all nonsense about brain cells dying off . . .'

He began to laugh. 'Hang about, hang about . . .' Then he stopped. She was plainly serious.

She explained earnestly, 'We've got so many thousands and millions of them that they can die off in droves every minute without anyone being any the worse. The only thing that ages people is a feeling of frustration – or boredom – or failure.'

'I've never had the time to be bored.'

'That's one reason why I feel no age gap when I'm with you.'

He looked at her and spoke gently. 'You are a nice lass. Much nicer, if you'll forgive me saying, than ever I realised at the start.'

She turned away again and concentrated hard on the water. He continued speaking, pretending not to see her embarrassment. 'But frustration. Yes. I know all about frustration. And I'm beginning to learn about failure. No, no.' He threw up a protective hand as she whisked round again. 'I know. Negative thinking. I'm learning.'

She laughed, and they turned and began to walk along the canal bank together, in friendly accord.

Chapter 12

With the ship delayed for repairs Sarah found herself with time on her hands. She accompanied Nick to Amsterdam airport to see him off on his flight to London. In the canteen he handed a newspaper to her.

'Triangle down another seventeen pence,' he said. 'How far will this go?'

'Reckon today's the day to buy,' she said calmly.

'What?' He stared at her. 'With the price still plummetting?'

'It'll rise today,' she told him. 'And sharply.'

'How are you so sure? More feminine intuition?'

'Bit more concrete than that. You'll just have to believe me – and wait. Bet me a fiver?'

'On what? Triangle shares zooming up?'

'Thirty-five to forty per cent during trading today,' she said with maddening calm. 'Then a steady upward climb. That's the picture.'

He gave a sharp nervous laugh. 'I'll take you on, but it's daylight robbery.'

'What are you going to say to Warrender?' she asked.

'I don't quite know. I'll have to play it by ear.' His flight was called. 'Here we go. See you later, perhaps. I'll be back tonight, but late.'

He gave her a quick peck on the cheek, and then was gone.

The day stretched before her, but there was a great deal to be packed into it. She started with a visit to the POHL Conference Centre at the Hague. What she found there confirmed her suspicions. With mounting excitement she called in at two other places, where the results of her investigations were also satisfactory. When she finally emerged, her eyes were glinting.

But gradually it was borne in on her that she had a new trouble to cope with, something quite unexpected, something that frightened her. It had started when she left the Hague, and as the day wore on she grew more certain, and more worried. Finally her nerve failed her and she called a taxi. But just as she was stepping in – rescue arrived.

'Matt, you don't know how glad I am to see you.'

He was not an apparition, but really there – accompanied by Tom and Jane, who had just come out of a bar and were in jolly mood.

'What's up?' Matt demanded. 'You O.K.?'

'I'm being followed. There's a man in a car. He's been trailing me from the Hague. I haven't been able to shake him and I don't like whatever he's at.' Tom and Jane approached and she lowered her voice. 'Don't say anything to them, please,' She raised her voice again for a greeting.

Ruthlessly Matt jettisoned Tom and Jane and had got into the taxi with Sarah before she had quite realised what he was doing. She stole a nervous glance in the mirror. The man was still following her.

'Now will you believe me?' she said to Matt.

Somehow, Mrs Carter thought, it wasn't as easy to talk to Marion as she'd hoped it might be. It hadn't helped having to go through that snooty secretary, and see her here in the office, where Marion sat formally behind a desk. And Marion was determined not to help her, she could see that. She took a long pull on her cigarette while she detailed her troubles.

'And you see, I can't seem to make ends meet. Now they say the flat's got rot in the kitchen, and I don't see how I can afford the builders.' Her voice became desperate as Marion's face remained stony. 'I can't afford to do it, and I can't afford not to do it.' Marion remained silent. 'And the rates have gone up again.'

Her heart gave a flutter of hope as her sister-in-law pulled open a drawer. But Marion only produced an ashtray, which she shoved forwards just too late to catch Mrs Carter's ash.

'You could give up smoking,' she said.

'If I could . . .' Mrs Carter shrugged helplessly. 'It wouldn't help all *that* much. A few packets of ciggies . . .'

'Quite apart from the money you pour down your throat,' went on Marion. 'You smelled like a pub when you came in here. What are you actually asking of me?'

Mrs Carter gulped. 'Oh Marion, you know what I'm asking and you know how it upsets me. It makes me feel so – cheap . . .' There was a silence. Marion did not contradict this. 'If your brother were still alive I wouldn't be having to come and ask you.'

'I'm a widow too,' said Marion flatly.

Mrs Carter stared, uncertain whether to laugh or cry at this.

'It is a bit different,' she said at last, in a wavery voice.

Marion's face did not relent. 'I have to fend for myself now George is dead. As I've had to all my life.'

Mrs Carter fought down the words that rose to her lips. The whole family knew how Marion had fended for herself – 'living in sin' with a rich man, that was how. And a quick marriage at the end to get her claws on his money. She'd fended to some purpose, had Marion.

'I've managed without a car,' she said at last.

'Yes, you're well served with public transport where you are.'

'But Marion, do you know what fares cost?'

'Go out less.'

'You're very hard,' Mrs Carter sniffled.

'Life is what you make it. I made something of mine – against odds. You didn't. That's the difference between us.'

'But I'm your sister-in-law.' The words were a despairing wail.

'I will not pay for your damp, nor your rates. What I will do is cover your expenses in coming here, so that your trip, though wasted of course, hasn't cost you anything. In the circumstances I think it's generous of me.'

Mrs Carter took the profferred cheque with a muttered 'Thank you.' There was no fight left in her for further argument. In the doorway she gave Marion a backward glance, looking like a rejected spaniel, fat, unwashed and smelly. Then she went, brushing against David West.

Marion jumped to her feet and strode to the window, longing to throw it open and let in some fresh air. She was amazed at the violence of her own feelings. She had not meant to be cruel, but the sight of her sister-in-law had brought back memories of a life she had hated and fled long ago. She knew she had been worse than cruel. She had been brutal. She could have screamed that David had seen her.

'Who was that?' he said.

'My brother's wife.'

'What did she want?'

'She came to beg. I gave her nothing, over and above the expenses of a wasted trip. It cost her nothing, so she's lucky.'

'You're a tough nut, aren't you?' he said admiringly. 'You could give that poor cow a hundred grand and put it down to tax loss.'

'I could. But I didn't.'

'She looks as if she could even be the head that goes into the gas oven,' he said indifferently.

Marion gave a cynical smile. 'Not here. Look, in effect I'm Barbara's mother. Oh yes, I didn't conceive and bear her, but if it comes to loving . . . my niece means a lot to me. But I'm a realist. I know my Barbara. Right now I'm where the money is and with my niece that counts. One day, perhaps . . .'

He spoke gently, 'Perhaps she'll love you for yourself.'

She smiled. David understood everything.

Later David West returned to his own offices to find Roger Powell waiting for him. Roger was just putting down the phone and his face was annoyed.

'That was Van Dooren,' he said, 'the man I've had following the Hallam woman today. He says he's been spotted and he's on his way back. She seems to have had an active day. First she saw Nick Stevens off on a London flight, after which she visited the POHL conference centre in the Hague.'

'What could that mean?'

'Then the public library, and then the head offices of Cosmopean Hotels.'

'How the hell could she have got onto that?' said David West sharply.

'I don't like it. I'm uneasy. But Christine did warn us.'

'You'll have to resign immediately.' Powell nodded, and David ploughed on, 'Of course you won't suffer financially, that goes without saying. We'll work something out for you, but I want your resignation, on paper, now.'

They would have been yet more alarmed if they could have overheard the conversation taking place between Sarah and Matt at that very moment.

'Tell me something,' she was saying. 'How easy would it be to tamper with the alarm-trip on the oil-filter?'

'Well,' he stretched his legs and leaned back on the park bench, 'it would have to be someone with a technical know-how.'

'Your kind of know-how?'

'Yup. 'Spose so. There are specialists, of course, who service alarms and relays.'

'Is it the kind of thing an 'instrument fitter' could have messed about with?'

'That's what those kind of service engineers call themselves. Why?'

'Because that course Christine was taking at the POHL conference centre – that was in instrument fitting. That's what I found out today.'

'Unusual course for a girl,' he said, whistling.

'D'you remember that's what Jane said when she couldn't remember what course it was Christine had been on all those years ago, when Jane met her? All she remembered was that it was a funny course for a woman. Apparently Christine was training to work on super-tankers. Then West discovered her, and gave her a job with Cosmopean. And that's not all. Cosmopean chain happens to be a wholly-owned subsidiary of D.R.W. Shipping.' She took out a sheet of paper and handed it to him. 'Take a look at the names on the board. That one – Roger Powell. Powell is managing director of Triangle. But he's also effectively a director of D.R.W. When he was appointed here he never disclosed that, and you know why? Because it's illegal.'

'Is it?'

'It is logically – and what's more important, legally – impossible to be on the board of two competing companies. By law, a director is bound to act in the interests of his own company. By the very nature of things, interests are going to conflict. So you see, the man's a fraud.'

He thought for a moment. 'You're going to tell Marion?'

She gave him an enigmatic smile. 'No, Matt. You are.'

Matt would not have known whether to be pleased or sorry had he realised that David West was forestalling him as they spoke. With Powell's resignation from D.R.W. in his pocket, the two of them had returned to her immediately. There was no time to be lost.

Marion was tense and agitated. 'I still don't understand *why* I was not told at the start.' She looked accusingly at Roger. 'It would have seemed natural to inform me.'

'Not really,' David purred. 'I think we simply didn't think it of sufficient import, did we, Roger?'

Roger shook his head. 'Quite immaterial. We had so much else to discuss. After all, the directorship of your outfit, David, was never more than a sinecure, was it?'

'No, nothing. When the penny dropped I simply had to ask Roger to resign from Cosmopean, which he very correctly did.'

'It's all really a matter of formalities,' said Powell smoothly.

'Honestly, Marion,' David took up the refrain, 'it just isn't one of the things you have to worry about. God knows you've got enough else, the way you've been thrown in at the deep end, having to run a really very complex business at a moment's notice. I'm constantly amazed at your acumen and enterprise and the way you seem to get to the crux of things. Aren't you, Roger?'

'Frankly, yes. It just shows the hidden resources people find when they have to pull them out.'

Marion bit her lip for a moment. Naive she might be, but not a complete fool.

'All very flattering,' she said at last, 'but a bit undeserved, I think.'

'Nonsense,' said David heartily. 'You've had a bloody difficult time, Marion, and I think you've coped well. Like one trained for the game, if I may say so.'

He could see she was beginning to soften. 'Will you have that drink now, before we go out to have a bite of dinner together?'

'Well, perhaps,' she smiled. 'Make it a small one. You may think I have a hard business head, but that's where it stops.'

David concentrated on getting the drinks. Powell was gathering up his papers. Each was making determined efforts not to look at the other.

Ted dashed into Sarah's office that evening, bleary but elated.

'I've found him,' he crowed. 'It was Erick Van Dooren. He's a private investigator.'

'That must be the man who was following me,' said Sarah. 'Ted, you're marvellous.'

He went out, his heart singing. He felt he might easily fall in love with Sarah, except that he hadn't yet decided whether an older woman was right for him. Time would tell. And, of course, there was Matt to be considered . . .

Charles Woodhouse had decided it was time to do something about his relationship with Barbara. Even to him it was obvious that he had lost ground with that little lady and the sooner he made it up the better.

He managed to accompany her (tag along would have been a better expression) on a shopping expedition in Amsterdam, and took the opportunity to remark, 'John's old enough to be your father, you know.'

'Charles, does it occur to you that perhaps that's exactly how I see him – as a father?'

'Don't believe you.'

'Your prerogative.'

'You see, I thought that you and I – well – were going along very nicely together.'

'We were. We are.' She gave him a kindly smile. 'Incidentally, you're old enough to be my father too.'

'Biologically perhaps, yes, but that's entirely different.'

'Of course it is.' She was sending him up. 'Look! Don't look so disappointed. I'm not the only fish in the sea.'

'Oh, I know that. My disappointment is because you've changed. I thought, perhaps, once, that you were my type.'

'And I'm not now?'

He gave a slight shrug. 'I have my doubts.'

'Then we both should be happy.'

'So you're not seeing the geriatric today then?'

'Mm?'

'The captain.'

'Ah, but I am. We're playing tennis.'

'Tennis! He'll have a heart attack. With a bit of luck . . .'

'Yoo hoo, Barbara! – Found you.'

Charles groaned. Judith Harper was advancing on them, and Barbara was showing every sign of pleasure.

'Got one. Hope it's the right size.' Judith pulled a tennis skirt out of her bag.

'Judith's going to umpire,' said Barbara.

Judith beamed at Charles. 'I did think of having a game but I'm not quite so quick as I used to be. What's the matter, Mr Woodhouse? It should be fun. Why don't you come along?'

'No thanks, I think I'll sit this one out.'

But fate had not quite finished dealing blows to Charles Woodhouse for one day. As he walked off, he clearly heard Barbara say to Judith, 'Don't worry, he's getting a bit past it these days.'

But at least he was spared from overhearing another conversation that took place between Barbara and John later in the day, when they were enjoying a cooling drink between games. Barbara had delivered herself of an opinion of Charles that did not flatter him.

'Jealous? Charles?' said John, divided between amusement and irritation.

'It sounded like it to me. He thought he and I were . . .' she made a flapping gesture with her hand.

'And now . . .?'

'He thinks that you and I are becoming – how do they say? – an item.'

'People are funny,' he mused. 'I mean, it's been marvellous being with you, I'm not going to pretend otherwise. Perhaps because . . . I wonder. What do you think?'

'When Charles said that you were old enough to be my father, I said, hadn't it occurred to him that that was perhaps exactly how I saw it?'

He nodded. 'Makes sense. You never having a father to remember . . .'

'And you more or less losing your daughter.'

'Well . . .' he shrugged, but said no more. Barbara was too young to understand the difference between a father you'd never known and a daughter you remembered with searing clarity.

'Exactly,' she said.

'All very reasonable.'

'And well thought out. Yes. Except,' she said unexpectedly, 'that it doesn't happen to be true. Right, one more set. And this time I won't let you win.'

The first thing Nick Stevens did when Sarah met him at Amsterdam airport was to hand her a fiver.

'You won our bet,' he said. 'Triangle shares are up 37p on yesterday's trading.' He regarded her quick smile with a mixture of affection and exasperation. 'Now the only thing I want to know is how you knew.'

Sarah tapped the side of her nose. 'Ah. That'd be telling.'

But she told him, and had the pleasure of watching his eyes pop. After that they went, by mutual consent, to inform Marion. They found her in her office, elated at the news and inclined to resent their serious faces.

'Why isn't everyone leaping about and swinging from the chandeliers?' she demanded irritably.

'It is exciting . . .' said Nick reluctantly.

'All right, tell me. Why did Triangle's shares inexorably slide down the scale and then, suddenly, this morning, shoot up again?'

'David West,' said Nick simply.

'Pardon?' Marion stared.

'Because of David West,' he repeated.

It seemed to convey nothing to Marion. She looked from one to the other.

'I'm afraid so,' said Sarah.

'*Afraid*?' Marion demanded.

Nick began to explain. 'Triangle's shares fell because of declining public confidence, right?' Marion nodded and he went on, 'Because of bad publicity. The sabotage, etc. etc.'

'I know!' she said impatiently.

'All of which happened *after* Triangle had gone public.'

'So what has this got to do with David?'

'I'm going to tell you. But you must listen until I've finished – no interruptions. He was responsible for the crisis.'

'I don't . . .'

'I said, wait until I'd finished,' said Nick in a sharper voice than he had ever used to her before. 'Those series of crisis were deliberately precipitated by David West for the sole purpose of making the shares fall in value. On top of that he sold his holding, ensuring that the fall in value turned into an avalanche. So then – are you listening? – when they were at rock bottom, at their cheapest, yesterday, he bought them all back, plus a great many more, for precisely the same sum of money that he obtained for selling them. The shares – naturally, if you understand the workings of the market – shot up again. So there we are.' He opened his arms as though seeking to encompass his whole explanation in one gesture. 'David West, by that very simple ploy, increased his holdings considerably, and, of course, his power in the company. That has been his idea – his plan – from the very beginning.'

Marion was silent a moment as though waiting to be sure he'd finished. Her eyes gave nothing away. 'I don't believe it,' she said at last.

'It's a matter of record,' said Sarah. 'It can't be denied.'

'That he bought and sold shares, yes, I'll have to take your word for it that that's correct. But not that he was responsible for the fall in the first place, the crisis that caused it . . .' She shook her head. 'No, never.' She caught the despairing look that passed between Nick and Sarah and said urgently, 'There must have been a reason.'

'I've told you,' said Nick.

'A *different* explanation.'

'Christine Harris . . .' Sarah began.

'I beg your pardon?' Marion turned sharply towards her.

'The deputy purser on board the *Anglia* was the saboteur,' Sarah explained.

Marion threw up her hands. 'More suppositions! More accusations!'

'She used to work for Cosmopean hotels, which tells us something,' said Sarah. 'The reporter who wrote all that damaging material . . . his wife testified that Christine Harris bribed him to write that article.'

Nick spent yesterday in London talking to Penny Warrender. She spilled all the beans.'

'All right, I must accept all of that as a possibility, but I still don't see what it all has to do with David West.'

'I've told you,' Nick said angrily.

She flared back at him, 'And I've told you that I don't believe you.'

Suddenly Nick lost his temper. 'Oh, this is impossible. If you won't see what's held up in front of your nose then . . . O.K. I've had it up to here with you.'

'Nick . . .' For the first time a note of uncertainty entered Marion's voice.

'You're so besotted with Mr David West that you've lost the power to reason intelligently.'

He stormed out before she could answer. Sarah followed him immediately, leaving Marion alone with her thoughts, and the wall chart with its climbing line – which now seemed a mockery.

It was night before she saw David. At her urgent request he arrived at the suite she occupied when she was in Amsterdam. He stood there looking elegant and superb, and her heart turned over within her. She uttered a silent prayer that his explanation would be a good one.

'This is going to be a little bit difficult,' he said when she told him why she had wanted to see him.

'I don't want it to be difficult,' she said hastily. 'Especially for you. You know what confidence I have . . .'

'Thank you . . .' He smiled warmly.

'It's just . . .' Her courage failed her.

'Why did I sell the shares?'

'And then buy them back.' She waited. 'David –' she said in a pleading voice.

'Sorry. It's not easy to –' he frowned. Then he seemed to decide something. 'O.K. It was because of you.'

'Me?'

'You must have some inkling about my – feelings – for you.'

She did not reply, but when she smiled he felt encouraged to go on. 'It seems to me that we get on so well, are sensitive to each other as people, and . . . I've never been afraid in business to come right out and say what I feel. I didn't want you to think that business had anything to do with the way I felt about you.'

'I don't quite . . .'

'The way to prove it was to sell all my shares,' he said quickly. 'Well, most of them. That way . . .'

'But then – please, I'm not doubting anything you say . . .'

'Why buy them back again?' he finished for her.

'It does seem . . .'

'Contradictory? Yes, it must. The point is, I sold my shares thinking only of . . .' he indicated first her then himself. He seemed almost too abashed to go on. 'And – what a confession for a business man to make – I didn't take the effect it might have on the company into the equation at all.' He gave an eloquent shrug. 'As soon as I realised what was happening – the possibly disastrous consequences it was having – I bought them straight back.' Marion nodded. Her eyes were shining again. 'Sorry,' he finished, 'it was very unprofessional. And, I pride myself, untypical.'

The look he gave her was almost sheepish, the look of a schoolboy caught stealing apples. His grin invited her to share the joke against him. She could not resist. With an impulsive movement she laid a hand over his.

'David . . .' she said softly.

She had been half aware of a faint noise but had pushed it to the back of her mind. Now the sounds resolved themselves into two voices, one of which she recognised as Barbara's. There seemed to be an argument, accompanied by some scuffling. It culminated in a shriek from Barbara, and in another moment the door was flung violently open and the girl stood on the threshold. Her face was tear-stained and full of hatred.

'There you are,' she said, her eyes fixed on Marion.

'What do you want?' Marion said angrily.

Barbara spoke with deadly calm. 'What does it feel like to be a murderess?'

'I beg your pardon?' Marion stared.

'My mother is dead!' Barbara waited, looking straight into Marion's blank pale face. 'Didn't you hear me?' she said, more loudly.

'Of course. I'm sorry, I . . .'

'Sorry? You might as well have held her nose and poured the pills down. She wanted a little bit of help, that's all.' Barbara flung out an arm to the room about her. 'Look what you've got, and you couldn't give her just a little when she was desperate.'

Marion began to recover her voice but her words had an air of frantic flailing. 'Oh no, look, I can't tell you how sorry I . . . but, Barbara, it wasn't . . .'

'Read it for yourself.' Barbara tossed a piece of paper into Marion's lap. 'Suicide note, that's called.' Barbara's voice rose to a scream. 'And as far as I'm concerned you can do the same thing yourself. Because I'm finished.' The last words almost vanished in her tears. Then the door banged and she was gone. Marion sat motionless, her head bent over the note until the slamming of the front door announced that Barbara would not return. She was trembling.

'Marion, what do I say . . .?' said David beside her.

'Nothing,' she said in a dazed voice. 'There's nothing you can possibly say that'll . . . nothing . . .' She seemed suddenly to become capable of movement and made as if to rise. 'I must comfort that child . . . I must . . .' Tears were pouring down her face as the truth began to sink in.

She found herself pushed gently back onto the sofa, and somehow David's arm was round her. It was too much for her fragile control. She dropped her head into her hands and sobbed with abandon.

'It's not right that you should have to take it all,' he said in a quiet voice, 'all on your own. I've been feeling this for a long time Marion. You need someone strong, to share, to take the load.'

She looked at him, tears pouring down her face.

Chapter 13

'Well?' John looked up sharply at Jane's arrival on the bridge.

'No sign, I'm afraid.'

'Have you tried her cabin?'

'Well, of course. There was no sign that her bunk had been slept in all night.'

'Oh hell. And everywhere's been searched?'

'Everywhere that she could legitimately be – assuming, of course, that she's not deliberately hiding.'

'That wouldn't make sense.'

'Is this a private worry?' said Matt. 'Or can anyone join in?'

'It's Barbara Carter,' said John. 'She's disappeared.'

'But people have stayed out before . . .'

John interrupted him. 'Her mother killed herself yesterday.'

'Oh hell.'

'She was given the news,' said Jane, 'and no-one's seen her since.'

'I'm going out to look for her,' said John suddenly.

'Amsterdam's a big place,' said Matt.

'I know that. But firstly I can't just stay here. And secondly I do have an inkling of an idea . . .'

He was gone almost before the words were out of his mouth. Matt shrugged. He had come to tell John the good news that the ship would be ready to move the next day. Now he felt spare and useless. He sought refuge in the ship's pub, with Nick and Sarah, and gave them the gist of what had happened.

'I can understand John's reaction, but how the hell he thinks he can find her in a city like Amsterdam, God only knows,' he said.

'Still, it's an attempt,' said Sarah.

'Good on him! It'll be better for her if John finds her, rather than some copper in a police car with its siren blaring. Anyway . . .' Matt broke off.

'Yes, let's get down to business. Christine Harris!' said Nick. 'I think we can implicate her all right in the sabotage, the bribery . . .

And we can get David West and Roger Powell in the company malpractice deal. But the problem . . .'

'Is how to link them together?' said Sarah.

'Right.'

'And that we have to do?'

'For the sake of the company, certainly. If we're going to prove that what's been going wrong lately was all a plot . . .'

'And what about Marion?' said Matt.

Sarah pulled a face. 'I don't think she'll see reason while she's besotted with David West. Not a chance.'

'What a silly lady,' said Matt, not unkindly.

'Oh, I don't know, Matt,' said Nick, 'I mean, running a vast organisation like Triangle! Well, it'd be tough on someone who's trained, worked their way up. But suddenly, from nothing; to be thrown in at the deep end . . .? Well . . .'

Sarah nodded. 'I agree. It must seem that without David to rely on she'd just sink in a morass of paper and meetings and decisions . . .'

'As far as she's concerned, he's the cat's whiskers,' said Nick. 'The feller with everything at his fingertips.'

'So where do we go from here?'

Jane's voice interrupted them. 'Ah, there you are.' She came and sat down beside them. 'I was just passing the purser's office, and the phone was ringing – and . . .'

'No Christine?' said Sarah.

'No Christine,' Jane observed.

Sarah threw a significant look at Nick, but Jane went on; 'So, being the dutiful lady I am, I answered the phone and it was Marion's secretary. She wants Matt, Tom and Charles to report to her office.'

'What will you say to her?' said Sarah.

'The truth,' said Matt. 'What does it matter? I can get a job anywhere!'

Instinct took John to the tennis courts where he and Barbara had played, and instinct had not deceived him. He saw her long before she saw him. Her eyes were staring blindly into the distance, and she had huddled her coat round her as though seeking shelter. She looked startled when he sat beside her.

'How did you know I'd be here?'

'Guessed. You've been here all night, haven't you?' She nodded.

'Had a lot of thinking to do, eh? Yes, well, often it helps to get away on your own for a while. Sort a few things out.'

'Trouble is, I haven't sorted anything out. It's all as confused as it was before.'

'I'm a very good listener,' he offered.

She didn't look at him but stared straight ahead, speaking as though the words were wrenched out of her. 'I was always such a bitch to her. My mother. Right from school days, to adolescence, to, well, all my life. All right, so she wasn't the best mother the world's ever known, but she had her troubles. I mean, she really had her troubles, and I . . .' she broke off and shook her head.

'Most people feel guity about their parents some time or another,' said John gently.

'I've got reason.'

'So have most people.' She looked at him quickly. 'Believe me. And it's only after they're . . .'

'Dead. It's all right, I've faced up to that.'

'Yes, dead, that they sit down and think, oh God, if only I'd done so-and-so, said this or that . . .'

She touched his arm in a timid gesture of thanks.

'I suppose, though, the main reason for my overnight vigil . . .' She gave a slight smile at her own slightly dramatic words 'was to try and exorcise my feelings for Marion.'

'Exorcise?'

'Hatred,' said Barbara flatly. 'Now that's true. I hate her, always have really. And now, after the way she treated Mother . . . It doesn't seem possible, does it? To have that much money and turn her sister-in-law down, when all she needed was a hand-out?' Her voice was harsh on the last words.

'You mustn't blame Marion.'

'I know. That's why I sat here all night. The thing is, I do. Maybe, one day . . .'

'I'm sure.'

'You're very understanding. So? What happens now?'

'Anything you like,' he said. 'To a point. For the immediate future, you can stay working on the ship.'

'Marion wouldn't . . .'

'Marion may be the biggest shareholder, but she's still only one of many. There's only one person who can actually sack you, and that's Sarah Hallam.'

'I know. But what happens when she leaves?'

'You can face that problem when it happens. Might be years yet.'

'She's working out her notice now.'

John looked at her sharply '*Is she?*'

'Didn't you know?'

He shook his head. 'How do *you* know?'

'Sarah told me.'

'You're quite close to her, then?'

'Only recently. Since I asked for my job back. I found out that I liked the lady. I admire her. A lot.'

He surprised himself by saying, 'And me.'

'I wish . . . well, this'll really sound adolescent, but what the hell! I wish I could be more like her. Sure, certain, unbending. Oh, I don't know. So back to my question: what will happen to me?'

'Anything you want. Look, if you're worried about college, you know, money, things like that, well you're not to. Funny thing – and I mean it, really funny thing – is that, in point of fact, I'm a millionaire.' She stared at him and he gave a rueful, self-mocking smile. 'It sounds even more peculiar to me than it does to you.'

'I didn't know.'

'On paper anyway. You see, I own five per cent of the company's shares. Doesn't sound much of a percentage, does it? But if you work it out . . .'

She looked down, lost in thought. After a moment she shook her head. 'Thank you for your offer but I don't want to live on people's backs any more.'

'You wouldn't be. It means absolutely nothing to me, money. And – look – there would be no strings. At all.'

'Thank you, but . . .'

'No thanks?' He was disappointed.

'No thanks.'

With a sudden resolute movement she got to her feet.

'Barbara . . .'

'I'll be all right. Thanks for your help.' She gave a self-depreciating shrug. 'It was, believe me.'

She moved off a few steps. He rose to follow her. Suddenly she stopped, turned back and ran to him. She threw her arms round his neck, kissing him hard but briefly on the lips. The she turned away again and burst into violent tears.

John stared at her, as completely lost as he had ever been in his life. After a moment he put a gentle arm round her shoulders and led her away.

In Marion's office Charles, Tom and Matt found themselves sitting side by side, like three schoolboys facing the headmistress. Marion regarded them from the other side of her desk, while David West stood at the window, eyeing the scene loftily. Marion's face was very pale, but she was in command of herself.

'Grasping the nettle, that's what this is called,' she said. 'I want to know – no prevarications – exactly where you three gentlemen stand.'

'On what issue, Mrs Terson?' said Charles.

'On the issue of Triangle, D.R.W., the sabotage, the bad publicity . . . need I go on?'

She waited, but there was silence while she looked impatiently from one face to the other.

'Shall I start?' said Matt when he could bear it no longer.

'Why not, Mr Taylor?' said Marion.

'I don't like any of it. I never have. The owner of D.R.W. being on the board of Triangle. And now talk of an amalgamation. An amalgamation that isn't.'

'What does that mean?' said Marion sharply.

'You know exactly what it means. It's really a take-over. Disguised, certainly, but a take-over none the less.'

'Who taking over whom?'

'You know.'

'*Tell me.*'

Matt shrugged. After all, why not as well be hung for a sheep as a lamb? Whatever he told Marion, there was going to be trouble unless it was what she wanted to hear. So he might as well be frank, and to hell with it. 'D.R.W. never had any intention for this to be a merger of partners. The idea from the start, was for D.R.W. to take over Triangle,' he said.

'David?' She looked at him.

'My shoulders are broad,' he said with an imperturbable smile. 'Anyway, people have the right to their own opinions.'

'Even if it does mean the chop for saying something unpopular,' said Matt.

Marion began, 'There's no question of . . .'

'Of course not,' Matt interrupted her with some irony.

'All right, David won't speak for himself, so I'll do it for him. I'd like to point out, here and now, quite categorically, that from the start Mr West's interest has been the company. What is best for the company is all that concerns him.'

'That's what he's told you,' said Matt, keeping his temper.

'I'm not a fool.'

Matt spoke carefully. 'In normal circumstances, no. But when personal relationships start taking over, then, to say the least, judgements get screwed up.' Matt turned a cynical eye on David West who was listening impassively, then looked back to Marion and said bluntly, 'He could scuttle the whole Triangle fleet and you'd think the sun shone out of him.'

'How dare you!' Marion flared. 'That's the most insulting thing that I've . . .'

'You asked for the truth. Sometimes the truth can sound insulting.'

She regained her temper. 'Anything else you want to say?'

He gave a little mirthless smile. 'I should have thought I'd said my last, wouldn't you?'

Marion regarded him stonily for a moment before addressing Charles. 'Do you agree, Mr Woodhouse?'

'With what?'

'With Mr Taylor's interpretation of events.'

'I'd say that Matt's seeing a little bit of what he wants to see.' Charles spoke cautiously. He wasn't certain yet which way this would go.

'Yes. I thought you might say that,' said Matt with a grin that showed he fully appreciated Charles' tactics.

'You've taken upon yourself to say what you think, you must allow me the same right,' said Charles heatedly. 'I really do think that, with the best will in the world, Matt's taken a totally wrong view of what's going on.'

'Who's side are you on?' Matt demanded.

'The company's, of course,' said Charles smoothly.

'*Which means?*'

'As far as this afternoon is concerned, Mrs Terson's.'

'Thank you. Mr Kelly?' said Marion.'

The phone rang. Marion looked at David.

'I'll take it next door, Marion,' he said, and left them.

'Yes, Mr Kelly?' Marion turned her attention to the only man who had so far kept silent.

Tom spoke reluctantly. 'I have to agree with Matt. In general.'

'Thank you. In fact, I'd like to thank all of you for coming and being so – frank. At least I know now where I stand.'

'That's it, is it?' said Matt.

'For the time being. Perhaps you'd like to stay for a minute or two longer, Mr Woodhouse?'

To her intense annoyance she saw Matt and Tom exchange a glance and a barely perceptible smile.

'See you back at the shop, Charles,' said Matt with a jeering grin, and left.

Marion smiled at Charles. 'May I offer you a drink?' she said.

When the three of them were alone David, Marion and Charles lifted their glasses in joint salute.

'To the success of the company,' they all said.

And Marion added, 'In spite of everything. I asked Charles to wait behind so that you and he could meet officially,' she added to David. 'I always believe in being direct. What do you think of him?'

David nodded towards Charles, whose eyebrows had shot up. 'From all the information I've heard, I gather that he's a fine officer. And from what I've seen in the last half hour he has his head screwed on the right way too. Quite a fair combination.

'That's very nice of you to say so,' said Charles cautiously.

'A very good judge of character, Mr West,' Marion added.

'So I believe,' Charles nodded.

'There's a reason for all this, Mr – Charles,' she went on. 'For asking you to wait behind, for discussing your attributes in front of your face. You see, there's a very strong chance of Triangle and D.R.W. merging.'

'In that respect Mr Taylor was right,' David West conceded.

'It'll be the biggest company in the North Sea,' said Marion.

'Sounds very exciting.'

'It will be,' said David. 'Believe me.'

'And there'll certainly be a place on board – a very important place – for good, loyal officers.' Marion looked at him as she spoke.

When she was alone again Marion sat with her hands in her lap, staring ahead of her. She felt desperately lonely. She was fighting off the memories of Barbara bursting in on her the night before, fighting off the accusing voice that told her she could have prevented her sister-in-law's death. The only memory she wanted was David West telling her he would shoulder her burdens.

Marriage. Something in her shied away from the thought of re-marrying so soon, but she could no longer go on alone, and David was so strong and dependable. Call it love, call it what you like, but she needed to rely on him now the others all seemed to be turning against her.

The telephone broke into her thoughts. It was Nick Stevens. This was the first she had heard from him since he stormed out of her office, but his voice was friendly and cheerful, asking her to have dinner with him that night. She smiled as her heart eased a little. It would be good to have Nick back on her side now he was showing signs of seeing sense.

'I'd love to,' she said, and she made her voice especially warm to show there were no hard feelings. 'Where did you say?'

He named the restaurant – one of the most expensive in Amsterdam.

'I'll be there.'

As she left her office and went out into the sunshine she was almost happy again.

Nick felt sick at heart as he put down the phone. He had heard the cheerfulness in Marion's voice and his whole being revolted at what he was doing to her. But he had no choice. Marion must be made to see sense, at whatever cost, before she destroyed the whole company, and now that chance had thrown the perfect opportunity in his way it would be criminal to pass it up.

It was so simple. A phone call from Sarah to say that Ted had been doing a bit of eavesdropping on a phone-call by Christine Harris, a call in which she had agreed to meet someone for dinner . . .

Christine never took her eyes of David West as he gave the waiter their order. Somehow she felt safer these days when she could see him. Of course he loved her, of *course* he did – but still . . . when she added up the things she could be caught for – libel, criminal sabotage, industrial sabotage, bribery – while he was still safe in his limousines and his board-rooms and his private planes . . .

She'd called him that morning in sheer panicky desperation, and to her surprise he'd immediately asked – no, *begged* – her to have dinner with him. That wasn't like David. Normally he tried to keep their meetings as few as possible, 'for safety'. But today he'd been anxious to see her.

She wondered just how much connection there was between that fact and a conversation she'd had with Roger Powell that morning. She didn't remember much about it, only the sound of her own terrified voice screaming, 'Don't forget, I can blow the whistle on the lot of you.' And the look of alarm that had washed over his face. He'd spent the next ten minutes trying to placate her. And what's the betting he'd got onto the phone to David the minute she was gone?

And here she was with David now, being entertained at Amsterdam's most expensive restaurant, and David was saying smoothly, 'You see? I told you it would all work out. And sooner than we could possibly have thought. Now that Marion's agreed to a merger I'll soon have complete control of the North Sea.'

'But you've only . . .'

'What do you mean, "only"?' he chided her gently. 'I have a hundred per cent of D.R.W. and I'll have twenty per cent of Triangle. That'll mean sixty per cent of the new company. A controlling interest.'

'But that's still not the whole of the North Sea.'

'All right. But you just wait and see. This is just a start.' He looked into her eyes. 'For the company, for you, and for us.'

'You mean that?' she breathed.

'Of course I mean that. As soon as everything's signed, sealed and delivered, I'll ditch that boring Terson woman, and you and I'll get married.'

He took her hand and smiled into her eyes in a way that made her heart seem to stop. After a moment he drew her towards him and kissed her.

Neither of them saw Marion Terson standing beside Nick Stevens, staring, white-faced and motionless as though rooted to the spot. Nick did not look at Marion's face. He could not bear to. After a moment she spoke in a dead voice.

'You did this deliberately, didn't you?' When he didn't answer, she repeated, 'Didn't you?'

He sighed. 'All right, yes, Marion, it was the only way to make you see sense.'

She was gone so quietly that at first he did not realise she had moved. He was looking across at David West and Christine, who were clinking glasses filled with champagne. He wanted to throw up.

By the following morning the ship's repairs were finished, there were only minor trials left to do, and Matt reported that they would be ready to sail the day after. Good news though this was, it caused almost as many problems as it solved.

'For a start, what are you going to do about Christine Harris?' Matt asked Sarah.

'There's no problem about a purser,' she told him. 'Dougie Evans is back.'

'Are you firing her?'

'No, she's going to resign.'

'Has she said so?'

'Not yet, but she will. It's going to make things very difficult. We still don't have any proof on the sabotage issue – and worse than that, there's still no way of imputing the responsibility to David West.'

'Except that they're having an affair.'

'So they're having an affair,' she shrugged. 'What does that prove? That Christine, on some misguided impulse – and totally unprompted by West – sabotaged the ship out of love for him. Leastways, that's what I'd suggest if I were West's defence lawyer.'

'Mmmmmm.' He turned to go.

'Have I said something?' she said, slightly hurt.

'Yeah, you've said a lot. And all of it frightens the hell out of me.'

She frowned, not understanding. 'Matt?'

Then he did something that took her totally by surprise. He came back and took her face between his hands, kissed her firmly on the lips, and released her gently. He was smiling. Flustered, she looked away.

'Why did you do that?' she whispered.

'To confuse you. I feel a lot better now.'

She watched him go, trying to calm herself. She wondered what he'd say if he knew how well he'd succeeded.

She forced her mind back to her work. It was the way she had always got the better of her sensations, and surely it wouldn't fail her now. After a moment's reluctance, it didn't. She managed to make her way towards the purser's office with a fair assumption of steadiness. There she confronted Christine with the evidence that it was she who had sabotaged the ship. Even to her own ears the evidence didn't amount to much. She would have to frighten the girl. She knew she was succeeding as soon as she asked Christine to account for what she was doing at the time.

'How could I possibly remember that?' Christine blustered.

'I think you could. If you tried.'

'That's, what, two weeks ago? Three weeks?'

'The eleventh of this month.'

'Nothing. There, look.'

'I hardly expected you to record it in the purser's log.'

'Record what?' Christine's face was a careful blank.

'Let me try to jog your memory. You were on duty, here, from six o'clock in the evening. At ten to nine, you spoke briefly to Barry Peters. Less than a minute later, the first officer, Mr Woodhouse, approached you and you asked him to relieve you for a moment. Twenty minutes later, Mr Woodhouse and Mr Kelly were discussing the fact that you hadn't returned. Five minutes later, there was an engine failure. Five minutes after that, you returned to your post.'

'What are you trying to suggest?'

'I'm asking you what you were doing between ten to, and twenty past, nine?'

Christine stared into the air as though trying to think. 'Yes, I do remember!' she said suddenly. 'I was taking a shower.'

'You asked Mr Woodhouse to relieve you so that you could take a shower?' said Sarah sceptically.

'No, I asked Mr Woodhouse to relieve me so that I could . . . Look, I don't know that I care to go into personal details with you.'

'All right, let's discuss something less personal. The POHL conference centre . . .'

She had the satisfaction of seeing Christine grow pale. 'Why don't you just say I sabotaged the engine?' the girl snapped.

Sarah smiled coldly. 'You acknowledge then that your course in instrument fitting might have been relevant? So far as I'm aware, instrument failure was never officially recorded.'

Christine tightened her lips. She was visibly shaken by her lapse, but it was not enough to make her crumble. 'And you hope to be able to prove this absurd . . . suggestion?' she said with a fair assumption of scorn.

'You had the means, the opportunity and the motive. No other person . . .'

Christine broke in derisively, 'What possible motive could I have?'

'The motivation was fairly complex – but you did it, basically, because you were asked to. By your lover, David West.'

There was a moment of dead silence. 'Ridiculous!' Christine sounded as though her mouth had suddenly gone dry.

'All right, we'll try another tack. Kevin Warrender.'

'What about him?'

'I have two statements, one each from himself and his wife, to the effect that articles written and published about this ship were neither in good faith nor the public interest, but were prompted by three separate payments, for which you are cordially thanked.'

The office was very quiet. Sarah kept her eyes on Christine's face. Not a feature moved but in the stillness Sarah knew she had won.

'What do you propose to do about it?' said Christine at last.

'For the time being, nothing.'

'I shall resign, of course.'

'Of course. But if you fail to serve out your notice, this company will sue you for breach of contract.'

Christine gaped. 'Miss Hallam . . . why aren't you . . .? If you believe all this, why haven't you informed the police?'

'Because I'm not concerned with the law and I'm not particularly interested in revenge. I just want to run an efficient company. If your prosecution helps toward that end, then you'll be prosecuted, make no mistake about it.'

When she had gone Christine stared at the telephone, trying to control the shaking in her hands. She longed to talk to David, but would he be angry if she called him now? Surely not, after the things he had said to her yesterday. She seized the receiver and dialled . . .

'May I speak to Mr West please? Do you know when he'll be back? Yes, it's Miss Harris. I need to speak to him urgently. Thank you.'

She slammed down the receiver and sat staring into space, her heart thudding.

David West too had had a somewhat fraught morning. His early attempts to get hold of Marion had failed. She was neither in her hotel nor her office, and no-one could tell him where she was. That worried him because it wasn't like Marion, and it thwarted his instinct to have control of everyone and everything all the time. Finally, when he was beginning to get really nervous, she had strolled casually into his office, smartly dressed and smiling.

'Marion, my dear – I've been trying to get hold of you all morning.'

'Yes, they told me.'

'But where've you been? I must confess I've been concerned – no, worried. I've been very worried, Marion.'

She seated herself. 'You're too kind to me, David. What could there possibly be to worry about?'

'That you'd been taken ill, perhaps, or that there'd been some terrible crisis. All sorts of fanciful notions come to mind when you . . . care about somebody.'

'Well, as you can see, I'm all in one piece, if a little breathless. I never realised what a pretty place Amsterdam is.'

'Oh Marion, you should have told me. I'd've accompanied you – what a lovely way to pass a morning!'

'And drag you away from your first love?' she teased him.

'My first love?'

She indicated the office. 'This.'

'This?' he laughed. 'Just a means to an end. It's a fool who lives to work. The wise man works to live.'

'I'll hold you to that. You can abandon it all, dismiss it from your mind . . and take me to lunch.'

'There.' He made a grandiose gesture. 'Consider it abandoned. Where would you like to go?'

'Not now!' she laughed. 'It's only eleven o'clock . . . and anyway, I must change.'

'No, wait!' He lifted the phone. 'Sharon? Will you tell Arthur to bring the Daimler round to the front of the office? No, to take Mrs Terson back to her hotel.' He replaced the receiver. 'And you'll be ready when?'

'One o'clock?'

'Arthur will be waiting for you. I'll come down with you.'

'No, no, no . . . I found my own way in, didn't I? You get back to your work.'

She was gone, with one last bright smile that had in it a hint of coquetry. As soon as West had shut the door behind her his face sagged into an expression of annoyance.

'Did you catch all that?' he said to Powell who had come in from an adjacent office.

'Eating out of your hand. Solitary walks in the morning? I thought only schoolgirls got it like that.'

'Yeah, well, that's love for you.' West rubbed his chin. 'All this old world charm gives me a pain in the jaw. Look, get onto Watson, will you – tell him I can't make lunch. He'll blow a fuse, but it can't be helped.'

He was there at the restaurant before her, rising to her with a courtly gesture as she swept in. She did not speak a word until he had ordered a large and elaborate meal, then she leaned back and regarded him over the rim of her glass. Her eyes were shining and almost flirtatious.

'How many meals is this, then, David? I feel there can't be many more restaurants left in Amsterdam.'

'Then we shall have to spread our wings a bit. Go further afield. Move out in ever-increasing circles until we've done a gourmet's tour of Europe.'

'Today Amsterdam, tomorrow the world. I'm sure all this eating doesn't do my figure any good.'

He took her hand. 'Marion, you're perfect – and change as you will, you'll *still* be perfect.' He proffered a cocktail stick with a cherry on the end. She leaned forward and pulled the cherry off with her teeth and he flourished the stick like a sword. 'And any man says Nay and I'll run him through . . .'

'Do you really mean that?' she asked with an odd little laugh.

'Try me.'

'And how would you have felt if, when George had died, he'd left everything to his daughter? And I'd just had the cottage in Suffolk?'

He closed his eyes in seeming ecstasy. 'A cottage in Suffolk? I'd've been enchanted. Marion, how could you ask? Am I so poor that I need to . . . to play the gigolo? Is that what you're asking?'

'Of course not.'

'D.R.W. Shipping is no smaller than Triangle – and it's all mine. One hundred per cent.'

'Now I've offended you.' She laid an anxious hand on his.

'Of course not,' he laughed.

'Do you believe in love? Or is that just an adolescent fantasy? I mean is it possible that at our age . . .'

Gently he interrupted her. 'Marion . . . Marion . . . Is that what you want to hear?'

'Please.'

'I'd've said it a thousand times already if it hadn't seemed . . .'

'What?'

'Presumptuous.' He looked into her eyes. 'I love you, Marion.'

'You do . . . want to marry me?'

'Want to . . .? Oh, Marion! Say you will and I shall be the happiest man in Holland. Holland? Dammit, the happiest man in the world!'

'Would Friday suit you?'

For a moment he did not realise what she had said. He stared stupidly, examining her words, one by one, trying to force them to yield up a meaning. 'Friday?' he said as last.

'It would make you happy and me happy. Why put off all that happiness?' she explained brightly.

'There'd need to be arrangements.' He began to recover his

tongue. 'We'd want it to be something of an occasion. Something worthy of us . . .'

'Just a simple service would be worthy of us. Something simple and . . . sincere.'

'Oh absolutely, but . . .' For the first time something in her face made him uneasy. 'Marion . . .?'

'That's what I'd like, David. Something simple, sincere . . . and soon.' Her voice came down hard on the last word, but her face remained full of bland naivety.

'Oh, and me – believe me,' he said quickly. 'It's a beautiful idea. My only regret is – and I say this to my shame – that I put in hand all the arrangements without first . . .'

'What arrangements?' she cut in.

'For the wedding. It seemed to me that . . . well, that . . .'

'The wedding?'

'Yes. In some respects, you see, I suppose I'm an old-fashioned man, and I was brought up to certain . . .'

'When?' she interrupted him again.

'It was to have been a surprise – a lavish surprise, admittedly, but with careful preparation . . . a formal proposal at a suitably romantic moment . . . I've been very guilty of planning, I'm afraid, when perhaps a younger man would have swept you off your feet in a moment of uncontrolled eagerness. You must forgive me.'

She smiled. 'How sweet of you. How very sweet.'

'I didn't dare presume that I could court you, woo you, win your trust and affection in so short a while – indeed, it seemed presumptuus to make the arrangements so early as the autumn.'

'By which time our companies would have merged.'

He shrugged. 'Indeed, though . . .'

' . . . business is of little consequence,' she supplied for him.

'Quite.'

She leaned back and regarded him. 'You're an incredible man, David.'

'Not really.'

'Oh, but you are. I've known a lot of people from various walks of life . . . different people . . . different situations . . . but I can honestly say that in a lifetime . . . and I'm not a young woman . . . in all my life I never met a more deceitful, detestable, or utterly evil man.'

Her voice never changed, and for a moment he did not realise what she had said. When he did realise he didn't move, but sat staring at his hands on the table. His face was bland, although inwardly he was cursing viciously. At last he raised his head and looked at her.

'Yes,' she said. 'The bubble finally burst.' She rose to her feet. 'I'll spare you the cost of a meal.'

She left the restaurant without a backward glance. It would have made no difference had she turned to look at him. She could have seen nothing through her tears.

David West finished his meal alone. He'd ordered the thing so he might as well eat it, and he wanted time to collect his thoughts. The last thing he wanted was to have to go back and talk to Roger Powell just yet. Powell was fast becoming a nuisance with his everlasting nerves. Lately he'd been talking about being done for misfeasance – which was hardly a crime. Well, it was, but not a crime as David West understood it. The wrongful use of lawful authority. But what was lawful authority for if not to use wrongfully and make a killing? But Powell was getting the wind up about his chances of a prison sentence, so David West imagined that before long he'd have to go back and quiet him down.

He was going to have to work out what to do about Triangle. He could see that his original idea was off, but he still owned twenty per cent of the stock. And Marion wouldn't want all this coming out. Perhaps that could be used as a lever to . . . oh yes, he wasn't finished yet.

Telling the whole story to Roger Powell was as much of a pain in the neck as he had always known it would be.

'I don't *know* how she knew. She just sprang it on me, out of the blue. "I want to get married," she said. "On Friday." Devious little cow thought she'd throw me. Well, she didn't. They should make me Foreign bloody Secretary for wriggling out of that one, I can tell you. So she just waffled on – then suddenly upped and called me an evil bastard and walked out. "I'll spare you the cost of the meal," she says – neglecting the fact that she'd ordered six courses round a fatted calf and they'd already brought the Chablis up from the cellar . . .'

'So what did you say?' said Powell curiously.

'Nothing. Not a word. I wouldn't give her the satisfaction.'

'What do we do now?' said Powell. He was trying to conceal the worry that gnawed at him.

'Well, the merger's gone out of the window, that's for sure.'

'Yes, I did manage to figure that one out.'

'But you're still managing director and I've still got twenty per cent of the poke . . .'

'For how much longer, though?'

David West shrugged. 'Until I care to relinquish it . . . which is a pretty good option in itself. Offload my shares and watch the price fall through the floor again. Conversely I could hang onto them . . .'

Powell's precarious control broke. 'But what about me?' he demanded shrilly. '*My* position? How can I possibly stay on that board now?'

'Why should you conceivably do anything else?' said West calmly.

'Because Marion will . . .'

'Marion can do *nothing*,' West gave a nasty smile, 'without blowing the gaff that she's got the I.Q. of a retarded rabbit. That woman made an idiot of herself over me. Any major change in policy would be tantamount to admitting it. Think about it. Christine, my love!' His tone changed smoothly as the door opened to admit Christine. The girl's face was white and drawn.

'Oh David, I've been so worried . . .'

West immediately took her in his arms, soothing her as he would have done a child. 'There, there . . . Tell me.'

'That Hallam woman. She knows, David. She *knows*.'

'All right, take it easy,' West chuckled. 'So she knows. So, too, we assume, does God – but as yet no fire and brimstone. No lightning bolts from the blue. No nasty little policemen knocking on doors. Knowing is one thing, my love, but . . .'

'I've had to resign.'

He pushed her away from him, all the easy geniality wiped from his face. 'You what?' he demanded sharply.

'I had to resign.'

'*Why*? Were you sacked?'

'No, but . . .'

'Did she *ask* for your resignation?' His voice was rising on a note of anger.

'Not in so many words, but . . .'

'So why did you do it?'

'I had to. She *knows*, David. She knows everything.'

'No she doesn't,' said West at once. 'She can't. Because if she did, you wouldn't be here now.' He watched her face as the truth of this dawned on her. His expression was brutal. 'You've been conned. Bluffed. Made a monkey of.' He turned away from her. 'Oh well, you may as well clear off then,' he said over his shoulder.

She frowned. 'David?'

Still with his back to her he waved a hand towards the door. 'Off. You're no use to me now, are you?'

She gave a little puzzled smile. 'What are you telling me?'

'That you've blown it. So off you go.'

'But I don't understand.'

He faced her and spoke slowly, as though to a half-wit. 'It's very simple. You walk to the door, you go through it, and you don't come back.'

She searched his face. 'What about "us"?'

He sighed, exasperated. Some women were so thick. 'There's no "us". There's you, there's me, and – I trust – an increasingly large distance in between.'

'When do you want me to come back?' she said, shaking her head as though to clear it and make the words mean something different.

'Listen. Let me spell it out to you. I took you on, several years ago, for a specific purpose. I trained you – in the best of my hotels – invested heavily in procuring for you the best background a purser could possibly have. Why? Because I wanted you to be a purser. For Triangle. Just like Roger here is managing director. For Triangle. *My* people. Where *I* want them. It's so simple, isn't it? And now you've blown it. You've resigned.'

'And our marriage?' she whispered.

He put an arm round her shoulders and began to edge her to the door, talking kindly. 'Christine. A little tip for you. A little worldly wisdom. Men are moved by three principles in varying proportions: power, money, and sex. If it's romance you want, look for a man who's poor and feeble. The rest of us have other things to do.'

She pulled away and faced him, her eyes burning. 'If I thought you were being serious, I'd go straight to the police and tell them everything.'

He opened the door. 'Of course you would, dear. Twenty years in prison? Just think of all the embroidery you could do . . .'

'You swine,' she screamed. 'You evil, lousy swine . . .' The slamming of the door cut her words off.

West gave a weary sigh and faced Powell. 'I'll never understand women . .' he said.

By that evening Sarah had still not solved the problem that was really troubling her, and their departure was perilously near. Matt came into her office to find her and Ted with their heads down, studying papers feverishly.

'So what's the state of play?' he demanded.

'Oh hello, Matt,' Sarah yawned.

'I've only said one line and you're bored,' he complained.

'No. Just tired.' She smiled at him. It was their first meeting since he had kissed her, yet she was aware of no feeling of embarrassment such as she would once have felt. Only a sweet pleasure at having him there.

Matt came over to look at what they were doing. He frowned.

'All very boring isn't it?' She smiled up at him.

'What's it all about?'

She ran wearily through the list. 'Commercial law, criminal law, tort. Just looking for anything . . . any little thing.'

'That we can pin David West to the ceiling with,' Ted added.

'I should've thought there were dozens of things,' said Matt.

'That's how it seems on the surface,' Sarah agreed.

'Sabotage, libel, criminal damage – all that company law he's supposed to have sidestepped . . .'

'Mmmm. We can build a pretty strong case against Christine – and against Roger Powell. We could also be a bit nasty to three other members of the board . . . all West's men . . . Yes,' she added as Matt looked at her sharply, 'I only discovered that today. But West himself? He's a clever fellow.'

'As clever as you?'

'Much more so. No, it's got to be conspiracy – but conspiracy to what? And how do we fix him?' There was a knock at the door. 'Come in.'

The visitor was Christine Harris. 'I just wanted a brief word . . . In private, if that's all right.'

'Of course.' Sarah made a sign for Matt and Ted to remain where they were, and followed Christine outside.

When she re-entered five minutes later, she was carrying a package and frowning.

'That didn't take long,' said Matt. 'Where's she gone?'

'To the airport,' said Sarah, not looking up. She began to tear the package open.

'Then where?' said Matt.

'A long way. I didn't ask.'

'She give you that?' Ted pointed to the package.

'Yes.'

'What is it?' said Matt.

'I don't know. She just said I might be interested.'

She tore off the last scrap of covering and laid the contents out on the desk. They were a mass of papers, letters, invoices, legal-looking documents, all photostatted.

'That's an invoice,' said Matt, seizing a paper.

Ted read over his shoulder. 'From Van Dooren . . . the private detective.'

'Made out to West.' Matt yelped.

'Hey, look at this! It's a letter from West to Powell,' said Sarah, her voice rising in excitement.

'So what was Christine doing with it?' said Matt.

Sarah didn't hear him. She was rummaging through the papers. 'And a photocopy of a letter from West's . . . I don't believe this. *And* it's dated!'

'Who's it from?' said Ted.

'Stockbroker.' She dropped it and seized another. 'Letter from Powell to West asking if it would be advisable to resign from the board of Cosmopean before taking up the Triangle appointment.'

'But where did she get all this from? And why?' said Matt, bewildered.

'It's her insurance,' said Sarah. 'She didn't trust him. Letter from West to Powell. Dated. "No reason to be hasty . . . no apparent or necessary conflict . . . cross that bridge when we come to it . . .".'

She looked at the other two, eyes shining with victory. 'We've done it,' she announced.

'I thought you was off to college anyway,' said Lisa. 'That's what I was told.'

They were stripping and making a bunk in a first-class cabin the following morning, early. Barbara gave her companion an exasperated look.

'Lisa, you of all people should know . . .'

'What?'

'That I can't.'

'Why not? Oh, I see! Yes – I didn't think of that. It would make it difficult. But then, how did you get on at school?'

'It was a private school. It's not that I'm stupid or anything – most subjects I was very good at. It's just the exams . . .'

Lisa began to back out of the door, clutching a bundle of dirty linen, still talking.

'Same with my cousin. He was fine until it came to exams and actually writing. *Oh, I'm sorry* . . .'the last words were torn from her by a collision with Marion, who was stalking past with an air of determination, and who did not even stop to remonstrate.

'That was your auntie,' Lisa hissed at Barbara. 'I copped her with the dirties.'

Barbara giggled. 'I'll get the other bundle and cop her on the way back.'

'Throwing dirties at the chairman of the board?' said Jane, putting her head in.

'Ah, well,' said Lisa, 'more thinking about it, really.'

'I was just wondering,' said Barbara, 'why my – why Mrs Terson was in such a hurry.'

Jane smiled. 'Not really our business what the upper echelons do, eh?'

'No, of course. Sorry.'

Just the same, Jane thought she could probably guess. Following its repairs the ship was putting to sea two days before Marion, or anyone else, had thought possible. Even John had cautiously opted for another two days in dry dock while tests were run. But Sarah Hallam had urged him to set out. She'd even nagged Matt into admitting that the tests were 'desirable' rather than 'essential', and John had yielded. Not everyone thought John was right. Charles, in particular, had made hay, accusing John of being 'taken over' by Sarah Hallam. John had overruled him firmly, but he could have done without Charles' presence on the bridge that morning when Marion came storming in.

'Marion.' John tried to greet her politely.

Without preamble she launched straight into the attack. 'Point number one. You will in future address me as Mrs Terson, Captain. The days of easy-going familiarity are over. As of now. Is that understood?'

He decided to humour her. 'No, Mrs Terson, but for the sake of a quiet life . . .'

'And I do not expect flippancy on the bridge of my flagship,' she snapped.

'No, Mrs Terson. Point number two?'

'Just what on earth do you think you're doing? Have you any idea – any conception – of what it feels like to arrive at a dry dock and find that twenty thousand tons of passenger shipping have evaporated over night? Do you know what that feels like?'

'No, but I can conjecture. Was it "surprising"?' His tight-lipped anger was now as great as her own.

'John, I am in no mood . . .'

'*Captain Anderson.*'

'I beg your pardon?'

He made one last attempt. 'Marion, I don't know what's eating you, but I'm too old and I'm too weary to have you or anybody else come up to my bridge and talk to me as though I'm a wayward adolescent. Now, would you like to go out, come back, and start all over again?'

'Captain Anderson . . .' to her fury he gave a heavy sigh and turned away as though she was an irrelevance to whom he had given enough time. Her voice became shrill. 'Captain Anderson! I want to know why this ship is here, now, taking on passengers.'

He turned back and spoke coldly. 'Because, Marion, that is its function. We sail at fourteen hundred hours.'

'At whose say-so?'

'Mine. I have a ship, a schedule, and right now, a very short fuse.'

'Why was I not told? Were you planning to sneak away without me knowing?'

For a moment John looked at her in disbelief. Then he spoke to Charles. 'Mr Woodhouse, would you kindly attend to Mrs Terson's problem? I have work to do.'

He moved off towards the chart room, ignoring Marion's cry after him. 'John, how dare you! Come back here.'

When he ignored her, Marion made to follow him but Charles touched her arm.

'Mrs Terson . . . please, I don't think that will do any good. You see . . . Captain Anderson hasn't been behaving . . . altogether rationally for the last two or three days.'

'In what way?'

Charles glanced up to make sure that John was out of earshot. 'Well, of course, there was the affair with your niece . . .'

'What affair with my niece? What are you talking about?'

'Didn't you know? Oh, that was . . . terribly indiscreet of me. I rather thought that everyone knew . . . insofar as they didn't try to hide it.'

'So that's it! I knew there was a reason . . . sneaking out of dock! He's eloping with my niece! In *my* ship.'

A tiny niggle of unease began to affect Charles. This wasn't quite how he'd meant the conversation to go.

'Actually, Marion – Mrs Terson — I don't think that was . . .'

'Of course it was! I've known that man of old. *All* men. I wouldn't put anything past any of you.' She turned towards the door.

'Mrs Terson . . .?'

'Don't say a word! I'm going back to the Sonesta to pack a suitcase. Then I'll be back.'

'Hello, Marion,' said Matt, meeting her in the door. But she ignored him and turned to call back to Charles.

'Don't say anything, Charles. This is going to be a surprise.' She hurried out.

'What was that all about?' said Matt.

Charles' dismay was almost comic. 'I think I've just made a rather stupid mistake.'

'Why? What've you done?'

'Eh? Oh, nothing . . . nothing at all.'

Sarah and her henchman were engaged in a small dispute: to prosecute or not to prosecute. That was the question, and the slings and arrows were flying fast.

'Either West has broken the law or he hasn't – and if he has, he should be prosecuted,' said Nick crossly.

'Nick, all I'm thinking of is the overall good of Triangle . . .'

'Right, fine . . . that's your job. I, on the other hand, happen to be a lawyer . . .'

'Now in whatever sphere the law has been broken – whether it be criminal, civil, moral or natural – the damage has been inflicted on Triangle . . . not on society at large. *Therefore* if the scales of justice should be balanced logically, the recompense exacted should be in favour of Triangle, not some abstract retribution imposed on behalf of society at large. Do I make myself clear?' He stared at her blankly. 'All I'm asking is: how on earth does Triangle benefit by West's being in prison for ten years?'

'It'll deter him from doing it again,' he said lamely.

She gave a short laugh. 'You don't honestly think we'll give him the *chance* to do it again . . .?'

'All right, we'll leave it all hanging over him like the Sword of Damocles.'

'Good.' To her relief she saw him smiling at her. 'Thank you Nick. It is for the best. Trust me.'

'Oh, I didn't doubt it for a moment. I only argue with you for the exercise. I never hope to win,' he said plaintively.

Ted hurried in and shut the door hard behind him. 'Wanna hear the latest newsflash? Mrs Terson's coming aboard. Well, actually she's been aboard and got off again, but she's coming back. Matt told me.' He became serious. 'Does it make any difference?'

'Yes,' said Sarah.

They knew now that there was no further time to be lost. Before they could speak to Marion, David West must be tackled. Nick had told Sarah about taking Marion to the restaurant, and how he had waited in vain the next day for any news of her. He wasn't sure what he had expected – apologies, excuses, tears, anything – but silence had ensued. He had no knowledge of how Marion had reacted, or if she had done anything at all. But whatever had or hadn't happened, it was vital to nail David West down in a position from which there was no escape.

Nick went to his office in Amsterdam and confronted him with photostats of everything Christine had given them.

'We have all the originals in the safe aboard ship. I'm not a criminal lawyer, David, but I do know enough to suggest to you, very reasonably, that we have a case,' said Nick.

'I'd be a fool to disagree. Conspiracy of one sort or another, yes?' Nick nodded. 'How many years? Five? Seven?'

'Two would probably be enough to kill you,' said Nick.

West gave a mirthless laugh. 'I'm not a sick man.'

'No, but you're a powerfully independent one,' said Nick quietly.

'Was. Miscalculated, didn't I? So what are you going to do?'

'That depends.'

'On what?'

'Partly on Mrs Terson.'

West gave a theatrical sigh and raised his eyes to the heavens. 'Oh well, that's that then. Straight to the dungeons.'

'No, it doesn't depend on her in that way. It's her instinct for survival that we're hoping to work on.'

'We?'

'Miss Hallam and myself.'

'I was afraid of that. Go on, what else does it depend on?'

'Yourself. All other things being equal, we're prepared to do a deal. First, Roger Powell and your other three minions resign from the board of Triangle as from now.'

'Consider it done. And?'

'You sell your shares.'

'Easy.'

'I haven't finished. You sell your shares – but very carefully indeed. Not all at once.'

'Anything else?'

'Yes. In the meantime I shall want an assurance – in fact, more than that, a binding, legal declaration – renouncing all rights to vote.'

'And if I fail in any particular?'

Nick indicated the photocopies. 'They're just the tip of the iceberg, David.'

'A very satisfactory deal. You've been kinder than I deserve.'

Nick too thought they had, but he managed to remain in command of himself. It was only when David West rose and held out a hand that his temper nearly deserted him.

'That really is pushing it,' he said, and left.

By the middle of that afternoon the ship was under way, although travelling at a speed much below normal. Matt came on deck to find Sarah leaning pensively over the rail, and joined her. She gave him a little smile.

'Last time you did this, the engine blew up,' she said.

'The engine is barely going, or hadn't you noticed?'

'No. But then I don't have an engineer's ear.'

'It's about as slow as I can get it without actually going backwards. For an hour. We might pep it up a bit then. But of course you know all that. From your time at the Department of Marine whatsits.'

'You like teasing me, don't you?' She looked up as she spoke and saw his eyes dwelling on her with a glowing look that made her turn her face away in confusion. 'Don't.'

'Don't what?' he said plaintively. 'Think?'

'Not those sort of thoughts.'

'Read minds as well, eh?'

'I can read yours. Sometimes. When you look like that.'

'O.K. I'll tell you exactly what I was thinking. Then you can tell me if you were right,' he offered.

'Go on then.'

'I was thinking how much I'd miss you if you left. Wondering what you'd do.'

'I don't know,' she said, realising it to be the truth. In a short time the *Anglia* had come to feel like home.

'You've had a rough time of it, what with one thing and another,' he said gently.

'I don't mind.'

'*I* do.'

She smiled. 'Ted helped.' Some instinct told her that this would pique him. She did not examine too closely why she wanted to pique him.

'Ah, my little rival,' he said lightly. 'I must remember to chuck him over the side.'

'That's what I was thinking when you came out.'

'About chucking him over the side?'

'No. How much I'd miss him if he left.'

He eyed her sardonically. 'You're saying that to make me jealous.'

'I'm saying it because it's true. I never had a kid brother.'

He relaxed. This was better. 'Is that how you see him?'

'Not necessarily,' she said, hastily recovering lost ground.

'You're learning fast, aren't you?'

'The wiles of woman? No, I suppose they're there all the time. They just need a bit of encouragement now and then.'

'Ted'll probably go to college. End up a captain.'

She gave him a sidelong glance. 'I think I might wait. Yes, I think I might.'

He grinned and gave her a friendly shove. It could rest there for the moment. Sarah was getting more interesting every minute.

Marion's eruption on board was proving every bit as disturbing as John had feared. She was tense, tearful and interfering, and he'd had enough.

'I demand to know why we're going so slowly,' she said, facing John on the bridge.

'Marion, I'm fast losing my patience with you . . .'

'Why are we going so slowly?'

'Because we have a recently overhauled engine which is being run in. Gently. Slowly. Sensibly.'

'And how in heaven's name are we to get to Esbjerg on time? Will you tell me that?'

He forced himself to speak patiently. 'We will get to Esbjerg at precisely the time our passengers have been told we will.'

'Never. At this speed, never.'

'Marion, we shan't . . .'

'I'm not totally ignorant. I have been to sea before. I do happen to know approximately how fast a ship has to go to cover a certain distance in a given time. Now will you kindly give the order to increase speed?'

He stared at her in disbelief before saying flatly, 'No.'

'Then I shall have no alternative but to relieve you of your command. Mr Woodhouse?'

'Yes, Mrs Terson.' Charles came near.

'I'm relieving Mr Anderson of the command. You will kindly order him from the bridge and take over.'

Charles never moved. He looked at John, who did not look back at him. Then he looked at Marion. But he made no movement to obey her.

'Well?' she shrilled. 'Are you going to do as I say?'

'No, Mrs Terson,' he said quietly.

To his dying day he could never have said why he replied as he did. But deep within him some instinct, not yet lost to decency, said the words for him. Perhaps it was caution too. For even Charles could hear the note of hysteria growing in Marion's voice, and that note warned him that if he gained his promotion in this way he would somehow regret it.

Sarah came onto the bridge just in time to hear Marion say, 'Charles, I don't think you understand. I am promoting you to captain. Isn't that what you want?'

'Yes,' he said bleakly.

'Then kindly assume the command and order Mr Anderson below.'

His voice was gentle. 'Marion, I think perhaps *you* should go below . . .'

'Charles . . .' she screamed.

'I mean it, Marion. Either you go below or I shall have you removed from the bridge.'

Sarah stepped forward. 'Charles, let me . . .'

Marion ignored her. 'John, are you going to let him speak to me like this?'

John might have replied that since he had been relieved of command if wasn't for him to 'let' Charles do anything. He didn't, however. He just looked at Marion in pity. To his relief Sarah took her arm.

'Mrs Terson. Mrs Terson, can you hear me?' She clutched hard at Marion who seemed about to faint.

'I feel dizzy,' Marion whispered.

Sarah led her towards the door. 'It's all right,' she said kindly. 'I'm here. I'll help you.'

At the door Marion stopped suddenly and buried her face in her hands. Her shoulders shook in silent grief. Sarah cast a helpless look at the two men before leading her out.

When they had gone John turned to Charles. But Charles had found something with which to occupy himself, and did not meet his captain's eyes.

Marion spent the voyage to Esbjerg and from there to Harwich lying in her cabin, alone in the dark, refusing all offers of comfort. The misery that she had suppressed under a bright determined face ever since her last meeting with David, had broken through at last, and left her helpless. She looked into the future and saw nothing but chaos. The hand she had thought was there to guide her had proved false. She was alone again, but more terribly alone than she had been after George's death.

And, in the darkness, it was the loss of George, piercing her with a sharp agony as though it had been yesterday, that made the tears run unchecked down her cheeks. Not the loss of David.

She said nothing when Sarah showed her the photostats of the evidence left by Christine. She listened impassively to Nick's account of how David had finally confessed. She read the paper he had signed. She went about in a daze. She was waiting for something to happen.

It happened the day after they finally docked at Harwich. There, in her office, in the presence of Nick and Sarah, she read a legal document that Nick had put into her hands. She read it right through from beginning to end without allowing a flicker of emotion to show in her face.

Then she said, 'How long have you been planning this?'

'Nothing was planned at all, Marion,' said Nick. 'It didn't happen like that.'

She held up the document. 'There's a lot of thought gone into this, Nick.

'Yes there has. I've spent the last two days with the best legal people I know.'

She gave a small grim smile. 'Just to catch Marion Terson.'

'No,' he said indignantly. 'Trying to safeguard your best interests. We didn't want you to lose one penny of the wealth George left you.'

'Or to retain one ounce of power,' said Marion, flicking her eyes over the paper again.

'Of course, you'll still have influence, a voice . . .'

'It's not the same thing, though, is it?' She looked round at them.

'Who's idea was this?'

Sarah turned from the window and exchanged a brief glance with Nick, which Marion saw.

'Mrs Terson . . .' she began.

'It's all right. You don't have to say anything. So, what happens if I don't sign?'

Nick took a deep breath. 'First of all, Marion, you've got to understand that even if you *do* sign, the issue isn't necessarily cut and dried. Reorganising a company's share capital is a complex business, a legal minefield . . .'

'What happens if I don't sign?'

'There'll be a full investigation by the Department of Trade, prosecutions, publicity . . . At the very best you'd be a laughing stock. At worst you could go down with David West.'

There was a long silence. Then Marion gave a little laugh.

'I was about to say I should have a word with my lawyer first.'

'I *am* your lawyer,' he reminded her.

'Quite.' Without another word Marion took the pen and signed. When she had handed the paper back to Nick she faced Sarah and said amicably, 'I don't know how, my dear, but I have a feeling *you'll* end up running this company.'

'That isn't what I want,' said Sarah, truthfully.

'But nevertheless, if you do —' Marion touched Sarah's arm gently, '— take good care of it for me.'

She gave them all a brief smile. John rose.

'Marion, there isn't, and never has been, anything personal . . .'

'It's all right, John. You needn't say anything.'

At the door she turned and regarded them all. Then she went out – a free woman.

For a moment the others all tried to avoid each other's eyes. Then Nick cleared his throat.

'She seemed to take it very well,' said John.

'Yes,' Nick mused. 'It might have been easier if she'd – created a bit.'

Every one of them felt awful. They were sitting staring at each other when Matt looked in, his face puzzled.

'What have you done to Marion?' he demanded.

'You've just seen her?' said John.

'Yes. What have you done?'

'Effectively we removed her from power,' said Nick. 'Set in motion a chain of events which hopefully will result in her shares yielding a higher dividend, while . . .' he faltered.

'Taking away her vote,' Sarah finished.

'How did she seem?' said John.

'Amused.'

They stared at him.

'*Laughing*?' Nick demanded.

'Trying very hard not to,' said Matt. 'Maybe she's relieved. Glad to be out.'

'Or maybe we made some glaring mistake,' said Nick worriedly.

He picked up the document. Sarah moved to read it over his shoulder. Matt and John stared at them, then at each other.

'I can't be doing with all this,' John muttered to Matt.

'You and me both.'

'Once upon a time, going to sea meant getting away from it all.'

'So what do you suggest?'

John glanced at his watch. 'Right now? Well, there's twenty minutes to last orders. What do you say?'

'I say thanks very much. Mine'll be a pint.'